How to Make a Friend

Fleur Smithwick

BANTAM PRESS

LONDON • TORONTO • SYDNEY • AUCKLAND • JOHANNESBURG

TRANSWORLD PUBLISHERS
61–63 Uxbridge Road, London W5 5SA
www.transworldbooks.co.uk

Transworld is part of the Penguin Random House group of companies
whose addresses can be found at global.penguinrandomhouse.com

Penguin
Random House
UK

First published in Great Britain in 2015 by Bantam Press
an imprint of Transworld Publishers

A CIP catalogue record for this book
is available from the British Library.

ISBNs 9780593073360 (hb)
9780593073377 (tpb)

Typeset in 11/14.5pt Sabon by Falcon Oast Graphic Art Ltd.
Printed and bound in Great Britain by Clays Limited, Bungay, Suffolk

Penguin Random House is committed to a sustainable
future for our business, our readers and our planet. This book
is made from Forest Stewardship Council® certified paper.

MIX
Paper from
responsible sources
FSC
www.fsc.org   FSC® C016897

2 4 6 8 10 9 7 5 3 1

To Steve, Max and Lulu

PART ONE

'. . . I would not wish
any companion in the world but you.'
Shakespeare, *The Tempest*

Prologue

'SAM, COME AND PLAY WITH ME.'

I spring up. I'm always happy to do what Alice wants. She's been dropping grass, brown-edged rose petals and soil into a blue plastic bowl and is stirring them, a frown of concentration creasing her brow. I inspect the mush and wrinkle my nose.

'Don't you want to smell it?' she asks.

'OK.' I breathe it in. It smells of earth and grass and not much of flowers.

Alice gives it another stir and I settle beside her. She looks at me expectantly.

'It's nice,' I say.

She sits up straighter and goes pink. I pick a daisy and she takes it and pulls each petal off and adds them one at a time. I count them in and sit back on my heels and feel the sun on my face. These are my favourite days, when nothing else matters, when I feel safe and happy. When it's just me and Alice and nothing in between. I think she's the most beautiful girl in the world.

'Do you want some?' she says.

'Boys don't wear perfume.'

'It's called aftershave when boys wear it.' She looks at me: 'You don't have to be a grown-up. You just have to put it on your chin.'

I shrug and jut my chin forward and she dabs some on my skin. Her fingers look like she's been washing in muddy water and I wipe the wet away with the edge of my T-shirt.

Alice jumps up and runs over to the tree house. Her father built it when Simon was little so it's at least nine years old. Simon hasn't used it for ages. He's a punk. He doesn't take much notice of Alice. He's ten years older after all, and when I see her following him, her eyes all hopeful, I want to shout at her to leave him alone because he'll only make her sad. But at times like that she never pays me any attention.

I watch as she clambers up the ladder. I'd climb up with her, but she doesn't ask me to and I daren't go uninvited. Sometimes she doesn't want me for days and at other times it's as if I'm the other half of her. Those are the best times. When her mother's making a fuss of her, which isn't very often, I feel like I'm sitting at the end of a long dark tunnel. Right now, I'm happy just to lie on the grass with my arms crossed under my head, watching her.

The neighbour's cat, a black, white and brown spoilt thing that Alice loves, slinks through a hole in the fence. The cat hesitates, the hair on her back rising, and then lets out a sharp hiss and stalks past me. I don't like her at all.

Alice laughs and calls it over.

I am distracted by the sound of Alice's mother chatting to one of her friends on the telephone and I can smell her cigarette smoke drifting out of the kitchen. Her name is Julia and she used to be a model. She's very thin and very beautiful with big blue eyes and a sweet smile that makes people think she's nice when she isn't. Sometimes Alice sits at her mother's dressing table, picking through her jewellery while Julia stares at her own reflection, pressing her fingertips on the skin above her eyebrows and lifting it. Alice is chubby and when they're with other people Julia often finds some reason to mention that. She cuts Alice's hair herself, as short as a boy's.

The sound of Julia's laughter goes up and down like children practising their piano scales. I pull a face. Alice is sitting on the balcony of the tree house, her legs hanging over the edge, the cat curled up beside her. Her feet are bare and dirty. She swings them to and fro and hums a tune. I wait, watching her, and she waves at me.

'Come up, Sam.'

I wrinkle my nose. 'Why?'

'Because you have to.'

'No, I don't.'

'Yes, you do. You have to do as I tell you.'

I shrug and wander over slowly, stopping to pick up a pigeon feather.

'Hurry up!'

'Alice, what're you doing?' Julia calls from the kitchen.

I hesitate, one foot on the bottom rung of the ladder, my hands clutching the sides and I draw back. The cat has already run away. I stare up at Alice and she pokes her tongue out at me. Her legs stop swinging.

'I'm playing with Sam.'

Chapter One

RORY NEVER HURRIED AND HE WAS RIGHT, BECAUSE WHAT WAS THE great panic? We always got there in the end. It was no good being cross with him either, because he knew how to defuse anger with humour. Ten years had passed since I met him on that dismal, sodden November afternoon and yet I still sometimes watched him the way I did at sixteen, thinking, Why did you pick me to be your friend?

He was on his mobile now, pouring balm on to the ruffled feathers of his boss, while Daniel and I waited, leaning against the car, chatting. I kept darting glances up the lane and when the church bells suddenly rang out, causing me to jump and birds to rise in a flurry of wings from neighbouring gardens, I lost patience and rapped on the window. Rory pocketed his phone, checked his reflection in the sun-visor mirror, picked up a silver-wrapped present from between his feet and swung the door open.

He grinned at us. 'Ready?'

I glanced at my watch, unimpressed, and set off.

'Alice,' Daniel said, hurrying after me. 'Calm down. It doesn't start for ten minutes.'

'I know but . . .' But what? 'I don't want to be crammed behind a pillar at my own father's wedding.'

'We're all doomed,' Rory muttered darkly, taking my hand and practically dragging me up the lane. 'Don't worry so much. Your family are not going to give you a hard time for being a few minutes late.'

He knew me far too well.

'Shh,' I said, as we hurried into the packed church.

From her seat near the front my sister Olivia frowned and beckoned me over, but as I hurried forward to join her, Rory and Daniel grabbed me by the arms and pulled me into a pew with them. I turned to Rory to complain, but at that moment the bells fell silent and I had to content myself with a disapproving scowl as we twisted round to watch Gabby's entrance. I was secretly pleased though, and anyway, as far as I was concerned, Rory Walker was family.

An hour later we poured out of the church, squinting in the afternoon light, fumbling blindly for our sunglasses. Dad had decreed that the sun would shine on his wedding day and so it did; only a few white clouds, shaped unfortunately like disintegrating skulls, moved lazily past the steeple. The bridesmaids and pageboy chased each other squealing around the ramshackle graveyard while the ushers and best man, my brother Simon, struggled to herd them in front of the camera. I didn't envy them their task. I'd had similar trouble on a magazine shoot yesterday, and those kids were being paid. Or at least their doting mothers were.

A woman in a tangerine dress and a green silk shawl was standing in a small group near the path to the lane, her hands moving as she spoke, her bracelets sliding up her arms. She did that on television too, those hands constantly in motion, as if words weren't enough to convey her enthusiasm. Even though I had known she was coming, her face still gave me a jolt. I had watched her history programme with an interest that, Rory complained, bordered on obsession. But then she was his brother's girlfriend, so he could afford to be blasé. I watched her place her hand on Jonathan Walker's chest and gaze up at him. There was something both proprietary and submissive about the gesture that left me

14

cold. When had I last seen him? A year ago at least, because I hadn't met this one.

I looked away. I didn't want them to catch me staring. 'So, what's she like?'

Rory made a face. 'His usual type. Highly intelligent, high-earning, killer heels.'

Daniel took my hand and held it to his lips. 'Don't worry, darling. You're much prettier than she is.'

'Flattery will get you nowhere,' I said, blushing.

'You'll like her,' Rory said. 'She's very smiley.'

'As long as she gets what she wants,' Daniel said.

'And what would that be?' I asked.

'They've been together a year now. What do you think she wants?'

'A ring on her finger?'

'A baby, silly.'

'Oh, I see. You think any woman over the age of twenty-eight will grab the first man who comes along. Megan MacLeod has a really interesting career.'

'Yes, but how old is Jonathan?' Daniel said. 'Thirty-five? Thirty-six? He's at that crossroads when a man starts to ponder his own mortality and to wonder whether he ought to get propagating before it's too late.'

'Procreating, Daniel,' I said. 'Propagating is what botanists do. I'm sure they'll settle down one day, but I doubt she's in a hurry.'

'Someone's a little tense,' he said, massaging my shoulders.

I pushed his hands away. 'I am not tense.'

Jonathan Walker was just a man. I would cope, albeit stone-cold sober, since I had naïvely promised to drive Rory and Daniel home that evening. They had to attend a christening the next morning.

I waited for my grandmother to emerge from the church and then we set off, with Rory and Daniel leading the way. They both looked dapper in slim grey suits, their hair close-cropped. Like Tweedle Dum and Tweedle Dee, I thought fondly, if it hadn't been for Rory's red hair.

'Lovely young men,' Gran commented, tightening her grip on my arm. 'It'll be your turn next.'

I had braced myself for this sort of comment but it still set my teeth on edge. Gran was wonderful, but she had never had much tact.

'It's not something I'm worried about.'

'Goodness, Adam's shot up,' she said.

Confused for a moment by the change of subject and trying to work out who on earth Adam was, I followed her gaze and spotted my ten-year-old half-brother, looking very grown-up in his suit, posing with his little cousins.

I tapped her arm. 'That's Archie, Gran.'

'I know that.'

I smiled at her. 'You said Adam.'

'Did I?' She looked around, almost as if she wasn't sure where she was, mapping the place with her eyes. 'I sometimes forget he's not here any more.'

Adam. Of course. The stepbrother who died in childhood. Her memory was becoming increasingly unreliable, often causing her to muddle the ancient with the recent. She was wearing a blue dress that I recognized from my nieces' christenings and it hung off her where a few years ago it had fitted perfectly. She was by no means decrepit and her mind was still sharp, but the moments of confusion were coming more often. She tried to cover it up and never complained, but it worried all of us. I leaned in and kissed her powdered cheek.

'Come on, Gran, I think you're needed for a photo.'

Back at the house a marquee had been erected at an awkward angle, half on the drive and half on the lawn, its position dictated by the apple trees. A string quartet filled the air with sublime music. Drooping ropes of yellow and white flowers, woven with leaves, garlanded the interior. Gabby hadn't wanted a formal sit-down dinner and instead had organized a big noisy party where everyone could mingle with whoever they liked and not be stuck sitting next to someone's cobwebby old uncle. Chairs and tables had been placed round the outside, for anyone who wanted to take the weight off their feet.

Rory dragged me up to Megan, introduced me, extricated her from an elderly fan and left us facing each other.

She greeted me enthusiastically; evidently one of those people who liked to shed their light on everyone around them. 'So you're Johnnie's photographer friend. It's so great to meet you at last. Johnnie says you're almost a sister to Rory. I think that's sweet. You're obviously very important to them all.'

I bristled. I didn't want the quality of my relationship with the Walkers to be pronounced upon by Jonathan – Johnnie's – girlfriend. I knew them first. I had known them for years. But I also knew my duty, both as daughter of the groom and as a civilized, sophisticated adult. 'They're my second family.' I smiled and looked straight into her eyes. 'I do love your programme.'

'Well thank you. That's very kind of you.'

'Were you frozen when you filmed at Loch Leven? You looked so cold.' Not the best I could have done perhaps, but not the worst either. Gran once said, in answer to one of my many teenage crises: Be interested, ask questions, listen to the answers and respond. Hey presto! A conversation.

'Not as frozen as Mary Queen of Scots.' Megan seemed amused. 'My next series is on the Cathar Heretics, so that should be warmer.'

'Oh, so much warmer,' I said, trying too hard.

I wasn't sure where we went from here. I supposed it depended on how important she was to Jonathan. His record for relationships was about eighteen months, so we were unlikely to meet again. I noticed how green her eyes were, enhanced by eyeshadow and the bright green shawl. Her lips were full, coated with crimson lipstick, and her blonde hair fell in thick waves around a heart-shaped face. I felt under-groomed, even though Rory and Daniel had both insisted I looked like a screen goddess when I did a twirl for them in my vintage polka-dot dress that morning.

'They're a wonderful family,' I said. 'You're very lucky.'

I hadn't meant to sound patronizing, but I could tell she had taken it that way. I turned to glance at Jonathan. He was standing a few feet away from us, looking impressive in his suit, very un-Jonathan. Megan would have tied his bow tie, looking up into his face, close to him. I hated that pretence. The man was perfectly capable of taking care of himself.

I dragged my attention back to Megan.

'I know I'm lucky,' she said, touching my arm gently. 'There are always other girls after Johnnie. He's very easy to fall in love with.'

'So I hear.' I smiled blandly and changed the subject. 'Who's that he's talking to?'

'Matt? It's a bit of a coincidence, him knowing your stepmother as well as Johnnie. The nicest man you could ever meet, but a mean drunk. He's a cameraman. Do you want me to introduce you?'

'Not yet. Maybe later.'

Towards evening, a car came to whisk Megan off to Gatwick to catch a flight to Carcassonne where she would be shooting an episode of her forthcoming documentary. I watched as Jonathan hugged and kissed her. She clung to him for a moment before sliding elegantly into the back seat. It looked like an act to me. Rory caught my eye and I smiled. I loved him.

Later, I saw Jonathan on the far side of the marquee. He was talking to Gabby's parents, but he turned, as if he sensed my gaze, and winked at me. I thought that was it, but he left them almost immediately and came over. He bent to kiss me and I proffered the wrong cheek; the corners of our mouths glanced against each other and there was an awkward moment while we sorted ourselves out. I managed to drop my blue pashmina. He was holding a half-drunk glass of champagne, but he stooped to pick it up with his free hand and replaced it awkwardly on my shoulders. I noticed that his hair had receded, but I didn't mind. I liked his crow's feet too. He looked worn in, not worn out.

'I haven't had a chance to say hello to you properly,' he said.

'I've been mingling.'

'Well, mingle with me for a bit. I don't know many people here.'

'I like Megan. I've watched her programme. She's good.'

'I'm very lucky,' he said, echoing his girlfriend with a lift of his eyebrows. 'What about you? Are you hooked up? I've been looking around, wondering, but there's no one here who fits.'

A waiter came by with a tray of canapés and Jonathan took one. I didn't because it looked like one of those social booby traps, too big to be eaten in one mouthful without strewing crumbs everywhere and getting something sticky on my fingers. Jonathan managed but I wasn't going to risk it. It was lovely to see him again. I had been half dreading it, half excited at the prospect. He had a habit of brushing me up the wrong way, but I came alive in his company and that was worth a bit of awkwardness.

'What type were you looking for?' I asked.

His mouth twitched into a smile that I couldn't resist returning, despite my irritation. 'Oh, I don't know. Someone a bit different. Attractively geeky, maybe. Someone who looks at you with dopey brown eyes.'

'From behind thick spectacles? Thanks.'

Jonathan laughed out loud. 'I've missed you, Alice.'

'You know what? I've always been on the end of a phone.'

Before Jonathan could respond, Matt clapped his hand on his shoulder. 'Aren't you going to introduce me?'

Disappointingly, Jonathan seemed more than happy to oblige. 'Matt, this is an old friend of mine, Alice Byrne. Alice, Matt Clarke.'

'Mike's daughter? You're a photographer, right?' Matt said, looking pleased with himself for remembering.

Jonathan shot me a glance that I hoped I had misinterpreted, like he thought he was doing me a favour. He moved off, leaving me trapped and powerless. I watched Olivia intercept him. Nothing ever changes, I thought, and looked away. She always flirted with Jonathan, as if she had a right to because she'd known him for so long and because she had always treated him that way. I felt a twinge of jealousy, but it was more to do with her ability to be perfectly at ease with him than the thought that he might be attracted to her.

Matt was waiting for a response. 'That's right.'

'What sort of photography?'

'Oh, you know. Fashion mainly. Magazines and catalogues. Not the big ones yet, but I'm working on it.'

'Are you taking the pictures today?'

'No,' I said stiffly. 'It's my father's wedding.'

I was a little ashamed. After all, even though Dad had hired a professional, I had brought the Canon compact that fitted neatly into my handbag, and had been taking snapshots with it. Gran, who was standing a few feet away, gave me one of her looks. I suppressed a smile.

'Having a good time?' I asked him, to make up for my rudeness.

His face drooped. 'To be honest, I'm not really in the mood. I've just split up with my girlfriend.'

'Oh, I'm sorry.'

'Don't be. I'm well shot of her.'

Quite aggressive, I thought, remembering Megan's succinct summing up of his character.

'I think the speeches are about to start.' I turned with relief to face the stage where my brother was standing beside Dad and Gabby.

I was sincerely proud of Simon. He had our mother's looks and our father's charisma and had somehow managed to get away, putting an ocean between himself and his family, while retaining his fondness for us. He was wonderful with Mum, one of the few people able to tell her what he thought without precipitating a torrent of aggrieved abuse, and he and Dad shared a bond that I envied. Considering how he had started out, he was probably the best of us three: the most diplomatic, the most patient and the most successful. And he looked great. His clothes were obviously expensive, he had given up smoking and had his teeth whitened, and his blue eyes blazed from a glorious Californian tan that implied a more than decent work–life balance.

He held up his hand for silence and a wave of anticipation spread through the collected guests. 'You can relax,' he said. 'He's my dad. I'm not going to be crude.'

After supper the band was replaced by a DJ playing the kind of numbers that had you up and out of your gilt-painted seat and on to the dance floor. I grabbed Olivia's little girls and we cavorted like idiots, my lack of rhythm going largely unnoticed. Olivia joined us and we held hands in a circle, Lottie and Elizabeth between us, their faces pink and shiny with excitement. When the song ended, I picked Lottie up and hugged her and the stiff netting under her bridesmaid dress crumpled in my embrace, earning me a sharp reprimand.

'Auntie Alice, you're spoiling my dress!'

'Oops. Sorry.' She really was the sweetest thing.

Olivia took her off me.

'You're looking lovely, Alice,' she said as we took seats at a nearby table. 'Have you done something different?'

I looked down at my dress. 'No. Just put some make-up on.'

'Well, something's put a sparkle in your eye. Is it a man?'

I shook my head. 'I'm naturally this gorgeous.'

Olivia wasn't listening; she'd spotted Lottie smoothing down her raw silk dress with sticky hands. She poured some water on to a napkin and cleaned her up, then turned back to me.

'I think it's a bit much, expecting the girls to be bridesmaids twice in two months.'

'I don't suppose that occurred to Mum,' I said. 'She probably assumed you'd be pleased.'

'Well, of course I'm pleased for her. It's just that she's so obvious, organizing her wedding within weeks of Dad's. She's like a child.'

I laughed. 'And that surprises you?'

But her attention had wandered again. 'Honestly,' she said, rolling her eyes.

I followed her gaze. There was something going on at the other side of the marquee, although it was hard to see what exactly. Just two men in suits squaring up to each other; Matt Clarke and a cousin of Gabby's. I was about to shrug it off and resume our conversation, when a fist flew out and Matt lurched backwards.

'Shit!' Olivia said, as I clasped a hand over my mouth.

I had never seen anyone being punched before, not in real life, and it was shocking. Olivia stayed put with her little girls but I leapt up. Matt fell hard against a chair, grabbed a tablecloth and hit the floor, pulling a shower of half-empty champagne glasses and scraps of canapé down on top of him. I winced as he got up, disentangled himself from the tablecloth and dived back in. He didn't stand a chance. The other man was built like a rugby player.

As one of a fast-diminishing group of sober guests, I felt duty-bound to step in before the pair of them turned the wedding into a farce. Dad would go ballistic, but the most important thing was not to upset Gabby. I wasn't going to let anyone spoil her day.

I hurried over just as Rory and Daniel pushed between the men and, in their endearingly polite way, tried to reason with them. It didn't work.

'Matt! Stop it!' I said, holding on to his arm and suppressing my revulsion. I could feel the sweat through his sleeve.

'Why the hell should I? He attacked me.'

His assailant lurched forward, eyes popping with fury.

Hovering behind him I could see a girl, her face torn between horror and delight. She grabbed ineffectively at his arm.

'Justin! He's drunk, it doesn't matter.'

Matt's nose was bleeding. Rory held out a handful of crumpled napkins and I passed them to Matt and then pressed my hand against his chest as he moved forward again. Simon and two other men were approaching, but Matt didn't see them, he pushed me aside and as I tried to stop myself tripping over my high heels I felt someone's arms go round me.

'I can manage,' I said, trying to free myself without losing dignity. Then I realized the arms belonged to Jonathan and redoubled my efforts.

'Wonderful, Alice, but I think those guys have it under control.' He pulled me straight and tapped my cheek lightly, as if he'd just rescued a small and clumsy child. 'Let them get on with it. I need some fresh air.'

'Good idea.'

I grabbed my shawl from the back of a chair as I passed and draped it around my shoulders. Jonathan caught his foot in the strap of a handbag and nearly went flying. I burst out laughing and gave him my hand and we slipped through a gap in the marquee cover.

Outside a light breeze rustled the leaves. Gabby had hung candles in jars from branches and it looked completely magical. The music and the laughter and the voices echoed through the night air. I felt part of it all and yet separate. I wondered how much Jonathan had drunk. He wasn't slurring his words, but that wasn't his style. He could hold his drink, unlike Rory, who was apt to behave like a schoolboy after a few beers. We walked across the lawn, my heels catching at the grass and digging into the soil. When we made it to the drive I breathed a sigh of relief. Jonathan seemed oblivious, walking along beside me, looking up at the stars. My feet felt as if they had swollen inside my shoes, so I stopped and bent down to take them off, hooking the straps over my fingers. Jonathan was unlikely to be impressed by my efforts at sophistication and I was more interested in being comfortable and walking normally than having sexy feet. Freed, I strolled along the verge.

Beside me, Jonathan grunted.

'What?' I said.

'I just realized that, for the first time since I've known you, I've completely forgotten that you're Simon Byrne's little sister and my brother's best friend.'

'I've always had my own personality, thank you.'

'Don't be like that. I know you have. But you were always such a familiar little thing and now you're a beautiful stranger. It's a nice feeling, getting to know you all over again.'

'I don't think I've changed that much. I wish I had.'

'Why? You're great the way you are.'

'The sort of woman who can only pull geeks? That's very flattering.'

'I was kidding. You're far too sensitive. You've changed for the better, actually.'

'I didn't realize I was that bad.'

'You were incredibly awkward, but it was understandable in the circumstances. Mum and I used to talk about it. She wanted to rescue you.'

'You make me sound pathetic.'

I shrugged his arm away, crossed over to the village shop and inspected the cards in the window. There was one offering free baby rabbits to a good home, with a photograph attached. They were adorable, but I didn't think either I or my flat would pass the test.

I could see Jonathan's reflection. He was standing with his thumbs hooked into his waistband, watching me. I stood my ground and finally he wandered over. After a moment he put his arm around my shoulders and drew me against him.

'I don't know what to make of you,' he said.

'That's interesting, because I don't know what to make of you either.'

'You've really grown up. I can't get used to it. Sorry, Alice. I shouldn't be talking to you like this.'

'No, you bloody well shouldn't be.' I felt pissed off and crowded. 'Nice men don't hug other women when their girlfriends are out of sight.'

He let me go and pouted. Pouting and Jonathan didn't work, it made him look ridiculous. 'It was just a friendly hug. I'm sorry.' He touched my hair and I flinched. 'Do you want to go back?'

I thought about it. I turned and looked up the lane towards the lights and listened to the music float through the stillness. I could imagine what was happening back there: elderly chins drooping on to elderly chests, bridesmaids and pageboys slumped in chairs, guests dancing cheek-to-cheek. The dance floor sticky underfoot. My father knew how to throw a party.

'Not yet.'

In spite of feeling irrationally uptight, it was lovely spending a bit of time alone with Jonathan Walker. It happened so rarely that it felt like a luxury; to have time to ourselves without Rory or any-one else. We had always got on a little too well, despite the ten-year age gap, and apart from a pathetic teenage crush and one badly misjudged incident in my early twenties we had navigated our friendship perfectly safely. For a moment, I considered kissing him. There was something in the air, a crackle of electricity, which made me want to throw caution to the winds and wipe the smirk off his face.

Something moved behind his shoulder, a shadow or a trick of the moonlight perhaps, and I had a feeling that I was being watched and judged; my conscience making a fleeting appearance. It came out of nowhere, but it put me on my guard. There are times in your life when you're faced with a decision that could have far-reaching consequences, and this felt like one of them. The consequences would be for me, not Jonathan. I must have looked distracted, because he took my shawl and wound it round me so that it roped me to him.

'What is it?' he asked.

'I don't know. I think I just had an out-of-body experience.'

'Space cadet.'

He pulled me against his side and dropped a light kiss on my hair. His hands were firm and warm on my arms and I knew that if I did kiss him he wouldn't reject me. I came within a nano of it. I could feel everything tense, my breathing become shallow. And then I panicked.

He was drunk and he didn't really mean it and it would be a disaster and he'd be embarrassed and I'd feel like the enemy. He was my friend and I didn't have so many that I could afford to play games and push him away. It was stupid.

'Sorry. I can't do this.' Flustered and confused, I drew away and twitched at my dress, smoothing the skirt and looking anywhere but at his face. 'I'm such an idiot.'

'Don't. You're right.'

'I don't know about that.'

He turned my face so that I was forced to look at him. 'Listen, Alice. Please don't think I don't want you. I do. But I don't want to hurt you because you mean so much to me, and I probably would. You know me well enough—'

'Jonathan! Shut up. For God's sake, I don't give a monkey's. I know perfectly well what you're like and I've no desire to be part of your oat-sowing process. Just because gorgeous women fall at your feet with mystifying regularity, doesn't mean I have to. We're friends, that's all.'

I felt a tight knot in my stomach. I adored this man and valued his friendship, but frankly, there were times when I really, really hated him.

He frowned and looked hurt. He undid his bow tie and jerked his collar loose. It was hard to tell if he was more aggravated with me, himself, or the constrictions of his hired suit.

'Sorry. My mistake. Look, this is a bad moment, and I've obviously made a complete prat of myself. I'll call you next week. We can meet for a drink.'

I had hit a sore spot. Tough. 'I'd like that,' I said. 'We can discuss your commitment problems.'

A movement in my peripheral vision made me turn and peer into the darkened shop and I thought I saw something that shouldn't have been there. A shadowy, diffused figure reflected in the window. I whirled around but there was no one else in the lane; only Jonathan, who was rubbing his jaw.

'I've been stung,' he said. 'Bloody countryside. Remind me never to move out of London.'

In the end, Rory, Daniel and I didn't leave until three in the morning. Daniel sat in the back of the car while Rory and I talked. There was something curiously harmonious about that drive, about the three of us; Daniel out for the count, so not winding me up, Rory humming a pop song when he ran out of energy for conversation, me joining in tunelessly. The road was clear, the night was cloudless and strewn with stars and Gabby and Dad were married. All was well with the world. Driving at night was such a peaceful experience, an opportunity for navel-gazing, if I allowed myself that luxury. I chose not to and thought about work instead. Vincent was making noises about leaving me to set up as a photographer. He was the best – actually, the only assistant I'd ever had, and he was fantastic. I didn't want to lose him, but neither did I want to impede his progress. I knew what it was like to feel that way.

Headlights from the other side of the central reservation threw white light across the car. I looked round and saw that Rory had nodded off, his head cradled by the seat belt, his arms lightly crossed over his stomach, his bow tie hanging louchely around his neck and his shirt untucked. He reminded me of his brother and, despite my best intentions, I found it impossible not to go there. I was still strung out over my conversation with Jonathan, replaying it in my head and coming up with things I could have said that would have been so much better, so much wittier. I had been too defensive – and for what? I'd love to have sat down and talked properly, deep into the night, but he never let me do that; never let me get under his skin. Ah well, if I wanted to spend hours putting the world and our souls to rights, there was always Rory.

A horn blared, cutting the night in two and I jerked back in my seat as the headlights of an oncoming lorry obliterated the darkness, blinding me. I swore loudly, wrestling the wheel, swerving as the lorry burst through the metal barrier and slammed into us. Rory and Daniel lurched out of sleep and we screamed as the car was forced into reverse, shunted backwards until we collided with the concrete legs of a bridge crossing the motorway. And then I was sucked away from it all and time seemed to slow down and I found myself somewhere beyond the pain and the mess. For some reason I thought of Sam. His image was so strong that I could have reached out and touched him. My little friend. My protector. And that was all. I closed my eyes and felt myself leave.

'One adult female,' the voice said. 'Not responding. Two adult males: one semi-conscious, one not responding.'

Then

I AM SITTING IN THE KITCHEN EATING MY LUNCH UNDER MUM'S watchful eye.

'Alice, sweetie, for goodness' sake, hold it with your fork and cut it with your knife. It's not that difficult.'

I know she's waiting for me to spill something or make a mess. I eat as carefully as I can, but knives and forks are really hard. I'm not like my big sister, Olivia, who is very pretty and does everything right. Mum says I have two left hands and two left feet. I frown and concentrate even harder. I'm always the last to finish meals, unless it's macaroni cheese or something like that; then I eat too quickly and get told off for bad manners. Sam never eats with me. That isn't allowed. My family mostly ignore him, except when they are being unkind.

'Were you having fun out there?'

I blink. 'A bit. Can we go to the park?'

'Olivia should be back from the shops soon. She can take you.'

'I don't want to go with Olivia. I like going with you and Sam.'

'Thanks,' Mum says with an odd lilt to her voice. 'I'm glad you put me first.'

I glance down at my plate. I know I've gone red because I can feel it.

'Have you had enough?'

Mum takes my plate and puts one of the crusts I've left in her mouth. She chews with her back to me and clatters the plate into

29

the sink and then cuts me a big slice of Neapolitan ice cream and watches me while I eat it. I finish it all then drink up my orange squash and push the glass away.

'Out you go then.'

She swipes up the bowl and gives me a quick push in the direction of the garden. I play with Olivia's old matty-haired Barbies; dressing and positioning them and taking their photographs with my empty Kodak Instamatic, just how I imagine Dad does when he's at work. After mud-perfume it's my favourite game. Sometimes I make Sam pretend to be famous so that I can take his picture.

The sound of Mum's laughter bounces out into the garden and I look up expectantly then go back to the dolls. After a few minutes the doorbell rings and I run to the house and stand with Sam just inside the kitchen.

'Maybe it's Dad,' I say.

From the hallway, we can hear Mum. She's not happy.

'Oh, for God's sake, I'm not doing anything of the kind. Anyway, Paula, I'm very busy right now.'

I glance at Sam. 'It's Gran. I hope Mum lets her in.'

'She will. Your mum can't fight Granny Byrne.'

'How do you know?'

Sam shifts his feet on the lino floor. 'I just know.'

'You're a know-it-all.'

'And you're a know-nothing.'

I giggle and hear my grandmother say, 'I won't be long. I would like to see my granddaughter.'

'You could have rung first.'

I stare through the door to the narrow hall. Mum really hates Gran and tells everyone it's because of her that Dad left, not because she kept being cross with him. I don't know which is true, but I wish he hadn't gone away. He's fun and doesn't get as annoyed with me as Mum does.

'I tried. Your phone's been engaged most of the morning. I don't call that looking after your child.'

'It's none of your business, Paula.' Mum moves back against the wall, her arms crossed, her face resigned. 'If you want to see her, she's in the garden. You can let yourself out.'

Gran comes over to inspect my bowl of perfume, dabs some on her wrists and sniffs it. 'That is gorgeous, my darling.'

My grandmother is small and a bit wide, like Dad, with black hair that Mum says is dyed and brown eyes, and she doesn't exactly stare, but she spends a long time looking at people.

I flop down on the rug and Gran joins me slowly, cranking herself into position.

'So what have you been up to?' she says.

I lean against her and she feels cosy and smells lovely. She wears a perfume that is faint like flowers that you have to go close up to before you can smell them. 'Playing with Sam.'

'That's nice. What were you playing?'

'Barbies.' I pull a blade of grass up and puff it away from my fingers.

Gran hesitates and then says, 'Poor boy. I don't expect he liked that very much.'

She glances around and then she sees Sam and goes still. The way she's looking at him makes me hold my breath. She stands up and turns away from me and Sam moves towards her. I can't see her face, but I can feel them staring at each other, as if they've met before somewhere. It goes through my body, prickling me. Sam has seen her lots of times, but I don't think she's really noticed him, even though she's told me she does. That's just like the rest of my family. But today is different.

'I'm Alice's friend,' Sam says. 'She asked me to come.'

He holds out his hand and touches hers and she smiles and he answers her by laughing, his face shining. Mum is leaning against the door frame, a cigarette drooping between her fingers, glaring. The moment passes and Gran turns back to me.

'Who do you play with at school, Alice?' she asks as she settles down beside me. 'Is there no little girl you can invite home?'

'I don't really want them to come here.'

'But why not? You have a lovely garden to play in and a pretty bedroom.'

I chew at my thumbnail and frown. 'Olivia gets cross when I take friends into the bedroom. It's better when I go to their houses.'

Sam holds out his hand but Gran ignores him. He looks down at his knees and I feel sorry for him and annoyed all at the same time. When he's unhappy it makes me feel guilty, even though it isn't my fault.

'Alice, I have to go now.' Gran starts to get up, but I grab hold of her sleeve.

'Please don't go yet. Tell me a story first.'

'Just one then. What sort of story would you like?'

I glance at Sam and he leans over to whisper in my ear.

'Sam wants one about Fred. About when you were a little girl.'

'Fred? You are funny. I'd no idea you remembered him.'

I remember him perfectly but I worry that I've asked the wrong thing and feel like I have to defend myself. 'You told me a story about him before.'

'Indeed I did. Maybe that wasn't so wise.'

I don't know what she means so I don't say anything. A moment goes by and then Gran starts to talk. She tells stories much better than Mum does, using different voices for different people. Fred has a clipped way of speaking, like chopping celery. Sam curls up on the rug, one hand against Gran's thigh, the other tucked into mine. His eyes are closed but I know he's listening. Sam always listens and always remembers.

'Sam is like Fred,' I say, after Gran has finished. 'Do you like him?'

Gran kisses the tip of my nose. 'I love him. You take care of him and he'll take care of you. He told me he would.'

After she leaves, Mum comes out into the garden. She stands

still, looking around, and then the cat darts past and she shrugs and goes back inside, leaving me and Sam alone, the way we like it.

Chapter Two

I WAS SURE I COULD HEAR DAD'S VOICE. OR MAYBE THAT WAS BEFORE. My mind, when I began to surface, was a muddle of dreams and memories, like strands of spaghetti tangling in a bowl. There were noises I didn't recognize coming from outside my head and voices inside. I felt unsafe and I wanted to cling to my father, but I couldn't and he began to sound as if he was talking through a wall. The brightness on the other side of my eyelids stung. A shadow fell across them and I opened my eyes, saw a form shimmering beside me and thought I must be dead.

It must have been much later when I opened my eyes again, because it was light outside. I closed them and gave it a few seconds, then tried again, squinting up at the ceiling. Polystyrene tiles and strip lights. I lay still, trying to work out where I was. From somewhere close by I could hear a foreign woman talking and the swoosh and click of closing doors and quick steps slapping down a corridor. The wedding? But it wasn't the sound of high heels on a wooden floor; it was more like cheap flats on lino.

What had I been doing? I felt my face, winced and moved my fingers up to my forehead and touched bandages. My ribs were agony. I closed my eyes and thought hard, searching for a definite moment in time, something I could use as a landmark. I saw Rory and Daniel strolling ahead of me and I felt gravel shift under my shoes. That was it. I had been to the wedding. And there was Dad waiting in the church, his greying hair neatly tied with a white velvet ribbon like a seventeenth-century courtier. There wasn't much else. I tried to picture Gabby's dress but I could only conjure her up in jeans and black leather jacket.

And then what? How did I come to be here? I must have fallen asleep waiting for Rory and Daniel to be ready to leave. But why had they let me? They had a christening to get to. Idiots. Perhaps if I dragged myself out of bed now, made us all some coffee, they'd still get there in time.

No, that wasn't right. I was confused. I was in hospital. I stared up at the ceiling and followed a section of white trunking, but it was too exhausting and I closed my eyes again. I concentrated. Church service. Reception. OK, got that. A little disjointed, but never mind. There was something else though that I couldn't grasp. It was too fleeting. God, I was thirsty.

A nurse entered the room and I opened my eyes. She hurried to my side and pressed the bell next to the bed.

'Alice, you're in hospital. You've been in an accident, but you're going to be fine.'

Within minutes I wished I had kept my eyes closed and slept a bit more. There was too much noise, too much going on and too many voices asking me questions.

Go *away*.

Did I say that out loud? I wasn't sure and I was too lethargic to care.

I had a vague impression of the doctor. He was black and had a lovely smile, but his face seemed to expand and shrink like a balloon being blown up and let down. I nearly laughed but thought he might be offended. He chatted about nothing in particular, shone a torch in my eyes, listened to my heart and checked my blood pressure. He told me that he was a neurosurgeon and that I had been in a coma for three weeks. He put his hand on my shoulder and the sense of authority and protection in the gesture made me want to cover it with my own hand and keep it there.

Rory? I opened my eyes and blinked, turned my head a fraction and saw a man sitting on the chair in the corner. Not Rory, I realized, and wanted to cry. But he seemed familiar all the same. I mumbled something but I didn't know what it was and neither did he, because he didn't answer. My eyelids drooped.

The next time I woke up I knew he was still there even before I opened my eyes. I thought perhaps he was a junior doctor or a medical student, but if that was the case, he was surprisingly relaxed. I pushed myself up with difficulty and drank some water. It was ridiculous to feel embarrassed about being in bed, but I couldn't help it.

'Are you my doctor?'

The man lifted his head and blinked at me.

'Alice, it's Sam.'

My mouth felt tacky and dry and my vision wasn't focused. Was I meant to know this person? Maybe I'd lost my memory. I frowned at him.

'I'm sorry, I don't . . .'

He came to my bedside and sat down, shifting his knees so that they weren't pressed against the side of the bed. He had fine features: long lashes, pale skin, a wide mouth and silky black hair. Was he my boyfriend? The effort of trying to remember, to place him, was exhausting. 'Sam? And are we . . . I mean, have I known you long?'

He smiled. 'I'm just Sam. Don't you remember me? I can't have changed that much.'

There was something about his tone, about the way he smiled, that took me right back, so clearly that I could smell toast and marmalade all mixed up with my mother's cigarettes, could feel

36

grass and grit under my bare feet, the rough grain of the tree house under my hands. Sam. No, it couldn't be.

'I've come back,' he said.

I shook my head, stared at him for a moment and then closed my eyes firmly. Silence. I dozed and when I woke he was still there but he was fast asleep. I stared at him, trying to find a hook, something about him that was irrefutably Sam, but once I started examining each feature separately my first impressions became elusive and I couldn't be sure. Eventually he woke and smiled drowsily at me and his expression caught me off guard because it spoke to me in a way his words hadn't. It reminded me of loneliness. God, I thought. He had been so real to me back then. Had I regressed twenty years?

I searched his face and tried to think sensibly, to create a chronology of events, but everything was mixed up: work with weddings; a bright flash that could be a camera taking pictures or a car crashing in the night; groups of people, their red mouths opening and shutting; laughter and music and the whirl of a silk dress as Gabby took to the dance floor, her white-blonde hair threaded with flowers.

'What do you remember about the wedding?' he asked.

'I remember dancing. With Lottie and Elizabeth.' I frowned. 'Not much else. The lights hanging from the trees.' I bit my lip. 'Were you there?'

'Yes, of course I was.'

'Sorry. This isn't right. It's lovely, so lovely to see you, but I know you aren't real. Next time I wake up you'll be gone.'

'So let's make the most of it while it lasts.'

'You've changed a lot.'

'Have I? What do I look like?'

'Don't you know? Your eyes are the same, and your smile. But you're older. You're handsome. Were you in the accident too? Is that why you're here?'

'I'm here because you called me.'

37

'I'm going to give you something to help you sleep.'

'No,' I said. 'Please don't. I don't want to go back there.'

'Nothing bad is going to happen,' Mr King said. 'We've contacted your parents so they should be here soon. In the meantime, one of the nurses will sit with you so you won't be alone.'

'They don't have to stay. Sam's here.'

Why did I say that? I was so disorientated. I picked up on a subtle change in the atmosphere, sensing it in my fingertips and the back of my neck. It was almost as though the objects around me had no real substance, like I could shut my eyes and open them again and they'd be gone. Proof to me that something wasn't right, that my brain was overcompensating for whatever damage had been done, creating things – people – who did not actually exist. It would calm down soon, with any luck, and return to normal. I had to relax, not get so anxious.

The consultant looked into my eyes. I noticed that he had extremely long lashes. At least his face wasn't warping any more.

'Alice, you haven't had any visitors yet,' Mr King said. 'Is there anyone you'd like us to contact? Sam, perhaps? Is he your boyfriend? We could certainly call him, if you like, let him know that you're conscious and of sound mind.' His laughter was a rumble, starting from his belly and stopping abruptly when he realized I wasn't smiling.

Should I tell him about the hallucinations? I wanted to, but I was getting tired again and I blinked away the urge to black out. I heard the doctor whisper something to the nurse and the shift of the chair as she sat down beside the bed. Then the consultant left and there was silence. I turned my head and opened my eyes.

'Can you get me a mirror?'

Sam was back, sitting in the chair that the nurse had vacated.

'How're you feeling?' he asked.

I looked at him suspiciously. 'Crap.' I reached up and touched my face. 'Do I look a mess?'

'Not too bad, considering you've been all the colours of the rainbow in the last three weeks.' His smile was mocking and warm. As if he knew me well enough to take the piss.

'And what colour am I now?'

'Yellow, with a lingering hint of purple.'

'I asked the nurse to get me a mirror. Is it here?' I couldn't turn my head enough to look.

'Not yet.'

'What's the time?' I asked.

'No idea.'

'Don't you have a watch?'

'I used to, but it was bizarre. I'd think an hour had passed, but then I'd look and it was only ten minutes. So I threw it away.'

I put a hand to my head. 'I have absolutely no idea what you are talking about.'

'No. I know that. Don't think about it. It doesn't matter.'

He put his hand on my shoulder and I felt the warmth of it, the real sympathy in the gesture. I didn't feel the need to explain. I thought he understood.

'You're awake,' the nurse said. 'Wonderful.'

I'd had another mini blackout. It felt as though I was living in a badly edited movie, the normal flow of life disrupted by clumsy cutting. I had a feeling someone else had come in while I dozed. A tall presence, moving around the room and then sitting by my bed. I was far too groggy to wake up and open my eyes. I wondered who it was, hoping it was one of the Walkers. Jonathan maybe. Visiting the boys. But that depended on what had happened to them. I felt my ribs tighten around my lungs.

'I've brought you a mirror, but don't be too shocked by what you see. Most of it will have disappeared in a few weeks and the scar on your forehead will fade. You can grow a fringe.'

I'd had a fringe once before. When I was nine I had hair that parted in the middle and went down to just above my shoulders. I had wanted a straight fringe like one of the girls in my class had, so I cut it myself. It was a disaster. Gran was looking after me because Mum was out on one of her rare modelling assignments and Mandy wasn't able to help out. When Gran saw what I had done, she told me off. I can remember my mouth dragging down at the corners, the tears coming.

'It'll grow out,' she said, softening. 'Don't worry, darling, and stop making that terrible face – the wind will change and you'll be stuck with it.'

I pressed my fingernails into my palms. It felt like the end of the world.

'Why aren't I pretty?'

'You are pretty.'

I looked straight into her face and caught the shift of her eyes. She was thinking one thing and saying another, just like all grown-ups.

'No I'm not.'

She twisted round on the sofa and cupped my cheeks with her hands. 'You're a child, Alice. Be patient and it'll come. You have lovely eyes, a beautiful smile and a pretty nose. Everything is in the right place; you just haven't grown into your potential yet.'

'What if I never do?'

'Well, you certainly won't if you think like that. For a start, you can take that look off your face and smile. I promise, by the time you're sixteen you'll be gorgeous.'

I wasn't convinced but I was eager not to appear negative. 'As gorgeous as Olivia?'

'Maybe even more so. Shall I tell you a secret? When I was your age I was an ugly little girl. But you've seen pictures of me when I was a young woman, haven't you? I was beautiful. Your grandfather fell in love with me the moment he saw me.'

I was so overcome with the romance of it that I hugged her too tightly. She laughed and prised my fingers off her waist. 'Alice, if I tell you something else, will you promise never to tell Olivia or Simon?'

I nodded.

'You are my favourite grandchild. You always have been, from the moment I saw you in Michael's arms. You have his eyes and his smile.'

'I'll leave you with it, shall I?' the nurse said, startling me out of my reverie. 'Have a look, get used to it, and I'll be back in five minutes with some breakfast. I'm sure you could do with a cup of tea.'

'Thank you. Could you get one for Sam as well?'

'Oh, let's wait until he arrives, dear, otherwise it'll just get cold.'

'OK. Thanks.' I had to get hold of myself.

She had been heading for the door, but she turned back. 'Oh, and a nice young man came in.'

I held my breath. 'What did he look like?'

'Tall. Black. Left you those flowers.' She indicated a fresh vase of freesias.

Vincent. My assistant. That was sweet of him.

'Just ten minutes then. We mustn't tire her out.'

Dad had brought flowers. He shifted three vases, placed his offering right in the centre of the windowsill and inspected the others. Knowing him, he probably wanted to make sure his were from the more expensive florist. I darted a glance at Sam and decided not to say anything. The hallucinations were hardly likely to go on for ever, so there was no point making a big deal of it.

'Sweetheart, you look like roadkill.'

'Thanks,' I managed.

That wasn't a very nice thing to say, but when I looked at him properly, I saw tears in his eyes. Dad had always been emotional; small of stature, big of heart.

He sat down and put his hand over mine. 'It's so good to see you awake. You can't imagine what we've been through. We thought we might lose you.'

What about Rory and Daniel? Why had no one mentioned them? My voice came out in a whisper. 'What happened?'

I looked up and saw that Sam had gone very still, his face frozen with tension. He needed to know as badly as I did.

'You were in a car crash. Either your mother or I have been here every day. I'm so sorry neither of us were around when you woke up. I'm gutted. It must have been very confusing.'

My lips felt dry and brittle. I licked them carefully. 'Dad? Where's Rory?'

'I spoke to your consultant before I came in,' he said, and I wondered if he had even heard me. But if he had and he wasn't ready to tell me then I wasn't ready for the answer. My body was heavy with drugs. I wanted to sleep.

Dad was still talking. 'He said you have to expect a few hiccups, but considering the knock your brain took, you're doing remarkably well. He expects you'll be in for at least another week.'

A hiccup? Was that what Sam was? 'How bad was my injury?'

Dad hesitated for a moment, and then said, 'Pretty bad. You had a subdural haematoma and fractured your skull and you've broken several ribs. You'll have to avoid laughing and coughing for a while.'

'I'll do my best,' I said.

Mum arrived and Dad let out a sigh of frustration. I had to struggle to focus on her. When I did, I thought she looked lovely. Bright and fresh. Her hair had been beautifully highlighted, her long legs were encased in tight white trousers and a sheer white shirt floated over a white spaghetti-strap vest.

'Darling, I'm so sorry. I would have been here sooner but the traffic was a nightmare. How are you?'

'Good to see you too, Julia,' Dad said.

42

Then

I HAVE STRICT INSTRUCTIONS TO STAY IN MY ROOM, BUT I CAN'T SLEEP. I'm too excited. Simon, who is in charge of me while Mum is away for the weekend, is having a party. Olivia is sulking over at a friend's house because he said she couldn't come. But he only said that because she refused to change her plans and help him look after me.

Sam and I creep around, trying to be inconspicuous, listening to the shouts and watching over the banister as groups of teenagers turn up at the front door, carrying six-packs and bottles of wine.

The party soon gets out of hand; there are too many people stuffed into our tiny house and the music is very loud. There's a lot of stupid yelling, mostly from the boys. We hear the sound of breaking glass coming from the front of the house and race into Mum's room.

'Piss off!'

The voice comes out of the dark, from the huge pile of coats on Mum's bed. It moves, rising like a monster, and I freeze and Sam drags me away and we jump on to my bed and wrap the duvet round our shoulders. At one point a boy and a girl open the door and let in a blast of music.

They spot me and the boy says, 'There's a fucking kid in here,' before they slam out.

'I want to go to the loo,' I say.

I open the door and stare. The party has moved to the landing.

A girl in a tartan miniskirt and fishnet tights is wrapped round a spotty, ugly boy and another sits cross-legged beside the bathroom door, drinking straight from a bottle of red wine while her friend kneels beside her, backcombing her sticky hair. We edge round them and try the door. It's locked and from behind it we can hear someone vomiting.

I rock from one foot to the other. 'Maybe I should get Simon.'

'I don't think so,' Sam says. 'He said you have to stay out of sight.'

'But I'm bursting.'

'Knock on the door again.'

I try not to cry but my bottom lip is trembling. 'When are they going to go away? When's Mum coming back?'

Sam doesn't know. He says he wishes she was here too. We wait but the bathroom door still doesn't open and eventually I give up and we push our way down the stairs but before we reach the bottom a boy with a bright blue Mohican shoves his booted feet against the banisters and raises his knees so I can't get past. 'What's your name, shorty?'

'Alice.'

'Alex? Is that a boy or a girl's name?'

I shrink against Sam and blurt out, 'I said Alice. It's a girl's name.'

'I don't think so. You look like a little boy to me.'

'I'm not. I'm a girl.'

The boy takes a swig of lager and looks me up and down. 'Nope. You're a boy.'

'I'm a girl,' I insist, outraged and confused by his persistence.

'Yeah? Prove it.'

'Leave her alone, Patrick, you wanker,' another boy says. 'She's only little.' He crouches down, takes a look at me and frowns. 'Jesus, she's shit scared, poor thing. Alice, is it?'

I nod.

'I'm Johnnie.'

Patrick sneers, 'Listen to you, Mother Teresa. You queer or something?'

'Piss off, you dickhead.' Johnnie grabs him by the shirt, brings his face in close and then shoves him so that he falls against the banister. He pats me on the shoulder.

'Don't listen to that idiot. Are you all right?'

'Stupid question,' Sam says.

I breathe hard and look up at my rescuer, rubbing my tears away with the back of my hand.

'I need a wee. They won't come out.'

'OK. Come on. I'll sort it.' Johnnie drags me back upstairs and thumps the bathroom door with the side of his fist. 'Come out, you jerks, some of us have to take a leak.'

'Naff off!'

'Get out, or I'm going to break the door down, you tossers.' He looks down at me and grimaces. 'Sorry. Put your hands over your ears.'

I do as I'm told and so does Sam. We stare at each other, petrified. Johnnie kicks the heel of his boot against the door and leaves a dent in it. I wince, thinking of Mum and the trouble Simon is going to get into. Finally, after a bit of shuffling, some whispering and laughter, the door opens and a boy and girl walk out.

'Keep your hair on,' the boy says as Johnnie thrusts me past him.

I close the door but it's too late. I sit on the loo and stare at my knees, mortified beyond words. I wonder whether I can stay in the bathroom for the rest of the night. That way no one will ever know. But I can't because other people will need it, so I get up reluctantly, drag Sam away from the mirror where he has been staring at himself for the last five minutes, and unbolt the door.

Johnnie is leaning against the wall. He pushes himself away with his foot. 'All right?'

I mumble something and my eyes well.

'What's up now?'

I gaze into his eyes, silently beseeching him to go away.

He frowns. 'Oh . . . right. Why don't you go and get changed? Then I'd stay out of the way if I were you. Go on. You'll be fine.'

I wish I could disappear into the floor. To my relief he leaves it at that, patting my head before throwing himself back into the party. The last we see of him, a black-haired girl has draped herself over his arm.

When we go back to my bedroom there are people on my bed and on Olivia's, kissing as if their faces are glued together, so we wedge ourselves into the airing cupboard and huddle up against each other. Sam says it's called French kissing. I knew that already. After a while, we hear shouting downstairs and creep out to see what's going on. A blue light is flashing on the other side of the frosted-glass front door and I'm about to go down when Simon charges up, grabs me by the arm and drags me into the bedroom. The kids who had been kissing leap up and run downstairs. We hear a commotion in the garden and peer out of the window as a mass of laughing and hooting teenagers scramble over the fence. Simon pulls me down.

'Get under the bed. And don't make a sound. The police are here.'

'I want Mum.'

'Well, she's not bloody here, you idiot, and this is an emergency. Look, Alice. I'm really sorry if you're scared, but it'll be fine. You have to hide now.'

'I don't want to. I was hiding before and it was horrible. You shouldn't have had a party.'

'Alice, for Christ's sake, I haven't got time to argue. Get under the bed.'

I fold my arms and shrink my neck into my shoulders. 'No.'

Simon screws up his face as if he's trying to stop himself losing his temper. 'If they find you they'll take you away and give you to another family.'

It's like a punch in the stomach. I don't want to be stubborn any more; I just want it to be finished. I'm tired and I start to cry but I do what I'm told and crawl under the bed and Sam and I lie there holding hands. Someone looks into the room and we see two sturdy black shoes and the bottom of a pair of sharply creased black trousers. Sam squeezes my hand so hard that it hurts. He murmurs 'Waltzing Matilda' to keep me calm. The shoes turn away and the door closes, and after a while everything goes quiet and Simon comes and slumps down on the edge of the bed. We wriggle out and I sit between Sam and my brother and he puts his arm around me.

He says, 'You stink.'

'I wet myself.'

'Mum's going to kill me.'

I look up at him and bury myself in his arms.

Chapter Three

I MUST HAVE DOZED AGAIN, BECAUSE SOMETHING SEEMED TO BE
missing between Mum's initial greeting and the whispered argument developing between my parents. By this time Sam had sat
down again, his chin dropped to his chest. He looked as though
he might be asleep. I was feeling more awake than I had done
earlier and although the pain was worse I didn't say anything
because I wanted my brain to stay unclouded for as long as I could
stand it. This, whatever it was – phenomenon? – surely wouldn't
last much longer. A coma meant a serious head injury, so it was
hardly surprising my brain was playing tricks. It'd settle down
soon, once I was stronger and back in control. It had to, because
this was disconcerting to say the least.

'I'd offer to have her but Larry and I are getting married
soon and the house is about to be sold. I'm completely snowed
under and the bedrooms are full of boxes. You and Gabby have
more space.'

'Julia—'

'Can I remind you that you are her father and you weren't
around when she was growing up? It's about time you pulled your
weight and put someone else first. She's going to need time and
space to recuperate and your house is much bigger than mine.'

'Julia—'

'And if she came to us she'd be reminded of you-know-what all
the time. She'll have to go to you.'

'Julia, shut the fuck up, will you! Of course we'll take her. I don't need you to tell me what's right and wrong. And as for not being around while she was growing up – Jesus, let's not go there . . . it just makes me angry.'

'Well, you weren't there, Mike, were you? And if you think buying her a flat makes it all right, it doesn't.'

'It didn't do any harm.'

'You could have thrown a bit of that spare cash at us when she was younger.'

I was drifting. It wasn't the first time I'd heard this sort of thing from my parents. They should never have married. But then again, if they hadn't, I wouldn't have existed. Would I have cared about that? I forced myself to stay awake. I was scared they would leave without telling me about the boys.

I opened my eyes. 'Mum?'

Mum took my hand. 'You rest, darling, and get better. I don't want you to miss my wedding.' She kissed me gently. So not like Mum. 'I'll drop in again soon.'

As soon as she left, Sam lifted his head and grinned at me. 'She hasn't changed.'

'No. She's getting married again.'

'I heard.'

'Are you asleep?' Dad asked, tapping my hand. 'You're not making sense.'

'Sorry.' I felt muddled and slightly embarrassed. Like when I was a child and all excited about having the right answer and put my hand up and it turned out that I was way off and the teacher sighed in a way that made the other children laugh.

'Don't worry about it. You're exhausted. I'll come again, and when you're feeling stronger I'll bring Gabby and the kids. They've been desperately worried about you. We all love you. We'll take care of you.'

I took a deep breath. My heart was pounding. 'What happened to Rory and Daniel?'

Dad took my hand, weaving his fingers through mine, his dark eyes filling with tears. 'Daniel's fine. Just cuts and bruises . . .'

'No,' I said, tears streaming. 'No, Dad. Please don't say it. I can't . . .'

'I'm so sorry, sweetheart, but Rory didn't make it. He died at the scene.' He pulled a tissue out of the box beside the bed and wiped my eyes before pressing it against his own. 'It wasn't your fault, Alice. Trust me. It was an accident. Some git of a lorry driver who hadn't slept in twenty-four hours. He came through it completely unscathed.' His voice choked. 'Please calm down, sweetheart. You're not doing yourself any good.'

'He's not dead. He can't be dead.' I started to wail. 'Dad, please don't go.'

He was getting up from the chair. 'I'm not going anywhere.' He eased his hand out of mine and went to the door, opened it and leaned out.

'Nurse,' he barked.

The nurse hurried in and I cringed as she came over to the bed. I don't know what I thought she was going to do. She poured me a glass of water from the jug and supported me while I sipped it.

'I'm going to give you a sedative, Alice,' she said brightly. 'You need your strength if you're going to get better.'

I took it without a murmur. All I wanted was darkness. I felt myself lose consciousness with a sense of relief. The last thing I heard was my father's voice, telling me everything was going to be all right. I knew it wasn't true.

When I woke to find that Dad had gone, I closed my eyes in despair. My head ached and I didn't think I had any tears left, but they kept coming, rolling down my cheeks. I had to fight the urge to howl.

'Why are you here?' I asked.

Sam rubbed his face and looked at me. He was tired. 'I honestly don't know.'

'Do you think I'm still dreaming? I must be. You can't really be real, it's impossible.'

'There's no point worrying about it, is there? Just get better. I'm here for you and I'll be your friend.' He broke into a smile. 'Do you remember how we were when we were small?'

It seemed easier to go along with it, whatever it was, than to fight. 'I remember.'

'Well, that's how it'll be now. Minus the Barbies though, if you don't mind.'

I smiled through my tears. 'But what does it mean?'

'I have no idea. This has never happened to me before. I could definitely get used to it though.' His brow furrowed. 'Do you mind me being here?'

'It's not a question of minding, is it? It's more a question of believing.'

I was holding the mirror, glass side down, on the blanket. I turned it over and lifted it slowly. I barely recognized myself. My face was bruised and ugly, my eyes bloodshot and exhausted. Sam took it from me and then leaned in close so that his head was next to mine on the pillow. We stared at our reflections, me probing my face gingerly; I dreaded to think what was under the bandages. Sam's smile slowly broke.

'Oh, Jesus,' he breathed. He touched his eyes, felt his jaw, his lips, his hair. He seemed energized; as if he couldn't contain himself. I felt tired just watching him.

'I thought you had died,' he said. 'I thought I would die with you.'

'I don't know what you mean.'

'Yes, you do. Don't fight it, Alice. Just accept me.'

That's it, I thought. I'm still in a coma. I'm dreaming. None of this is real. I'll wake up any minute now and I'll be back at the wedding and Rory will still be alive. I'll crash on the sofa and Rory and Daniel can get the train home and everything will be as it should be.

I woke feeling woozy and dizzy, my mind and body heavy with painkillers. I couldn't focus without an effort. Sam was there, but his figure was unsteady. I blinked and tried again and he became solid, hard-edged, and three-dimensional. I shivered and pulled the blue blanket over my shoulders. I desperately wanted to touch his face, to feel the shape of his nose and mouth, the texture of his skin, like a blind woman absorbing a lover's features through her fingertips, but something stopped me touching him, some latent spark of self-protection. As if reading my mind, he took my hand and pressed it to his chest. It's hard to explain the effect the gesture had on me; it was a drink of water after a long walk; it was good news after an anxious wait; a burst of lightning after a heavy, sultry day.

'Can you feel my heartbeat?' he said.

I closed my eyes and nodded. I could feel the strength of his hand round my wrist, the warmth of his skin through his shirt, the strong beat of his heart. 'But no one can see you.'

'They're not interested in seeing me. They never were.'

I reached up and placed my hand against his jaw. 'You need a shave.'

'It's been a bit of a vigil, watching over you. I haven't had time.'

Chapter Four

AFTER I WAS DISCHARGED FROM HOSPITAL, THE FIRST THING I WANTED to do was see Rory's family, and Dad, reluctantly, agreed to make a detour. I could understand why none of them had come to see me in the hospital, but every day I still hoped for and dreaded a visit. I hoped that at least Jonathan would look in, but I didn't really expect Rory's mother. I could only imagine how devastated Emma must be; how much had been ripped from her. Not seeing them hurt me so much, but if I thought about it, which I did – there wasn't much else to think about – I knew I was being unreasonable. I wasn't family. Their grief was private. But I was in agony too, tormented by the loss of Rory, submerged by the guilt, made nauseous by the *what ifs*. What if I had left fifteen minutes earlier instead of faffing around saying goodbye to people who were too drunk to remember or care if I did? What if I had never met Rory that day, nearly ten years ago? And then there was the place I couldn't go; the words I didn't dare say even to myself, let alone to anyone else. I shuddered and thrust the thought away.

I could not get my head round the fact that Rory hadn't been at my bedside, cracking bad jokes to cheer me up. Every time I thought about him it sent a wave of horror through me. I couldn't imagine the nightmare ever going away.

The police came to the hospital with an accident investigator to complete their witness statements. It was strange, being taken back to that day, trying to fit the torn pieces together to make some sort of whole. Even stranger, trying to divest it of the waves of emotion that pulled me back and flung me forward. I remembered little of the car journey. Only a feeling of contentment, of taking care of two sleepy men, like a mother picking her inebriated teenagers up from a party.

I tried to answer their questions. I tried my hardest to remember what had happened but nothing seemed to stick in my mind for long enough to seem real. They wanted to know if anything had distracted me at the fatal moment. They meant, I supposed, had I not been alert when I needed to be? I didn't know. They asked me about the wedding, about why I had chosen to leave in the small hours, rather than wait for a more sensible time. I explained that Rory and Daniel had to be somewhere in Oxfordshire by ten the next morning.

I would be able to sue the lorry driver. They told me that as if it was something good, that I'd get a lot of money. I didn't care about money. I only cared about Rory and the Walker family. They advised me to do it anyway, because at the very least I'd need a new car. It was routine and my insurers and lawyer would deal with everything. I didn't want to think about how I would feel driving again, so I didn't think about it. It would happen when it happened.

Dad was very good at telling me what I ought to be doing, which was helpful, sort of, but the result was, I felt infantilized. I knew I wasn't well enough to go back to the flat, but that didn't mean I wasn't desperate to. Sam agreed, but he was more rational than me; he saw things the way I did, but he also knew how things were. He had observed the people around me for long enough to understand them.

He was in the back of Dad's Mercedes when we left the hospital. Why didn't that bother me? Couldn't I see it was completely bizarre and totally irrational? Perhaps I was mad. A head injury could cause distortions of the mind and most people would assume that that was what Sam was. I had heard of people who had survived strokes only to find they were speaking in a foreign language. I didn't know what he was, and nor did he, but we were agreed that he wasn't a ghost or a figment of my imagination, and if he was an anomaly, he was a warm and solid one. There was certainly no getting away from the physical reality of his presence. If I could touch him and hear him and he looked like a man, then surely he was a man?

So I was mad, obviously. On the other hand, I didn't say anything to Mr King or any of the nurses. Why was that? Did I want to keep him? Was I like a child hiding an insect in a match-box so that my parents wouldn't put it back? The truth was that I wasn't frightened, I was intrigued. I wanted to know how far this would go before he popped like a bubble and disappeared for good.

A car hooted and Dad swore as a Japanese woman walked across the road, ignoring the pedestrian lights. She turned and gave him a withering look. Sam laughed and I looked round at him and felt a gentle warmth steal over me. It was strange but he gave me such a strong sense of belonging and I'd never really had that before, I'd always felt peripheral to other lives; to family, friends and the people I worked with. Something that was supposedly natural seemed to require so much unnatural effort. Apart from Rory. I swallowed and turned to gaze out of the window at the people in the streets and wondered how they fitted, whether their lives were neat and well constructed, and how many were like me, trying hard to be part of a whole just to get by. Probably more than anyone realized.

We pulled up outside the Walkers' house and Dad turned to me. 'Are you absolutely sure?'

He had tried to persuade me that I should wait until they contacted me and I was beginning to regret not listening. I felt physically sick. It was the hardest thing I had ever had to do.

'Do you want me to come with you?' Sam asked.

'Yes.' It was easier to answer them both at the same time.

'I'll wait until I see you go in. Just in case.' Dad leaned over and kissed my cheek. 'I'm going to get a coffee. Good luck, sweetheart. Call me as soon as you're done and I'll be back in five minutes.'

I walked up the tiled path and rang the bell on the black front door and glanced up at the windows, hoping that they wouldn't see me before they answered. I had a horrible feeling they were waiting in silence, knowing it was me and hoping I would walk away. Sam stood beside me and I could see his face reflected in the glass. His fingers caught mine. Emma opened the door and we stared at each other. I cracked first, stepping towards her, and to my relief she hugged me fiercely. She had lost so much weight that I could feel her bones through her clothes.

'I'm so sorry to turn up like this,' I said. 'I should have checked first.'

She made a visible effort to pull herself together. 'Don't be silly. It's wonderful to see you.' She dried her eyes on a crumpled tissue and looked beyond me to Dad, waiting in the car. She nodded briefly at him. 'Come in, darling.'

I followed her in and heard the rev of Dad's engine as he drove away. There was an awkward moment when I sensed Emma was trying to work out how to handle me and I felt hollowed out inside and had to stop myself from running after the car.

Sam had moved ahead of me but he turned and held out his hand. 'Come on, Alice. You knew it wasn't going to be easy.'

I bit my lip and nodded and he smiled at me.

'Good girl.'

Dotty, their Labrador, padded up and I bent to stroke her but she drew back and snarled, her tail tucked tight between her hind legs.

'Dotty,' Emma said. 'Don't be silly. It's only Alice.'

I tried to look like I didn't mind, but I was hurt. I had known her since she was a puppy.

'How are you feeling?' She brushed my hair away from my forehead, gently passing over the dressing that still covered my scar.

'All right. A bit fragile.'

I felt an ache in my throat and put my hand over my mouth because my chin was wobbling. I followed Emma into the kitchen. This was my second home but it felt as though I was visiting it for the first time.

Brian put a tray of potatoes into the oven before turning to greet me. 'Sorry, Alice, we're all upside down. Sit down. I'll make you a cup of tea.'

'I won't stay long.' I hovered nervously by the kitchen table and then drew out a chair. 'I'm so sorry. I miss him so desperately. I wish I could have been at the funeral.'

'We're having a memorial service on his birthday,' Brian said. 'We want you there. You were such an enormous part of his life.'

Why would there be any question? 'Of course I'll come.' I pulled a hanky out of my sleeve and blew my nose. 'Is there anything I can give you a hand with?'

Sam was inspecting the photographs that decorated the walls. There were two that included me and he lingered near those: one of me and Rory walking through Richmond Park, taken from the back. Rory was pointing at something and my head was turned in that direction, following his finger with my eyes. Even without our faces you could see so much affection there. The other was of me, Jonathan and Rory lying flat on our backs in the garden. I missed those days.

'No,' Emma said. 'You don't need to do anything.'

I felt a creeping sense of isolation. I recognized it for what it was, but it still made me desperate. I started to talk, knowing that I should just shut up but unable to stay silent.

'I don't want to intrude, but I want to help. I want to feel like I'm still a part of your lives.' I caught the glance that Brian shot Emma and started to tremble from the effort not to cry. 'I don't want to lose you.'

'We know what happened that night,' Brian said. 'It was just appalling bad luck. As far as Emma and I are concerned you are as much a part of this family as you were before Rory . . .' He stopped and shook his head. 'Before Rory died. You mustn't ever think you're not welcome.'

The doorbell rang and I looked up anxiously, reaching for my mobile.

'It's only Jonathan and Megan,' Emma said, her pale face regaining a little colour. 'Stay for a few more minutes, won't you? They'd love to see you. Megan's been absolutely wonderful. I don't know what we'd have done without her. She's kept me from disintegrating completely.'

I smiled a little wanly. 'I'll call Dad anyway. It'll take him ten minutes to get back here.' I was shocked at how jealous I felt.

I listened to the bustle as they came into the hall and waited awkwardly while Jonathan fussed over Dotty, Megan behind him talking quietly to Brian. I felt engulfed by loneliness. I sensed that Jonathan knew I was there, even though I was outside his line of vision, and wondered why he was taking so long to acknowledge me, where the tension had come from. A memory nagged at me, but I couldn't pin it down. Sam had gone very still and was staring at him.

Eventually, Jonathan squeezed past Brian and came over and kissed me on the cheek.

'Alice. How are you? I'm so sorry I didn't get to the hospital.'

'It doesn't matter,' I said. 'You've had enough on your plate.'

And then I had a flash of memory and frowned. Something had happened but I wasn't sure what. Sam snapped out of his trance and came and stood behind me and wrapped his arms around my waist. For a moment I leaned into him but it felt all wrong. We were both tense.

'Are you cold?' Jonathan asked.

'No.'

The silence lasted a fraction too long before he said, 'So, are you staying for lunch?'

'No. Dad's on his way to pick me up. I'm going to stay with him for a couple of weeks, until I feel stronger. Though, to be honest, I feel strong enough already, but he's insisting.'

Did Jonathan look relieved? Yes. They all did.

'Oh, Alice, sweetie,' Megan said. 'You poor thing. You've had a hell of a time, haven't you? Is there anything I can do? Just call me if you need help with shopping or anything.'

'Thank you.'

I saw how relaxed Megan seemed in that kitchen; like I had once been. But that was a different time and things had changed. I watched as she opened a cupboard and took out two mugs and set them on the counter and filled the kettle. Emma and Brian didn't appear to question her dominion over their home; they even seemed to welcome it.

Sam nudged me. He wanted to go. I desperately wanted to leave as well but I couldn't bring myself to say what was needed. I didn't want to feel that I didn't belong or to think that as soon as I left they would breathe a collective sigh of relief and get down to the business of living again. I especially didn't want them to realize that they were pushing me away, because I knew they didn't mean it. It was just that Megan represented the future and I was the past. It was heartbreaking, but I had to face it.

I glanced at Jonathan and caught him looking at me. He gave me a half smile and I swallowed. I had a feeling that I had exposed myself in some way.

'Come on,' Sam said. 'Let's get out of here. You can't compete with the perfect girlfriend.'

'I'm not.'

I grimaced, realizing that I had said it out loud. This was going to take a bit of getting used to. No one seemed to notice, thankfully. Emma had begun to set the table, a clear signal that I should either leave or dig my heels in and outstay my welcome for the sake of making a point. That was one thing I could never do.

'I really ought to get going,' I said.

Sam put his hand on my shoulder. No one tried to stop me. Emma gave me a hug.

'If you want to say something at the memorial service,' she said. 'We would be very grateful.'

'I'd be proud to. I love you all as much as I loved Rory. Whenever you need me, I'll be there.'

'Why don't you come round to us for a quiet meal sometime?' Megan said. 'Just spag bol. Nothing fancy.'

'I'd like that.'

I looked over at Jonathan and felt Sam's hand tense.

'It's all right,' I said. 'I'll be fine.'

'Of course you will,' Megan said.

A car hooted and I extricated myself. 'That'll be Dad.'

I said goodbye and Brian hugged me so hard that I could barely breathe.

'Interesting,' Sam said, once the door had closed behind us.

'What is?'

'Megan.'

I tried my best to be nice. 'She seems like a kind person.'

'I'm not so sure of that. She was manipulating the situation.'

'What do you mean?' I had a feeling I knew, but I needed to hear him say it. There's something illicitly thrilling about having others voice the bad things you're thinking.

'She wanted to make sure you knew where you stood. She's possessive.'

'And you got all that from five minutes in her company?'

'Of course.' His voice became gentler. 'Alice, you did notice she was wearing an engagement ring, didn't you?'

The pavement seemed to melt under my feet. I looked at the house. The door was closed and the windows stared back at me, empty. I felt like a child, lonely and lost and shut out of other people's lives. They were all there, in the cosy, Aga-warmed kitchen, supporting one another, and they didn't need me. I had that disconnected feeling again and held on to Sam just to feel the warmth of human contact.

I breathed out. So it was over now, that part of my life. The engagement explained some of the tension. They hadn't wanted to tell me because it wasn't a moment for congratulations.

Sam pressed my hand to his lips. 'You mustn't mind. They're just trying to move on to the next stage. Megan is a life raft.'

I forced a smile. It was only what I had been thinking, after all. 'She's right for him. They'll be happy and it'll give Emma and Brian something good to focus on.'

'Alice.' Dad had jumped out of the car and was crossing the road towards me. He took my arm and his voice was tinged with anxiety. 'Come on, sweetheart. Let's get you home.'

Then

MUM HAS A BOYFRIEND, NICK, A GOOD-LOOKING BUILDER WHO IS ON medication for schizophrenia. I don't like him but I hate conflict and tension, so I don't say anything. There's only Mum and me in that house, and without Simon and Olivia to dilute the mix it pays to keep the peace. Maybe Mum's the same. Maybe we tread on eggshells round each other. I don't know. We never have that sort of conversation. Anyway, it's because of Nick that she leaves me properly alone a week after my sixteenth birthday. I don't tell a soul about her going away. I feel a bit ashamed, I suppose, of Mum for leaving and of myself for minding.

For some reason Monday is more than usually bad at school. Girls give me a wide berth when they pass me in the corridor, as if I have something contagious. By the time the final bell rings my throat aches from keeping the tears back and my stomach churns. I grab my bag and coat from the hook and run all the way home.

Outside the front door I put my hand in my blazer pocket and discover I've forgotten my keys. Just to be certain, I tip everything out of my satchel and repack it methodically: text books, pens, random bits of ink-splotched paper, empty cartridges. I scan the street, looking for an easy answer, but none of the neighbours hold our keys. Olivia does though, and her flat is only a twenty-minute walk away, so I turn up the collar of my blazer and set off just as it begins to drizzle.

By the time I arrive it's dark and the drizzle has turned to heavy rain. Olivia rents a flat with her boyfriend on the first floor of a smart red-brick Victorian villa in a pretty tree-lined street. I ring the bell and shelter under the shallow arch above the door. There's no answer and I check my watch. Five o'clock. They're probably only just leaving work.

I stamp my feet against the cold. I can't stay here for an hour, but I don't have enough money for a café. If one of the other tenants comes back, I suppose I might at least be able to get inside out of the rain. But what if Olivia is going out after work?

I feel helpless. It's cold, dark and wet and no one knows or cares where I am. Normally if I start feeling sorry for myself I get angry at other people for not wanting me, and that way I cope. I'm not coping very well now. I feel as if desperation has taken hold of my ribs and is squeezing them round my heart. I try to distract myself and start to sing a pop song under my breath, but I lose the thread. And then I see someone walking along the other side of the street, looking straight at me, as though he knows me. He crosses over and stops where the pavement meets the open gate.

'Hi, Alice.'

I walk down the steps, stalling for time as I search my memory for a name. I think I know him – I must do, because he plainly knows me – but I can't for the life of me put my finger on it. And why does his face make me feel happy and guilty all at the same time? I decide to bluff in the hope that he will give me a clue.

'I haven't seen you for ages. Where have you been?'

Rain is dripping from his fringe. He wipes it away. 'I've been around. What's up?'

That's not a lot of help. I still can't place him. 'I'm locked out. I thought my sister might be here, but she's not.'

There's something about him that is intensely familiar, not so much his face, but his presence. I want to reach out and touch him, but I don't, because that would be weird. I've a fairly good idea, by this time, of what is weird behaviour and what is not.

He smiles. He has a gorgeous smile. 'I thought you'd forgotten all about me.'

'Of course I haven't. Don't be silly.' I feel myself going bright red.

An estate car pulls into the kerb and parks and I glance at it, instinctively shrinking back into the doorway.

He puts his hand on my arm, recalling my attention to him. His voice is urgent: 'Ask me to stay.'

I'm confused, but at that moment a white van blares its horn and I watch it swerve to avoid the car door as it swings open. A woman's voice shouts, 'Sorry!' and the driver yells something misogynistic before speeding off, headlights catching the rain.

'What did you say?'

But the boy has gone and as I peer through the darkness a name pops into my head. Sam. I can't see him anywhere. I step back into the shadows, leaning against Olivia's door and tuck my freezing hands under my arms.

Two people emerge from the car. One of them, a woman, hooks her jacket hood over her head, while the other, a teenage boy, stands in the downpour watching her. He's probably about my age and not particularly good-looking, but he's not bad either. There's something about him that makes me want to keep looking. He has red hair, which I don't much care for, but he's carrying a guitar case, so that sort of cancels it out. His black school blazer is too big for him and his shoes don't look like they've ever been polished. I glance down at my own feet. They aren't so great either.

Embarrassed to be caught hanging round someone else's property, I open my satchel and pretend to search for my keys.

'Rory,' the woman says. 'You're getting drenched. Let Stinker out and get inside.' She acknowledges me with a smile. 'Are you waiting for someone?'

'My sister.' I hesitate and then add, 'Olivia Byrne. She lives here.'

Rory is coaxing an obviously rain-averse black Labrador out of the back of the car. He succeeds eventually and slams the boot closed. His mother unlocks their front door and then comes round to my side of the fence. Her hair is red too. I can see curls poking out from under the hood of her jacket. She has the same steady gaze as her son.

'They're away until Friday,' she says. 'I keep their keys for emergencies. Come in out of the rain for a moment and I'll find them for you. I'm Emma Walker, by the way.'

'I'm Alice. Alice Byrne.'

I have a horrible feeling that this woman knows what's in my head and can sense that I'm on my own in more ways than one. It's humiliating to be caught out like that. I am wary but at the same time I feel a curious tug. It isn't recognition of a kindred spirit, or anything silly like that; it's just an odd connection, as if I've been waiting to meet her. Either that or the loneliness of the past week has finally got to me, blowing the tiniest shred of human kindness completely out of proportion.

I follow Emma inside. The door closes behind us and I feel a rush of warmth. The hall is wide and dark and one wall is floor-to-ceiling books. The other has pictures, hung close together, all the way up the stairs. I've never seen so many. I hold out my hand to Stinker and he sniffs it politely.

Emma Walker switches on a light and I look beyond her to the kitchen door, at Rory. He is a typical teenage boy, part child, part man. His arms are a bit too long for his body and his jaw is angular, although the rest of his face is soft and immature. His hair is cropped very short. When he looks up at me, his blue eyes shine under thick sandy lashes. He is cool but he's also a bit goofy. I dread to think what his impression of me is, but I can hazard a guess.

Emma pulls her hair into a clip and wipes a drop of rain from her cheek. She's a comfortable-looking woman, I decide. Not beautiful, but she has lovely kind eyes and dimples when she smiles. She wears jeans and cowboy boots and her coral earrings clash with her red sweater, which clashes with her hair. She opens a drawer in a mahogany side bureau, finds the keys and hands them over.

'Don't forget to drop them back before you leave.' She looks at me properly then, at my wet hair and shiny nose, my school uniform and bag. I probably have steam rising off me as well.

'Why don't you have a cup of tea with us first?'

Their kitchen looks so inviting and she is so kind, but kindness is the last thing I need. It'll only set me off.

'No thank you.' I turn away.

Rory catches my eye and murmurs, 'I don't blame you. I'm only here because she invited me in for tea five years ago.'

Emma lets rip a snort of laughter and thumps him. I stifle an urge to giggle and, holding my satchel above my head, run back round to Olivia's flat.

Inside, I scoop up the mail from the hall floor, chuck my coat and bag on the sofa and lock myself in the loo. I sit hunched over, clutching my knees hard enough to leave nail marks. Eventually, I make myself get up and look in the mirror and I see what Rory Walker must have seen. A pathetic, miserable excuse for a sixteen-year-old girl. I grit my teeth and try desperately not to cry. I hum a bit too. It sometimes works.

Olivia's flat is small with just one bedroom. The sitting room looks out on to the street and has three sash windows with roman blinds. It's been painted wall-to-wall cream and is very boring. If it had been mine I would have used bright colours. I rummage around for the spare keys to Birch Street but can't find them in any of the obvious places, or the less obvious ones for that matter. I know Dad and Gabby are on holiday somewhere exotic so I'll have to go round to Mum's friend, Mandy, and ask if I can stay. That would be a fate worse than death. I'd almost rather sleep rough than spend time with her.

Tears stab at the back of my eyes and ache in my throat and I feel myself beginning to slump into a fog of self-pity, so when the doorbell rings I nearly jump out of my skin.

I pick up the intercom. 'Hello?'

'It's Rory. From next door. Mum sent me round.'

I pause for a moment and then buzz him in and leave the door to the flat open. I walk back into the kitchen and pour some water into the kettle. My hands need something to do.

'You all right?' His gaze rests on my tear-stained face before he looks away.

'I'm just . . . I'm making tea.' I can barely speak. Why is he here? What does he want? I realize I'm humming again and stop abruptly.

Rory pulls a CD from the shelf and inspects it before putting it back.

'Mum said I ought to check on you. She's a teacher so she thinks she's got a sixth sense about yoof.'

I shake my head but it's too late. It's like those films about submarines, when the last hatch bursts and a great wave of sea water comes crashing through. The poor boy didn't realize what he was letting himself in for, but he does OK, taking over tea duties while I sob.

He hands me a mug. 'What's the difference between roast beef and pea soup?'

I sniff. 'I don't know.'

He sits down, slouches over his tea and blows on it. 'Well, you can roast beef but you can't pee soup.'

I laugh almost as hard as I cried. In fact, it makes me cry even more. I don't hang out with boys, or anyone else for that matter, but it seems oddly natural to be sitting in the kitchen with Olivia's neighbour. He's nice.

'I've locked myself out. Olivia has a key to my house, but I can't find it.'

'Where's your mum?'

I avoid his gaze by staring into my steaming mug. 'Away.'

'Don't you have any friends you can stay with?'

'Well, yes, but . . .' I chew at a fingernail and then realize what I'm doing and put my hand in my lap. I shrug. 'Not really.'

Rory laughs. 'And you're not even a ginger. Come next door. Mum's inner nurturer is threatening to explode. I think there's some cake left.'

'You can sit in Jonathan's place,' Rory says, that first evening.

I've been taken in like an abandoned puppy. Stinker originally came from Battersea Dogs Home, so that makes sense. Rory, it turns out, is very black and white about people and he has decided he likes me. It's that simple. He has none of the cattiness of the girls at school; there's no undermining, no bitching and no subtext that I can't understand. He is just Rory and I'm just Alice.

'You've got a brother?' I say.

'Oh yes. The wunderkind. He lives in Bristol.'

'Don't you like him?' That surprises me. Or maybe it doesn't. My experience of brothers is mixed, to say the least. Sometimes they're kind. More often they're vile.

'Yeah. I'm only taking the piss. He's cool.'

'What does he do?'

'He's a journalist for a local paper.'

That sounds impossibly glamorous.

'And Mum thinks the sun shines out of his arse.'

I grinned. 'How old is he?'

'Ancient. He's twenty-six. You should meet him. You'd like him, everyone does.'

At that moment a middle-aged man walks in and drops his briefcase down on one of the kitchen chairs.

'Dad, this is Alice,' Rory says. 'I was telling her about Jonathan.'

'Who?' His father has gone straight to the fridge and is peering inside.

'You know. Your first-born?' Rory slumps in his chair and sighs.

Mr Walker shuts the fridge door and holds out a large hand. 'Alice. How marvellous. I hope Rory has been hiding his true personality.'

I push myself up, lean over the kitchen table, shake his hand and try not to stare. Brian Walker is a giant of a man; broad-framed with a hang-dog expression and skin pitted by what must have been horrendous teenage acne. But his smile is huge and his personality so reassuringly paternal that I love him immediately. Emma with her kindness and her gravelly, dirty laugh is my idol. I want to be part of the family so badly it hurts.

I spend the two nights before Olivia gets back in the Walkers' spare bedroom and it doesn't seem odd at all. It feels as though I've known them for ever. Emma washes and dries my clothes and sends me to school with my bus fare and a kiss on my cheek. It's a revelation. This is what mothers are supposed to be like.

Jonathan comes to stay on my last evening because he has to be in Central London early the next morning for an interview with a national newspaper. He turns up on his bike, which he leaves lean-ing against the bookshelves in the hall, his shirt tucked half in and half out and one trouser leg cinched in with a bicycle clip. Brian has cooked a roast and Rory's brother sits down opposite me. He drags his fingers through shaggy brown hair, pushing it away from his face, and to my surprise I experience a jolt of recognition, which dissipates quickly, leaving me doubting my first impression. I don't think I've ever seen him before, but it's not impossible, I suppose. I risk another surreptitious glance and he catches my eye and there it is again, that same electric shock, and at the same time adrenalin surges through me.

'Jonathan,' Emma says. 'You were at school with Alice's brother, Simon Byrne. You remember.'

The penny drops. I know exactly where we met and what the circumstances were.

He shifts his gaze to me and smiles. I can feel myself going beetroot and study my food as though it's the most interesting plate of roast lamb I've ever seen. When he doesn't say, oh yes, you're the girl who wet her knickers, I risk a glance in his direction. Everything about him makes me weak-kneed. He is at least as tall as Brian, but narrower and rangier. He has a thin mouth that curves into a crooked smile and great cheekbones. Brown eyes shine with intelligence from under arched brows and a long, kinked nose provides an attractive and, I think, very dashing asymmetry. It's a man's face: square-jawed, high-cheekboned and gloriously self-assured, rather like his father's but with far less obvious scarring. Beside his big brother, Rory looks ridiculously young.

'That was in Jonathan's punk days,' Rory is saying. 'But he was always a bit of a soft punk, weren't you, bro? About as scary as Dad in a bad mood. He'd get ready to go out, all dressed up and full of bad attitude, and kiss Mum goodbye. Pathetic really.'

I have a mental picture of Jonathan pushing his face into another boy's, sticking up for me. It makes my skin prickle and it's only then, reminded of that night, that I remember the other boy, the one who came out of the rain, and for a moment my mind wanders. It's Jonathan's voice that brings me back.

'Shut up, Rory, you were only a kid. Of course I remember Simon. He was funny, used to make us all laugh . . . So what's he up to now?'

He's talking to me. I force myself to look up and hold his gaze and that's it. I'm in love.

Jonathan isn't my first crush. Because I don't know any boys I have a terrible tendency to fall for anyone: the kid in the street who stares at me and mutters something smutty as I walk by; the son of the local butcher in his white, blood-spattered coat who watches me covertly as I pay his father for half a pound of mince and two chicken breasts (he generally has at least one raging zit and it seems to pick a different place to erupt every time I go in, as if it's slowly mapping his skull); the guy who sells tickets at the cinema with his long, lank hair and Black Sabbath T-shirts; the half-Indian man I occasionally babysit for with his rubbery face and extraordinary, mobile eyebrows. Anyone with a pulse, really. But Jonathan is special.

The few days I spend with the Walkers do much to restore my faith in humankind and in myself. They like me, therefore, I'm likeable. And that's a big deal. I'm really happy and forgive Mum completely. If it wasn't for her total disregard for my wellbeing, I would never have met them.

Chapter Five

'JULIA'S CALLED TWICE,' GABBY SAID. 'YOU'D BETTER CALL HER BACK.'

I had no doubt Mum was making a point. 'I'll call her in a minute.'

Gabby nodded. She was diplomatic where my mother was concerned. She knew her own power and didn't need to be defensive or antagonistic with any of my family. Mum she tolerated with compassion, Gran with patience and a singular ability not to take offence and Olivia with a mixture of both. Simon was different. He had moved in with her and Dad when he was sixteen and they were extremely fond of each other. As for me, I was only six years old when we met, but she was the best thing that could have happened to me. Before I met Emma Walker, Gabby was the only person who understood, who helped me keep a sense of perspective when things went wrong. She encouraged me to look my problems in the face and not be scared. I had spent weekends with them and had found sanctuary in their spare room from time to time. Gabby had even helped me decorate my flat, rolling up her sleeves and tying back her hair. She had scraped wallpaper, attacked the mouldy bathroom and picked up a paintbrush. Mum had gone to John Lewis and bought me some bed linen, which was sweet of her. Olivia had given me her old sofa and some cushions that the girls had spoiled with yellow felt-tip. Only on one side though.

'Alice, darling!' Mum said. 'Thank goodness. I've been so

worried. I'm sorry I couldn't have you to stay, but you do understand, don't you? I'm literally up to my ears here. I wouldn't be able to give you the attention you deserve.'

I found myself apologizing to her. Gabby didn't comment when I gave her back the phone.

Later, Gabby went up to bed, leaving me alone with Dad. Except for Sam, of course. He was still with me, sitting on the vast sofa, one leg hooked over the other, his arms along the back, watching us. Dad's kitchen was enormous, a great white box with enlargements of his black-and-white photographs and paintings by Archie and Millie on the walls. Impressive floor-to-ceiling glass doors ran the width of the room, there was enough granite to have left a hole in a mountainside and a sea of polished limestone covered the floor. The abused-looking sofa was upholstered in a dark slubby green and with the help of the children's artwork did a fine job of making the room feel less like a designer desert.

While I was in hospital Dad had gone round to my flat and picked up my laptop, but, bar glancing at my inbox, I hadn't done anything about the emails that had come in since the accident. I sat down that afternoon and started responding to clients, reassuring people that I was fine and would be back at work soon. In the last year I'd begun thinking about getting an agent, but I was neither desperate nor busy enough to have moved beyond the thinking stage. Dad had one, but Dad was different. There was no way he could organize himself. Plus he was highly successful. For now, I was happy slowly increasing my list of clients through word of mouth. Personal contact was important to me. Without it, I was too apt to retreat into my own little bubble.

There were several messages from magazine editors and mail-order companies saying they were sorry to hear about my accident, and would I call them when I was back. I replied to them all, sounding upbeat and energetic. The worst thing I could do was show frailty. Fashion was not a business that had time for weakness of any sort. All you had to do was be out of touch for a few weeks and your clients would bury you, mentally. So I made light of my injuries and told them I missed them. That done, I was exhausted and ended up watching a DVD curled up between my half-brother and -sister on the sofa in the den.

The house was quiet now, the children theoretically asleep. Dad poured me a glass of wine, then picked up his cigarettes and lighter and went outside. I followed him, and, after a few moments, so did Sam. He and I sat with Dad between us along the edge of the decking with our feet in the grass, the warm night air fragrant with the white roses that rambled along the fence. Dad flicked his lighter in the darkness and Sam turned his head and stared at the flame.

Even though I had become accustomed to Sam's presence, I still couldn't comprehend him. There was something about the night and the brightness of his eyes that took the edge off my grief. The really odd thing was that it felt right, even desirable, to have him near me, as if he filled a vacuum. It wasn't that he cheered me up or left less room for dark thoughts, it was what I'd felt when I was at my most vulnerable, in the hospital: that he stopped me from drowning. Sam was surreal, but surreal was just a notion, as, to my mind, was God. I believed in good and evil, but only as it emanated from mankind. We are our deeds. Maybe Sam was my deed. Surely he had been caused by the trauma of Rory's death and, whatever anyone said, I'd had a hand in that, however un-witting. The thought made my eyes prick. I wouldn't think about it now. Another day, when I was stronger, I'd face it.

I breathed in cigarette smoke as Dad breathed out.

'That's better,' he said.

'Given up giving up, then?' I tried not to sound too miserable. Dad didn't deal with other people's emotional turmoil particularly well.

'Don't start.' He dragged unrepentantly on the cigarette, let the smoke out in a slow spiral and then patted his stomach. 'If I didn't smoke I'd be fat, so that balances out the risk.'

'Yeah, Dad. Whatever you say.'

Sam stood up and stretched the kinks out of his shoulders. He looked down at my father. 'Do you remember when he met Gabby?'

I nodded.

'I can still picture him charging after her with his ponytail bouncing up and down and your brother howling with laughter.'

'Olivia was mortified,' I said.

'Eh,' Dad said. 'Mortified about what?'

'Oh, nothing. Just thinking out loud.'

Gabby had found me when Sam and I got lost in Portobello Market. I was really too big to sit on her shoulders, but she put me up there anyway and walked from under the flyover almost as far as Westbourne Grove, where Simon spotted me and came running over. She had been about nineteen at the time; tall, thin and punky with spiky white hair, a denim jacket and drainpipes. I was too used to Simon to find her scary and Dad, who was thirty-seven, had been instantly smitten. After she had handed me over and walked away he had stood in a trance for a few moments, before shoving me at my brother and setting off in hot pursuit.

'He did look ridiculous.' Sam lay back on the lawn and stretched his arms out. 'Nice to know some things never change.'

I could see his eyes in the light from the kitchen. He breathed in and out and his fingers brushed the grass.

He patted the spot beside him. 'Come and lie down next to me and tell me what all this means.'

I wanted to but I shook my head and he propped himself up on his elbows. 'I still can't believe I'm here with you. It feels like heaven.'

'It's not though, is it?' I said. 'This is my life, not my death.'

'You always were literal.'

'Sorry.'

Dad grunted. 'You're staying at least a week, preferably two, sweetheart. Doctor's orders.'

Sam sat up and put his hand on my bare foot. It tickled and my foot involuntarily jerked. He caught it and held it tight and murmured, 'What do you think I am?'

I frowned at him. 'A ghost,' I said. Then I added, 'I don't believe in ghosts.'

'Neither do I,' Dad said. 'Is there something wrong?'

'I honestly don't know.'

Sam let go of my foot and looked up at the stars. 'Alice, you worry too much. I'm a good thing, aren't I?'

I wrinkled my nose at him. A moment passed. Dad smoked, looking into the darkness, probably thinking about what he had to do in the morning, and I studied my fingernails. I had painted them a pearlescent pink for his wedding and the thin crescents of white moon reminded me of how much time I had lost.

'Dad?'

'Hmm?'

'Since I woke up, there's been someone with me all the time.'

'Alice . . .' Sam groaned.

'In what way?' Dad asked. 'Do you mean that you feel like Rory's still around? That's natural with bereavement.'

'What would he know about bereavement?' Sam said.

'His father died when he was fourteen.'

Dad's cigarette was suspended inches from his mouth. 'What did you say?'

'I was talking about your dad. I was telling . . . the other person, that you understood bereavement.'

'The other person?' Sam said. 'Well, I suppose it's better than "ghost".'

I nudged him with my toe.

Dad grunted. 'You're telling me you think someone else is in the garden with us?'

I looked up at the sky. There were a few blue-grey clouds but the stars were visible between them. I scratched an itch at the side of my nose. Sam might be finding the situation amusing, but it was taking me a little longer to adjust. I wanted someone, Dad I suppose, to understand what was happening to me, and to care. However much I adored Sam, I was worried that if I wasn't very careful I would become disconnected from the rest of my life. I didn't know where to start. Dad put his arm around me and we sat in silence.

'You will get through this, Alice,' Sam said. 'I'll help you. I loved Rory too.' He had stopped smiling. He was staring into my eyes.

'I loved Rory too,' Dad said. 'He was a great kid. I'm so glad he found Daniel. At least when he died he knew he was loved.'

I caught a sob in my throat. 'Can I ask you something?'

'Anything.'

'Did Mum ever talk to you about Sam?'

I rested my elbows on my knees and my chin in my hands. Sam came and sat beside me, kissed me on my cheek and gave my hair a friendly tug. The warm night and his body close to mine calmed me.

'The Invisible Sam?' Dad asked.

'You don't have to explain me,' Sam said. 'It's all right.'

'No, it's not.'

'Lots of kids have imaginary friends. It's normal and you were on your own a lot. Your grandmother was a little concerned, I remember that. But you grew out of it. You were an awkward child and we should have helped you form friendships.'

'Instead of humouring me, you mean.'

'Believe me, I feel bad about that, but it seemed like the right thing to do at the time.'

I didn't comment. What was the point? 'But Gran had Fred, so she knew what Sam meant.'

'Fred?' Dad frowned.

'Yes. She used to tell me stories about him. He was her imaginary friend. So she must have been lonely too.'

Dad nodded. 'She was, at least until her mother remarried. She adored her stepbrother.'

'Adam. I know. But she hardly ever talks about him.'

'Yes, well it was a long time ago and he died so young. It was a very painful time for her.'

Dad finished his cigarette and stubbed it out in the grass. I could feel tension in the arm that Sam pressed against mine.

'What if I told you Sam was sitting beside me?'

Sam buried his head in his hands and at first I thought he was crying. Then I realized his shoulders were shaking with laughter. I didn't think there was anything to laugh about but I was feeling a little hysterical and my diaphragm ached with the effort not to join in.

'You think he's here?'

'I know he is.'

His smile faded. 'No, he's not, sweetheart. Jesus, I think we'd better get someone to take a look.'

'Sam, do something,' I said. 'Just do something to prove you're here.'

Sam wiped a tear from his eye. 'Alice, I can't do anything when we're not on our own. It's almost as bad as it was before . . .' His gaze shifted to my father. 'Anyway, what's the point? He can't see me.'

My voice rose. 'Because I want him to believe me. At least tell him something that I couldn't know. You can do that, can't you?'

'Hey, calm down. There's nothing to prove. Your father loves you and so do I. What am I supposed to say to him anyway? I don't know any more about him than you do.'

'Just say something.'

He sighed and thought for a moment. 'OK. Tell him that when you were in the coma he told you that Rory had come up to speak to him at the wedding. Rory said how beautiful you were that day and your dad looked over and saw you dancing, laughing your head off. You were radiant. And then Rory tucked his arm through your dad's and they just stood and watched.'

I repeated what he said, watching Dad's profile intently. He rested his head in his hands. 'That poor boy.'

'Yes.' I paused. 'Is it true? Did Rory say that?'

Dad nodded. 'But you could have heard me, Alice, and stored it away. There's no one here except you and me.'

I rubbed my eyes. Tiredness had crept over me, pulling me down by the shoulders.

Dad stood up, took my hands and hauled me to my feet. 'Time for bed. We'll talk some more tomorrow.'

That night Sam and I lay flat on our backs holding hands and it reminded me so strongly of my childhood that I couldn't help but smile. Sam hummed the tune to 'Waltzing Matilda', and I turned over and eventually gave myself up to sleep with the song beating a rhythm in my head.

Chapter Six

'WHY DO YOU TALK TO YOURSELF?' MILLIE ASKED.

It was the end of the week, Saturday morning, and Millie was sitting on a stool at the kitchen island, eating Coco Pops, and was on to her second bowl. Archie was making himself toast.

'Millie! Don't be so rude,' Gabby said.

She was wearing skinny jeans that made her legs look endless, and a pale pink linen shirt. Even after having children, she still possessed the rangy figure of a model and I envied the way she carried off her clothes. Her white-blonde hair was like a perfectly ironed piece of fine silk and she used mascara and a flick of eyeliner to enhance pale blue irises rimmed with black.

I swallowed a mouthful of coffee before I replied. 'I really don't mind. You can ask me whatever you want.'

Millie put down her spoon and glanced from me to her mother. She was eight years old; a mini replica of Gabby with the same big smile, the same air of mischief.

'I've heard you. You talk to someone. I thought you were on the phone first of all, but then the other day your phone was in the kitchen, ringing in your bag, and I went up to tell you and I heard you talking.'

Sam nudged my leg with his toe.

I cast him a rueful smile before answering Millie. 'Sorry. I've always talked to myself. It's a habit.'

Millie didn't blink. 'But it's not like you're saying, "What am I going to do today?" Or, "Oh God, I'm knackered," like Mum does. It's like you're listening to someone and then answering.'

'Millie's going to be a detective,' Gabby said. 'Don't let her bother you.'

'Mum, I was only asking.'

'It sounded more like a cross-examination.'

Archie buttered his toast and reached for the strawberry jam. 'I think it's cool to have a mad half-sister.'

'Cheeky little bastard,' Sam said.

'Shut up.' I was very fond of my half-brother.

'Archie was only trying to be funny,' Gabby said.

'Oh. No. I'm sorry, I didn't mean Archie.' I felt my skin heat up.

Gabby wasn't mollified. 'Who did you mean then?'

'I was thinking out loud. I was telling myself to shut up.'

I cast around desperately for a distraction. Dad was in the garden, barefoot, resplendent in a black silk dressing gown, his hair loose, filling the birdbath with water from a jug. He made me smile. He was such a strange man, such a mixture of charisma and insecurity. More trouble to Gabby, I imagined, than either of their children.

'Alice, you're digging yourself a hole,' Sam said.

I covered my glowing cheeks and whispered, 'Stop it. Go away.'

'OK, Alice, it's all right.' Gabby stood up and came round to my side of the island.

Archie, oblivious to the subliminal stuff going on around him, or possibly not, grinned at me. 'I don't care if you're barmy. I think you're cool.'

'I do,' Millie said. 'I don't think people should talk to themselves.'

'You talk to your dolls. You're all, "Oh, Brad, I love you so much. Oh Jenny, you are so beautiful I want to sex you."'

Millie was outraged. 'I do not say that word. Mum, tell Archie I don't say that word with my dolls.'

'Oh, yes you do.'

'That's enough, Archie. Can you talk about something different, please? And leave Alice alone.'

81

Sam burst out laughing and I was hard put not to. At any rate, it broke the tension. A robin was pecking around under the choisya and the morning sunshine had just caught the edge of the lawn. I watched for a moment. Sam had his head in his hands and he glanced at me through his fingers. I wrinkled my nose.

'Well, she does talk to herself,' Millie said.

'Buzz off, you two,' Gabby snapped. 'I want a word with Alice.'

Millie jumped down and took her bowl to the sink, followed by Archie with his plate. They maintained an expressive silence as they left the room.

I rubbed at my temple. 'I'm sorry, Gabby. I need to get home.'

'Aren't you happy here?'

'It's not that. I have to get on with things. I've got follow-up appointments at the hospital and work, and I want to help Mum with her wedding and there's the inquest.' I could hear a note of hysteria creeping into my voice. 'On top of that, I have to chase the insurance and think about getting a new car.'

'We'd be happy to help, if you'll let us.' Gabby put her hand over mine. 'Darling, you don't have to explain. I understand, of course I do. But talk to me. I want to know how you're feeling.'

I picked up my mug but the dregs were tepid.

'Not great, to be honest. It's like there's a loop in my head and I don't know how to make it stop.'

I had a horrible urge to tell her, to spill my guts, to say the unspeakable. But even though she was possibly the one person I could have told, I was too afraid of what voicing it would mean. Would she urge me to tell the Walkers the truth or convince me to keep my mouth shut? It would be unfair to make her complicit. It was my burden.

'You have to.' Gabby picked up her cardigan and wrapped it around her slender frame. 'Alice, if it's that bad, being on your own isn't going to make it any better. Please stay. At least for a couple more days.'

I glanced at Sam. He shook his head.

'I can't.'

My stepmother studied me without saying anything.

'Gabby, I'm twenty-six.'

It was childish to mention numbers and unnecessarily defensive. She pushed her fingers through her hair and dragged it back.

'OK. This is what your dad and I are worried about. You seem detached a lot of the time. Sometimes it's like you don't even know we're here, and Millie isn't the only one who's heard you talking to yourself. I glossed over it just now, because I don't want her to start worrying, but, darling, it isn't normal. We think you ought to see a professional.'

I shook my head. 'Gabby, really, I don't want—'

'Your father will pay.'

'It's not about the money.'

'But you admit you're finding it difficult. Surely it would help to talk to someone who understands these things?'

Sam leaned towards me and frowned, his chin on his knuckles. 'Doctor, this woman is an interesting example of ego-induced delusion compounded by paternal abandonment and maternal narcissism. I say we operate.'

He was only trying to joke me out of it, but I refused to laugh. I wasn't in the mood. 'Stop it.'

'See? You're doing it again. What was that? You cannot go round talking to someone who isn't there.'

'But he is here.' I felt the certainty in my voice and was surprised by it. It's extraordinary how adaptable human beings are, how easily we come to believe, how much we can take in our stride.

'Who, Alice?' Gabby took hold of my wrists and pulled my hands down. 'Who is here?'

I shook my head and swallowed hard. 'Sorry. That came out wrong. Someone has come back into my life and it's very confusing, that's all. I didn't mean anything else.'

Gabby looked bemused. 'A guy?'

I nodded.

'Well, why didn't you say something before? Is he someone special or just a friend?'

'He's a good friend.'

'Could he maybe stay with you for a while?'

'Yes. He can always stay with me. I'll be fine if he's there. So, I'll go home tomorrow and you needn't worry about a thing.'

She didn't look convinced.

Dad wandered in from the garden. 'What are you two plotting?' He switched on the kettle, opened a cupboard, peered inside and closed it disconsolately.

'Alice is planning on leaving us tomorrow.' Gabby took his favourite mug out of the dishwasher, washed it up and handed it to him. 'I was trying to persuade her not to go quite yet.'

He looked at me and shrugged. 'She's an adult. We can't make her stay.'

'Thanks, Dad.' I wasn't sure how to take that.

'But come down to your gran's with me tomorrow. She's been worried about you. Then I promise we'll get you home.'

A few minutes later I headed up to the bathroom and went straight to the mirror. My hair was growing back where it had been shaved for the operation to reduce the swelling. My bruises were beginning to fade, leaving smudges of yellow around the eye area, a bit like nicotine stains. I felt unattractive and a little pathetic. I inspected the livid scar on my forehead. I could imagine the piece of glass or metal slicing through it, narrowly missing my eyes. Behind the scar, my brain had been jolted against the inside of my skull with the force of a battering ram. I had been lucky, I suppose, but what about the injuries I couldn't see? Had the impact to my frontal lobe caused Sam? But that didn't explain his presence during my childhood.

Or was I imagining that as well?

I'd had more than one MRI scan in the last two weeks, but they hadn't shown up anything that my neurologist didn't expect. So what else could it be? Maybe it was something deeper, something locked away in the depths of my subconscious that the impact had liberated. Sam came and stood beside me. I put my arm around his waist and we stared into the glass. I smiled. Whatever the reason for his continued presence, I really liked having him around.

'Where have you been all my life?' I said.

'Never far away. Handsome, aren't I?'

I jabbed him in the ribs. 'Don't be vain.'

'Before the car crash, I couldn't see my face.' He raised his hands and covered his cheeks and jaw, pressing his fingers into his flesh. 'I don't want to lose myself again.'

I held him tighter. He felt warm and real. And if I didn't believe that, there were the involuntary workings of his body to convince me: the rise and fall of his chest as he breathed and the rhythmic beat of his heart.

'Do you think I should see a psychiatrist?'

He took my hand and pressed it to his lips. 'Absolutely not.'

It felt as if he were sealing a bargain. I was beginning to under-stand how vulnerable he was, even though he hid it well. There was so much more to Sam than charm and devotion. He needed me as much as I needed him. He reminded me of King Louie in *The Jungle Book*, wanting to stroll right into town. I felt sorry for him and it must have shown in my face because he scooped me into his arms and gave me a resounding kiss on my cheek. When he hugged me I felt like a child, content not to question any more. I held him tightly.

'I love you, idiot,' he said. 'So don't look so anxious.'

'How do I know I'm not imagining you?' I mumbled into his shoulder.

He pulled away and pressed his forehead against mine. 'I don't think you are.'

'I know you don't, but that doesn't mean . . .'

There was a knock on the door and Millie said, 'Alice, hurry up. I need to clean my teeth.'

Chapter Seven

GRAN'S HOUSE WAS HEATED, DESPITE IT BEING JULY. HER SITTING room had windows in two walls but the red velvet curtains were closed across the ones behind the sofa, presumably so that the sun wouldn't reflect on the television. It was oppressive. The first thing Dad did, on entering, was draw them. On the walls there were some impressive paintings, mostly landscapes left unsold when Gran's antiques business was wound down. Sam wandered over to a dresser crowded with framed photographs. I watched him try and push one over. Nothing moved. It was as if they were glued rigidly to the surface. We had worked out that Sam could only do what he wanted if we were on our own, otherwise he had no impact whatsoever on the solid objects around him. He said it felt as though his hands were numb, his fingertips like cotton wool. It made him feel sick to even try.

None of the pictures on display featured Mum and there was only one of Gabby. Mostly, they were pictures of my late grandfather, Dad and her grandchildren. At the back, in a silver frame, was one I had been fascinated by as a child, a photograph of her when she was a little girl, sitting on a sandy beach next to her stepbrother, swaddled against the wind in a coat and thick scarf. Their faces looked so serious. I saw Sam touch it and frown. Then he dropped his hand and turned away.

Gran poured tea from a silver teapot through a strainer. She had always liked a bit of ceremony. We waited while she added milk from a porcelain jug and stirred it with a little silver spoon. I could feel the tension rolling off Sam. In the car on the way down he had been on edge, twitching with impatience, making it hard for me to concentrate on what Dad was saying. This visit meant a lot to him. He was convinced that my grandmother had once spoken to him and I knew exactly what he was talking about because when he described that moment in my garden twenty years ago, it raised the hairs on the back of my neck. I hoped for his sake, as much as my own, that she would give him some sort of reassurance.

'Paula.' Sam crouched down beside her chair and covered her hand with his. 'Paula, can you see me? Just give me a sign. Anything. Mike doesn't need to know.'

Gran either ignored him or had no idea he was there. I suspected the latter and I could feel his frustration. He kept trying to catch her eye but her gaze eluded him, and even when he spoke directly to her his voice became lost somewhere in the space between them. I felt for him. He had set so much store by this meeting.

'Paula,' he said. 'I'm doing this for Alice. She needs to know that she isn't alone.'

I flicked him an irritated glance. Gran wasn't strong, mentally or physically; she was eighty-seven, her hearing had deteriorated and although there were still plenty of days when she was completely her old self, there were also days when she wasn't, when her mind was fuzzy round the edges.

'She needs time, that's all. This is a leap of faith for her. She knows I'm here. It's just a question of making her understand how important this is to you.'

'Give it a rest.' I spoke firmly and he sat back, but he didn't take his eyes off her face.

'What planet are you on?' Dad said.

Sam raised his head and stared at him. 'I think your dad could be the problem. His personality is too strong. Maybe if he leaves the room she might be able to see me.'

I made a face, shrugging my shoulders.

'Please. This is too important.'

'You were an unconventional little thing, Alice.' Gran's comment seemed to come out of nowhere. She turned and snapped at Dad. 'Why on earth did you leave the poor child with that woman?'

Dad made a visible effort to control his irritation. 'That woman was her mother.'

'Well, so what?' Sam said. 'You knew she was screwing her up.'

'I'm not that screwed up,' I said. 'And will you stop talking about me like I'm not here.'

'But Paula's right,' Sam said. 'They chose not to see how unhappy you were. It was just all too much effort.'

'Can we not have this conversation now? Dad, would you mind leaving us on our own for a few minutes?'

He shot up out of his chair. 'Fine. I'm going outside for a fag. You girls have a nice chat and then we should get going.'

He closed the door behind him. Sam went over to the mirror that hung above the fireplace. I couldn't see his reflection. He turned round.

'Ask her about Fred.'

'What?'

He repeated himself and I did as he asked, leaning forward, my elbows on my knees.

Gran didn't bat an eyelid. She blinked and pursed her lips, the pink lipstick cracking. 'Does he live in the village?'

'No.' I spoke gently. 'He was your imaginary friend when you were little. You used to tell me wonderful stories about him.'

'Think, Paula,' Sam urged her. 'Please try.'

There was a long silence and my heart began to beat very hard, the blood rushing to my ears. Sam could barely keep still.

'Gran. Please try and remember.'

'There were lots of children. They used to play in the streets.'

'But Fred was different, wasn't he?'

She became a little more animated then. She seemed to have found her way out of whatever mist her mind had become lost in. 'I suppose he was. My mother didn't allow me to play out. She said the children were rude and dirty and I'd pick up bad habits. Fred and I used to watch them from the window.'

'I remember them,' Sam said. 'Little bastards. Tell her I remember the day we hid in the garden for hours when they called us names. She was supposed to be visiting her aunt but she doubled back. Her mother smacked her for it.'

I thought he'd gone mad but I repeated what he said.

Gran's smile was mischievous. 'I just wanted to play with them. But I've told you that story, Alice. Don't you remember? When you were a little girl.'

I frowned. Had she?

She patted my hand. 'Alice, dear. There isn't anyone else here.'

Sam grabbed the side of the dresser and closed his eyes. He looked dizzy and I had to restrain myself from rushing to support him. I stood up slowly instead and pretended to look at the photographs. I kept my back to my grandmother.

'Sam?' I whispered, pressing the back of my hand against his.

He opened his eyes and I smiled tentatively at him, but then Dad walked back in, his humour evidently improved by the combined hit of fresh air and nicotine.

'Right, Mum. Time we were heading off. I'll come back in a couple of weeks. Don't get up.'

That was my father. Never could stay still in one place for long. A clock-watcher and a pacer. Time was fleeting. In Dad's world there was no point stopping to mull things over. Just do. Move. Keep avoiding time, avoiding the inevitable. Since Rory, I understood his need to grasp life where he could find it.

Gran gripped his arm as he kissed her cheek. 'Take good care of her.'

Sam turned to the wall and crashed his fist against it. I felt the vibration go through the house but Dad and Gran seemed oblivious. One of the pictures was slightly askew though.

'Alice,' Sam hissed. 'Did you see that?'

I nodded, trying to remember if it had been that way before. It must have been.

'It moved.'

'Possibly.' I hugged my grandmother. 'I'll come back soon, I promise.'

I let her go and Sam put his arm around me and held me close while Dad spoke to her. I heard her tick him off about the size of his gut and smiled. She might have been losing it a little, but she could still be a tyrant when she chose. Sometimes I suspected she exaggerated the confusion to get his attention. I went outside and got into the car, but Sam didn't come out. I opened the door again, just as Dad was pulling his seat belt across his stomach.

'Sorry, Dad. Forgot something. I won't be a sec.'

Inside the house Gran was holding the photograph of herself with Adam. She looked stricken. Sam was standing close to her.

'Sorry, Gran. I think I left my scarf.'

She didn't respond so I took the photograph from her and replaced it on the dresser. 'Is everything all right?'

'Of course it is, darling. Off you go. Michael will be getting impatient.'

I turned to Sam and whispered, 'For God's sake, get in the car!'

Chapter Eight

AT THE END OF A WEEK'S CONVALESCENCE GABBY GAVE ME A LIFT home. I tried to convince her that I was perfectly able to take the tube, but she insisted. We dropped Archie and Millie at their summer holiday club and drove down to Battersea.

'I still think you're going home too early,' she said as she backed expertly into a tight parking space.

I undid my seat belt, got out and looked up at my windows. For once, they didn't seem welcoming. 'You might be right.'

Sam climbed out and stretched. There was something farcical about the situation, and unsettling at the same time. I couldn't get my head round the fact that Gabby, along with everyone else on the planet, was completely unaware of him.

The place smelled musty and abandoned and the summer heat had sucked the life out of it. I hurried to open a window. Living under the roof, I felt the extremes of weather, the sun battering down, or the rain. I liked the storms, but not the mugginess.

Everything was just as I had left it several weeks ago, only dustier and smellier. Still, it was good to be back home in my quirky little flat with its odd angles and the sloping windows that drew in the morning light. I'd gone mad when I first took possession, slapping vibrant pink paint on to the bedroom walls, sea blue in the bathroom, sunshine yellow in the sitting room and kitchen. My favourite black-and-white shots hung in the bathroom where they looked great against the blue and where, amongst the photographs of friends and cityscapes and things that caught my eye, I had smuggled in more than one that featured Jonathan.

In the rest of the flat there were books on every surface, and pictures, mainly found amongst stacks of dross at car boot sales, covered every spare inch of wall. I had been trying to recreate Brian and Emma's house – with some success, I thought. At least, I liked it. In the bedroom I had hung a brightly coloured plastic chandelier that I'd once thought was amusingly ironic.

Now the flat seemed to have developed a split personality; familiar and unfamiliar. That would go soon, once I was used to it again. In the meantime, it felt as if I was catching up with an old friend.

Gabby picked up an empty coffee cup from the table by the sofa, wrinkled her nose at its contents and took it into the kitchen. Sam made a face and I frowned, disconcerted. I didn't know what he wanted of me – to explain him to Gabby, or pretend he wasn't there. She had gone quiet.

'What?' I asked.

'I'm not happy about this, Alice. You're expecting too much of yourself. You haven't had time to get used to Rory not being around and it's going to hit you hard. I don't want to leave you here on your own. Please come back home with me.'

I shook my head. 'I can't. I have to start rebuilding my life. You've been so kind, but staying at your place just makes me feel like a child again, and I can't afford that luxury.'

She waited a moment before she replied, choosing her words carefully. 'I know I'm not your mother, but I might as well be. I care about you.'

'I know.' I wished she would stop. Kindness was terrifying in its ability to break down self-control.

She plumped up the cushions on the sofa and straightened a pile of books. 'Will Julia come over, do you think?'

'I'm sure she will. Don't worry, I won't let myself get depressed. I'll keep busy.'

I wanted her to go, but when she left I felt a loneliness I hadn't expected. I sorted through the post and junk mail while Sam rummaged around. Sam. In my flat. Showing no signs of leaving. I felt like weeping.

'This place is a tip,' he said.

I pulled myself together. Dissolving now wasn't going to help. 'It's my tip.'

He shrugged. He seemed ridiculously at home and his relief at being here was infectious. I felt my misery slip away because he was with me, keeping me company, making me laugh, not piling on the pressure.

Then I noticed the discarded wedding wrap on the table and the Sellotape and silver ribbon. Sam followed my gaze and gave me a hug, his hand on the back of my head, pressing me gently against his shoulder. He let me go, picked it all up and took it into the spare room.

I could hear a distant siren and laughter and the yells of young boys out to make trouble. All familiar sounds. Despite everything, it was good to be home. I picked out an envelope that looked official, opened it and unfolded the sheet of paper. It was from the insurers, acknowledging my claim. There was a form with it as well, that would have to be dealt with, but the questions included: *Was any person/persons injured as a result of the accident?* My hands shook as I put it down. I couldn't avoid it for ever, but it could wait a little while longer. I also had a letter from the police confirming that the driver of the lorry had not been injured and letting me know that my car was at the recovery yard. Once it had been examined, I needed to collect the contents, such as they were. I didn't know if I could bear it. My handbag had been retrieved by the paramedics at the scene, but there might be something of Rory's. I had a vision of his shoes lying in a pool of blood and almost screamed. I knew I wouldn't go.

I opened the rest, but apart from one payment advice note, a hefty enough sum to see me through the next few weeks, it was all bills and final demands. Which reminded me: I needed to invoice for the children's fashion shoot the day before the wedding. I glanced at my laptop, feeling curiously dispirited. Later, maybe. I fetched my camera from the spare room, took it out of its case and kissed it because I was so pleased to see it. I sat down on the sofa, raised it to my eye and framed Sam. He affected a model's pose; hips jutted, shoulders back, eyes piercing. I laughed and took the picture then put my camera down, my hands trembling. The shots from my last job would be on the memory stick, but my other camera, the smaller one I'd taken to the wedding, would have pictures of that day. Pictures of Rory. I'd have to look at them eventually.

Sam folded up an old newspaper, dumped it in the waste-paper basket and took my holdall into the bedroom. I could hear him muttering. He knew my flat well, that much was obvious. He knew where I kept things, which drawer, which cupboard. Why was that? Because he was in my head or because he had been here before? I did question it, of course I did, but when you are in a room with another human being you know that they are there in all sorts of different ways. You see them and you hear them; they brush past you; they turn and laugh at something you say. They respond to you. Well, Sam did all that and at no point did he break the rules of human existence. He didn't vanish and reappear on the other side of the room. He didn't walk through walls or speak in voices. He was just a bloke doing bloke things in my flat.

It was too confusing; all mixed up with the emotional fallout from Rory's death and Jonathan's engagement and the physical fallout from my injuries. What was it soldiers suffered from? Post-traumatic stress disorder. In which case, I should definitely be seeing someone. Only, I didn't want to be given pills to make Sam go away, or shunt him into a back area of my brain where he'd stay until the next disaster. Whatever was going on, I wanted to see it through without science getting in the way.

Sam reappeared holding a mug, went into the kitchen, opened

the fridge and recoiled. 'Jesus. It would have been nice if your family could have at least chucked the food out. This is revolting.'

I lobbed a cushion at him but it fell short and landed on the floor, disturbing the dust. He closed the fridge and picked the cushion up and brandished it at me, laughing, and I grabbed the camera and snapped.

I thought the same, but out of loyalty to my family I didn't say it. Mum and Olivia could easily have taken my keys and sorted the fridge out, picked up the post. I would have, if it had been my daughter or sister lying comatose in hospital with machines beeping and tubes poking out everywhere. To give Olivia her due, she had been in to pick a few things up and had dropped them round at Dad's, but otherwise, nothing had changed. I followed Sam, tackling the plastic-wrapped loaf of greenish-blue bread before opening the fridge and gingerly removing the stinking chicken breast and furred cheese and dropping the whole lot, including an unopened bottle of milk, into a black bin-bag. This I tied by the handles and took straight outside, then came back and sat down heavily on the sofa. I tired so easily. Sam pulled me up by the arms.

'What am I?' I protested. 'Your cleaner?'

'We could hardly accuse you of that, could we?'

I ignored the slur. There were other things on my mind, questions that needed to be answered. I was curious about him.

'How much have you been around since I was a child? Were you with me all the time?' The mind boggled.

He flung himself down on the sofa. 'Some of it. It depended. When you were lonely, I was there. When you were otherwise engaged, I wasn't. Sometimes I just hung out.'

I made a face and joined him, curling up into the cushions. 'So you didn't see me with boys?'

He drew his chin in comically, like a turtle. 'Do you mean, did I see you making out with your boyfriends? No, I bloody well did not. What do you take me for?'

'Sorry. There weren't many anyway. I was a late developer.'

His voice softened. 'I think you were aware of me sometimes, on some level.'

'I think so too. When I was desperate I would talk to you. I think I even saw you once or twice, but those times felt surreal.' I paused, and then asked, 'Were they real? Were you there?'

He went still. 'It was like those dreams where you never manage to get where you're going, where something frustrates you every time you get close.' He sighed. 'Alice, I just want to be real, and if I can't be real, I want to be safe.'

'From what?'

'From nothing. From a vacuum. It's our bond that's made me. Break that bond and I'm . . . I don't know what.'

The flat seemed to shrink. I started to feel anxious. It was as if he already knew that he was on shaky ground, that one day I might let him down. I stood up and when he held on to my wrist I pulled away.

'Sam. What do you want from me?'

His jaw tightened. 'I think the reason I'm here is because you need me and I'm scared that I won't exist if you stop needing me, if you don't let me stay with you.'

I hesitated before I responded. I felt I had to be careful with him. On the other hand, if he was going to stay, it was important to know what was happening, what would happen. At the moment my immediate future was looking hazy. I said tentatively, 'So we need each other.' When he still looked anxious, I added, 'Sam, I don't know what I'd have done without you. I'm terrified of what not having Rory around will mean.'

'I'm not Rory though.'

'No, but you're here and that's what matters.' I smiled at him. 'But we have to think this through, because, if you are here to stay, my life will change. I'll have to assimilate you into it somehow, and still function as a normal human being.'

He hugged me hard and things just seemed to slot into place; I didn't feel the need to panic over our odd situation. When I was a child I never questioned him. He was simply there. Those other odd visitations during my teenage years I could put down to hormonal changes, phases, adolescent anxiety attacks and loneliness. But not this. I was twenty-six years old and embarking on a close friendship with a figment of my imagination. I wanted to burst out laughing.

Then

'ALICE.'

I jerk awake. 'Yup?'

Rory shoves at me with his toes. 'I don't believe it. You were asleep.'

'I was not.'

'Your nose was touching the page.'

'I was absorbing information.'

I sit up and pick bits of grass off my knees and shins. Truthfully, I had dozed off, the pages of my very dry A-level history book blurring and reconfiguring into a dream about Rory's big brother. I'd had a late night.

Rory is sitting cross-legged, a book open on his thighs, but I don't believe he's been revising at all. I can hear Capital Radio coming from somewhere along the terrace of Victorian cottages. On the patio, Mum is sunbathing in her black bikini, a copy of *Vogue* shading her face.

Rory lets his book slide to the ground and lies down on the rug beside me. 'Do you want to hear a joke?'

'No.'

'Why are there no painkillers in the jungle?'

I snort. 'Dunno, Rory. Why?'

'Because the parrots eat 'em all.'

'Hilarious.'

He's silent for a moment. He's doing it more and more these

days: going off into a dream. It bothers me because I'm not used to this side of him. I am the quiet one. I prefer it when he's mucking around.

'Alice, do you ever wonder what the point of all this is?'

'No. I know what it is. It's to get me away from here. I'm going to pass my exams if it kills me and then I'm going to art school to study photography.'

'You won't get far if you're dead.'

He sits up and starts to plait my hair while I go back to my revision. I begin to feel sleepy again and doze off, and when I open my eyes and look round he's lying on his stomach absently picking the petals off a daisy and dropping them one by one into the cold dregs of my tea. It stirs a memory. I nearly say something about déjà vu, but the doorbell rings. Mum puts down her magazine and stands up. Rory turns and gives me a drowsy smile. I pick up my camera and take his picture. Rory, with his pale-lashed eyes and angular face, is my muse. I use Mum sometimes, but I have to be careful; an unflattering portrait can put her in a foul mood for days.

A few moments pass. An ant marches on to my book and I brush it off and follow its progress across the fringe of the rug and through the grass. I hear the rise and fall of the laugh Mum saves for attractive men and I sigh and grind my forehead against my fists.

'Oh, God.'

Jonathan Walker strolls out of the house behind my mother, casting his benign, slightly weary gaze over us. He pulls the frayed strap of a canvas bag over his head and drops it on the grass. A lock of brown hair sticks out at an odd angle above his right ear and one of his trouser legs is tucked into his sock, presumably to stop it getting caught in his bike chain. I am pathetically happy to see him.

I give a little wave and then feel like an idiot. I wonder if he's noticed my bare legs and midriff, or the way my hair flows over my shoulders and the straps of my blue bikini dissect my back.

'Hey, bro,' Rory says, brightening up. 'What're you doing here? I thought you had a job.'

'I'm going to put the kettle on,' Mum says. 'Would you like a coffee, Jonathan?'

'No, thank you. I'm not stopping. I need your keys, Rory. There's no one home and I forgot mine. I thought I'd probably find you here.'

'Where's your bike?'

'Outside.'

'You have locked it up, haven't you, you dork?'

'No,' Jonathan says patiently. 'My bike key is on my ring.'

Rory shoves his hands into the pockets of his shorts and pulls out a packet of chewing gum and a screwed-up bus ticket. 'I've dumped my set somewhere inside. I'll go and find them for you. I'll bring your bike in if you want.'

'Thanks, mate.'

Rory disappears with Mum. I know they'll get talking. It's the one thing I don't understand about Rory. He adores my mother.

Jonathan scratches the side of his neck and looks uncomfortable. After a moment he sits down on the rug next to me but he doesn't touch me and I'm certain that it's deliberate. That's what I choose to believe, anyway. He's wearing chinos and a tired striped shirt. He takes his shoes and socks off, chucks them aside and rolls up his sleeves. I do my best not to stare at his forearms but I can't help myself. They are tanned with just the right amount of hair and his hands are long, his fingers strong and elegant, like I imagine a pianist's would be.

Rory leans the bike against the fence outside the kitchen. We hear the jingle of an ice-cream van and he turns his head. He's like a dog, pricking his ears up at the sound of Pedigree Chum being scraped from a can. 'Anyone want anything?'

'No, thanks.'

Both of us speak at once. I would actually love a Strawberry Mivvi but I'm worried about appearing unsophisticated.

I sink my head into my arms. I don't see Jonathan often and when I do I jabber at him like an idiot. I would rather say nothing at all. I want to look at him but I won't let myself do that either and I don't need to. I know his face by heart. I love his scruffiness. I itch to steal his sweaters and wrap myself up in them, stick my fingers through the holes in the elbows. I want to touch his hair. It isn't rough like Rory's. It's softer and untidy. He looks so sleepy and careless, but he's sharp. He looks as though nothing matters to him, but when things do he can get very angry. I want him to get angry with me, but he never does. He just smiles his lazy smile and humours me. The little sister he never had.

'How's Sarah?' I say.

Jonathan picks up my camera and inspects it. 'We're not really seeing each other any more.'

'What does that mean? Not really seeing each other? You either are or you aren't.'

'Don't be so nosey.'

'I'm sorry. Did she dump you? That must make a change.' Facetiousness is my only defence. I take the camera out of his hand. I'm naturally possessive of it.

'No, she didn't dump me. It was mutual. We ran out of things to say to each other.'

I pretend to yawn.

'Sorry if I'm boring you.'

He flicks my shoulder lightly, not realizing what tumult his touch can throw me into. Like all ugly ducklings, I can't quite believe that my feathers are fine.

I prop myself up on my elbows and look down at him and his lips slowly curve into the smile I love. I lift the camera to my eye and take his photograph.

Jonathan sits up. 'What do you see when you're taking pictures?'

101

I shrug. 'It's more what I look for.'

He raises his eyebrows. Jonathan is genuinely curious about people. He told me that was why he chose to study journalism with psychology. He doesn't say anything and I feel a bit uncomfortable, as if he's moved into my territory.

'The story, I suppose. I want to see something in their eyes that tells me something's gone before and something's yet to come. You know what I mean?' I look at him hopefully. 'Don't you?'

'Yup.'

He makes a movement as if to get up, but stops and sits back again. He isn't relaxed. I hope he'll stay, but he doesn't have time. He seems to come to an internal decision because he puts on his shoes, stuffs the socks into his bag and then stands up and stretches.

'Good luck with your exams, Alice.'

I want to ask him something, but Rory has reappeared and the whole thing's become a bit embarrassing. I glare at my friend but he doesn't take the hint. It's now or never.

'Dad and Gabby are house-sitting for Gabby's parents in July. Olivia and Simon are coming for the weekend and Dad says I can invite whoever I want. Rory's coming. Would you like to come too? It's in Kent.'

He'll say no. I know he will. Rory is staring at me as if I've grown a second head.

'That's sweet of you.'

Sweet? I die a death.

'Oh, well if you don't want to, that's fine. I just thought . . . well, you know . . . it might be a laugh.'

He looks down at me from his great height and I squint up at him, the sun in my eyes. 'I'll do my best but I can't promise. I may be sent on an assignment at the last minute.'

'Alice,' Rory says when Jonathan has gone. 'Do you have a crush on my brother?'

Chapter Nine

MY MOBILE HAD BEEN LOST IN THE CRASH SO IF ANYONE HAD TRIED to reach me, maybe to offer me a fortnight's fashion shoot on a Caribbean beach – miracles do happen – they wouldn't have been able to. I went shopping with Gabby and bought a new one and the network managed to retrieve my old number and some of my stored information, so hopefully, I would be back in the loop soon. And then Dorothy called from *Her Week*.

'Alice, for heaven's sake. I couldn't believe it when I heard. How are you, darling?'

'I'm fine. Up and about. Going a bit stir crazy. You know. It wasn't that bad – just a bump on the head.' I grimaced at the gross understatement.

She didn't sound convinced. 'But you were in a coma.'

I resisted the urge to say, *yes . . . yes, I was and it was so, so awful*. 'Not for long. Honestly, I'm OK. Just trying to get back to normal.'

'Ah. Well, that's why I rang. I've got a couple of days for you, if you really think you're up to it.'

If she'd been in the room I would have kissed her. 'Of course I am. I'd love to do it.'

She gave me a few details, but before she hung up, she said what I'd been dreading. 'And your friend . . . Vincent told me. I am so sorry, Alice.'

My throat started to ache. I just wanted her to stop. 'Yes.'

'If you ever . . . I mean, if you want to talk to us about it. Our readers would want to hear your story. It would help other people to know how you've come through it.'

But I haven't, I wanted to shout. 'Maybe. Not yet.'

'Of course not. Well, I'm so pleased you're up and about. I'll drop you an email.'

I don't know if it was hearing a voice from my other life, or just her kindness, but I suddenly felt as though I was going to cave in with grief. It came out of nowhere. I said goodbye and retreated into the bathroom, sat down on the side of the bath and pulled off a strip of loo roll. I pressed it hard against my eyes and hunched over, gulping back the tears.

Sam knocked on the door. 'Are you OK?'

I didn't answer and after a few moments I heard him walk away. There was something wrong with me. Oh, Rory.

When I came out, Sam was leaning against the wall, as real as anyone I'd ever met. He was flicking a cigarette lighter on and off. I went over, took it gently from him, and dropped it back in the kitchen drawer where it belonged.

'Poor Alice,' he said, searching my face.

I leaned against him and he held me tight and I wanted to stay like that for ever, warm and safe and comforted. He kissed the top of my head and I felt my tears soak into his shirt. It was such a relief to have someone there who wasn't trying to buck me up or sort me out. Someone who would just hold me.

There was a moment later that evening when I began to feel twitchy. I wasn't sure what Sam expected. We had shared the spare bed in Gabby's house, but even though it had been perfectly innocent, I couldn't pretend we were still children. Wherever he came from, Sam was a man and I was a woman and I didn't want him to get the wrong idea. Or me for that matter. I decided matronly efficiency would be the best approach.

'Right. Let's get you settled. We need to sort out the spare room.' It was where I dumped everything. I'd miss the space. 'I think you'll be more comfortable there, don't you?'

He gazed at me, distracted. 'Fine.'

'So you don't mind?'

'Don't mind what?'

I almost stamped my foot. 'Not sharing a bed. You know what I'm talking about.'

He smiled sweetly. 'Of course I do.'

I was prepared to be mollified. Grudgingly. 'Yes, well, I just wanted to be sure you didn't have other ideas.'

'I wouldn't dream of it.' Amusement flickered in his eyes. 'You've gone red, Alice.'

'That's because I'm embarrassed.'

'Dope.' He tugged my hair. 'You're like a sister to me.'

It wasn't the first time a man had told me that.

The phone rang and I went to answer it, relieved at the interruption.

Peter Jones's posh frock department wasn't really me, but it was easier than traipsing from shop to shop and it was for a wedding outfit anyway, not work, where trendy jeans were de rigueur. Sam was fascinated by the place, wandering from rack to rack, running his fingers over the clothes, loitering while I tried on dress after dress, picked out by Mum and Olivia, who seemed to have a fixation with floral-print pastel numbers. I behaved like a tame dog, accepting each offering, pathetically grateful for the attention even though the colours they chose made my complexion look sallow. Olivia and Mum cooed and admired everything in-discriminately. The shopping trip had been my mother's suggestion, backed up with suspicious enthusiasm by Olivia. Presumably they had a particular Alice in mind – a grateful and obedient one.

'You look lovely,' Olivia said as I walked out in a pale blue dress splashed with large white flowers, made from some sort of wispy nylon. 'You could do with a necklace.'

I wandered over to a stand where a pink dress had caught my eye. I liked it. Its retro, fifties edge was much more my thing.

'Try it on,' Sam said. 'The rest of that stuff is crap. You look awful.'

I glanced down at the dress I was wearing. 'Thanks. That makes me feel so much better.'

'Well, what do you want? I'm not going to tell you that you look good when you don't. Try it on.'

I shrugged and took the dress back to the changing room while Sam waited with Olivia and Mum. When I came out he grinned.

'You look like a film star.'

I wasn't so sure about that, but it was a definite improvement. The vibrant colour at least suited my olive skin and the shape was flattering. It gave me curves.

Mum pursed her lips and tilted her head to one side. 'I'm not sure.'

'Oh, come on,' Sam said. 'She looks gorgeous.'

'I don't know,' Olivia said. 'I think it's a bit loud for you. The cream one suited you better. It was subtle.'

'I like it,' I said. 'It's fun.'

'It's brash,' Olivia said. 'Try on the other one again. It's much prettier. And then let's go and get some tea.'

Sam was livid. He turned on my mother and Olivia, and was about to launch into an invective when I came over and pinched him hard on the arm, as if I thought they would hear him, which obviously they wouldn't. He rolled his eyes at me. I changed and after a minute he followed me into the fitting room and studied his very solid reflection in the long mirror while I smoothed down my hair. After slipping in and out of so many dresses, it looked as though I had rubbed a balloon on it.

'You shouldn't let them bully you,' he said.

I pushed my feet back into my pumps. 'It is Mum's wedding,

Sam. If she doesn't like the dress then I won't get it. Anyway, maybe it didn't look all that great, maybe you're just biased.'

'They're jealous of you.'

'Don't be silly. Why would they be?'

'Because you're more beautiful than them and you're real. You can hardly call Olivia real. Her face barely moves.'

That was interesting. 'I didn't notice. Do you think she's had Botox?'

'I think they both have. Alice, really, you're as short-sighted as they are.'

'God, sometimes you sound just like Rory.'

There was a long silence. My hands shook.

He sank back against the wall. 'Buy that dress, Alice. You look incredible in it.'

I wrinkled my nose. 'No. Just for once, I'm going to be a good daughter.' I put the pink dress back on its hanger, running my fingers over it one last time, feeling a little regretful. 'Move, Sam. You're sitting on my bag.'

'Are you all right in there, madam?' the shop assistant asked, twitching at the curtain.

'Fine. I was on the phone.'

'Ah.' There was a brief pause. 'Why don't you hand me the things you don't want.'

I paid for the state-approved dress with Sam making irritated noises beside me and then followed Mum and Olivia up to the fifth floor. Sam was just ahead of me on the escalator.

'Aren't you missing something?' he asked casually.

'Like what?'

Mum turned and stared at me. 'I beg your pardon.'

'Your cardigan,' Sam said.

'Oh, flaming Nora. Mum, I've got to run back. I left something in the fitting room. Just order me a cup of tea, could you? I won't be a minute.'

'OK, Alice,' Sam said, as we took the down escalator. 'Change

107

the dress. Never mind your bloody family. You don't need their approval. I don't know what's got into you.'

I didn't know either. He was right, I was being pathetic and it wasn't like me at all. I retrieved my cardigan then found the pink dress again, held it against myself and swung its hem.

The sales assistant walked over. 'You should get it. It definitely suited you better than the other ones. You looked amazing.'

'You could have backed her up before,' Sam said.

I almost responded; it was so hard to remember that, for everyone else, Sam wasn't there. It was only me on Planet Weird.

'OK,' I said, pointedly addressing the assistant. 'I'll swap them.'

I was flattered and also, out of my family's immediate orbit, I had snapped back into myself. Then I heard a voice behind me and turned round and there was Megan MacLeod, fresh and glamorous, her blonde hair bouncing as she approached.

'Hey,' she said. 'Fabulous dress.'

'Do you really think so? Mum thinks I should get this one.' I held open the bag and Megan peered inside, fingering the material.

'No. It's too mumsy. The other one's young and fun. I'd change it, if I was you.'

'There you go, Alice,' Sam said. 'You can't argue with that.'

'Listen, I've got to run,' Megan said. 'But come to supper on Saturday. It'll just be me and Johnnie, nothing special. You wouldn't have to dress up or anything.' She put her hand on my arm and added gently, 'I think Johnnie would like a chance to talk to you before the memorial service.'

I glanced down at her hand, at the emerald and diamond ring on her finger. 'I'd love to come. Thank you.'

'So we're on then? Brilliant. Seven thirty. And, Alice . . .' Megan added. 'You should wear that dress to the service. Rory would have adored it. Emma and Brian don't want everyone in black anyway.'

I flinched. She would know that, wouldn't she? I held my breath until she walked away.

Up at the café I put the bag under the table and sat down. Mum and Olivia had bought me tea and a large chocolate brownie. I really was flavour of the month.

'You were ages,' Mum said. 'What on earth have you been doing?'

'Sorry. I bumped into a friend.'

'A friend?' Olivia had just forked a piece of carrot cake. It hovered close to her mouth. 'What friend?'

Then

EVEN HEAVILY PREGNANT, DAD'S GIRLFRIEND, GABBY, IS STUNNING. She has a big heart and a big laugh and has embraced the three of us, despite being barely older than my brother. They are an odd couple and we were all surprised that she stayed. We keep our fingers crossed and pray that she'll never leave him.

Gabby's parents own a converted oast house on the outskirts of a village close to the Kent–Sussex border. It's built on a small rise and is approached by a long gravel drive lined with rhododendrons on one side and conifers on the other. To the front the lawn slopes down to a round pond and close to that there are four enormous oaks. The ropes and swings that Gabby used to play on with her sisters are still hanging there, waiting for Archie, my two-year-old half-brother, to be big enough to use them.

Jonathan turns up on the Saturday morning and for the next day and a half I lurch between happiness and misery. Olivia seems determined to embarrass me in front of him. On Saturday evening we play cards in front of a completely unnecessary fire – Dad's bright idea – and when Jonathan says how kind it was of me to invite him along, Olivia pipes up, with a stupid laugh, 'She asked Sam first, but he was otherwise engaged.' For God's sake! I'm eighteen years old. It's as if Olivia is trying to remind me that I'm so much younger than Jonathan is. The baby. Luckily, the remark is completely lost on Jonathan, who just looks bemused, but it leaves me feeling as if I've been deliberately set apart.

On Sunday Dad forces us to go for a walk. Only Gabby and Archie are exempt. We tramp obediently along the lane and on to the footpath that skirts the fields, the ground rough under our shoes. Simon talks to Dad, and Olivia monopolizes Jonathan.

I'm envious of Olivia. She has a curvy body, can flirt unashamedly and holds a deep-rooted conviction that no man can resist her. And at the moment she and Jonathan are both unattached. Although probably not for long, I reckon. At least for Jonathan. Rory's theory is that, for all his independence, his big brother doesn't like being on his own. He can't cook and his idea of looking after himself and his flat is hazy to say the least. It's only a matter of time before he asks someone to marry him. When I think about that it makes me feel panicky, as if I've been given a deadline.

Rory is behaving oddly, he's permanently either moody or overexcited, and I wonder if he has a problem with Olivia. Maybe he secretly fancies her? I tuck my arm through his and drag him along until we catch up with Simon. His brow clears and he becomes almost too merry, involving Simon in a ridiculous debate about communism. Somehow he knows exactly how to push my brother's buttons. Simon, over from LA only for a fortnight, has bought all the kit and is wearing a tweed jacket, cords and Hunter wellies. Whatever happened to my punk brother? Rory and I think it's hysterical.

I can't keep up with their conversation. I don't feel left out, exactly, because I'm not, but I do start to get that leaden feeling, as though everything is too much effort. It's easier just to let them talk. I join Jonathan and Olivia. I can feel her irritation with me, but I don't care. It's my turn. Dad wants to talk to her anyway, so she's finally forced to concede defeat.

'You and Olivia seem very happy together,' I say to Jonathan.

'Is that right?'

Jonathan has a bouncy walk. From a distance, even out of focus, you can pick him out from a crowd.

'Do you fancy her?'

He fields the question. 'I can see I'm going to have to teach you the rules of good interviewing.'

His stride is longer than mine and I have to jog every few steps to keep up. But I like talking while we walk. He can't see my face and doesn't notice when I blush and I don't have to look at him and make those impossible calculations, like how long to hold his gaze.

'You certainly don't need lessons in evading the question.' My adrenalin has kicked in with a vengeance.

'Leaving silences encourages your interviewee to open up,' Jonathan says. 'I'm waiting for you to say something.'

He stops walking and crosses the verge to a gate where a pony is standing, its nose over the iron bars. Jonathan tugs up a hank of grass and offers it to him.

I reach out and stroke the animal between its ears and it butts my hand. 'Why do you flirt with Olivia?'

'I don't.'

'Of course you do.' In my heightened state of awareness it feels as though the animal is bridging the ten-year gap between us, its muzzle acting as a conducting rod. 'Anyway, I don't care what she does. And you can go out with whoever you like.'

'Thank you so much.'

I turn away and start walking. Jonathan catches up with me. I look straight ahead.

'And she's gorgeous,' I say. 'So I wouldn't blame you.'

'Don't be cross, Alice. I'm not going to date your sister. It'd feel incestuous.'

'Yuk.' I wonder where that leaves me.

Just then Olivia insinuates herself between us and laughs up into his face. I want to hit her.

'You have to have a word with Rory,' Olivia says.

Everyone apart from us is slumped in the sitting room:

112

Jonathan and Rory playing cards with Dad and Simon; Gabby and Archie fast asleep on the sofa. Olivia doesn't look at me when she speaks. She's tying an apron around her waist. I have been delegated the peeling.

I take a handful of carrots from the crateful of Gabby's expensive organic veg. 'What about?'

'You know what about,' Olivia says.

'No, I don't. Why don't you tell me?'

'Well, if you're going to be like that, I won't.'

I don't reply. I chop a carrot and drop the segments into the saucepan.

'So, you haven't noticed?' She raises her voice to be heard above the sound of sizzling onions. 'You haven't noticed that your best friend is obsessed with your big brother. You're either blind or totally naïve.'

I feel myself go cold. 'No, I haven't.'

'I'm surprised he hasn't told you he's gay. I thought he told you everything.'

'How can you possibly know that?' An odd, unpleasant feeling creeps over me, as though I'm on quicksand and my friends are walking away.

'For goodness' sake, Alice, grow up. It's patently obvious.'

'No, it isn't. If it was, I would have known. He would have talked to me about it.'

Olivia cocks her head. I want to scream.

'Maybe he's afraid you'll be shocked. Oh, come on, Alice, don't look like that. I'm sure he would have told you eventually.' She seems to realize she has gone too far and adds gently, 'You're just too close to him, that's all. The poor boy must be absolutely desperate to tell someone, he just can't quite bring himself to say it. That's why he's dropped so many loaded hints to me and Dad.'

I pick up another carrot and start slicing it. 'But not to me.'

'Sorry,' Olivia says, exasperated. 'But you do have an air of innocence and you're a bit of a square. He'd be worried how you'd react. We all would.'

I turn the knife over, then put it down carefully, wipe my hands on a dishcloth and walk out of the room and out of the house. I hear Olivia call after me. Sod her and sod them all. I run to the end of the garden, climb over the gate into the field and follow it round until I come to a stream. I sit down on the bank and put my head in my hands. It isn't that Rory might be gay. I couldn't care less about that. It's that he doesn't feel our friendship is deep or strong enough to tell me. But there have been signs, I acknowledge with a pang of guilt, and plenty of them.

I lie down on my back and bend my arm over my eyes. I'm not disgusted or even shocked. I'm devastated. Why hasn't he told me? I'm his best friend. Big tears roll down the side of my face, tickling my ears. The sun beats down, quickly drying them.

'Alice.'

I open my eyes, squint into the sunlight and see a young man standing over me. He crouches down and I realize that I know his name; that I don't even have to think about it.

I shade my eyes with my hand. 'Sam?' The light is odd and nothing is quite as it should be. I decide I must be dreaming.

Sam sits back on his haunches. 'I thought I'd never see you again. God, you're beautiful.'

My smile widens. 'Am I? Where've you been?'

'Here and there.'

He makes himself comfortable, matching my position, leaning against his knees, his head turned towards me. He seems real, but he doesn't fool me. I know I'm asleep. It must be a guilt dream, because I let him go so easily. I couldn't have been a very nice child.

'You're not really here, you know,' I say. 'This is a dream.'

'If you like. Listen . . .' He picks up a leaf. 'You can see this because your eye sends a signal to your brain and your brain accepts it and acknowledges it.'

'Now you're getting technical.'

He drops the leaf with a sigh and I watch our reflections ripple in the water and then I hold out my hand and he takes it and clutches it tightly. His eyes seem to reach right inside me, as if he wants something from me. But I don't know what it is.

'Who are you really?' I say. Then something tickles my nose and I yelp and flick it away. When I open my eyes, Rory is crouched beside me. I feel completely disorientated.

He grins. 'Were you dreaming or just delirious?'

'Dreaming. Was I talking in my sleep?'

'Mumbling like a loony. I've been looking for you.'

I sit up and bend over the water's edge. 'You scared the life out of me.'

'Sorry.' He undoes a loose shoelace and reties it. 'So, what're you doing here?'

I hunch my shoulders, wrapping my arms around my knees. 'Olivia was driving me nuts. I had to go for a walk before I said something.'

'You said, *Who are you really?* Who were you dreaming about?'

'I don't know.'

'Jonathan?'

I shove him over and he bursts out laughing then clutches my wrist and tries to pull me over too.

'Get lost, Rory. You are such a berk.'

He brushes himself off and sits up again and we both gaze out across the water. It's an idyllic afternoon. I wonder what he's thinking. I'm not sure whether I should repeat what Olivia said. If it's true, then he must be going through hell trying to work out how to let his family know and all I've been worried about is why he hasn't told me. I feel ashamed. He needs my friendship and here I am, sulking.

'You would tell me if anything was wrong, wouldn't you?'

He rests his chin on his knees and picks at the grass. 'Like what?'

115

I shrug. 'I don't know. It's just, you seem a bit withdrawn lately. You don't make as many jokes.'

He smiles and takes hold of his earlobe, twisting it. 'Vroom vroom. What am I?'

'Engine-ear. I've heard that one before.' I hesitate, scared of saying the wrong thing and pushing him away, but wanting to help. 'Are you unhappy?'

He won't catch my eye. 'Why do you ask?'

'Because of something Olivia said and because of the way you've been lately.' I turn my head but he looks off in the other direction. His shoulders are set. 'Are you gay?'

'I think so.' He picks up a twig and snaps it and then jumps up. 'We'd better show our faces or they might think we're up to something.'

I know Rory better than to press for more. He's broken his silence at least. It'll be all right now. I fight the urge to give him a huge hug because I don't want to overdo it, and content myself with squeezing his arm in a friendly manner. Then I look down at the water and just for a moment it darkens as if evening has crept up on us. Glancing up, I expect clouds, but the sky is an uninterrupted blue. I bite my lip and turn to Rory.

'Race you.'

Chapter Ten

IT WAS THE EVENING OF MEGAN'S DINNER. SAM DIDN'T THINK I WAS ready; in fact he was sure I wasn't, but I insisted on going. I had to reassure people that I was coping, otherwise they'd worry about me. Sam came along as well; although he didn't say it, I knew he was scared of what would happen if I left him alone. We hadn't been apart since the day I began to see him again and we were no closer to an answer. We still didn't know whether he *was* or *was not* when I wasn't with him.

'Alice,' Megan said, her lips pursing briefly close to my cheek. 'Come in. Listen, it's not just us. We decided it would be too solemn, so I've invited a couple more people.'

'That's fine.' I glanced at Sam and he smiled.

'Do you remember Matt, from the wedding?'

'Not sure. I don't remember much about it, to be honest.'

'Dumped, drunk and belligerent,' Sam muttered. 'Let's hope he's not going to make a git of himself tonight.'

It still didn't ring any bells.

'Great,' Megan said. 'That means he has a second chance to make a good impression. So, there's a friend of mine here too. Hannah. Just so you don't think you're being set up. She's going to be my matron of honour. Ready?'

She led me into the sitting room. Jonathan and Matt, who I vaguely recognized, stood up at once, both holding on to their bottles of beer. Jonathan stepped forward first, all friendly reassurance, kissing me on both cheeks before introducing me to Hannah.

'Do you have a drink?'

'I'm just getting her a glass of wine.' Megan disappeared back into the kitchen.

Matt looked sheepish. 'Good to see you again.'

Hannah was an impressive woman: tall and slender with a beautiful, haughty face and brown hair tied back in a thick pony-tail. She didn't smile much and when she did it was mostly at Jonathan, who she looked at with a subtle lowering of her lashes. Even though the collar of his shirt was frayed and he was wearing socks and no shoes, I could tell she envied Megan her luck. I was in no position to mock her for that. She had also ignored the instruction not to dress up and was wearing a short black dress with high heels. I had kept it casual with white cropped trousers, blue cardigan and strappy sandals; my concession to formality, a pair of dangly glass earrings.

'Oh, the fight!' I said, without thinking, and the room went silent. 'Sorry, I've only just remembered.'

Matt visibly squirmed. 'I know I was out of order . . .'

'Oh, God, I didn't mean that. I don't think Dad and Gabby even realized it was happening.'

'You can sit down now,' Megan said, smoothing things over with a radiant smile. 'Everything's ready.'

The table was at one end of the sitting room and Megan had placed three candles stuck into antique teacups along the centre. We watched Jonathan light them one by one and then Sam held his hands close enough and for long enough to hurt the tips of his fingers. I held my breath, horrified. He glanced at me and shrugged before backing away from the table as the others took their seats.

I sat between Jonathan and Matt and opposite Hannah. Megan turned the lights down low and served the food.

'Have you done all this yourself?' Hannah asked, admiring the table.

Megan curled a lock of hair behind her ear. 'Well, yes. But Jonathan vacuumed.'

'It smells absolutely delicious. Is it Nigella?'

She blushed sweetly. 'No, it's something my mother used to cook.'

'God, I don't know how you do it,' Hannah said. 'I know I couldn't.'

'It's nothing really. My mother cooked beautifully and taught me not to despise domesticity. I have to say, I don't do this often, but when I do I find it immensely rewarding.'

'Pass the sick bag,' Sam said.

'What about you, Alice?' Hannah said. 'Are you a domestic goddess?'

'Hardly.'

'Alice's mother wasn't exactly a nurturer,' Megan said. 'It makes such a difference.'

I stiffened and shot Jonathan a dirty look. He had obviously discussed me. He mouthed an apology.

'No, Mum isn't the cosy type.' I smiled coolly at Megan. 'But she's still my mother.'

There was a pause, quite a pregnant one, then Megan laughed and said, 'Johnnie's hopeless around the flat. But if we were ever marooned, he could build a shelter and a raft, and catch and kill our food.'

'Very heartening,' said Matt, and there was a rumble of manly laughter.

I drank steadily as the evening wore on, even though I'd meant to stick to one or two glasses. At one point, Matt turned to me and said in a low voice, 'I hear you were in a coma for three weeks.'

Sam had been looking bored but he stood up, interested in the turn the conversation was taking. I caught his eye and half smiled, trying to pretend I was reasonably sober.

'Yes,' I replied politely.

Sam came and crouched beside my chair. 'You've had too much to drink. Take it easy.'

'Mind your own business.'

He burst out laughing. 'Alice!'

I bit my lip, stifling a giggle. Matt's smile dropped and he went for his wine glass, nearly knocking it over in his haste. He slugged some back and glanced around nervously, but no one else had heard.

'I didn't mean to pry,' he said.

I smiled to cover my slip. 'I'm sorry. It wasn't as interesting as it sounds. I was unconscious and then I came to. There was nothing in between, no long white corridor with a bright light at the end.'

Sam circled the table and stopped close to Megan. He touched her hair and looked at Jonathan, staring at his face, his eyes tracing his features. What was he looking for? Was he threatened by him? Chances were I'd find a boyfriend sooner or later and Sam would have to accept that. I wished it could be Jonathan, but that wasn't going to happen. I glanced at Megan, chatting away to Matt, showering him with sparkle and warmth. It wasn't that I couldn't compete, I had accepted that I wasn't made that way; but what I still had to learn to accept was that this was what Jonathan was drawn to.

Hannah, who was sitting on the other side of Jonathan, was attempting to charm him with a mixture of sexual allure, wit and determined eye contact. 'A journalist with a degree in psychology,' she murmured. 'Should I be worried?'

I caught Sam's eye and he smiled at me and raised his eyebrows. My lips twitched in response.

Jonathan smiled. 'No, I don't think so.'

'But don't you have all sorts of theories about people? When you talk to them, don't you automatically check out their body language?'

'He doesn't need a qualification to interpret yours,' Sam commented.

120

'If I was interviewing you, quite possibly, yes. It's useful to have that background. If nothing else, it helps me to understand what people aren't saying.'

She leaned back and lifted her glass to her lips, gazing at him over the rim. 'What about us?' she murmured. 'Look at Alice and Matt. Can you tell if she likes him or not? Do some decoding for me.'

Jonathan glanced at me. I was sitting with one elbow resting on the table, my fingers propping up my cheek, the other hand holding my fork. He didn't answer Hannah's question, which, to me, raised several about himself. Instead he put down his glass and prodded me on the shoulder. I was relieved to be rescued. Hannah looked peeved.

'How're you doing?' Jonathan said.

'Fine. It's a lovely dinner.'

'I was hoping to get a chance to talk to you about Sunday week.'

'It's odd,' I said. 'But I'm looking forward to it. I feel as though I'm going to be seeing Rory again.'

'I know. I feel the same way. It's as if it's been got up as an excuse to visit him. Like a surprise party. I'm so glad you came tonight.'

'Thank you. I'm glad you invited me.' I hesitated, looking away from him at Megan, who was laughing at something Hannah had said. 'I haven't congratulated you both yet. I'm very happy for you.'

Jonathan didn't say anything for a moment and in that time Sam had moved so that he could see his eyes when he answered me. The candlelight rested on Jonathan's face, making the hollows beneath his cheekbones appear deeper, his eyes like dark caves.

He spoke softly. 'I know it seems very sudden—'

I interrupted him. 'No, it doesn't. You've been together a while.'

'I meant after Rory's death.'

121

Jonathan was staring at me. Matt reached for the bottle and started topping up wine glasses.

'Have you set a date yet?' I asked.

'End of October.'

'Oh. That's soon.' I had expected to have had at least six months to get used to the idea. The end of October was just over three months away.

'Megan didn't want to wait,' Jonathan said, glancing at her.

I silently finished his sentence. To get pregnant. 'No, well, she's probably right.'

He smiled quickly and ate another mouthful of Megan's delicious stew. I had lost my appetite.

'Can I ask you something?' I said.

'Sure.'

I grimaced. 'This is going to sound a bit stupid, but do you know about people who see things?'

'Do you mean psychics?' He was relieved to change the subject. I could hear it in his voice.

'No. Not exactly. I don't think so, anyway. Just an alternative reality. One person seeing things that other people can't, but that appear real.'

'There've always been other ways of experiencing reality. No two people are the same. The world would be a boring place if they were.'

I sighed. 'I don't know what I'm asking really.'

He smiled and tapped the side of my head with his finger. 'Maybe you're a right-brainer. That's the creative side of your mind. Anyone who professes psychic ability uses the right-brain function. It hasn't been scientifically proven, but there've been plenty of studies. Left-brainers tend to be more cynical and less artistic. So what's it all about?'

I shrugged. 'I've had some odd experiences since the accident.'

'Such as?'

'Oh, nothing that interesting. Someone who shouldn't be there.

He's a good presence. Not scary. Not a poltergeist or anything like that.'

'Have you heard of synaesthesia?'

I shook my head. 'No.' At least he hadn't laughed.

He ate a mouthful, and then spoke, waggling his knife at me. 'It's supposedly a cross-wiring of the brain. People who see the world differently. Kandinsky had it, or was thought to. Or there's Carl Jung's theory of synchronicity. It was his way of making sense of the paranormal; events that defy rational explanation. He had a spirit friend called Philemon who he used to talk to regularly. There's plenty of information out there, if you know what to look for. So who are you seeing?'

'Oh, well—'

Megan interrupted: 'Johnnie's writing a book on psychology, aren't you, honey?'

He smiled at her, showing the barest glimmer of irritation. 'Not psychology in itself. It's about how journalism has manipulated and contributed to the evolution of psychology over the last hundred and fifty years, and vice versa.'

'Really?' I said. 'That's so interesting. I had no idea you wrote books.'

'Book,' Jonathan said. 'It's my first. I'm fascinated by the human mind. I've always liked digging around in people's heads. So what were you about to say?'

Megan reached over and tapped me on the arm. 'I am such a bad hostess. I've hardly spoken to you. How have you been?'

'Oh, you know. Up and down. It's really nice to be out in the evening again. I've felt a bit cooped up lately.'

'Has your mother been looking after you?'

I laughed. 'You are joking, aren't you? No, I stayed at Dad's. It was meant to be for two weeks but after one, they decided I was nuts, so I thought I'd better make a move before they had me committed.'

'So, how nuts?' Hannah asked.

I fiddled with my wine glass, twisting it between my forefinger and thumb. 'I talk to myself.'

'Don't we all?'

'Only I don't.' I leaned back in my chair and looked over at Sam and widened my eyes. I thought he looked weary.

'They're all so rat-arsed,' he said. 'It isn't going to make much difference what you say. Tell them, if that's what you want.'

Matt frowned. 'Don't what?'

'Talk to myself. I talk to Sam.'

The conversation around the table went dead. Jonathan gave me an odd look and I wondered what was going through his mind.

'So who is Sam?' Megan asked. Her eyes settled on mine.

I felt myself go pink. 'He's a friend. I've known him for years. I haven't seen him for a long time, but now he's back.'

Sam walked over and stood behind Hannah. Jonathan was tight-lipped. Matt seemed pleasurably bewildered, as if a slightly constrained evening had suddenly and inexplicably become entertaining.

'We should go home, Alice,' Sam said. 'It's late and it's your first night out. You mustn't overdo it.'

'I'm not overdoing it. I'm fine, really. I'm having a good time.'

Megan was instantly apologetic. 'Oh, Alice. I'm so sorry, I didn't think. Of course you mustn't wear yourself out.'

'So how long have you been seeing this guy?' Jonathan asked. There was an edge to his voice.

'Well, I'm not exactly seeing him.' Sam blew me a kiss and I smiled. 'At least, not in the way you mean.'

'What does he do?' Matt asked.

'I don't know.' I looked up at Sam. 'What do you do, Sam?'

'I look out for you.'

'He looks out for me.'

Hannah twirled a stray lock of glossy hair around her finger and I wondered if she was aware the gesture was sexy and that

Matt was staring at her. I tried it with mine but it didn't have quite the same impact.

'I'm confused,' she said. 'Is he some sort of carer? Does he not have a job?'

'Well, not really.'

I felt a wave of heat rush to my cheeks. The worst thing was that Megan was trying to catch people's eyes to tell them to shut up. Unfortunately, my alter ego just kept on going.

I put my finger on my lips. 'It's a secret.'

Sam groaned and I added, as if this were an entirely rational conversation, 'No one can see him so he can't get a job.'

Jonathan put his arm around my shoulders, drew me to him and kissed me on the temple. Megan frowned and Sam went very still.

Hannah asked, 'So is he here now? In the room with us?'

I nodded. 'Yup.'

'Wow. What does he look like?'

I tilted my head and chewed at my bottom lip. 'He's tall. He has beautiful dark-blue eyes and black hair. He's slim and gorgeous.'

Sam made a face. 'Thanks, Alice.'

Hannah said, 'Sounds too good to be true. Can you conjure one up for me?'

Matt tried to top up my glass again. Jonathan attempted to stop him but I thought that was a cheek and pushed his hand away, knocking half a glass of wine across the table.

'Oops. I'm so sorry.' I slumped back in my chair and stifled a belch.

'You're not going to throw up, are you?' Sam said.

'No.'

'It doesn't matter,' Jonathan said.

He picked up the glass and dabbed at the stain with his napkin, making things worse. Megan fetched some paper towel from the kitchen and for a moment they were distracted.

Hannah hissed at me across the table, 'Where is he now?'

I leaned forward and hissed back, 'Standing right behind you.'

Hannah jerked round. Sam grinned at her. She settled back into her chair and fiddled with her earring.

'Put your hands behind your back,' I said. 'I'll tell you how many fingers you're holding up.'

'Alice,' Sam said. 'Don't turn me into a parlour game. You don't have to prove anything to this lot. And don't look at me like that. If you do this you'll make an issue of it. People won't leave you alone.'

'Once. Please.'

He held up his hands, surrendering like I knew he would. 'Once then.'

I mouthed thank you and the room fell silent; an awkward mixture of embarrassment and pity killing conversation. Hannah put both her hands behind her back and folded down her fingers.

Sam held my gaze. 'Three.'

'Three.'

'Wow.' That was Hannah, her slightly disdainful look momentarily replaced by awe.

Matt leaned back to check. 'Lucky strike. Do it again.'

But Sam turned his back on us and walked over to the window.

'Jesus,' Jonathan said. 'You made my hair stand on end. How did you do that?'

'I told you. Weren't you listening?' I shoved back my chair and stood up, lurching. 'Sorry. Not feeling so great.'

I stumbled out of the room, closed the bathroom door, threw myself at the loo and vomited. After the first bout, I rinsed my mouth and opened the door a crack, only to hear Hannah saying, 'Do you think . . . I mean, I don't believe in ghosts or anything like that, but do you think she's psychic? That was quite impressive.'

'No, I don't think so,' Matt said. 'I think she's neurotic.'

'Oh, for fuck's sake,' Jonathan exploded.

That made me smile.

'Johnnie, really. There's no need to shout at Matt.' Megan

sounded genuinely concerned but she was probably less worried about Matt than the possibility that she would be expected to hang around A & E for the rest of the night. 'Do you think I should go and check on her?'

'No, I'll do it. Why don't you make everyone a coffee? It's probably time to call cabs anyway.'

He was angry and I wondered, hopefully, if he was angry with me. I closed the door quietly and my stomach lurched again.

Chapter Eleven

WHEN JONATHAN AND SAM CAME IN I WAS SITTING ON THE FLOOR beside the loo, sweaty-browed, grey-complexioned and mortifyingly aware that I looked revolting. I shrank into myself. I didn't feel great about one man seeing me with my dignity in shreds, let alone two. I wished Sam would go, and then I felt disloyal. He looked so worried.

Jonathan smiled down at me and I raised my head slowly. 'Is Megan annoyed? I ruined her dinner.'

'A one-woman demolition gang? Don't be daft. I was dying for them all to go. She's calling a cab for Hannah.' He paused for a moment and then said, 'You can stay the night here. There's a spare bed in my office.' He crouched down beside me. 'God, you look awful.'

His eyes and his tone said something different and even in my sad state I experienced a frisson of awareness. Sam frowned and seemed to study me, as if he was trying to see me the way Jonathan did.

Jonathan pulled my hands away from my face. There was a softness in his expression that I hadn't seen before and I badly wanted to kiss him. Fortunately for both of us, I felt far too disgusting to make the attempt.

Sam snapped, breaking the tension. 'Too late for that, my friend. You had your chance four years ago.'

So he knew about that, did he? I half-laughed. He was so

melodramatic sometimes. I couldn't take him seriously. When Jonathan let me go I wrapped my arms around my legs and rested my chin on my knees. 'The room's spinning.'

Sam sat down on the side of the bath. He was behaving like my chaperone.

'Go away,' I mouthed.

He looked as if I had slapped him, and I suppose I had. It was like when we were children and I was in charge, telling him when he could and could not play with me. It was a low blow and I was sorry for it, but I was drunk, ill and incapable of great depths of compassion and sensitivity.

'I can't leave you with him.'

I didn't answer because I couldn't. Jonathan was rinsing out a cold flannel. He handed it to me and I covered my face with it, pressing it against my eyes. He tucked my hair gently behind my ears and then let his hand rest on the back of my head.

'That was quite a stunt you pulled in there.'

'Oh, I'm full of surprises.' I peeked over the edge of the flannel. He had such a beautiful smile.

'You certainly are. Is Sam still here?'

'You bet I am.'

'Was that a trick question?' I asked. 'Or are you humouring me because you think I'm deranged?'

Jonathan laughed. 'I'd call you eccentric. And I ask because I'm interested. Hannah thinks you might be psychic.'

'Honestly, Jonathan, it was a guess. And have you considered that maybe Hannah pretended I'd got it right? To shake us all up.' I sighed. 'Dad and Gabby think I need to see a shrink. They're probably right. Only, I can't be bothered. I've got enough to do without sitting in a clinic, baring my soul to someone who won't understand. I can deal with this myself.'

He pried the flannel out of my fingers, rinsed it again and wiped my forehead, earning another filthy look from my guardian. Sam was beginning to look as ill as I felt. He held out his hands and turned them over. Even I could see they were trembling. He curled them into tight fists.

'By getting drunk?' Jonathan looked amused.

'Yes, maybe. If I feel like it.'

I could feel the tension in Sam. Any other time, this totally innocent yet verging on illicit conversation with Jonathan would have been a moment in my life that I could obsess over for years. As it was, I felt like an awkward teen trying to flirt under the watchful gaze of her unimpressed father. I just wanted Sam to go.

I added, childishly, 'And anyway, Megan said it was only going to be you two. I don't do dinner parties at the best of times. Hannah and Matt are very nice—'

'No, they aren't. Matt's a prat and Hannah's a nightmare.'

'Yeah, all right. But that's not for me to say. She fancies you, by the way.'

'Lucky me.'

'Megan says we all do.'

'We?'

I felt the blush coming but there was nothing I could do. Jonathan had appropriated the flannel again. 'I meant women in general. We all fancy you. Apparently. Anyway, you should be careful. You could get into trouble.'

Sam crouched down and stared into my eyes. I tried not to acknowledge him, but I couldn't hold out.

'Stop flirting with him, Alice.'

When I dragged my gaze away, it was as though I was physically detaching myself from him.

'Thanks for the warning,' Jonathan said. 'How're you feeling?' He rubbed the back of his neck. The last time I had seen him looking this awkward was after I had kissed him in the street. But that was a long time ago, in another life.

'Horrible. I'm never going to live this down.' I added, apropos of nothing, 'I like Megan.'

'So you keep telling me. Can you stand? Only this is bloody uncomfortable.'

'Sorry.'

'Not your fault. I shouldn't have let Matt ply you with drink. I was distracted by all those women who fancy me.'

'I don't.'

Jonathan levered himself up and held out his hands. 'Up you get.'

I took them and he drew me into his arms. We stood close together, me with my nose pressed against his shoulder, my feet against his. My fingers strayed to the place where his shirt had come untucked. I felt his skin and he drew in a sharp breath.

'Alice,' he muttered. 'Behave. You've had too much to drink. Don't make things worse.'

He gently pushed me away and Sam came right up into his face, breathing into his nose. 'Take your hands off her.'

He turned from Jonathan abruptly and stared into the mirror. His image had faded to a spectral shadow. He thumped the side of his fist against the glass.

'What was that?' Jonathan put his hand on the mirror and frowned.

'Hannah's gone, Jonathan,' Megan called. 'You can come out now.'

We both relaxed our shoulders. It was the door to the flat slamming, that was all. But Sam was ecstatic. I glared at him, the muscles in my face tensing with the effort to make him understand that he wasn't welcome, that he should go. He shook his head slowly. I turned away.

'Bit of a dramatic exit,' Jonathan commented.

'I expect she was leaving in a huff because you're in here with me. I really am sorry. I shouldn't have drunk so much.'

'It doesn't matter. At least the dinner was memorable. Which is more than I can say for most parties I go to.' He rummaged in the bathroom cabinet and found a spare toothbrush, which he placed on the side of the basin. 'Clean your teeth. You'll feel a million times better. I'll go and sort out the bed.'

He touched my cheek and I didn't release my breath until he had left the room. And then it came back to me. A snatch of the conversation we'd had at my father's wedding. What he had said to me about wanting me but not wanting to hurt me because I meant too much to him.

And what I wished now had been my response: *I don't care about that, I just want you to kiss me.*

After he had gone, Sam stood in front of the door, blocking it. 'Don't stay here.'

'Don't be ridiculous. I can barely stand up. I just want to collapse. We'll go home first thing in the morning.'

'I don't understand you.'

I was holding the toothbrush under the tap. I turned to face him.

'I don't understand me either. I don't understand why I see you, why I feel you and hear you and nobody else does.'

We glared at each other. I didn't want to start feeling hostile towards him, but he was pushing and pushing me. It was emotional blackmail and I didn't like it.

There was a sharp tap on the bathroom door. 'Alice? Are you OK in there? Do you need anything?'

I opened the door and Megan handed me a pair of green-and-white striped pyjama trousers and a white T-shirt.

'These should fit you – if you don't mind the bottoms being a bit short.'

'Thanks. Has everyone gone?'

'Yup. Matt took a taxi with Hannah. Johnnie's stacking the dishwasher. Why don't you go to bed and sleep it off?'

I allowed myself to be led down the corridor and into the small back room. There was a desk under the sash window with a laptop closed on top of it and a wall of bookshelves beside it, piles of papers everywhere and an overflowing waste-paper basket. One of Jonathan's sweaters hung over the back of the chair. The bed was narrow and was obviously used as an alternative surface because papers and books had been hastily removed and stacked on the floor. Jonathan's leather bag looked rather forlorn where it lay slumped against the leg of his desk.

If I hadn't been so ill, I'd have been fascinated by this room. I'd have waited until Megan had left and then explored it, checked the titles on his shelves, tried to analyse the way he ordered his papers, looking for clues to his inner life in every corner. I wondered if Megan sensed this as she switched on the bedside light then leaned over the cluttered desk and closed the blind.

'Sorry it's such a god-awful tip. It's the one place that's out of bounds for me. Will you be all right?' She pulled a carrier bag from under the desk, took a book out of it and handed it over. 'Just in case you need to vomit again.'

I sat down and felt the bed. 'The room's going round but it's OK. I'm not going to be sick.'

Megan's face relaxed. 'It was fun. But maybe a little too much, too soon? See you in the morning then. Sleep tight.' She closed the door.

I lay down and drew the blankets over my shoulders, then Sam climbed in between me and the wall. He stared up at the ceiling.

'I feel like shit,' I said.

Sam breathed out and squeezed my hand. The hostility had vanished. 'Serves you right.'

'You're mean.'

I tried to settle but I was wide awake, turning things over in my mind. Eventually, I propped myself up on my elbows and looked down at him. 'So, let me get this straight. I'm never allowed to fall in love? It'll just be the two of us from now on? I'm going to have to resign myself to people thinking I'm a batty old spinster? It's not a particularly attractive prospect, Sam. And how will it work anyway?'

His eyes held mine and there was defiance in his expression. 'I don't know. I'm learning on the job as well.'

'Sam, please understand—'

'Just sleep, Alice. Everything will be all right in the morning.'

Chapter Twelve

SAM AND I HAD TIME TO SPARE WHEN WE ARRIVED AT THE CHURCH for Rory's memorial service because I had been so worried about being late, I had overcompensated. We walked down to the river and strolled along the path, watching the boats and ducks on the flat water. As instructed by Megan, I wore the pink dress I'd bought for Mum's wedding.

And so there we were, Sam and I, wandering along the river path like any ordinary couple. Sam was happy. He always was when he had my undivided attention, and he was very engaging with it. We didn't talk about complicated things, and I think he assumed that I was like him, that I didn't need anyone else so long as we had each other. On one level he was right. With him I had company; someone who really seemed to understand me, who was in many ways a part of me. But he wanted too much and he thought that, by offering his protection and his undying love, I would have everything I could possibly want. The trouble was, I wasn't a child any more. I didn't need a shield against the world.

We watched some boys row by in an eight in their matching blue-and-white kit. They were focused, staring back at their wake, their arms pulling rhythmically on their oars, their splash quiet and controlled. We stopped outside a pub where tables were laid out on a small jetty above the river. It was crowded but one of the tables had just been vacated so we grabbed it and sat down to kill a few minutes.

135

Two young men approached, armed with pints of beer and a packet of crisps. 'Do you mind if we sit here?'

'Be my guest,' Sam said. 'Just don't sit on me.'

I looked up at them, shading my eyes. 'Not at all. We . . . I mean, I. I'm not staying.'

One of the men sat down sideways on the bench and pulled his legs over, then shifted up for his friend. He ripped open the crisps and offered them to me. I shook my head and they wolfed them down, leaving the empty packet on the table between them. Sam touched it and the edge lifted, but it could have been the breeze. A toddler padded over and stared up at us and Sam brushed the salt off his fingers and poked it on the nose. I thought that the child looked surprised, but the expression was so fleeting that I could have imagined it, and then he babbled something and pointed a sticky finger at the crisp packet. His mother scooped him up, smiling an apology, and deposited him, protesting, into his buggy.

Sam took hold of my wrist. 'Do you think he sensed me? Babies are a bit like animals, aren't they?'

'Yeah, maybe,' I whispered, distracted by a text from Vincent and forgetting that I wasn't meant to talk to him in public. 'Give me a second, Sam.'

The men looked at me. One of them said, 'Sorry? Do I know you?'

'Oh, I wasn't . . . I mean, I'm going to be late. I have to go.'

'But I'm Sam.'

'That's nice.'

I extricated myself as elegantly as possible from the bench, smoothed down my dress and hurried away. I was beginning to feel shaky as the minutes ticked by and the sight of the church as we turned the corner brought home why I was there. I tried to slow things down but it was no good and within moments we were only yards away. I chewed at my lip, staring at the people waiting outside in the churchyard, examining expressions in the way I did with air stewardesses, for reassurance that the turbulence meant nothing sinister, that I would get safely home.

'Are you going to be OK?' Sam said, looking at me with concern. He patted my shoulder awkwardly.

I pulled myself together, wiped my eyes and blew my nose. 'Yes. Sorry. I'm terrified I'm not going to get through this.'

'You will. You owe it to Rory not to break down. Just don't look at Emma.'

'I know. That would be a disaster. Oh God, Sam. What if I can't? What if I forget the words?'

He put his arm around my waist. 'Come on, you know them by heart. You've practised enough. Hold my eyes and you'll be fine.'

I glanced round and spotted Daniel hurrying along the path, glancing at his watch. I waved and he approached us. He looked drawn, but he managed a smile and a kiss.

'You look amazing,' he said. 'This is crazy, isn't it? Rory should bloody well be here.'

Brian, Jonathan and Emma were standing outside the little red-brick church, greeting their friends. Emma and Brian saw us first and waved and we picked up our pace and hurried over. Then Jonathan turned from the woman he had been talking to and stared at me and my heart missed a beat.

Daniel was effusive in his greetings, hugging and kissing them. Neither Brian nor Jonathan seemed to mind the physical contact and Emma appeared to love it, sinking into his arms and embracing him with equal enthusiasm.

She dabbed at her eyes. 'Darling Daniel. And Alice. Thank you both so much for being here. If you go in, Megan will show you where to sit and explain the order of service.' She opened hers and scanned it, as if she hadn't a hundred times already. 'Daniel is up first, then you, and then Jonathan will speak at the end. I'm so grateful to you.'

I was alert to every nuance. The *thank you for being here*, as if it had been a choice, rather than the natural course of events. I

137

hadn't realized until that moment quite how desperately I wanted to be back in the fold. But things would never be the same between us, no matter how hard I wished for it. My eyes blurred and I had to blink to clear my vision.

'In you go.' Brian propelled us forward.

Jonathan caught my eye as I walked past him and I smiled a greeting. We stopped for a moment just inside the door. The church was full of flowers, like a wedding. Garlands of white roses and ivy hung from the ends of the pews; vast arrangements stood like angels on either side of the altar. It was glorious, but all I could think was, why didn't they ask me to help? Megan hurried up to us and Daniel held his hands out and laughed out loud.

Thank God for Daniel, because my greeting stuck in my throat.

'My God, he would have adored this. Well done, Megan love. You've done him proud.'

'Thank you, Daniel.'

She squirmed out of his arms, smoothed down her dress, explained what was required and directed us to the pews at the front. Sam kissed me on the cheek then walked to the back. We waited for the bustle to die down and the first hymn to strike up. When it came to my turn to speak, I was determined not to let Rory down. It was the only thing that stopped my legs collapsing underneath me. Jonathan, who was sitting next to me, gave my arm a reassuring squeeze as I stood up.

I searched for Sam and my eyes found his and it gave me the injection of resilience that I badly needed. I took a deep breath. 'Rory was my best friend. He was my family. I never told him how much he meant to me, but I hope he knew. He would have laughed. Rory drew people to him effortlessly and they stayed because they shared his love of life; he was born generous.'

My voice wobbled. I took another deep breath and held it together.

'Rory, my thoughts are with you, through our past and our future, regardless of the constraints of reality. They go with you, wherever you go. Rory loved his Shakespeare, so this is for him.

> 'If the dull substance of my flesh were thought,
> Injurious distance should not stop my way;
> For then, despite of space, I would be brought
> From limits far remote, where thou dost stay.'

I was shaking. I did not want to cry. I knew the words, but I dropped my gaze from Sam and looked down at them and, to my dismay, they began to lose definition. It threw me so badly that I nearly forgot what came next. Then I raised my head and Jonathan's eyes locked with mine and held them. It was as if he was gripping me by the shoulders and ordering me to keep it together.

I took another breath.

> 'No matter then, although my foot did stand
> Upon the farthest earth remov'd from thee,
> For nimble thought can jump both sea and land
> As soon as think the place where he would be . . .'

I managed to finish without dissolving, but it did take several minutes for my heartbeat to calm down afterwards. Another hymn followed, giving me a chance to pull myself together, and then Jonathan stepped up to the lectern.

Jonathan was masterful. It surprised me, although perhaps it shouldn't have. He understood public speaking and he understood his audience. He recounted stories of the scrapes Rory had got into, of his innate kindness and irrepressible sense of humour, of his love for his family and loyalty to his friends. There was enormous strength in the way he stood there, broad-shouldered and straight-backed, speaking to our hearts. To me he became a man then, a hero in the truest sense of the word. He described his brother with huge pride but also with a pinch of fraternal exasperation that made people laugh. When he returned to his seat I wanted to hold his hand. Megan touched his face and he leaned away from me, into her.

When we came out, Sam was sitting on a gravestone. He seemed distraught. He must have been overwhelmed by the service as well. But I couldn't go and comfort him, not now. This wasn't about him. I waited for Gabby and Dad to emerge and then got into their car and we drove back to the Walkers' house. Sam didn't come with me but I didn't worry overly. I resented the fact that his attention-seeking had left less room in my head for Rory. Gabby turned round in her seat and reached over to press my hand. She smiled at me. This was normality. This was real and it was what counted. Not my imaginary friend.

Chapter Thirteen

'ALICE, COULD YOU GET THE SAUSAGE ROLLS OUT OF THE FRIDGE?'

It was obvious that Megan was in charge. I wasn't sure how I felt about that.

'Don't want the oldies drinking on an empty stomach,' she added, smiling over her shoulder.

I was on edge around her. I'd gone to their flat and behaved like a teenager at her first party, getting incoherently drunk and salivating all over the hostess's boyfriend. Not good. I tore open the packet and arranged the rolls on to a baking tray. Megan took it from me and put it in the oven. It was as if she was my mother, allowing me to think I was helping. That stung.

I washed the flakes of pastry off my fingers and dried them before I spoke.

'I want to apologize for the other night.'

Megan straightened up, took off Emma's oven gloves and laid them carefully on the side.

'Alice, this is not the time. Really.'

'OK. But can I help?'

I stepped forward, looking around the kitchen and thinking that it had a different energy to it. Megan's energy. It even smelt of her perfume. Nothing had changed here and yet everything had. I felt as though I'd drifted into a parallel universe where all the familiar things refused to acknowledge that I had history with them; from the mugs I had hooked my fingers into, to the chairs I'd sat on, I was afraid to touch them for fear of rejection.

'Do you want me to take some of these round?'

'No. You go out and talk to people. I've got it covered. I'll be out in five.'

I wanted to argue. I wanted to say that I had a historic right to be in that kitchen, but she was so smiley and so confident that I felt even more like a visitor. It was horrific how quickly my relationship with this house had changed. It had been so much a part of my life and yet without precisely thrusting me away, it had raised barriers. Its walls meant as much to me as the walls of the house I'd grown up in, but perhaps that was only my perception, and now, without Rory, I had somehow become unglued from its fabric.

It doesn't matter, I thought, as I turned round and left the room.

Outside, the older generation sat on the patio on chairs that had been brought out of the house or borrowed off neighbours, and the younger ones, Rory's friends and cousins, sat or stood in groups on the sun-dried lawn while Emma and Brian watched. They were smiling, awed by the number of people paying tribute to their son, telling them how gorgeous he had been, how much they missed having him in their lives.

My small family were well represented. Dad and Gabby were here without the children, as were Olivia and Mum, who had arrived at the church together and only hung around for half an hour, much to my relief. They had been fond of Rory, particularly Mum, but they didn't like Emma and Brian. Simon wasn't there because he'd already arranged to fly over for Mum and Larry's wedding. For once my sister didn't seem inclined to bat her eyelashes at Jonathan and at one point, when I was on my own, she came over and held my hand. I dropped my chin as I struggled not to break down. Olivia's softer moments were so rare that, when they came, they hit me hard.

'We all liked him so much, Alice. It's rotten for you.'

'Worse for his family,' I muttered.

'I know, but it's you I care about. If you need anything, if you just need company, please call me and come round. I can't bear to think of you sitting in that flat all on your own.'

To be on my own was exactly what I wanted, but I thanked her anyway. I thought she might hug me and I started to move away just in case. There was only one person I wanted to go to, and he was out of bounds.

Sam glowered in the background, but I decided not to take any notice. This was Rory's day and if I had done something to piss him off, it would have to wait. I saw Daniel and watched him for a moment, feeling wistful. I sincerely hoped we wouldn't lose touch. I missed our daft arguments. He winked at me and I nearly burst into tears. I wanted to run over and throw my arms round him, but Brian was walking towards me.

'How's my honorary daughter?'

His pitted cheeks were a little flushed, his eyes bright, and I wondered how much he had already drunk to get himself through the ordeal. I hugged him and reached up to give him a kiss.

'Did you realize he was so popular?'

Brian nodded and gazed at his son's friends, maybe seeing some of them as small children, as stroppy teenagers, remembering the tramp of their feet through the house and up the stairs to Rory's bedroom, the music thumping through the walls, the laughter and the shouts.

'When this is over, when we've got used to life without him, I will be all right.'

'Of course you will.'

I was dismayed at the change in him. His large frame was less fleshy, his face gaunt. He had lost his vigour.

'For Emma's sake. That's what's so wonderful about Jonathan and Megan's engagement. It's given Emma something to hold on to, something to plan for and hope for.' He drew a deep sigh and said, 'Thank God. Ah, Jonathan . . .'

Jonathan put a hand on his father's shoulder and the two men stood side by side looking at me. Then Brian turned away to greet an old friend.

The brief silence that followed made me want to run away. And if that wasn't bad enough, Sam was watching, making every word I did manage to spit out sound laboured. I wished to God he hadn't come.

'Thank you for the reading,' Jonathan said. 'It was beautiful. It summed up everything I was feeling.'

'That Rory hasn't really gone?'

He nodded. 'Yes. All we have to do is ignore earthly boundaries and we can be with him. Oh Christ, Alice. How are we ever going to get over this?'

There was so much that I wanted to talk to Jonathan about: about Rory, about the way I felt about his family, about how cut off I felt. But all my thoughts sounded so selfish. What did I matter? I didn't know what to say to him. I couldn't commiserate; we had done that; we already knew what we had each lost, and I couldn't bring myself to mention his engagement. Fortunately Jonathan came to my rescue.

'Do you remember that weekend we all spent with your dad and Gabby?' he asked. 'When Archie was a toddler.'

'Yes.'

I remembered it perfectly. I remembered the smell of the day, the sounds of it. I remembered Jonathan so close to me that I could barely breathe. I also remembered how he had allowed Olivia to monopolize him. I wasn't proud of the way I had behaved.

'We are friends, aren't we?' he said. 'Just like we were then. Just because Rory isn't here any more, doesn't mean we're going to lose sight of each other.'

I looked at him steadily. What was he trying to tell me? That I'd imagined what had happened on the night of the dinner party? That he wanted to believe that I was too pissed to remember? That he wanted me to act like it had never happened?

I blinked first. 'I can't see Megan inviting me round for dinner again.'

At the mention of that evening, he dug his hands into his jacket pockets and hunched his shoulders and I felt something lurch inside me.

His smile was attempted rather than spontaneous. 'Don't be silly. She understood.'

I looked into his eyes and thought, You are an idiot, Jonathan Walker. And then I broke into a smile. It was his face that made me grin. I couldn't help it. It was as if I had been programmed to react positively to him.

He put his hand on my arm. 'That's better.'

Sam was sitting on the ground, his arms hanging loosely across his knees, watching us. He obviously hadn't got over whatever it was that had put him in a mood. He stood up slowly and walked towards me. I didn't remove Jonathan's hand. I wanted to push Sam's buttons.

'What's up?' Sam said.

'Everything's fine.'

'Christ, I wish it was,' Jonathan said. He rubbed his fingers through his hair in a familiar gesture. 'But nothing's fine any more. It all seems so unreal, everything: Rory's death, my engagement. I feel like I'm playing a part – and not very convincingly.'

'Don't listen to him,' Sam said. 'He's making excuses. It doesn't mean anything.'

There was no point letting Sam wind me up. If he wanted to sulk, that was his lookout. I ignored him. 'Jonathan, let's just get through today. Tomorrow you'll wake up and things will look better.'

I was talking rubbish. It was stupid to allow myself to slip into the well-worn grooves of a teenage infatuation. Jonathan didn't want me; he might occasionally fancy me, but he had Megan and he didn't need me making a fool of myself over him, particularly right now. And anyway, I knew him too well to kid myself that I stood a chance. At that moment, Emma called him over. He sent me an apologetic smile and walked off.

I wasn't happy with Sam and I wanted him to know it. I turned and hissed, 'For God's sake, what are you doing? Rory was my friend and I want to be part of this party, and if I want to talk to his brother, I will. If you don't like it, just bugger off. I don't understand why you're being like this.'

'Don't you?'

'No, I don't. Everything was fine. You know it was. If you're in a foul mood now, it's not my fault.'

'Um . . . Alice,' Megan said. She had come up behind me, holding a tray of canapés which she carefully set down on the grass. 'Why don't you come inside for a minute, get out of the sun?' She added, whispering, 'People are looking at you. You're talking to yourself again.'

Gabby and Emma joined her and guided me into the house, effectively screening me from the other guests. I went with them meekly and sat down on the sofa. Sam stood framed in the doorway, watching us.

'I really don't think you should be living on your own, darling,' Gabby said. 'It's too soon. You're not ready yet.'

I bent over and rested my forehead in my hands. 'I just want everything to be normal again.'

'I know you do, honey,' Megan said. 'And it will, I promise, but it could take a few months. This happened to a cousin of mine, so I know what I'm talking about. You've had an almighty bash on the head and you can't expect things to be exactly the same. You've been lucky, but you won't have come out of it completely unscathed and you need to learn to adjust to whatever that means. Maybe you should go home for a while, to your mum, I mean.'

I groaned. 'There is no way I'm living with Mum. She'd hate it as much as I would, and it would hardly be conducive to straightening my head out.'

146

'Well, come back to us then,' Gabby said. 'Just for a short break. The kids would love it.'

'I'm working next week, but I will think about it, I promise.'

I wondered what Sam would say. Quite a lot, probably. At any rate, it was unlikely to happen. I had to stand on my own two feet.

'Come today,' Gabby said. 'If we give you time to think, you won't budge.'

'I didn't realize you were all so worried about me.'

'Well, of course we are,' Emma said. 'When Brian and I heard you'd left your father's house and gone back to the flat, we were horrified.' She hesitated. 'Alice, I want to ask you something, and you don't have to answer straight away. We're spending the rest of the summer in France and we'd love you to join us for as long as you like. It would give you a break.'

'Are you sure?'

Part of me was ready to panic at the thought of spending time alone with them; part of me wanted to throw my arms around Emma and cry my eyes out, but the last thing she needed was to have to deal with someone else's broken heart. Perhaps they wanted me there to dilute their own grief, so that they didn't choke on it. Whatever the reason, I was overwhelmed by their kindness. If it was at all possible, I wanted to be there for them and help them. I couldn't emulate Megan's confident empathy, but they knew me well enough to understand that I loved them.

'Yes,' Emma said firmly. 'Come as soon as you can. We'll be back in September.'

The sun was going down and its light glared through the train windows, broken from time to time by rows of houses. Through Mortlake and Barnes it flickered against our faces, making me squint. Sam was still in a vile mood and his anger and my irritation sat between us like a surly sprite, draining all the positive emotion from the day.

I dropped my keys on the small IKEA cabinet beside the door.

147

Sam walked over to the window and stared out, his shoulders stiff. Of course I knew his mood had to have something to do with Jonathan. What else was there? I was beginning to understand that Sam had a frightening capacity for jealousy. When he finally turned round, he was ashen, his eyes dark and angry.

'Please tell me what I've done,' I said. 'I can't bear this silence.'

He advanced on me and I recoiled, my back pressing against the kitchen counter. It obviously shocked him because he stopped abruptly and his eyes searched my face.

'Did you think I was going to hurt you?'

'I'm sorry. You just looked so angry. You're frightening me.'

'Tell me how you feel about Jonathan.'

I set my chin, prepared to do battle if that was what he wanted. 'I can't help it if I find him attractive, Sam. But apart from that, I like him and he cares about me. Anyway, he's getting married. He's in love with someone else, so you don't have to feel threatened.'

'You're not stupid, Alice, so don't pretend.'

'I'm not. I'm just telling it like it is.'

'Then why,' he said, pressing the heel of his hand against his forehead, 'why did you look at him? I told you to look at me if you needed to. You held his gaze like you were fucking drowning in it.'

'I don't know what you're talking about.'

'Yes, you do. When you read the sonnet.'

I remembered then. I had looked down, breaking my connection with Sam, and when I looked up I had searched for Jonathan, not him.

'I'm sorry.' I sighed, defeated. 'I don't know why that was. I think he was looking at me, you know, and he caught my eye and then I just hung on because I was trying to get through it. But that was all, Sam. I swear it didn't mean anything.'

'What were you talking about later on?'

'Nothing. You didn't give me a chance to say anything. Sam,

148

stop it. You know how I feel about you.' I touched his face and he gripped my wrist and pulled my hand down to my side.

'Don't try and manipulate me, Alice. You don't know what you're playing with.'

I was tired. It had been an emotional day and I could do without Sam laying into me. 'Will you stop it! You are not real, you bastard! Get the hell out of my head. Go away!'

'You know you don't want that.'

He sounded so patronizing that I completely flipped, lashing out and slapping him across the face. He grabbed my arm and shoved me away so that I fell against the sofa. I yelped with fright.

He rushed to help me up. 'I'm sorry. I'm sorry. I didn't mean to hurt you.'

I could have let rip but I didn't because I was as angry with myself as I was with him. After all, I had provoked him. His reaction shouldn't have come as a surprise. He would always want more of me than I was prepared to give and there would always be that conflict between us. What on earth was I going to do?

He walked over to the table and gripped the back of a chair, hunching his shoulders and dropping his head. He looked up at me through his fringe.

'You're safe with me.'

I could only nod mutely, aware that in giving in I was creating more problems for the future. I had a horrible feeling I'd live to regret it.

Then

I ARRIVE PUNCTUALLY AT AN ADDRESS IN STOCKWELL AND SPOT Jonathan's bicycle already chained to the railings of a tall and shabby stucco-fronted house. He called two days ago, offering me the chance to shoot a high-profile writer for a national paper because the photographer who would normally have taken the job was stuck on location in South Africa. I am nervous and excited and desperate to make the right impression: unflappable, professional and good at what I do. Just because I've been scratching around for assignments, begging features editors to glance at my portfolio and making ends meet by working in a pub, it doesn't mean I'm not capable. I'm so grateful for the opportunity I could kiss his feet.

I park and get out of the car, looking up at the building. The plaster is cracked and buddleia sprouts from behind the drain, but it's still far more beautiful than my red-brick Battersea terrace. I scrutinize the names against the doorbells and press the second one.

Jonathan buzzes me in and thunders downstairs to greet me. He is looking unusually smart in a charcoal-grey corduroy jacket, black trousers and white T-shirt. Even his socks match. I notice this anomaly as I follow him up a scruffy staircase and through an open door. The flat must have been grand once and still is, in its way. Only now it looks tired, the paint flaking off the ornate mouldings that frame the high ceiling, the old-fashioned, schoolroom-style radiators peeling. In the sitting room, at a desk in front of one of the two French windows, a woman is sitting. She's small and fine-boned with greying hair and greyish eyes and she looks as nervous as I feel. Jonathan introduces us and then starts his interview while I set up my equipment.

I've never seen him work before and I find myself wondering whether his technique is different depending on whether it's a man or a woman. I reckon it is. I can imagine that the way he comes across – reassuring, affable, shaggy and kind – instils confidence in people. It seems to be working on Connie Wells. Add to that a natural bent for flirtation and you have a potent mix.

When the interview has finished and the photo session begins, I'm not nervous at all. Both Connie and I have been expertly warmed up by Jonathan, so it's easy to appear confident and professional. I tell a couple of Rory's better jokes to make her smile seem less fixed, show her how to angle her body and how to keep her hands looking relaxed, keep up the patter while I take the pictures. I'm surprised how natural it feels. Perhaps it's the Jonathan effect.

When the front door finally closes behind us, he says, 'Well done. That was excellent.'

I go straight to the car with my laptop and camera while he holds the rest of my kit in his arms or crammed between his leg and the railings.

'You're surprised?' I say.

'A little.'

I pause and then think better of making a smartarse remark. 'Well, I hope they're good. I took enough.' I stash the laptop in the car and run back for the rest.

'Do you want to grab some lunch?' Jonathan asks.

I have my keys in my hand, but I glance at him hopefully. I'd love to have lunch with him. Apart from anything else, it feels as though it would be the right way to end the morning. Then I grimace and shake my head. The area is a little too edgy, the elegant Georgian streets a mixture of pristine, moneyed homes and the down-at-heel; islands of aspirational elegance surrounded by grey acres of council estates. Most of the downstairs windows are barred.

'I'd better not. I wouldn't be able to relax with all my stuff in the car. The camera was Dad's. They cost a fortune new and he'd kill me if I lost it. And there's my laptop. Sorry.'

'Bring the car with you. There's a great tapas bar along the South Lambeth Road. You can park outside.'

'A little off your usual beat, isn't it?'

He shrugs. 'I've been there before, once or twice.'

'Are you going to leave your bike here?' I have a moment's panic, wondering what might be knocking around in the footwell of my car and then realize it wouldn't matter, not with Jonathan. He wouldn't notice if I tipped the entire contents of my dustbin into it.

'I'll bring my bike and meet you there.'

I find the restaurant easily and, as luck would have it, a white van is just pulling out. I nip into the space and as I'm paying at the meter, Jonathan cycles up. We go in together, although at the last minute I go back and retrieve my camera from the boot of the car.

It's weird, walking into a restaurant with Jonathan Walker. I feel energized in a way I never have before as I sit down in the window and shuffle out of my jacket. I don't know what to say, or where to begin. It all feels so new, so full of potential. For the first time ever we're alone and face to face across a small square of table, our knees practically touching, no other distractions apart from the menu, no escape for either of us until the meal is over. It feels both illicit and natural. We are going to have to have a proper conversation, just the two of us.

Jonathan peruses the menu then puts it down. 'I'm bloody starving. I could smell cooking all the time I was in the flat. What did you think, by the way?'

'Of the smell?'

'No, idiot, of the job. How do you think it went for you?'

'I don't know. But it felt all right. I am so grateful to you. It's such a relief to photograph something I can show off to Dad.'

Jonathan laughs. 'Your dad? Is that all you're worried about?'

'No, of course not. I'm trying to persuade someone to take me on as an assistant, but it's tough out there. I've been banging on doors for the last six months. Now I've got something other than pack-shots and arty portraits of Rory to put in my book. It's brilliant.'

He smiles and something in his eyes makes my nerves jangle. 'I honestly think it's all going to start happening for you. Aren't you glad you didn't give up on yourself?'

'Of course. Look. What do you think?' I turn the camera towards him so that he can see the tiny screen and then click slowly through the images. My heart is beating too fast. It's so important that he thinks they're good, not just workmanlike. Workmanlike isn't going to impress him or move my career along another step.

He leans over and studies them closely, getting me to start again and take it more slowly. I'm aware of the texture of his skin, the tiny mole close to his ear. 'She's not the easiest subject, is she? So serious and intense. Here – this one. That's when you found it.'

I peer at the image and then at the previous one. There is a difference. It's subtle but important. It turns Connie Wells from a rather severe-looking woman trying to be relaxed, to a woman with a twitch to her lips and a light in her eyes. 'Yes,' I say. 'I think I see what you mean.'

'See, this is where it gets interesting. That's what I love about interviewing – that moment when you find the electricity, when your subject comes out from behind the wall they've built. You did that, Alice. You should be proud of yourself.'

I glow like a child receiving praise from her favourite teacher. 'You warmed her up.'

He leans back and grins. 'Yeah, but I've been doing this for a long time. Remember what you told me years ago – that you look for what came before and what will come after. That's always stuck with me, and you were absolutely right. Keep plugging away at it, Alice, keep beating down those doors. You're going to do just fine. Shall we order? Do you know what you're having?'

I can't focus on the menu at all. 'You choose.'

'I'll get a selection. We can share.'

He catches the attention of a waiter and reels off a list of tapas: razor clams and eggplant chips, stuffed peppers, patatas bravas. It all sounds wonderful, but I'm far too wound up to care what I eat. My mind is turning over various avenues of conversation. Jonathan is highly intelligent, educated, extremely well-read and well-travelled. I rack my brains. What have I read recently? What films have I been to see? My mind has gone blank. If he'd dressed with his usual lack of care, I would feel more comfortable. It's this smart thing. I'm not used to it. I can't tease him when he looks like that. My gaze keeps lingering on his mouth. Because I'm driving, we only order coffees, although I really want a glass of wine. We smile at each other.

'So . . .' I say.

'So?' He tilts his head and waits.

'You suggested lunch. You can pick a subject.' I sip my coffee, looking at him over the rim of my cup.

He laughs. 'OK. Do you have a boyfriend?'

So he isn't expecting anything erudite from me. I feel resentful. I might have studied photography, but that doesn't mean I have no other interests. 'Not at the moment, no,' I say tartly. 'How's your love life?'

There isn't much leg room under the table, and my feet keep touching his. I move mine away. I don't want it to be my fault. Then I realize that might look even more obvious and put them back. His don't move so perhaps he can't feel mine through the leather.

'She's called Isabel and she's Spanish. She's gorgeous.'

Hence his expert knowledge of local Spanish restaurants. Perhaps the woman lives around here somewhere. I'm seething with jealousy, but I keep a breezy smile on my face. 'I'm sure she is. What does she do, besides making you look good?'

'She's a dancer.'

I'm sure I detect the ghost of a satisfied smirk. 'So you're a stage-door Johnnie? Do you hang around after her performances clutching bouquets of red roses?'

'Sometimes.'

We look at each other and I feel a blush creep up my neck. My napkin slides off my knee and I bend to pick it up, grimacing as I do so. I'm making a fool of myself. Jonathan waits, watching me.

'Can we talk about something else?' I say. I can feel myself getting snappish. He has a curious ability to make me angry even when I'm desperate to kiss him.

'Of course we can. I'm reading a really good book at the moment.' He reaches into his battered leather bag and takes out a well-thumbed paperback.

'I've read that. Rory lent it to me. It's wonderful, isn't it? I couldn't put it down.'

'How is my brother?'

'He's absolutely fine,' I say.

I'm not sure I want to get into discussing Rory with Jonathan. I don't know how much he tells his family about his lifestyle and how much he keeps back to stop them worrying. Fortunately the waiter comes over, and the next few minutes are absorbed in tasting and discussing the food. After that I resolutely steer the conversation, anxious to appear interesting and interested. Jonathan responds and loses his laconic, slightly mocking air, getting stuck into a discussion about psychology, his favourite subject.

When we finish, I try to pay my way, but Jonathan refuses to let me.

'I think about you sometimes,' he says, sliding his credit card back into his wallet.

'Do you?' I glance at his lips and then up at his eyes. He looks amused.

'It was strange, the way we first met, wasn't it? Like fate.'

Why does he do this to me? Is it deliberate or does he really not know? I lift my head and hold his gaze. His brown eyes are frank and open. He isn't playing games with me, not on purpose anyway. But that's what's so maddening about him. He genuinely likes me and wants to please me, but he just doesn't understand.

'Are you ready to go?'

I nod and push my chair back, dissatisfied and yet aware that something between us has moved on. I think that he's finally acknowledged that I'm an adult. He's taken his time, but he's there. It can only get better, surely?

Outside, Jonathan puts his arms around me and holds me tight, his jaw pressed against my temple. I breathe him in and slowly circle my arms around his back. It feels bony under the jacket, and warm.

I lift my head and for a moment we just look at each other, then an old woman with henna-dyed hair, pulling a shopping trolley, jostles us and we move apart.

I mumble something incoherent and have to start again. 'I'll see you around.'

'Of course you will. I'll make sure our paths cross.' He hesitates and then says, 'You're lovely, Alice. Never change.'

I force a smile and when he puts his hands in his jacket pockets to find his keys, something snaps inside me and I walk back to him, stand on tiptoe and kiss him on the lips. There's a moment when his body tenses and I feel his response. It isn't imaginary. When I pull away and look into his eyes, his have darkened, his breathing quickened, like mine. He starts to say something then seems to change his mind and fiddles with his keys instead. He doesn't look as if he wants to repeat the experience.

'Listen, Alice—'

My face is on fire. 'Don't.'

'OK. So we don't talk about this? Is that what you want?'

I shrug, feeling like a sulky teenager. 'What is it you want, Jonathan?' I turn away from him abruptly and try to fit my key into the lock but my hands are shaking so much I only succeed in scratching the paintwork. 'It was just a kiss. Don't worry about it.'

Jonathan puts his hands on my shoulders, pulls me round and envelops me in a huge hug. 'Darling Alice. You know I love you, don't you?'

'I suppose so,' I mumble into his chest. What did I expect? For him to go down on one knee and swear undying lust and passion? Idiot.

'Like a little sister.'

I nod and he drops his arms. 'I love you like a brother too.'

'So kiss me like a brother then.' He bends and proffers his cheek. I kiss him and then laugh, but I am mortified.

'I've hurt your feelings.'

You don't know the half of it. I study him for a moment and catch something fleeting in his eye. Curiosity? Puzzlement, perhaps. Maybe it's progress or maybe I've scared the hell out of him and taken two steps back. 'No you haven't. I'm meeting someone else this evening anyway.'

He nods, but I detect something fondly mocking in his expression. He doesn't believe me.

'Good. Good. I'm pleased. I hope it's someone I'd approve of.'

'Because you're my big brother?'

'Exactly. Listen, Alice. I've got to get going. Good luck, OK. I'll let my editor know that you were fantastic.'

'Thanks. I look forward to reading your article.'

I jump into my car, shove the key into the ignition, reverse into the bumper behind me and drive off with a shriek of tyres. I feel total and utter despair. Is he never, ever going to see that I'm entirely different from the child he rescued all those years ago? I have breasts now, for God's sake. And long hair. And I might not be beautiful, I might not be glamorous, blonde and scintillating company, but I'm pretty and I have a brain. In the rear-view mirror I can see Jonathan watching, so I wait until I've turned the corner before hitting the steering wheel with the heel of my palm and letting rip.

'Jesus, bloody Christ! Oh my God, oh my God, oh my God. What the hell was I thinking?'

'Alice, hush.'

I pull up at a set of traffic lights and at the sound of the voice I turn with a sharp intake of breath. The air in the car goes eerily still. Cars flash by, people cross the road but they seem set apart from me somehow. And then a horn blares and I lift my hand in apology and shoot through the green light, my heart pounding.

Chapter Fourteen

'SHE'S BEEN HIGHLY RECOMMENDED,' DAD SAID. 'AND IT'S ALL private. Not the NHS. No waiting around with a bunch of loonies and freaks. Anyway, I've paid for it and she was bloody expensive, so you have to keep the appointment.'

I had hoped to avoid this. Sam couldn't understand why I couldn't, or wouldn't, see that Dad was only doing this to make himself feel better. I did see that, of course I did. I'd have been a fool not to. But I really didn't care. Dad needed me to need him. Well, fine. I could deal with that. It was better than Mum's insistence that she was entirely independent of her children; that Olivia, Simon and I led our lovely, blessed lives and she led hers.

'OK, Dad. I'll go. Give me her address.'

What harm could it do? It might even do some good, maybe help me find a balance.

I didn't have a car to transport my bulky kit to the location in Shoreditch, but that was what taxis were for. Sam and I had patched up our disagreement and he came with me. We couldn't stay angry with each other for long. I found my need for him confusing. It wasn't physical, unless wanting to be hugged counted. I must have badly needed an emotional crutch. Thinking about it kept me awake at night. I'd veer from panicking that this was now my life, that he would never go away, to wondering what it would be like to have him grow old beside me. If I couldn't have

Jonathan, I didn't really want anyone else. Men would come along from time to time, if I was lucky, but I doubted my ability to stay the distance with someone who would always be a compromise. Sam might have been an enigma but at least he was never boring.

I found the day physically exhausting, in a way that I never had before. My camera felt heavier, my shoulders and ribs ached and my head, by the end of the morning, was banging. I hadn't taken my painkillers because I didn't want to risk feeling fuggy, but in retrospect that was probably a mistake. There were moments when I had to clench my teeth to stop myself from crying out. I thought I managed to hide it, but when we stopped for lunch the hair and make-up artist, who I had worked with before on many occasions, came up to me, brandishing her concealer.

'Would you like some tips on scar camouflage? I can make it disappear.'

I only just stopped myself from throwing up my hands to ward her off. 'No. But thanks.'

'Why not?' Sam said.

I'd been prickly. I apologized. 'I don't like touching it myself, let alone anyone else.'

'I don't blame you. I can do your eyes, if you like. It would pick you up.' She finger-combed some of my hair over the short patch. 'I could do something about this.'

'I don't look that bad, do I?'

'No.' She sounded unsure. 'You just look tired and your skin's a little lifeless. Fresh air and exercise will help. And make-up.'

I let her get on with it. To tell the truth I found her persistence oddly reassuring. I quite liked the results, but the make-up felt heavy and tight, and as soon as I got home I cleaned it off. I had made it through the day. I'd proved myself. Now all I wanted was to have a large glass of wine and curl up on the sofa in front of a movie.

First, though, I put the memory card into my laptop and opened the file with the new photographs. The location was a Georgian house that had been meticulously restored to its former glory. The models looked exquisite in their evening dresses against the back-drop of shadowy panelled rooms and draped elegantly over antique furniture. It gave me a sense of satisfaction to discover that the accident hadn't affected my eye for shape, colour and light. I scanned the images until I found the ones that would earn the money and please the client, and selected a few extra that pleased me and copied them into my jobs file.

Sam pulled a chair round and sat down beside me. 'Let's have a look.'

'They've turned out really well, don't you think? This one's good. The light's perfect.'

'They're beautiful.' He studied each frame carefully, then sat back. 'Where are the pictures you took of the flat?'

I didn't know what he was talking about. 'Which ones?'

'When we first came back here. You got your camera out. You can't have forgotten.'

I frowned and concentrated. 'I'm not sure.' I scanned the menu and clicked on an icon. A dozen images filled the screen. 'Do you mean these ones? They're quite dull.' I went through them slowly.

Sam had gone very still. 'Stop. Go back. OK, that one.' He stared at a picture of the square arch between my sitting room and kitchen.

'What?' I asked.

I tried to work out what was so interesting and something sputtered in my mind like a car engine coming to life on a cold morning. Since the accident, my brain seemed to take its own sweet time to flush out memories. It was frustrating. I didn't have a clue why I had taken the photographs. Sam swore under his breath and rubbed his forehead with the heel of his palm.

'Do you really not remember?' he asked.

I shook my head. 'Well, no. What am I supposed to be seeing?'

'It's what you're not seeing, Alice. You were taking photos of me.'

'Ah.' I shut my eyes and tried to picture it and slowly the memory came back. 'Oh, Sam. I am sorry.'

I didn't know what else to say. The photographs showed no sign of his presence. There was no distortion, no shimmer of energy and no man. I thought about the implications. It was my first real proof that Sam was not actually with me. The camera told the truth and it was my mind that was changing the facts to create a new reality. Probably because I couldn't cope with the old one.

'It doesn't mean you aren't here.' I placed the back of my hand against his cheek. 'You're warmer than I am. You don't need to prove anything, Sam. I can see you.'

'But the camera sees with its lens and it only sees what's there. You see with your brain, so your brain can distort images.'

It was only what I'd been thinking. 'Most people's brains don't.'

'Most people haven't had a major head injury.' He jumped up and paced the room before coming back to me. 'Let's face it, Alice. I function as a part of your mind. I do what you think I can do, even if you're completely unaware of it. There is no other explanation.'

I had only looked at the first few images, but now I checked them properly, one by one. And then I saw it and smiled.

'Look at this.'

The cushion was suspended in mid-air, caught in the afternoon light. I turned to him as a slow smile transformed his face. His expressions could really delight me, like a child's could delight its mother. Not that I felt particularly maternal towards him. Or maybe I did. I might have to think about that one later. He bent and put his arms around my shoulders, his cheek against mine. And then he let me go with a groan.

'You threw it at me. It doesn't prove anything.'

'I'd have had to be bloody quick, and anyway it would be blurred.'

'Alice, this is pointless.'

I tried to sound encouraging. 'We can take some more. Something that would be irrefutable.'

'Don't bother. There's always an explanation for everything. I might as well be the Loch Ness monster.'

I laughed at him but he didn't laugh with me, so I refrained from making the facetious comment about UFO sightings that had popped into my head. 'But look how much progress you've made.'

'In here, with you, perhaps. But I don't have any effect outside this bubble.'

'Yeah? So what about the toddler at the pub? You thought he sensed you, didn't you?'

'I forgot about him.' His voice was a grumpy, non-conciliatory mumble. 'But even that doesn't prove anything.'

'Come on, cheer up. I have high hopes for you.'

'So, tell me, Alice, why have you come to see me?'

The psychiatrist, whose name was Carol Margulies, took one of the chairs placed in front of her desk. She was slender and mild looking, in the way that a sandy beach is: one pale colour and soft curves, no edges. She wore bronze-framed oval spectacles that every now and again she took off, inspected and replaced over grey eyes. Her black hair was laced with iron and silver and seemed edgeless too, springing gently round her face. The consulting room was in the basement of her house; a clean, calm space with a wide window looking out through security bars on to a small patio. I thought the bars were an unfortunate touch, given the nature of her clientele. Beyond them, stone steps led up to the garden.

Carol was waiting, still smiling, absolutely patient.

'I was in a car crash,' I said. 'I was in a coma for three weeks.'

She nodded thoughtfully. 'That must have been confusing for you, losing all that time.'

'I lost my best friend. Time doesn't matter.'

'Are you finding it hard to come to terms with the loss? I can help you with that.'

163

'I . . . that's not really the reason I'm here. Not the reason Dad booked the appointment, at any rate.'

'Your father organized for you to see me?'

'Yes.'

'Why was that?'

I looked down at my hands. I hadn't let Sam come in with me. To my mind, a conversation between psychiatrist and patient should be private. His presence would make me watch my words. But maybe that was what he wanted. At the moment he was outside, twiddling his thumbs. At least, I assumed he was. There had been a bit of a row, because neither of us knew what would happen when we weren't sharing the same space, but in the end I dug my heels in and insisted we find out. We had to do it sometime. It might as well be now.

'An old friend has come back into my life.'

I felt a chill and rubbed at the goose bumps on my arms. It was hot outside, but cool down here in the bowels of her house and I was only wearing a thin shirt.

'Well, that's a good thing, isn't it?'

I smiled. 'Yes. Yes, it is. It's wonderful. But the point is, I knew him when I was a child. He was my best friend.'

I had grown rather expert in skirting around the issue of Sam's presence. I could probably spend the whole of my allotted hour avoiding the absolute truth and I was tempted to. What good would explaining it do? It was bad enough that my closest friends knew. God, I wished I had never gone to Megan and Jonathan's that night.

Carol leaned forward and adjusted her glasses. 'So this is someone your family doesn't approve of? They think he's bad for you?'

I glanced at the door and felt my hands shaking. I don't know why I was so anxious. Sam wasn't nearby, couldn't scowl at me or tick me off for saying the wrong thing.

'I'm not judging you, Alice. It doesn't matter to me who your friend is, or what he's done. I only want to help you. Is he hurting you in some way? Is that what they're worried about?'

'No, it's not like that. He'd never hurt me.' I put my face in my hands, pressing my fingertips into my eyes, squeezing them shut. I drew a deep breath. 'It's just that they can't see or hear him.' I sat back and breathed out and added bluntly, 'So that's why I'm here. Because I'm a grown woman with an imaginary friend and my family think I'm mad.'

'That's not a term I'd use,' Carol said. 'Perhaps we should backtrack. Tell me something about yourself.'

I told her, and when I got to Olivia and Simon she asked me to describe my relationship with them.

I thought for a moment. 'Retrospectively, needy, I suppose. Especially with Simon. I was a bit of a nuisance, but sometimes they were kind to me. A lot of the time, they weren't there anyway.'

'So you were left to your own devices?'

'Pretty much.'

Carol's pen scratched swiftly across her pad. 'And what about your parents? Do you have a close relationship with them?'

'It's getting better. They split up when I was two. Dad's remarried and Mum's about to marry for the second time. She's very beautiful and he's very successful.'

As I spoke I could almost hear what Carol was thinking. Ambitious father with no time for her, vain mother saddled with an unwanted third child too far removed from its siblings to be of any interest to them. Lonely and isolated within a dysfunctional family unit. Classic something-or-other. I was beginning to feel trapped and I wanted the session to end. We talked about my early life, about Paula and my mother and father, about Rory and his parents. I didn't mention Jonathan. It felt disloyal to Sam.

'So what's your friend called?' Carol asked.

I looked her in the eye, searching for something beyond professional interest. 'Sam.'

'And how old is he?'

'I don't know. About the same as me, I suppose. I haven't asked him.'

'So he's aged?'

'Yes.'

'And is he with you now?'

I tensed. This was the sort of thing that made me uncomfortable. I hated being humoured. I'd had too much of that when I was a child.

'No, he's not,' I said a little too sharply. 'He's waiting for me outside.'

'Would you ask him in?'

I sighed. 'Look, I know you're trying to be open-minded about this, but you don't have to say things you don't believe. It makes you look ridiculous and it's patronizing to me.'

I was shocked at my outburst. Since when had I become so assertive?

The psychiatrist looked flustered. 'I'm sorry. Let me put it differently. I'd like you to ask the man you believe is waiting for you to enter the room. I want to see you speak to him, whether he exists or not.'

'OK.'

I went upstairs and stood just inside the front door, on the seagrass mat. Outside Sam was either there or not, there was no way of telling. I couldn't sneak up on him, get there before myself and see him materialize. It was pointless even trying. I opened the door. Sam was sitting on the steps and he twisted round when I came out.

'So?' I said. 'What happened?'

'Nothing.' He shrugged and smiled at me. 'I've just been sitting here.'

'Are you sure? I mean, has time passed? Have you seen a car go by?'

'Yes and yes.'

'That's good, isn't it?' I said uncertainly. 'Unless I'm making all this up in my head. There's something a little bit chicken-and-egg about the situation.'

He smiled. 'You don't say. Are we done then? Can we go?'

'Not quite. She wants to meet you.'

'Well, go back in and pretend I'm with you. I'm not getting involved in this.'

I sat down beside him on the warm stone and took his hand, but he pulled it free and raked his fingers through his hair. I stared at his feet, shod in black-and-white sneakers. If I concentrated hard enough, perhaps I could alter their colour, or swap his blue jeans for black. Surely I should be able to make whatever change I liked, if he lived in my head. I kept staring, at his shoes, at his legs but they stayed the way they were.

'I'm not going to lie,' I told him.

He looked straight at me. He was serious. 'And I'm not going to turn you into a circus act. What are you expecting to gain from this?'

I shrugged as a cloud of gloom descended on me. 'I don't know.'

He touched my face. 'Are you all right?'

'No. Not really.'

'You've lost your footing,' he said gently. 'And you don't know what to do to get steady again. You want that family. You always have. And now, with Rory gone, you are literally terrified of losing them.'

Sometimes he took me by surprise. Sometimes he seemed more grown-up than me. It was hypnotic.

And then he could spoil the moment. 'And Jonathan . . .' he added, leaving the tail end of the sentence hanging.

'What about him?'

'I'm not saying you don't find him attractive. He is attractive. All I'm saying is that, for you, he represents a path back into the life you had before. But he's not the answer. You can't expect the Walkers to save you all over again. You have to do it for yourself.'

I bit back a retort but he had made me really angry. It wasn't like that at all. I didn't need saving. 'So are you coming downstairs with me or what?'

He laughed but he sounded exasperated. He took my hand, turned it over and examined my palm. 'I don't see why I need to.'

'Because I hate the way she looked at me when I told her your name. I want her to understand that I'm serious.'

A woman turned into the street, pushing a pram. Sam nudged me.

'Watch this. I've been practising. Quick, while she's still looking at you.'

He concentrated hard, tensing his face, his eyebrows meeting and then he flicked at a pea-sized ball of scrunched-up sweet wrapper. Nothing happened.

'Wait. I can do this.' He tried again and again but nothing happened. The ball didn't even twitch.

'It's OK,' I said. 'It really doesn't matter.'

The woman darted a glance at me as she passed. I took off my shoe and pretended to shake out a stone.

'It worked before.'

'But there was no one there, was there?'

'No.'

He scraped the pavement with a piece of broken glass. It didn't leave a mark. I took it off him and threw it away.

'Come in with me, Sam. Please.'

He groaned. 'All right. Five minutes, and then we're out of here.'

Carol looked up and smiled. 'As far as you're concerned, Alice, is Sam with you?'

'Yes.'

'Can I ask him something, or would you rather I asked through you?'

I shrugged. 'Ask him anything you like.'

'Sam.' She paused and smiled wryly, as if she couldn't believe she was doing this. That was annoying. 'Sam. Do you feel like you are a part of the world around you, or like someone looking in? What I mean is, do we feel real to you or surreal?'

'Real enough for you to be bloody irritating,' Sam said.

I smiled and repeated his words. Carol looked disconcerted. She got up and went round to the other side of her desk. I watched, without much expectation, while she wrote on a scrap of paper.

'Sam, can you read what I've written?'

He glanced at it and then strolled over to the door, throwing a word over his shoulder with a derisive sneer. 'Harvey.'

I'd got what I wanted and I nearly repeated what he said but something stopped me. At first I didn't understand what the matter was, but it was simple. It was the thought that he might have got it right and that she would want more, that both terrified and repelled me. I didn't want her digging around in my psyche. She had picked the name Harvey as if it was all a joke and now, however seriously she took it, I would always worry that on some level she found the whole thing amusing. It was a stupid mistake but, in the end, I was glad she had made it. It saved me from worse.

'He doesn't want to.'

'Why not?'

When I didn't answer, Carol glanced at her watch. 'We're going to have to finish up now, I'm afraid. But, just tell me, is your relationship with Sam sexual?'

Sam walked over, placed his hands on her arms and his cheek close to hers. 'You are really twisted, Ms Margulies.'

'No. We're just good friends.'

'Do you want my help?' She smoothed her hands down her skirt. 'I can't see you against your will, but if you come to me I will do my best to get to the bottom of this. Sam isn't real, however strongly you feel he is. He's there because you need him badly enough, that's all. You've created someone to make you feel wanted and special. My job is to find out why you need him, and try and help you make things right so that you can go on to lead a normal life. I won't press you to make another appointment now, but I strongly advise you to do so.'

'I'll think about it.' I picked up my handbag and hooked the strap over my shoulder.

'Wait,' Carol said. She rested her fingers on the edge of her desk. She had beautifully shaped nails. 'Alice, I see a lot of clients and, apart from my professional knowledge and expertise, I do get an instinct for what's going on. I sense that you are a naturally happy person, who for one reason or another has been made to wear the skin of an unhappy one. It's an unnatural state for you, Alice, and I have a feeling that it might be at the root of all this. You aren't the person you should be, and it's been going on for an awful long time, not just since your accident.'

I frowned, not agreeing with her at all, but for some reason my eyes pricked.

'I'd really like to see you again, Alice. I think you have a lot to explore.'

I bit my lip and nodded. 'Look, I don't know. I'll think about it.'

She reached over and touched my arm and the gesture was kind, not invasive. Kindness was my Achilles' heel and, as the front door closed behind us, a tear ran down my cheek. I wiped it away and shot a glance at Sam, wondering. Was she right? Was this really all down to the strain of not allowing myself to be happy? I took his hand. It was warm. Then I reached up and kissed his cheek.

'What's that for?'

'For putting up with me.'

My odd behaviour drew a surprised glance from a man pulling a suitcase out of a taxi. He was unshaven, a little dishevelled, wearing jeans and a pale pink shirt with the sleeves rolled up. He looked at me and frowned and then broke into a smile. It was Matt Clarke.

'What're you doing here?' he said.

'Just visiting a friend.'

He glanced at the door I had come out of. 'Say no more. I won't pry.' He paused and looked at me speculatively. Sam stood by with his arms folded, his lips drawn into a contemptuous sneer. 'Do you want to come in?'

I shook my head and tried to look regretful. 'I've got to be somewhere. Sorry.'

His face fell. 'I only moved in the week before I went away. Celia and I bought it together, which has turned out to be a pain in the arse. At least come in and take a look. Be my first guest. It's a bit depressing otherwise.'

I was about to say no and then found myself hesitating. Why not? It seemed a small thing to do. Sam raised his eyes to heaven.

'OK,' I said. 'But just for a minute. I really have to get going.'

'Great.' He slung a large black man-bag over his shoulder and lifted his suitcase. 'Would you mind grabbing that?' He nodded at a bag of duty-free alcohol.

I picked it up, putting my hand underneath it to take the weight.

'Drowning your sorrows?' I asked.

He flushed. 'Most of that's for my dad actually.'

'I'm sorry. I didn't mean to imply anything.'

'No worries.' He went inside and opened his door with a flourish. 'Ta dah! Home sweet home.'

I put the duty-free down on top of an unopened removals box and looked around. Sam wandered in after me. He didn't seem particularly impressed. Matt took me into the kitchen first, pointing out its glories. It was basic but light, with a large window looking out over the basement flat into a pocket-handkerchief garden.

'It's wall-to-wall magnolia, but it used to be a rental. I've got all sorts of ideas for doing it up.'

'Oh yes, it's a blank canvas,' I said. It didn't hurt to be generous.

'Don't patronize the poor bloke, Alice,' Sam muttered.

I frowned at him.

'Garden's mine. You get to it through the bedroom, which is a bit of a nuisance, but it's good to have it. I'm going to have to put bars on the windows at some stage. The neighbours were burgled recently.'

'Poor things.' I peered through the door. The room housed a double bed and a dark wood wardrobe. The carpet was brown and tired.

'Yeah, well. Hey, would you like a cup of tea? I haven't got any milk yet, but there's a newsagent's down the road. I could run out and get some.'

He spoke fast and I could sense his anxiety. He didn't want to be on his own.

'No, that's all right. Thanks, though.'

I explored the sitting room, making all the right noises, picked up a photograph of him with a pretty girl, presumably Celia, and put it down quickly when he saw me.

'I've got to move on,' he said, taking it and shoving it face down into a drawer.

'You'll find someone else.' I stood by the window and looked out. Sam had lost patience and was outside, leaning elegantly against a car. 'I'd better go.'

Matt raised his eyebrows, sceptical in a friendly way. It annoyed me inordinately.

'I'm so glad I met you again,' he said. 'I don't suppose you'd like to go out for a drink sometime?'

'Maybe.'

'Well, you know where to find me now. I enjoyed the dinner, didn't you? I thought it was brave of them, but I suppose it's important to try and keep things normal. Jonathan's bloody lucky to have found Megan.'

He was following me outside as he spoke, anxious to prolong the conversation. I felt sorry for him but my smile muscles were

172

beginning to ache from the effort. A car started, and I turned my head automatically, and caught Carol's eye. She nodded at me and then pulled out. I don't know why that should have disconcerted me. Maybe because in my head she didn't exist outside her little white consulting room any more than, to children, teachers exist outside their classrooms.

'Thanks for coming in,' Matt said. 'I appreciate it. It's a pill coming back to an empty flat.'

He pulled his wallet out of his pocket and found a business card. It read, *Matt Clarke, Lighting Cameraman*. I put it in my bag and then relaxed and grinned. Sober, he was all right really. Just a bloke. I set off down the road at a stroll even though I felt like running. It was a beautiful day and it suddenly hit me that I was alive when I could very well be dead, that life still retained its possibilities, that there were so many things to be thankful for.

Behind me, I heard Matt let out a yelp. I stopped and looked back. He was on his knees, one hand on the step.

'Are you all right?' I was doing my best not to laugh.

'I'm fine. Just tripped, that's all.' He smiled bravely but couldn't quite meet my eye. I thought it was sweet that he was embarrassed. It humanized him.

I ran back. He put his hand on my arm and I helped him up.

'Thanks. Don't know what happened there. Sorry, I've got blood on you.'

I looked down at my sleeve. His blood had smeared across it in a thin arc. 'It'll come out in the wash. How bad is your hand?'

He grimaced. There was a nasty cut on the heel of his palm and on the ground near him lay the piece of broken glass that I had so carelessly discarded. He picked it up and inspected it before dropping it into the gutter.

'I'd better go in and clean up,' he said.

Feeling guilty, I unzipped a pocket in my bag and found him a plaster that I kept for blisters, and then, on impulse, leaned forward and kissed him on the cheek. I felt bad leaving him with his injuries and his empty, soulless flat, but Sam was growing impatient. As I walked away, Matt's apologies for ruining my shirt were drowned out by the sound of a passing car.

Sam caught me up quickly. He seemed to be bubbling over.

'Poor man,' I said. 'He hurt himself quite badly.'

He stopped in his tracks and pulled me round to face him. His eyes were alight. 'Alice, I tripped him. I stuck my foot out and he fell over it.'

'Sam!'

'OK. I'm sorry. Maybe I shouldn't have done that.'

'No, you shouldn't.'

'But, Alice . . .' His smile was irresistible, like a child caught out in a prank. 'Can't you see how amazing it is? What it means? I made it happen.'

'Just don't do it again – at least, don't hurt anyone. They might blame me.'

It struck me how extraordinary it was that Sam's presence in my life had come to feel normal. There was a living, breathing man walking beside me, a gorgeous man, but I knew that if he sat down on the tube some fat oaf would inevitably plant themselves on top of him. I wondered how that would actually work. If Sam was, as everyone else would have me believe, just a product of my damaged brain, then surely anyone who sat on him would go straight through him. Funnily enough, although the tube was reasonably busy and there were few seats to spare, no one sat next to me. Perhaps they sensed an invisible force. Or perhaps I had a bad aura.

I spent the next week ignoring the phone. Carol Margulies had unsettled me and I didn't want to talk to anyone. Mum called several times, leaving long messages about arrangements for her wedding on the following Saturday. I had promised to help her and, what with one thing and another, I hadn't been able to face it. I read yet another of her texts and dropped my phone with an exasperated groan.

'You do like to punish people, don't you?' Sam said.

'No I don't.'

'Then be a bit kinder to Julia.'

I looked at him with surprise. 'That's so unfair. I'm not horrible to her.'

'No, but you make it plain you don't have time for her. Alice, Rory adored your mother. Surely that tells you something?'

'Shut up, Sam. You don't know anything about it.'

He really didn't and I felt incredibly resentful. Who was he to judge me? I was the one who'd had to live with Mum, who'd had to support her through every financial and emotional crisis and listen to her endless complaints about my father and my grandmother. The world had revolved round Julia Byrne and I'd had to as well. It had taken an effort of will to prise myself out of that. I didn't see why I had to change the way I behaved towards her. If I had distanced myself in the last few years it was because I had to. It didn't mean I didn't love her. Sam could bloody well mind his own business.

He shrugged. 'She's not that bad. She never was.'

'Since when did you become a fan?'

'Since I came back. I'm not a child any more and my point of view is different. I've matured.'

'Well, bully for you. Are you saying I haven't?'

He tried to put his hands on my arms but I pushed them off. My irritation had become physical.

'No. I'm only saying that you need people around you, so don't push them away. That's all.'

'I thought you were supposed to be all I needed.'

'Don't be ridiculous. I'm not trying to isolate you.'

'You could have fooled me.'

He let me go. I could feel the hostility in the air between us. I couldn't live with this. It was awful. It was like having a blistering row with a friend and not being allowed to walk away and cool off. All I could do was shut myself in my bedroom and read my book until I'd calmed down enough to go back out. When I did, Sam acted as though nothing had happened and I had to let it go. It wasn't worth it.

The only person whose call I picked up was Emma's. She was calling from France, to repeat her invitation. I said I really wanted to come but that I had to work a few things out.

After I hung up, I sat in silence. Would it be unbearable or was it what we all needed. I should have discussed this with Carol. I should have talked about my sense of responsibility for Rory's death, my fear of losing my friendship with his family and my insecurity around them, when all I wanted to do was help. That would have been more useful than the farce over Sam. I just wanted to be told how to be with the Walkers, without the awful confusion of guilt and pain. But then I'd have to talk about the conversation I'd had with Rory the day before the wedding, and she might urge me to tell them as well, to help the healing process. I couldn't do that. It might help heal me; it certainly wouldn't make things better for them.

Then Gabby phoned to ask when I was coming to stay. She called back a few hours later to say that she knew I was there and would be round to help me pack. I grabbed the phone.

'I can't move in with you,' I said. 'It's not a good time.'

'Alice, seriously, you need to get out of that flat. Shutting your-self away from the world is not going to help you get better. Come to us. We won't intrude.'

'Gabby, I have been out! I've worked. I've been to the ruddy psychiatrist. I've been shopping. I'm not a hermit, I swear. I can't afford to be. Just let me get through Mum's wedding and then I promise I'll think about it.'

Then

OLIVIA AND I SIT ON HER MULBERRY-RED SOFA, OUR FEET ON A
hessian rug and a tray of tea and home-made ginger biscuits on
the coffee table in front of us. Her mantelpiece is crowded with
silver-framed photographs and embossed invitations, some of
which are out of date. Elizabeth is playing with her toys at the end
of the sitting room allocated to anything plastic or brightly
coloured.

Up until my niece was born, Olivia worked in recruitment.
Now she's producing babies, and doing very well at it. Thirty-
seven weeks pregnant and in blooming health, her hair glossy and
sleek, her skin glowing, she is a goddess.

We chat about this and that and I wait for her to get to the
point, which she finally does but only after Elizabeth tires of her
toys and starts whingeing. When she pads over on her chubby
little legs, Olivia pulls her on to her knee. I think she finds it easier to say what she has to say with my attention distracted by my
adorable niece.

'So how's the photography going?' she asks, waggling a plastic
rattle in front of Elizabeth's fingers.

'It's fine.'

'You're still working at the pub?'

'Well, yes. I can't afford not to.'

Olivia sighs. She turns Elizabeth round so that she's facing me.
I reach out and she clutches my fingers and giggles.

'Don't you think,' Olivia says carefully, 'you ought to have a fallback? You need to start thinking seriously about the future.'

'It's incredibly hard trying to break in.' I don't know why I'm protesting.

Her lips curve into a tight smile that isn't a smile really. 'Maybe it's a bit too hard, Alice.'

'What do you mean? I'm building the business up. You can't expect it to happen overnight.'

Since that shoot with Jonathan things have progressed, although it's been painfully slow. But that just makes me more determined to succeed. I'm not going to waste all the effort I've put in since that day by giving up now.

'I'm not disputing that you're talented, but in order to get on you need more than that. There are loads of people out there desperate to get a foot in the door, all just as talented as you are. The ones who make it in the end are the ones who're more like Dad.' She pauses to tease Elizabeth's fingers out of her hair. 'Elizabeth, stop it.' The little girl squirms and Olivia sets her down. She sits at her mother's feet gazing up at me. 'It's that social thing,' Olivia adds. 'You have to be able to talk to people.'

I keep my eyes fixed on Elizabeth. 'You're saying I don't have the personality for it?'

'No, I'm not saying that. You have a great personality.'

'Thanks.'

'You do.' Her expression is understanding and yet insistent. 'It's just that you're not a team person or a group person. You're so much better one-to-one. When you come to our drinks parties, I can tell you find it hard, you have this wall that springs up round you the minute you find yourself in a social situation. You struggle.'

I have a mental image of standing in Olivia's drawing room, faced with a dozen beautifully groomed couples, thinking, *I've got to walk in and join them. Shit.* My brain emptying. And then Olivia introducing me to three women who obviously know each other extremely well through NCT classes, or something like that, deep in conversation about local schools. When they discover I don't have children, conversation quickly dries up. Olivia throws her parties about three times a year. I avoid them if I can.

'But your parties are full of the sort of people I don't particularly like. I'm sure they're lovely, but most of them work in banks, or have just had babies. It's not my scene.'

'So you go to lots of parties and talk to lots of people?'

'No. But I work in a busy pub.'

'You're behind the bar. You're protected. You've always needed that, Alice.'

Sod off, Olivia. 'I'm not socially inadequate.'

'I didn't say you were.'

'Yes, you did. And you think I should get a proper job that doesn't rely on my non-existent talents as a crowd pleaser. What does it matter to you anyway?'

'You're my little sister. I feel responsible.'

I laugh and Olivia looks offended.

'Well, you needn't.'

'I know, but I do. Look, Alice. Please don't take this the wrong way. The fact is, you have to make sure that you can support yourself, just in case.'

I raise my eyebrows. 'Just in case I can't find a man to look after me?'

Olivia looks me squarely in the eye. 'Yes.' And then places her hand on her stomach and smiles softly.

I glance around the room and decide I can do without the things Olivia has, without the John Lewis furniture and the curtains she spent weeks deciding on or the tasteful décor and the pictures and rugs. This is not a choice. I don't have to opt for this life or the apparently living hell of being on my own. There are other things and all different sorts of people and places. Olivia with her pregnancy and blue-eyed daughter is so deep in self-love that she can't see beyond it.

I stand up, stinging with hurt. Today's visit hasn't been successful and, as always, it disappoints me because I want more. 'I'm only twenty-two. You don't need to start panicking quite yet.'

Olivia doesn't move, just pats the sofa beside her. 'Don't be like that. Sit down. We can talk about something else.'

'I should go.'

Even if she wasn't pregnant, I wouldn't confide in Olivia. Her sense of her own rightness is as ingrained as religion. But more than that, I am a little afraid that she's right and I will never make it. It's just never occurred to me that the obstacle might be my failure to sparkle at parties.

Chapter Fifteen

'DARLING. WHAT HAVE YOU BEEN DOING?'

Mum brushed the air close to my cheeks with her lips. She smelled of perfume and powder and looked fantastic. Botox? Sam thought so. Virgins' milk? Whatever she was on, it was working.

'Nothing much, just resting.'

She shook her head and pursed her lips and I felt thirteen again and caught out in some trivial misdemeanour. Like allowing my hair to get greasy. I had been thinking about what Sam had said, trying to look at her from a more mature viewpoint, and I'd reluctantly come to the conclusion that I did like her. I didn't feel connected, though, and I didn't have that friendship thing with her that Olivia seemed to. But that was all right. She was who she was. She wasn't going to change and come over all mumsy without a personality transplant and, as long as I didn't expect it, we would get along just fine. Well, up to a point. Once I'd come to that conclusion, I felt I had been quite grown-up about it.

She sat down on the arm of the sofa and flicked her hair dramatically. The gesture reminded me of Olivia.

'I cannot believe you've made me come all the way over here.'

I tried to look contrite but it didn't cut any ice. Sam was obviously amused and I had a feeling he understood her better than I did. She was by nature jealous, so the pair of them had that in common at least.

'I haven't made you do anything.'

'Don't be deliberately obtuse. You know exactly what I mean. You appear to want people to worry about you. You enjoy being the centre of attention. I have so much to do, you cannot possibly understand, and you are being absolutely no help.'

I couldn't think of anything to say to that, bar mumbling, 'Sorry.'

'Alice,' Sam said. 'You have to stick up for yourself when she does this. Don't let her take the moral high ground.'

I raised my eyebrows. It was all very well for him to tell me what to do. He didn't have to deal with her.

'You are so utterly selfish,' Mum added. She moved over to the small table where I ate my meals, and pulled out a chair. I had assumed from the way that she'd perched herself on the edge of the sofa that she wouldn't be staying. Now though she seemed to settle in. 'You've always been wrapped up in yourself.'

'Mum, that's a bit harsh.'

'You've had everyone running around after you, worried sick, when, frankly, I'm the one they should be worried about. Well, aren't you going to offer me a cup of tea?'

'Would you like a cup of tea?'

She fixed her beautiful eyes on me. 'Yes, I would. Thank you, darling. You know, it's really hard for me at the moment. You underestimate the strain I'm under. Olivia is wrapped up in her family and Simon is thousands of miles away. In your situation, on your own, you should offer to help more. You haven't once asked me if there's anything you can do.'

'OK, Mum.'

I walked into the kitchen and switched on the kettle and stood with my back to her, breathing slowly. There was no point reacting or attempting to justify myself. Besides, she was absolutely right. I did have too much time on my hands at the moment. Two days' work did not constitute being busy. Convalescing was no excuse. I should be helping more, being a better daughter. Something else to feel guilty about.

Sam wandered in. 'Don't let her get to you.'

I nudged him out of the way, poured boiling water over a teabag and took the milk out of the fridge.

'She's just being Mum,' I whispered. 'And it's not as if I'm not used to it.'

'Your brother,' Mum called, 'has been absolutely wonderful. He's insisting on paying for everything and he's phoned me almost every day. He is so supportive.'

'I offered to take your pictures. You said no.'

She sniffed. 'I don't expect you took the photographs at your father's wedding. I imagine he paid through the nose for a professional.'

'Yes, I'm sure he did. It was just a way of helping you, Mum. I wasn't implying you couldn't afford it.'

'Well, I didn't want you to over-tax yourself.' She paused. 'Simon is paying for a photographer.'

I sighed and placed her mug on the table. 'I can't wait to see him.'

'He's thinking about flying you over to LA to see his shrink.'

I hastily suppressed a yelp of laughter. 'Oh, come on. That's way over the top.'

'Well, what do you expect? You talk to yourself. You refuse to answer calls or open the door. No one sees you from one day to the next. You pretend to have a boyfriend who, quite frankly, we all know doesn't exist. If you carry on like this, Alice, I'm going to have to cancel my honeymoon. Your selfishness, your utter disregard for other people, is going to ruin my happiness.'

I pulled out a chair and sat down. 'That's ridiculous, Mum. You're over-reacting. I don't need looking after and I certainly don't need Simon interfering.' I hesitated, not knowing whether it was any of her business and then decided what the hell. 'Anyway, I've seen a psychiatrist. Dad organized it. It was a complete waste of time.'

'Oh, so when your father asks, it's fine, but not when it's the mother who brought you up and sacrificed her youth for you.'

She was like a petulant child. I felt the beginnings of role reversal and shuddered inwardly. It struck me that might be what she wanted; to be someone's petted child, to absolve herself from responsibility. Poor old Larry was going to have his work cut out.

'Mum, you're about to get married. Forget about me. Just think about Saturday.'

'That's all very well, but how am I supposed to enjoy myself when my daughter is living in la-la land? Olivia suggested you should go into the Priory for a few weeks.'

Sam snorted at that remark. 'Olivia can talk. If anyone needs therapy, she does.'

'Keep out of it,' I said sharply and he raised his eyebrows. 'Please.'

'Don't tell me to keep out of it,' Mum said. 'I'm your mother. Until you have your own children, which is looking fairly doubtful right now, you will never know what it is to love a child, to worry yourself to death over her.'

'You're looking pretty good on it,' Sam said.

'Sam.'

He raised his hands, laughing. 'OK, OK.'

'This is precisely what I mean. I'd have thought you'd have grown out of your imaginary friend by now. Or are you as incapable of making real ones as you were when you were a child?'

'Nice,' Sam commented.

'I have as many friends as I need. You don't have to worry about me, and you certainly don't need to cancel your honeymoon.' I made a split-second decision. 'In fact, I won't be here anyway. I'm going to France after the wedding, to stay with Emma and Brian. So you see, I'm fine.' There was the inquest to get through as well, but there was no point mentioning that to her. Dad would come with me.

Not that I didn't know that Mum's was an empty threat. There was no way she would cancel any pleasure of her own for someone else. I added, in the hope of appeasing her, 'I am sorry if you think I've neglected you. I didn't mean to.'

'You should try a bit harder, Alice. And please, when you come to my wedding, remember that it's my day, not yours. For God's sake, don't start talking to . . . to what's-his-name.'

'His name is Sam.'

Mum tapped her fingernails on the table. 'The last thing I want is a photograph of my daughter gabbling away to a tree. In fact, bring someone with you, one of those friends you insist you have. Bring a man.'

I groaned inwardly. 'I don't have to prove anything.'

'No, but it's the least you can do for me. I want a normal, happy family around me on Saturday, not two sensible children and one . . . one . . .'

'Nutcase,' I supplied. 'OK. I'll bring a male friend.' I would ask Daniel. It would be nice to catch up.

'Not Daniel,' she said, reading my mind. 'He's as camp as Christmas. Bring a real man.'

'So,' Sam said, after she had gone, leaving a trace of her scent in the air along with a few bad vibrations. 'You aren't going to take her seriously, are you?'

I slumped down on the sofa, leaned my head back and closed my eyes. 'About what?'

'About bringing another man and not bringing me.'

My eyes snapped open. 'Why? You're not jealous, are you?'

'Yes.'

'Well, don't be, you idiot. Sam, you need to trust me. I'm really not interested in getting into a relationship right now.'

The moment I said it I thought of Jonathan and my heart started to race. I still thought about him in a way that I knew I shouldn't. I dreamed about him too, and the dreams often contained scenes that were disturbingly physical. Sam must have sensed something because he drew back and stared so intently at me that I was thoroughly disconcerted.

'Be reasonable, Sam. You have to accept that this is bound to happen from time to time, whether you like it or not. I need to be able to mix with my family. It's all right being alone if you know that there are people out there that you can see and talk to, but not if you've cut yourself off completely.'

'I've never asked that of you. I'm not stupid. All I ask is that you understand that if you stop needing me, I'll lose all this. I don't mean I want you to be miserable, but I can only be here because you need a friend. That's all,' he added. 'That's all I am.'

We were silent for a moment and then Sam smiled and said, 'So who are you going to invite?'

I released the breath I'd been holding and with it some of my tension. 'Matt Clarke, I expect. He was at Dad's wedding, so he might as well come to Mum's too. He doesn't inspire me with unbridled lust, so you can rest easy.'

Then

RORY WANTS ME TO GO OUT FOR A DRINK BECAUSE HE'S MET someone and has been on two dates with him and now wants the poor bloke to meet me. I try to dissuade him but he isn't having it.

'This one's special,' he says, when I mention washing my hair and watching TV.

'I'm really not in the mood. You'll be all loved up.' I was still smarting with resentment from my conversation with Olivia.

'I won't, I promise. Please, Alice. You'll like him.'

He's just changed out of his suit – the one he wears for his proper job as a newly fledged accounts manager at an advertising agency – the job he walked into because he knows how to get along with people – and is wearing black jeans and a dark-blue V-neck jumper. His red hair is beginning to grow out of its last cut, kinking over his ears.

'I don't know.' I stare disconsolately at the television set. I know perfectly well that if I let him go on his own, I'll only end up sitting in front of the TV with a plate of microwave lasagne, feeling sorry for myself.

He looks at me closer. 'What's up?'

'Nothing.' I turn away and go into the kitchen. Rory follows me and we stand in the small space, me looking at my feet, Rory, arms crossed, eyeballing me.

'Honestly, it's nothing. Olivia's pissed me off, that's all.'

'What did she say?'

'It doesn't matter.' I look up at him and smile. 'I'll come with you, but if I start feeling like a lemon, I'm going to leave and you have to promise not to try and stop me.'

When we reach the pub, Rory's new friend isn't there and I'm worried that this is going to be awful, that Rory is going to be hurt and disappointed. I hate the man already, whoever he is. Rory deserves better. He's funny, intelligent and a true friend. What more could anyone possibly want?

We go to the bar and I order half a lager and Rory has a pint. While he's paying, a man comes up behind him and touches him on the shoulder. When Rory turns and smiles at the stranger, his expression tells me everything, but I still feel protective and wary.

'Daniel, this is Alice,' Rory says. 'Alice, this is Daniel.'

We eye each other and shake hands. Daniel passes that test with flying colours at least. Then he orders a glass of sparkling mineral water, because he's detoxing, which is annoying, and we take our drinks to a table and sit down. I sit with my back to the wall, the men opposite me, like a panel.

'I feel like I'm here for an interview,' I say.

'No. I think that's me,' Daniel says.

Relief washes through me. He's funny and a bit eccentric and his ears stick out. He has charm, but not so much that a best friend would be suspicious and when I speak to him he looks at me as if he's really interested in what I'm saying. He's a few years older than us, early thirties at the most, and works in the city and presumably earns pots of money, although he never mentions it. Nor does he tell me how much his watch cost him, or what sort of car he drives. He is low-key. Under the table I keep my fingers crossed.

'So what did Olivia say to upset you?' Rory asks. 'Olivia is Alice's big sister,' he adds for Daniel's benefit. 'A bit like one of Cinderella's ugly sisters, only she's gorgeous.'

I breathe out and roll my eyes. It's difficult to explain it to Daniel without a nagging feeling that he might be on Olivia's side because he's more her age than ours. Rory I don't worry about, he believes in me.

'She thinks I should give up trying to make it as a photographer and find some safer employment, just in case I never find a man to support me. She basically thinks I won't be successful because I'm not sociable enough.'

Daniel raises his eyebrows. Rory roars with laughter.

'How much do you want it?' Daniel asks.

'Completely.' My hands curl into tight fists. I see Daniel looking at them and blush. 'It's part of me. I can't just get a normal nine-to-five and take pictures at the weekend. It would be soul-destroying.'

He places his hands, palms down, on the table. 'I know a photographer whose assistant is emigrating to Australia. He's looking about for someone else.' He pulls his phone out of his pocket. 'How are you on the digital stuff?'

'Absolutely fine,' I say, starting to tingle with excitement.

'Do you want an introduction?'

'That would be amazing. Are you sure?'

'Rory says you're very good and I trust him.'

Rory gives me a fraternal pat and Daniel texts his friend and five minutes later I have a date for an informal interview.

'Something to tell Olivia,' Rory says.

I shake my head. 'I'll leave her alone for a couple of weeks. I might say something I regret.'

'I think it's about time you did. You shouldn't let her win all the time.'

I shrug. 'Anything for a quiet life.'

'Why?' Daniel asks, interested. 'Is that what you really want?'

I hold his gaze and then I feel my smile widen into a grin. 'No one's ever asked me that before. Maybe I need to start telling people what I really think.'

'Yeah, well don't go overboard,' Rory says. 'I am quite sensitive.'

189

I laugh. 'Maybe I'll wait until she's had the baby.'

And then my phone rings and I glance at the caller display. 'Talk of the devil.'

'Are you going to answer it?'

I very nearly don't and then just before it cuts off I pick up. 'Olivia.'

All the lights are on in Olivia's house when we pull up in Daniel's car, and a harassed James, Olivia's husband, opens the door. I can see Olivia behind him, sitting at the bottom of the stairs clutching her stomach, and I give her a little wave. James looks beyond me to the two men sitting in the car, the engine humming.

'This is so kind of you,' he says. 'Olivia's ready to kill your mother.'

Mum was supposed to be keeping herself available should Olivia go into labour during the night when the nanny wasn't around, but she's away for a couple of days with her boyfriend and Olivia is three weeks early.

Rory gets out and leans over the roof. 'Anything you need?'

'No thanks, Rory, we have everything. Sorry to spoil your evening.'

'No worries.'

'Why don't you come in and have a drink? There's a bottle of wine in the fridge and plenty to eat. No reason why Alice should be on her own.'

Rory ducks down and confers with Daniel. Olivia pushes herself up with a groan and, supported by James, staggers to the door. My irritation has vanished in the excitement and I give her a quick hug and to my surprise she returns it. It feels strange; uncomfortable, but at the same time, rather touching.

'Good luck,' I mutter into her hair.

I walk to James's car with them and wait while she climbs in and draws the seat belt over her belly. Then I stand back. At the other end of the street a man is watching us from the shadows. I stare at him and then Daniel says something and I turn round. When I look again the man has gone. It was nothing, just a stranger wondering what all the drama was about, but it leaves me with a feeling of unease that I can't quite shake off. Rory and Daniel stay for an hour, making the most of James's hospitality, then they leave me alone.

Upstairs in the spare room I stand by the window and watch the street for a while. It's quiet, the sort of place where people have young families and go to bed at a reasonable time. Is this what I'm supposed to be aiming for? Would this make me accept-able to my sister? Obviously Olivia is right about being able to support myself, but I don't need her telling me that; it's only what I've been trying to do. I pull the curtains across, look in on Elizabeth, who is sleeping soundly with her hand curled round a bar of her cot, and then go to bed. Street light shines through a crack in the curtains and the occasional car drives by. I lie awake while the digital clock beside the bed marks one hour and then two. Something is going to happen. Something is coming. I know it's the night talking, that in the morning I'll remember and laugh at myself, but it doesn't make me feel better. I close my eyes tight and picture Elizabeth snuggled up, try to put myself in the child's place, safe and warm, and shut out other, more troubling thoughts.

I wake up to the sound of the front door closing. The light out-side is watery. I stretch and make my way down to the kitchen where James is standing, bleary-eyed, staring at the kettle.

He brightens when he sees me and smiles hugely. 'It's a girl.'

The next day Olivia texts me to say that she's received an enormous bouquet of pink roses from Daniel and Rory.

Daniel and Rory. I feel so overcome with emotion, I nearly burst into tears.

Chapter Sixteen

I ARRIVED AT RICHMOND STATION ON SATURDAY AFTERNOON, FOR Mum's wedding, feeling like I was bunking off school, exhilarated, guilty and as light as a feather. I hadn't realized how much Sam's presence weighed me down. Matt waved at me from the top of the station steps and I smiled and picked up my pace.

'You look lovely,' he said, kissing me on the cheek. 'Look, we match.' He tweaked up his trouser leg to show a bright pink sock.

'Very dashing. Sorry I'm late.'

'If it's because you were making yourself gorgeous, I'll forgive you. It was worth it.'

In black tie and clean-shaven, Matt looked very different from the weary long-haul traveller I had bumped into the other day. Perversely I had preferred him that way. Still, he had a big, engaging smile that instantly dispelled my nerves.

I laughed off the lame compliment and we walked out of the station and into Richmond, making our way to the Register Office where a modest crowd had gathered to witness Mum's second attempt at wedded bliss. I hovered by the door, scanning the guests. I saw Olivia and James with their girls and recognized a few of Mum's friends including horrible Mandy. I took Matt by the hand and we made our entrance. Simon waved at me.

We pushed our way through and Mum, turning to greet me, gave Matt a blatantly appraising look, her smile at once surprised and grudgingly impressed. Matt kissed her on the cheek and told her she looked absolutely beautiful and I felt a mixture of relief and pride.

'So, where did you two meet?'

She didn't even comment on what I was wearing. I was disappointed.

'Matt was at Dad's wedding.'

A cloud passed over her face. I had been tactless. But what else was I supposed to say? Gabby and Dad's wedding had been a huge affair compared to this one and she knew it.

She leaned into me and whispered, 'You haven't brought anyone else, have you?'

I looked around, pretending not to know what on earth she was talking about. 'One man at a time,' I said. 'Mum, you look fabulous.'

She smirked and preened. 'The Registrar thought I was Olivia's sister.'

'I bet she did.'

Later, at the hotel where the reception was being held, Matt and I strolled out on to the terrace and stood with the other guests, taking in the spectacular view of the Thames curving round past Ham House. Waiters appeared with canapés and champagne and my little nieces moved between the adults like foraging cats.

Olivia came over. She leaned on the wall and sipped her champagne. 'What a perfect day.' She looked me up and down but didn't say anything. I was beginning to think she and Mum had made a pact – don't do anything to set Alice off.

I introduced Matt, suspecting that he was the reason she had approached me in the first place. Then Lottie wandered over and asked him who he was.

His attention temporarily lost, Olivia said, 'You were so right about that dress. You look fabulous.'

I was too surprised to respond.

193

'How's the head?'

'The head's doing just fine.'

'Are you sure?'

'Well, of course I'm sure. Why do you ask?'

She raised her eyebrows. 'Alice, you do know people think you're having a breakdown, don't you? Listen, I wouldn't normally interfere, but Mum's worried about you and so am I.'

I couldn't help laughing. 'Olivia, do you know what you sound like?'

'Sorry, I didn't mean to offend you.'

'You haven't. I'm perfectly aware of what people think, and frankly, I couldn't care less. I don't see why everyone has to get their knickers in a twist over me. I'm just doing what feels right.'

'That's what we're concerned about. I'm not being mean, Alice, but what feels right to you, feels a bit peculiar to everyone else. I know you've been through a lot—'

'But you think I should have got over it by now?'

She knew she had said the wrong thing, but she was never any good at saying sorry. 'Don't be silly. I don't think that. But you do have to move on. It isn't healthy, dwelling on things like this.'

I could feel myself getting angry. 'It's only been two months, for God's sake. Besides, how do you know what I dwell on?'

'There's no need to be defensive.'

'I am not being defensive. I just don't want to be told when it's time to move on. I'm not ready and I'm not going to force it. I'll know when that time comes without being alerted by you or Mum or anyone else.'

'OK,' Olivia said slowly. 'I apologize. I won't say another word about it. But just so you know, I'm here for you . . .'

Luckily for Olivia, the band chose that moment to go quiet and everyone stopped talking so I had to bite back a sharp and not very polite response. To the delight of their guests, Larry picked up a guitar, struck up a riff and started singing 'You're Beautiful', his eyes fixed on his bride. How sweet, I thought, as Matt put his arms around my waist. I wasn't entirely sure I liked being pinned against him, but I let it pass. We were having a good time and I didn't want to spoil it.

Mum was grinning from ear to ear and I couldn't help smiling. There was no way I was going to say it, but laughter lines suited her. I really loved her in that moment. She was like a child, blossoming in the limelight. For once in her life, she had absolutely no excuse to complain that she was neglected. We actually felt like a normal family, delighted with each other.

'Your stepdad is so chilled.'

'He's going to need to be.' I prised Matt's arms away and put a little space between us. 'Matt, we are just friends, aren't we?'

'Of course we are.'

'I mean, I don't want you to read anything into this.' I was turning myself inside out with embarrassment.

Matt put his hands on my shoulders and looked into my eyes. It was disconcerting. I could smell champagne and smoked salmon on his breath.

'Alice, don't worry so much. Just enjoy yourself.'

'I am.' I sounded like I was protesting too much, which wasn't what I wanted. 'I asked you to come because I felt I could, not because . . . well, oh you know what I'm talking about. I want to be clear, that's all.'

'And you are. Perfectly. I'm not ready for a relationship either. I still think about Celia a lot.'

He didn't look like I had hurt his pride, but I wasn't sure. I wished I hadn't invited him. I should have dug my heels in and brought Daniel along.

Simon appeared with his girlfriend, a slender blonde in an aquamarine dress who moved as though she expected the crowd to part, which it did. Matt immediately focused the full force of his attention on her. I was more amused than put out and it meant I didn't have to share Simon with either of them.

'I'm so sorry about Rory,' Simon said. 'I know how close you two were. He was the brother I should have been.'

Tears stung my eyes. I couldn't say anything.

'That bad?'

I nodded.

'Christ, it must have been awful. His poor family. Do you see them?'

'Yes. I'm going on holiday with his parents next week. They've been very kind to me. But I miss him so much.'

'How are you doing? I mean, head-wise?'

'Oh God, not you as well.'

'Olivia got there first, did she?'

'Yup.' I contemplated letting it go and nearly did. But then something odd happened and it all came out in a rush. The things I had promised myself I wouldn't say, because growing up meant letting go of ancient resentments, were suddenly tripping off my tongue. 'You two were happy to vanish into thin air when I was small. If I was worried about my sanity, it would be because of those years alone with Mum, not because of anything that's happened recently. I've had a bump on the head that may or may not have affected my mental state, but it's nothing compared to my childhood.'

I spoke so emphatically that he took a step backwards. He finished his champagne then handed the empty glass to a passing waitress.

'God, I didn't . . . I mean, I didn't know it was that bad. I suppose we were selfish, just getting on with our lives, but you seemed fine. I adored you, Alice. I never told you that, and I'm sorry.'

'I think I knew. Anyway, Simon, it really doesn't matter now and there was nothing you could have done. I wasn't your responsibility. If anyone should have done more it was Dad, but he was so busy and he had Gabby.'

Mum told me this story once, about when Simon left. I

196

remembered it quite clearly although my memories inevitably came from a different angle than hers. Simon had gone to live with Dad after that fateful weekend when Mum had come home to find the house damaged and empty cans and cigarette butts littering the garden and had threatened to kick him out. She hadn't meant it of course, but Simon had gone anyway.

It was two weeks later and I was sitting at the kitchen table, drawing Sam and our neighbour's cat poking their heads out of the tree house. Mum said I put down my felt-tip pen and asked her when my brother was coming home. She had been painting her nails and I distinctly remember her holding the tiny brush still for a moment and then dragging it delicately across her little fingernail.

'He's not. He's decided to live with his father.'

'But he lives here. With us.'

Mum shrugged. 'He's sixteen, he can go where he pleases. He obviously doesn't care about us any more.'

My ears started ringing, my stomach turned over and I was breathing too hard. Mum's great joke was that I went so red she was terrified I was going to pop. Apparently I threw my head back, opened my mouth and let out a long, miserable howl, like an abandoned dog.

After that Mum thought I was having some sort of fit because I began flailing about, but actually, Sam was trying to hug me and I was pushing his hands away, screaming and shoving. The bit she doesn't admit to was grabbing me by the arm and slapping me across the face. We heard footsteps pounding downstairs and Olivia appeared.

'What on earth's going on? I thought someone was strangling a cat.'

By this time Mum had pulled me on to her knee and was holding me too tight. 'She's upset about Simon.'

'Oh that. Well, at least she gets his room.'

Mum thought my reaction was amusing, but at the time losing

Simon had broken my heart. I thought about telling him this story and decided no, I'd save it for another time. I'd said enough to make him feel bad without adding another layer.

Simon scratched the back of his head. 'I suppose with parents like those, we were bound to turn out selfish bastards.'

'Well, yes of course. I'm not saying I'm Little Miss Compassionate and Empathetic. In some ways, I'm probably as bad as them. The only difference is, I know it. Mum has no self-awareness and she's insensitive, and Dad is, well, Dad's just Dad. They get away with it.' I groaned. 'I like to think, if I ever have the opportunity, I'll do it better.'

'And so you shall,' he said, as his girlfriend extricated herself from Matt. He slid his arm around her impossibly slender waist. 'Surviving?'

By seven o'clock, Lottie and Elizabeth were high on sugar and had morphed from mischievous little girls into unspeakable brats. Olivia's exhausted and tearful nanny rounded them up and they headed home. Simon and his girlfriend went into Soho to have dinner with some film business contacts, and Matt and I walked along the river, admiring the boats.

'When I'm rich,' Matt said, 'I'm going to have one of those.'

'Me too. I'm going to have that stonking great big one over there.'

'I've already put down a deposit, so you can't have it. You can have the little one that all the pigeons have shat on. I'll invite you over to mine occasionally.'

I giggled. The champagne had definitely got to me. 'I love the river. I really miss living round here. There's a boat moored further up towards Twickenham that belongs to Rory's family. We used to go out on it a lot when we were teenagers.' I gazed upriver and was instantly gripped by a sense of things lost. 'I should go home.'

I pictured Sam waiting for me and felt a twinge of guilt. I was dealing with him, but I was aware that I couldn't rush things. Today had been an experiment and I didn't want it to turn into a massive issue. Apart from his jealousy, I knew he had a low boredom threshold. That wasn't a healthy combination.

'Why?'

'I've got stuff to do.'

'Alice, it's Saturday night.'

We turned back and retraced our steps to Richmond. I was surprised how easy a companion Matt was. He talked about himself a lot, which wasn't great, but on the other hand, with my mind so full of Sam, I didn't have much to say anyway.

Once we were back in town, I tried to steer him up the slope and away from the river but he resisted and kept walking until we were outside a busy pub. A small crowd had spilled out on to the riverside walk and the air carried the scent of beer, perfume and cigarettes. Matt breathed it in appreciatively.

'One for the road?'

I shook my head. 'Nope. Sorry, but I'm late as it is.'

'For what?' Matt looked at me hopefully. 'Just one drink, then we'll go.'

I hesitated and prepared to dig my heels in, but then I realized that, for one thing, I had no viable excuse up my sleeve and, for another, I didn't want to go back to the flat. Matt was right, it was Saturday evening and most people were out socializing. What harm could it do? It had been ages since I'd gone out for a drink with a friend. And poor Matt, he probably wasn't looking forward to his lonely bachelor pad. I nodded and ignored a tiny pin-prick of fear.

Matt and I finally left the pub at ten thirty. It wasn't late, just later than I had promised Sam I'd be. Outside the station he approached a line of taxis. I tried to draw him away.

'It'll cost a fortune.'

'The day hasn't cost me much yet, babes.'

'Babes?' I gave him a look which I hoped was withering but it only served to widen his smile and I grinned back at him. 'Don't push your luck.'

'Hop in then.'

It was dark and warm in the taxi and the sound of the diesel engine ticking over was soothing and hypnotic. I discovered that I didn't object to Matt's thigh being lightly pressed against mine. I couldn't pretend that there was any real chemistry between us, but there was enough for me to feel a low-level anticipation. This was what life could be like if Sam ever left, and if I could bring myself to accept that I could never have Jonathan. I could have a safe, conventional boyfriend who went out to work each day. It was a nice, comforting thought. Shame Matt wasn't The One.

'So what about you?' Matt said.

I hadn't been listening. 'What about me?'

'What turns you on?'

'Why do you want to know?'

'Because you interest me. I can't seem to get a handle on you.'

At that moment, I was absolutely sure he was going to try and kiss me before the end of the journey. It had come to the point where I could take a different route if I wanted to. I wondered what would happen if I invited him in. If I took him to my bedroom. I glanced at Matt's hands and imagined them exploring my body and felt a frisson of awareness. I could do it. I could allow him to seduce me. Would Sam vanish like a genie back into his lamp? I couldn't believe I was considering having sex with someone I didn't want, as a means to an end. It was horrible.

Matt smiled at me. 'Are you sure you don't have any dark secrets?'

I scowled. 'If you're going to mention my visit to your neighbour, then don't. It's rude.'

'I wasn't. I was more interested in your invisible friend.'

I hung my head. 'Oh, don't. I was pissed and not making any sense at all. I don't know why I came out with all that.'

'That's what I like about you. You're completely potty.'

He took my hand and I raised my eyebrows. He smiled back, slightly leery. The cab by this time had almost reached Battersea. I gazed into Matt's eyes and felt a small stirring. Not exactly a body-blow of sexual excitement, but at least he made me feel like a normal person: liberated, ready to take control of my life, able to make choices. I knew I was thinking too much but it made no difference. Whichever way I looked at it, I had no real intention of getting into a relationship with Matt Clarke because I didn't love him. I knew what love felt like because I had been in love with Jonathan for ten years. Twenty, if I counted from our first meeting. I despaired of myself sometimes.

I wondered what Sam was doing now. Was he weakening? Was he angry or disappointed and afraid? I needed to be at home. Something wasn't right. It felt as if my world was out of kilter. The taxi seemed to be driving very slowly. Or maybe it was time that was slowly stretching, making me feel as though I would never get to where I wanted to be. My thoughts weren't making sense, but that was hardly a novelty.

'Can I ask you a personal question?' Matt said.

I tried to appear relaxed. 'You might not get an answer.'

He took that as permission. 'Do I scare you?'

That made me burst out laughing. It came out as a snort and sounded quite rude. I put my hand over my mouth and nose and apologized through my fingers.

'Jesus, you have a lot of defence mechanisms,' he said.

The cab drew to a halt outside my flat. Matt pulled my hands gently from my face and I found myself twisting round and kissing him. I parted my lips and felt his teeth against my tongue. He tasted of beer and I felt a little anxious that I wasn't enjoying it as much as I should. For one short moment his mouth opened, his tongue rubbed wetly against mine and his hand slid from my shoulder to my breast.

It really wasn't a nice first kiss; it was deliberately sexual and

201

probably sprang from my need to feel real and connected. I knew that the energy came from me, not him, although he wasn't unwilling, but it was all wrong. There was a huge, frustrated void inside me and kissing Matt was not going to fill it, not in a million years. It only made it yawn wider.

Matt pulled away and coughed nervously.

'I'm sorry. I'm not ready for this. Please don't be offended.'

I straightened up and smoothed down my dress, mortified. 'It doesn't matter. I understand, really.' I was desperate to wipe my mouth.

How could I have misread the signals so disastrously? I must be losing my touch. Maybe I had never had a touch. All I wanted was to get out of the car, get away from him. I found it difficult to meet his eyes and when I did, because he forced me to, I made a silly face, screwing up my nose. 'Sorry.'

'I'll call you.'

I shook my head. 'I'm going to France.' Thank God.

'When do you get back?'

'Couple of weeks.' I dived out of the cab, slamming the door behind me.

Matt pulled down the window. 'I mean it. I want to see you again. You don't have to be embarrassed.'

'I'm all right. Really. It didn't mean anything.' I fished desperately in my handbag for my keys and pulled them out with a flourish. 'I'll let you know when I'm back.'

'Text me.'

'About what?'

'Anything. Send me a text from France so that I know I'm back in your good books.'

As the taxi pulled away, my next-door neighbour came out of his house with his dog, a Jack Russell bitch with a tendency to bare its sharp little teeth at Sam.

'Been out carousing?' he asked, looking envious. He and his wife had recently had a baby.

'Sort of. Mum's wedding.'

I glanced up at my window. The lights were off but I thought I saw a shadow move. Had Sam been watching? How much had he witnessed? I shivered. 'Good night.'

The communal hall was in darkness and I pressed the switch fruitlessly. The bulb must have gone. I couldn't shake off a feeling of foreboding, even though I was home and safe and the front door had shut out the night, and good-natured Charlie Clifford was outside somewhere with his dog. There was nothing to worry about and it wasn't as if it was pitch-dark. A thin strip of light crept from under the door to the ground-floor flat and a street lamp shone through the leaded window above the front door. Any other evening its soft glow would have been comforting, but tonight it felt sinister. I waited for my eyes to adjust and then I walked forward, deliberately making a noise with my heels on the tessellated tiles. My hand touched the small side table where the mail was stacked. I picked up a letter and held it to the light but I couldn't read it. I peered at my reflection in the cheap gilt-framed mirror that hung above the table. The dimness made me look fuzzy and unfinished. I touched my lips and wondered if the kiss showed in my eyes, in the way I held myself.

The darkness made me shiver. I dropped the letter and ran upstairs, my fingers sliding along the banister. Outside my flat I was barely able to hold my hand steady enough to fit the key in the lock. When I turned it and pushed the door, I hesitated, held my breath and listened before opening it fully. The only sound came from a passing car and the rush of blood in my ears as my pulse quickened. Something was wrong. I had a strong sense that I shouldn't go in. But that was ridiculous and where else was I supposed to go? This was my home. And Sam would never, ever do anything to hurt me. I walked inside.

The flat was gloomy and I couldn't see him. I reached for the light switch and nearly jumped out of my skin when his hand gripped my arm.

'Jesus, Sam. You scared the life out of me.'

His eyes looked unnaturally bright. 'Where've you been? I was worried about you.'

He let go of me and I put down my bag and keys. My hands were trembling. 'I went for a drink after the wedding. I lost track of time.'

'With Matt?'

'Yes, of course.' I couldn't hold his gaze. I picked up an envelope, opened it and pulled out a bank statement, glancing at the page without reading the figures, before I looked at him again. 'It was still so sunny and lovely when it all finished and it was gorgeous down by the river. It seemed a shame to leave.'

'And come home to me?'

I dropped the statement. 'Don't be silly. It wasn't like that at all. He just wanted to talk about Celia.'

'And what did you want to talk about?'

'Families,' I said, more irritated now than afraid. 'We talked about families because we had been to my mother's wedding, and we talked about holidays because he's just been on one and I'm about to go. There. Is that all right?'

'So while I was waiting here, wondering where the hell you were and what you were doing, you were down by the river, enjoying a romantic moment with that worthless prat.'

I lifted my head and frowned at him. Matt might not ever make the *Sunday Times* Rich List, but he wasn't worthless. He was a perfectly nice bloke who would make someone a perfectly nice boyfriend. Just not me.

Sam studied my face. He didn't speak for a moment and then he said, 'Do you know how that makes me feel?'

'You sound like my mother.'

He stared at me, his eyes ice cold. 'What the hell is that meant to mean?'

'Nothing,' I said quickly. 'It isn't meant to mean anything. I'm tired, Sam, and I'm going to bed. You can do what you like.'

I looked into his eyes and felt my mood shift. Behind the anger I saw something else. He had been really scared. I knew what I had done and I knew what that did to him and I felt guilty. He was petrified of losing me just when he was beginning to get a foothold in life. I could only imagine what his day must have felt like; the long wait and the fear and frustration.

This wasn't good. I had to steel myself. I couldn't let pity guide the way I behaved. Maybe, I should have come back sooner and not left him on his own, though. It had been hard for him.

'Sam,' I said gently. 'We talked about this. We talked about you letting me live my life.'

'You kissed him.'

Something nasty wormed its way round my belly.

'No. He kissed me.'

It was the first lie I had told him and it didn't banish the fear; it made it worse.

'Why?' He sounded interested. 'Did you give him the impression you wanted it?'

'No, of course not. I wish you could hear yourself. You sound like a jealous husband.'

Sam's face contorted with anger. 'Don't pretend you don't understand what's at stake.'

'I do understand, but that's all the more reason why you shouldn't push me away by smothering me.'

There was a freezing silence. I drew a long breath and reached for his hand. He didn't take it and I dropped mine. I was shaking. It was time to calm things down.

'I honestly don't know why it happened.'

Sam didn't comment, so I staggered on, faltering over my words.

'The day was so much more fun than I'd expected it to be. Larry is really wonderful and Mum looked so happy with him. I had a warm, fuzzy feeling when I left, like I actually belonged to a proper family. Matt's just a bloke, and it was just a kiss, but I'm sorry if I hurt you. I was having a nice time. I was happy.'

'I thought I made you happy. What the hell am I here for if I can't do that? Alice, look at me.'

I looked. While I was with Matt I could almost believe that Sam had been a dream. But here he was. I could feel him and hear him. I was so tired. Stupidly, I began to cry.

Sam's expression softened. 'It's all right, Alice.' He drew me into his arms. 'Go to bed. I understand.'

As I left the room, he added, 'It was hell not knowing.'

After the row with Sam I knew I wouldn't sleep so I took a pill and then lay staring at the ceiling. My digital clock seemed to move faster than normal, because it was midnight at least half an hour before I expected it. I turned my pillow over so that the cool side was against my cheek.

When I finally drifted off it was only to lurch awake again, disturbed by an insistent ringing. I fumbled for my clock, thinking it was the alarm, and then realized it was the phone.

'Hello?' There was silence. 'Who is this?'

When they still didn't reply, I told whoever it was to sod off, rolled over and dragged the duvet over my head.

I tried to relax but I sensed a shift in the atmosphere. I slipped quietly out of bed and went to the window. The occupant of the second-floor flat opposite was evidently still up and there were a few brightly lit windows picked out randomly along the terrace like a half-opened advent calendar, but otherwise my neighbours were asleep. I tried to imagine what Rory's response to my situation would be, but I doubted Sam would have happened if Rory had still been around. It was confusing and it was very late and letting questions like that take over my mind was unhelpful.

I turned away, feeling uneasy, and went to the bathroom. Before I went back to bed, I switched on the light in the corridor, pushed Sam's door open a crack and listened. I couldn't hear him breathing. After a while my eyes adjusted to the darkness and I saw from the flattened blanket that he wasn't there.

That was odd. Sam was angry and disappointed but still, he had never gone out without me. Did it mean that he had ceased to exist because of Matt? Maybe he wasn't coming back. Maybe that was it. I felt a surge of hope. I would be alone again.

I went back to bed and woke up with the dawn light creeping through the gap in the curtains. I thought I heard a noise and when I rolled over I saw Sam standing near the door, watching me. I scrambled up into a sitting position and stared at him.

He stepped forward. 'I need to talk to you.'

I groaned. 'Go back to bed, Sam. It's far too early.' I glanced at my clock. Four thirty. What a night.

In the semi-darkness Sam's eyes flashed. 'You cannot order me around! We are not six years old any more.'

'No we're not. We're adults. But right now you're behaving like a child.'

His tone changed. 'I'm sorry. I just needed to see you, to speak to you. I couldn't sleep.'

'Where did you go?' I rubbed my eyes and tried to focus.

His eyes widened. 'I haven't been anywhere.'

'I checked your room, you weren't there.'

'Maybe you just couldn't see me. That's what I'm afraid of. You spend time with another man and I vanish.'

I frowned. I wasn't going to tell him that that was precisely what I had thought.

'Look, I'm not stupid. I know that I've turned your life inside out . . .' His voice was conciliating, but it wasn't having the desired effect.

'Stop. Please, Sam. I'm too tired to have this sort of conversation. I can't think straight. I need to sleep.'

He looked as though he had plenty more to say but in the end he sank down on to the bed beside me. 'Can I stay with you for the rest of the night? I don't want to be alone.'

I shrugged and moved over. Neither of us spoke again, but I didn't sleep until long after I felt his body relax.

I woke up close to nine o'clock, rolled out of bed and stood under the shower for as long as I could stand it. I felt trapped. My flat was beginning to feel like a gaol and Sam my gaoler. What was he offering me in return for his existence? Undying affection? Great. Lucky me. I never asked for that. Then I pictured myself sitting in the tree house as a child, talking to myself, wishing I had a friend, wishing someone, anyone, wanted me. So maybe it was my fault.

I listed the things that he craved – proof of life, corporeal form, my withdrawal from anyone who cared about me – and I scrubbed harder.

And what did I want now? I wanted to feel safe. I wanted not to feel guilty. I wanted to connect with real people. I wanted to be alone with Jonathan, to have a conversation that wasn't distorted by knowing that Sam was watching and judging and drawing conclusions. I wanted my old life back. If I got it, I'd make more of an effort with my family; I'd be more tolerant and forgiving of my mother; I'd learn to respect Olivia; I'd be less selfish; I'd be generous, sociable, warm and confident. I'd be me, but better, wiser and nicer.

When I came out, wrapped in a towel, Sam was waiting for me. The set of his shoulders was tense, his expression contrite.

'Please don't hate me,' he said.

My mouth felt dry. I went into the kitchen and poured myself a glass of water and drank it down before I replied, 'I don't hate you.' I forced myself to smile at him. 'I'm going out for a while, alone, to get my head straight. We can talk later.'

The atmosphere in the flat was stifling. It didn't feel like my sanctuary any more. I shut the door of the bedroom before I pulled on jeans and a T-shirt. When I came out Sam was sitting at the table, his arms crossed. He followed me with his eyes as I got ready to leave. I slipped my feet into flip-flops, looped a cardigan around my shoulders, picked up my bag and keys and went to the door.

'Don't be long.'

I stopped in my tracks and looked at him. 'I'll be as long as I like.'

Then

MY PHONE RINGS AND I PULL IT OUT OF MY POCKET. 'RORY. What's up?'

'What's that noise? Are you working?'

'Well, not right this second.' Behind me in the studio two small boys are chasing each other round with mini-guitars, their hair slicked into quiffs, while their mothers help themselves to the generous lunch that *Her Week* has provided. I am knackered and we're only halfway through. The intern has turned the music up. I cover one ear with my hand and press the phone harder against the other.

'Great. Listen, I'm on my lunch break, trying to find something for Mike and Gabby. What do I get them?'

'I don't know. Where are you?'

'Outside Agent Provocateur.'

I shudder. 'Fine, but please don't tell me about it.'

He laughs. 'Jonathan says he's looking forward to seeing you.'

'That's nice.'

I silently thump my forehead against the glass.

I haven't seen Jonathan in about a year and it's been four since I irretrievably wrecked our friendship by kissing him. Time enough to get over it, one would think, although, judging by my reaction just now, a lifetime wouldn't be sufficient.

'Just to warn you, he's bringing Megan.'

'Good,' I say firmly. 'I'm longing to meet her.'

210

'Alice, listen. Let's take the train. It's daft you driving.'

'It's fine, Rory. You'll never make it to your christening if I don't, and you can't have both godfathers not turning up at the font. It would be unforgivable.'

'So would you not being able to get pissed at your own father's wedding.'

'I don't need to get pissed. I'm a grown-up. Honestly, don't worry about it; I'd rather take the car. It means I'm not trapped.'

'But I feel so bad. I can go online right now and check connections. If there's a way of getting to Oxfordshire by ten, I'll book it. We can get a cab to Wadhurst station.'

'Don't be ridiculous. We'd need to book hotel rooms as well and it's far too late for all that. Look, I'm driving and that's final. I've got it all worked out in my head.'

'If you're absolutely sure . . .'

'I absolutely am.' The cost of a train ticket is enough to put me off. But also, I've thought it through and I'm happy with the arrangement. And, of course, Rory and Daniel would owe me.

PART TWO

For I have sworn thee fair, and thought thee bright,
Who art as black as hell, as dark as night.
Shakespeare, Sonnet 147

Chapter Seventeen

I WRIGGLED MY TOES AND STRETCHED. I HAD BEEN IN FRANCE FOR four days, and I was already tanned. In the fields, the lavender had dried and the harvest had begun and I could hear the sound of tractors toiling through the neatly spaced rows. Emma and Brian had rented a converted farmhouse in Provence. The building was white and low with green shutters, a terrace, a stretch of dry lawn and an orchard. Perfectly beautiful in a perfect spot. The house had two bedrooms and a one-storey annex, consisting of a den with scruffy sofa, TV, a desk and a stark little bedroom looking out on to a courtyard. My room looked on to it as well, but I also had a view of the olive groves. Emma and Brian's room was on the other side of the house. After the last few days in London it was such a relief not to be cooped up with Sam. At least here I had a change of scene and company.

After I walked out on Sam that morning after Mum's wedding, I called Daniel and asked him to meet me. It felt like I had taken my first independent steps since the accident. Being with Daniel was like escaping from a stagnant pond and diving into a moving river. He kissed me effusively, steered me into the café, sat me down and fetched me a coffee and a large sticky bun. He was wearing a trendy jacket, well-fitted white T-shirt, jeans and pointy brogues. I felt inordinately proud to be seen with him and rather ashamed of my flip-flops. We talked about how he was coping and then, when I thought I was going to get away without mentioning my problems, he asked how I was with such genuine concern that it all came tumbling out in a rush.

I waited while Daniel absorbed what I had told him.

'Wow. That's quite a lot to take in.'

'Am I going mad?'

He steepled his hands around mine. 'No, you're not, darling girl. But there has to be some reason why this is happening to you. It could be linked to depression.'

'Only, I'm not depressed.'

'You've been through a hell of a lot and you haven't really given yourself a chance to catch up. You may well have the beginnings of it without even knowing.'

I shook my head. 'You don't understand. I've looked it up. It's not that, and I'm not having some sort of psychotic episode either, and I'm not schizophrenic. I'm not hearing voices in my head. Sam is physical. He's no different to you or anyone else. I can see and touch and hear him. He breathes, he sniffs and he breaks wind. He is about as real and human as you can get, except I'm the only one who can see him.' I hesitated, not sure how much I should say or how much Daniel would understand. 'He scares me.'

'Scares you? How?'

I fiddled with my napkin, tearing it into strips until Daniel put his hand firmly over mine and then teased it out of my fingers.

'Sorry,' I said.

'Tell me, Alice.'

I leaned back and put my hands on my lap where Daniel couldn't see them. 'I can't explain it. He hasn't threatened me or anything, but he needs me so badly. He's desperate and it makes me nervous. And he's unpredictable. You're going to tell me I need help now, aren't you?'

'Alice. What do you expect me to say? Of course you need help.'

216

I bit my lip and grimaced. It was so hard to explain Sam to people, but I wanted Daniel to understand, the same way I would have wanted Rory to. I took a sip of coffee.

'OK,' I said. 'There are three ways of looking at this. Either I'm right and Sam is real and capable of hurting me physically and emotionally, or I'm hallucinating.'

'And the third?'

'I've made it up. I'm doing it for attention. I'm sure Mum and Olivia think I have Munchausen's syndrome. Pick one.'

Daniel rubbed the side of his nose in a way that reminded me forcibly of Rory.

'I'd love to believe he was real.'

'Don't sit on the fence or anything. God, this is doing my head in. You have to believe me, Daniel. Sam inhabits my world. I don't know how and I don't know why, but he's there and he wants to stay.' I couldn't stop my small moan of despair. 'He's never going to let me go.'

'Maybe you're the one who should be doing that.'

'Believe me, I've thought about it. Do you think I need to kick him like you kick a habit?'

'It wouldn't be a bad way of looking at it. You should step back and try for some objectivity. If Sam's a habit, does he give you a buzz?'

'Sometimes, yes. It's pretty extraordinary, after all. And he was lovely at the beginning.'

'Good. And then you became dependent.'

'I don't know about that. I . . .'

He held his hand up to stop me. 'Let's run with this. You can't go cold turkey; you're too fragile right now. What you should do is take it slowly, one step at a time.'

I frowned. It wasn't that simple. 'So what do you suggest?'

He blew out a breath. 'I don't know. What would be the easiest step for you to take?'

'Being with other people, I suppose. Limiting the time I'm on

217

my own. I'm going to spend a couple of weeks in France with Emma and Brian.'

Daniel smiled. 'There you go. You're sorted.'

Was I?

'Alice. About the inquest tomorrow. We'll go together.'

I nodded and took his hands in mine. 'I'm so sorry, Daniel. So, so sorry.'

He swallowed and nodded. 'I know, sweetie. But please don't be. Nobody blames you. Least of all me.'

The inquest came and went and somehow I got through it despite it feeling unreal. I thought it would help me move on at least a step, but it didn't. Rory was still a presence in my mind, a friend who I wanted to see but somehow was unable to. It was awful. Like someone telling me all over again that he was dead and I was involved. Hammering it in. Emma hadn't come, but Brian had flown back from France and Jonathan had been there too, and Dad. And Sam, of course. He sat behind me, his presence oppressive and aggravating. In the end the hearing was, as Shoba Kabir, Dad's lawyer, had forewarned us, immediately adjourned. The coroner didn't give a date for the full inquest, but Shoba said to expect to wait several weeks. We filed out into the sunshine. Brian hailed a taxi and he and Jonathan said goodbye to me and left. Daniel went back to work and I had lunch in a pub with Dad.

'I'm so glad you came,' Emma said. We were sitting beside the pool watching Brian pottering round, picking up mugs and discarded magazines. 'It's lovely to have a distraction. You're good for me.'

She was wearing a floaty pale-green dress and her hair was precariously piled on top of her head with a butterfly clip. Strands had fallen out and curled softly around her neck and shoulders. I noticed greys that hadn't been there before.

'Good,' I said, feeling inordinately pleased.

Later, while I was reading in the shade of a large canvas parasol, I heard a car draw up on the other side of the house and the sound of its door slamming. Sam was somewhere in the hills, walking off his energy, unable to sit still for more than fifteen minutes at a time. I pushed myself up on my elbows. I could hear Emma's voice, slightly high-pitched. Whoever had arrived was obviously a welcome surprise. Emma called me and I picked up my sarong, wrapped it round my hips and tied a knot.

'Look who's here!' Brian said as I walked through the French windows into the kitchen. His eyes were shining.

Jonathan held out his hand and I went to him and found myself locked in the sort of bear hug Brian usually gave me. I rested a moment, pressed against his shirt, feeling his ribs and the beat of his heart. Then I pushed myself away with an awkward shuffle.

'What made you decide to come after all?' Emma said, reaching for the kettle.

Jonathan put a carrier bag containing bottles and a newspaper down on to a kitchen chair.

'I'm trying to finish the book and the whole wedding thing is so bloody distracting. I decided to come out and work on it in peace. Megan's stressed, but she might fly over at the end of the week if she has time.'

'Is everything all right?' Emma said. 'You haven't had a row, have you?'

I had been wondering about that too and I felt rotten, because I secretly would have loved the answer to be yes. I risked a quick glance at his profile but didn't let my gaze linger. I reminded myself of the excruciating embarrassment of the Matt episode. I had texted him from the airport, just to prove that I was cool with it all, but he hadn't replied. No surprise, really. I had made a fool of myself that night, but if that humiliation saved me from doing worse now, then it would have been worth it.

'No. Far from it,' Jonathan said. 'It's just that we're both busy and people keep phoning all the time, demanding immediate answers: does she want to go with whites, or whites with an accent of green? How many silk rosebuds on the bridesmaids' dresses? Christ, it's doing my head in. I don't know why we can't just have a few friends and family at the town hall. The bloody thing's snowballed and, because of her programme, the women's magazines have got in on the act and she's had to factor in interviews with them. We had *Marie Claire* at the flat the other day.'

Emma made a sympathetic noise. 'Poor thing. She's taken an awful lot on. But I suppose she could always say no.'

'And have the press decide she's an arrogant bitch? She's far too canny for that. So anyway, I'm here to spend time with my parents and to get some peace and quiet.'

I studied him. Like his mother, there were dark shadows under his eyes, a trace of tension around his mouth. He glanced at me and caught my eye.

We took cold drinks outside. Jonathan sat at the edge of the pool with his feet in the water, a bottle of beer beside him. The afternoon was almost over and I was beginning to wonder where Sam was, and to dread his reaction when he got back. Jonathan was unusually expansive; manically so. A bit like Rory used to get when he was trying to pretend everything was all right. I decided his dark glasses made him look leaner and harder and very attractive.

When Sam returned, I was sitting on the edge of the lounger. Jonathan floated in the bright blue pool, ignoring the wasps that alighted on the sparkling water. His hair was wet and slicked back, his brown eyes gleaming. Sam cast no shadow but I knew without looking that he was behind me. Jonathan swam away and, where he had been, I saw Sam's reflection shimmering. I looked up but I didn't say anything. Brian and Emma lay quietly dozing, their books on their chests, their glasses askew.

'What's he doing here?' Sam said. 'Did you know he was coming?'

I couldn't speak so I just shook my head. I tried to keep my expression neutral but I was never very good at acting.

＊

The following morning, I woke up early and lay in bed with my eyes shut, listening to Sam's steady breathing, unable to get back to sleep. Across the courtyard, I could hear the sound of Jonathan typing in the den. After a while I slid out of bed, crossed the floor silently, and looked down. Jonathan's window was open and his desk-light shone brightly through the thin curtains. I took my dressing gown off its hook, closed the door behind me and crept downstairs. The kitchen smelled of freshly brewed coffee. I poured myself a cup and opened the doors to the garden. The lavender that edged the stone terrace was wet with dew, the air was fresh and the morning sunshine had begun to dilute the dawn.

I could still hear Jonathan if I strained my ears. I listened for a while and allowed my mind to drift and only realized that the typing had stopped when Jonathan, barefoot and rumpled in an old T-shirt and pyjama trousers, stepped outside.

'Good morning,' he said, slouching into the chair beside me.

'You're up.'

There was something disconcerting about seeing him this early in the morning, unshaven, his hair still mussed from bed.

'Well, yes.'

'Oh, all right. It's a little too early to expect me to make intelligent observations.'

He laughed. 'So, Alice . . . ?'

'Yes, Jonathan?'

'Is this a good time to ask you something?'

'Depends what it is.'

I leaned on the table and smiled at him over my coffee. I felt happy and free. Not exactly relaxed, but as though it was the right place for me to be: sitting here in the early morning sun, enjoying the company of a man I couldn't have.

'That business over dinner at my place, was it for real?'

I didn't answer immediately. I suppose I should have expected it, but it still embarrassed me. I shaded my eyes and frowned at him.

'Jonathan, this is really hard for me. I feel such an idiot.'

He scratched at his stubble and yawned. 'Sorry. I should keep out of it. It's only, after what happened that evening, I can't help wondering.'

'So, are you asking me as a friend or is it professional interest? You told me Hannah thought I was psychic.'

'I didn't think she was serious. Mind you, for a moment, you even managed to suspend my disbelief. I was jealous. You talk to him and not to me.'

I blushed. 'I can't talk to you, not properly.'

Jonathan looked at me intently. He seemed suddenly less shambolic and I could see the professional in him, the man who persuaded people to open up.

'Why in heaven's name not? I've known you long enough. I've always made it plain that I care about what happens to you. You are part of our family, Alice.'

I bent my head and let my hair shield my profile. 'I was.'

'You still are.'

There were tears gathering behind my eyes. I forced them back. 'Do you really think so? I know you're trying to be kind but I also know how difficult it is for your parents. Maybe I shouldn't have come.'

'They want you here. Obviously, it's very hard for them, but they adore you. It will be all right; just give Mum time. You're definitely their surrogate daughter. Dad will be fighting Mike for the privilege of leading you up the aisle when you get married.'

I sniffed and wiped my eyes and smiled up at him. 'Ha ha.'

'Ha ha, you're not getting married, or ha ha, our fathers won't be competing over you?'

'Don't you have a book to finish?'

'Knowing you were outside contemplating your navel or what-ever you were doing, I couldn't resist the chance to talk to you on your own.' He narrowed his eyes. 'You are on your own?'

'Yes.' I picked up my mug and drank some of the coffee. When I looked up he caught my eye.

'Do you know how gorgeous you are?' he said.

'Don't say things like that to me.'

When I blushed he smiled his slow, teasing smile and my toes curled with pleasure.

'I really should get back to work.'

He started to push his chair back, unaware that he had once again succeeded in awakening my inner adolescent.

'Jonathan . . . ?' I hesitated and he didn't fill the gap. I felt myself go red. 'If you tell me what's bugging you, I'll answer your question.'

He sat back down, stretching his legs out. His feet were long and bony. 'You go first.'

'All right. Yes, it was for real. Sam was in your flat and he's here now, asleep. Your turn.'

'Can't we explore the subject of Sam?'

'No.'

'OK. Although I don't think you're playing fair. I have the wedding jitters.'

I felt a tiny thrill which I immediately quashed.

'That's normal. You've put off getting married for so long, it was always going to be tough once you made up your mind.'

He leaned his elbows on the table. 'It was an impulse. I asked her because Rory had just died and we all . . . I . . . needed something to cling to.'

'Jonathan, you've been through so much and you've had to stay strong for your parents and I know that can't have been easy. I think you've been amazing. And maybe your impulse was right, maybe Megan is the woman you need.'

'You're very sweet. And I do love her and I am going to get married.' He waited a moment before adding, 'Alice, I keep wanting to say something to you but I'm not sure what it is. I think I may even have come out here to see you.'

Sam appeared then. He stopped abruptly a couple of metres from where we were sitting.

'I should go back in,' I said. I could have strangled him.

Jonathan went quiet and then he shaded his eyes, squinting into the sky.

'And I'd better get back to the grindstone. Do you want to cycle into the village to pick up some breakfast later?'

'I'd love that.'

'And I was thinking we could all go to Les Baux. It's only about fifty kilometres away and it sounds incredible. There's a thirteenth-century fortress.'

I laughed at his sudden enthusiasm for tourism. 'Have you been reading the guide books? Actually, I'd love it. Your dad was talking about it yesterday. Maybe in the afternoon, when it's not quite so hot. I'm sure they'll both be up for it.'

In our bedroom, Sam closed the door and leaned against it. 'Did I interrupt something?'

'No. He'd only been out a couple of minutes. We were just chatting. Nothing earth-shattering.' I hoped to God I didn't look as guilty as I felt.

Sam's expression was brooding. He chewed at the inside of his mouth. I stayed quiet. If he wanted to have a go at me, he would, without any prompting.

'When Matt kissed you,' he said. 'Please tell me it didn't mean anything.'

Why were we back to Matt? I shouldn't have told that lie. It had been a childish, spur-of-the-moment decision that I now regretted. 'It was nothing to do with Matt. It was me who kissed him, not the other way round.'

Sam was silent for a long time. 'You should have told me the truth.'

'I was embarrassed. Can we back up a bit? Not make demands on each other, just relax and have a good holiday. It will work. I promise. You need to be patient. And you mustn't get so angry.'

'Angry?' He seemed bemused and a little lost. 'I'm not angry with you, Alice. I'm just disappointed.'

Through the windows I could hear Emma and Brian and I wondered what they were talking about. Not me, I didn't think. More likely Jonathan and Megan. It would be easier to fix on them than to dwell on the past. It had to be tempting to think about weddings, and even future grandchildren, when the heart has been ripped out of your family.

'I'm back Sunday week. So I can certainly do the Tuesday or the Wednesday.' I was talking to Kitty Goodwin who ran a fashion label called TeaCake from her house in Kent. Women's clothes with a vintage edge.

'That's brilliant, Alice,' Kitty said. 'I'm so pleased you're getting back into the swing of things. I'll email you the details. Take care of yourself.'

It was great to have work, but not so much for the money. Before the accident I would always rearrange my diary to suit a client and would work even if I was ill, but recently I had found myself entertaining an uncharacteristic and not very sensible *no worries* attitude to my financial situation. What I craved far more than a cheque in the post was the feeling of purpose that I hoped work would give me. Since Rory's death, my life had seemed dangerously pointless. Taking photographs of beautiful people? So what? I had to find the passion again, or I was lost.

The closest village was only a couple of kilometres away, but it took half an hour to cycle the distance because Jonathan and I kept stopping to admire the countryside and listen to the crickets. I was finding it very difficult to think of things to say and the frequent silences made me self-conscious. It wasn't the comfortable silence that you get between long-standing friends and lovers. It was the kind that falls between two people who either like each other too much or too little. To me anyway. For all I knew, Jonathan might very well have been mentally rewriting a particularly tricky paragraph.

We bought croissants and baguettes and put them in his rucksack and set off back to the house. When we were within sight of it, Jonathan stopped and pushed his bike on to the verge. He walked through some scrub grass into a field and I followed him.

'You look really worried,' he said, examining my face. 'We are alone, aren't we?'

I nodded. I was thinking that if I could see the house, maybe Sam could see me. It made me feel like prey.

'I can't believe I asked you that question.'

I shielded my eyes from the sun with my hand and glanced at him. 'Then why ask?'

'Because I'm curious. A couple of hundred years ago, you would have been dunked in the village pond or burned at the stake.'

'Oh, well, that's helpful.'

I sat down on a bit of humped grass, burnt to the colour of pale straw. A lizard scooted across the rough ground. I hugged my knees and tried to ignore the tension.

Jonathan stood over me. I studied his legs and thought they were rather nice.

'What do you want, Alice? Do you want Sam to go away?'

I fiddled with the strap of my sandal. 'It's complicated. I want to be normal, but he dominates my life. I feel so guilty about him.' I paused. 'If I look at it objectively, which I promise you I do, I can see that Sam is a part of what makes me, me. How could it be otherwise? Sometimes I hate him, but it's all mixed up with anger at Rory's death and blaming myself for what happened.' I stopped. My hands were shaking.

He sat down beside me. 'Go on. I'm listening.'

I chewed at my lower lip. 'You're a journalist and you have a journalist's nose for sniffing out stories and you told me you liked digging round in people's minds. I'm not sure I want you shoving your spade into mine.'

Jonathan laughed. 'I wouldn't mind writing about you, when the time comes. But not until you're ready.'

'That will be never then. I don't fancy being a laughing stock.'

He slapped a fly away from his arm. 'You stopped me talking to you this morning.'

No, Sam had done that. 'I'm sorry.'

He studied my face, as if he was searching for answers. But I didn't know what the question was. I wished I did. I wanted to help. The way he was looking at me threatened to turn me to jelly.

If he kisses me, I told myself firmly, it'll ruin a long friendship and chances are I'll lose him as well. And Sam will guess because it'll show on my face. Jonathan had picked up a stone and was tossing it from hand to hand. The moment had passed. Disappointment made me feel sick at heart. Why could I not read men?

He drew some lines in the dirt. 'Noughts or crosses?'

'Noughts.' I found a small twig and drew a circle.

'Alice, I am really confused. I don't know if the way I've begun feeling about you is bound up in Rory's death, or if it's always been there. Jesus, I've cocked up royally.'

I didn't look at him and I knew he wasn't looking at me. We were both pretending to concentrate on the game. I drew another circle. It was the not looking that was doing the damage.

I muttered, 'I'll tell you a secret. I've had a crush on you since I don't know when.'

'I never noticed.' He twisted round and we stared at each other but the look in his eyes was not what I wanted. It told me he was torn.

'This isn't the right time, is it?' I said, forcing myself to lean away from him.

He smiled ruefully. 'When has it ever been?'

'It's your fault. You're the one who always has a girlfriend. If you took a break now and again, I might get a look in.'

That made him laugh. 'I'm not that bad, am I?'

227

'Yes.' I over-emphasized the word. I was feeling muddled and upset. 'We should get back. Your parents will be wondering what's happened to their breakfast.'

'It wouldn't be right, Alice.'

'No,' I agreed. It wasn't exactly what I thought but at least I had been the one to say it first. That helped.

Jonathan stroked my new fringe away from my face, his fingers carefully touching my scar. 'Does it hurt?'

'It feels a bit weird.'

He touched my forehead with his lips and then pulled me up and we made our way back to the house. I could have done it. I could have crossed that invisible line and kissed him. But I'd been there before and I wasn't about to repeat my mistakes. If anyone was going to cross a line it would have to be him.

Chapter Eighteen

JONATHAN'S PLAN TO GO TO LES BAUX PROVED POPULAR BECAUSE WE were all feeling guilty about wasting our days lying prone under the sun. We decided to leave after lunch and spend the hottest part of the day in the air-conditioned hire car, aiming to arrive at about half past two. In the meantime, we took our books and laid cushions on the recliners. Emma swam a few gentle lengths while I covered myself with suntan lotion. Jonathan took the bottle from me and did my back. I couldn't breathe. Sam was watching and I caught his eye once and stopped Jonathan as soon as I could because I could see Sam hated it and I was sorry to cause hurt. All the same, I resented his interference in my life. He wasn't my lover.

I picked up my book and read for a few minutes, then jumped up and went to the side of the pool, hesitated and dived in. It was foolishly ambitious on my part. I narrowly missed a belly flop.

As I surfaced, Jonathan burst out laughing. 'What the hell do you call that?'

I splashed him crossly. 'Don't laugh. I don't know how to dive properly.'

He came to the edge of the pool and looked down at me and I squinted up at him.

'I hated swimming lessons,' I said. 'I can just about manage breaststroke, but diving is a nightmare.'

'I'll teach you.'

He held out his hand and pulled me up. I sat near his leg,

dripping wet in my black bikini, fully aware of the effect I was having on him. Emma was watching. I slid back into the pool.

Jonathan sat down and cooled his feet in the water. The moment was so fraught with tension that the only thing I could do was swim away.

'I know what he's up to,' Sam shouted. But I took a big breath and dipped my head. I didn't want to hear.

On the way to Les Baux, Sam sat in the back of the car between me and Jonathan. Brian was driving. I spent most of the time watching the scenery slide by, admiring the fields of lavender and the pretty villages while Emma talked about the impending wedding, wondering out loud if Megan was likely to come over and join us.

Once there, we split up. Emma and Brian, in sunhats and sandals, walked at a slower pace than Jonathan and I. They wanted to inspect details and linger over interesting arches. Brian had brought the guide book from the house and had appointed himself expert-in-chief. We walked over to a wall, leaned against it and scanned the view of the hills and the flatter lands in the fore-ground. It seemed to have a profound effect on Sam. He spread his fingers against the warm stone and gazed at our surroundings. We could see vineyards and, in the distance, the limestone boulders of the Alpilles.

'It's sublime, isn't it?' Sam said. His eyes were shining. He looked as though he had been injected with life. He pressed his palms against the ancient walls. 'I feel like I've been around for as long as these stones.'

Jonathan groaned. 'Dad's waving. He probably wants to show me something.'

'What have you said to him?' Sam asked. 'Alice, stay here for a minute. I want to talk to you.'

I couldn't answer. Jonathan was looking at me as if he was expecting me to go with him but I decided to get it over with. There were a few things I could get off my chest too.

'Would you mind if I stayed here for five minutes? Come back and find me. I just need a moment.'

Jonathan looked as though he might argue, then he seemed to think better of it, nodded and walked away.

I turned so that I was facing away from the street. Just another tourist admiring the view. I scanned the horizon then brought the camera up to my eyes and clicked. 'This is hell, Sam. You have to give me some space.'

He leaned his lower back against the wall, raising his face to the sun. 'What do you need space for? To find out how you feel about him?'

I was silent for a moment. Then I said, 'No. I know how I feel. It's not that. It's just that I can't think straight. You're in my head all the time, making me feel bad when I've done nothing to feel bad about.'

A middle-aged couple, wearing ill-fitting jeans and socks with their sandals, stopped in their tracks, looked at me and grimaced at each other before walking on. I dissolved into laughter and for a few minutes Sam and I were happy with each other, almost like we had been up until Mum's wedding day.

I watched a bird of prey skim across the sky, following it with my eyes until it vanished into the glare.

'I've seen the way he looks at you,' Sam said. 'He has an agenda.'

I thought it was all a bit too good to be true. 'Please give it a rest. Jonathan is kind to everyone he likes.'

'So you think Megan would be happy if she saw how you two are together? Don't take me for an idiot, Alice.'

'What do you think is going to happen? I'm going to get off with Jonathan and you're going to go up in a puff of smoke?'

I strode off, leaving him behind. I wondered why he didn't follow, but I wasn't going to argue. I wandered around on my own for a while, deliberately avoiding both men. Then I saw Jonathan. Sam was heading in his direction, crossing towards the ruined part of the town. Jonathan climbed up to what once had been a window and stood with one hand pressed flat against the stone, his feet apart, firmly planted in the dust. I watched from a distance as Sam joined him and my blood ran cold.

Jonathan shaded his eyes and turned. Sam put his hand against his chest and tried to push and I started to run. Instinctively, Jonathan slammed both hands against the wall then Sam crouched down and ran his fingers through the dust. Neither of them had seen me yet.

'Shit,' I muttered, as I rushed over. 'What are you doing?'

Sam turned his head. 'Don't sound so worried. I was just admiring the view.'

'Admiring the view,' Jonathan echoed.

I climbed up and joined them, holding on to Jonathan with one hand, the wall with the other. 'It's beautiful,' I breathed, determined to appear as if nothing was wrong. 'Inspiring. I could live somewhere like this.'

Jonathan seemed to pull himself together. 'I don't know. I suspect it's dead in the winter and obviously it's crawling with tourists in the summer. If one season didn't drive you mad, the other would.'

'Grouch. The air is fantastic and it's just so still, so peaceful. And I wouldn't care about being isolated in the winter, I think I'd like it, especially right now, with my family trying to tell me how to run my life.'

Jonathan kissed the top of my head and put an arm around my waist. I froze. 'Careful what you wish for.'

'I wish you were a million miles away,' Sam muttered.

'Alice,' Jonathan said. 'I know this is stupid, but is he here? Was he here when you showed up?'

I nodded.

'I thought . . . I mean I felt like I wasn't alone.' He laughed. 'I expect it's my mind playing tricks. Too much sun, probably.'

'You're just going to have to make your own mind up about that.' I sounded sharp but I felt a glimmer of hope.

I turned to go and missed my footing. Sam caught me by one arm and Jonathan by the other, but my bag slipped off my shoulder and my purse fell out. I bent to pick it up and my hair stood on end. A crude letter S had been formed in the dust. It could have been a trail left by a lizard; it could have been done by the toe of Jonathan's shoe. It could have been Sam. I hastily brushed it away with my fingers. Sam smiled at me.

'Go away,' I whispered.

Jonathan held out his hand to pull me up. 'This place is starting to give me the creeps.'

'I'm not leaving you on your own with him,' Sam said.

I exploded with irritation. 'I don't need a minder.'

'I never suggested you did,' Jonathan said.

Sam looked from me to Jonathan. 'Alice, all he wants is to have sex with you. Don't kid yourself that it goes any deeper.'

'Go. Away.'

He held his hands up, surrendering.

'Alice . . .' Jonathan shaded his eyes. 'Jesus. Are you for real? Sorry. I didn't mean that.'

'What did you mean, Jonathan?' Where had my hostility come from? 'Look, I can't deal with this now. I'm going to get something to drink.'

Jonathan jumped down and then he looked back, squinting into the light. His white shirt was open at the neck. Even though I was annoyed I couldn't take my eyes off him.

'Talk to me, Alice.'

'Are you saying you believe me?'

He looked confused. 'I can't say I believe he's here, but I do believe that you genuinely think he is. Honestly, I'm at a loss.'

I threw up my hands. 'At a loss? Great. I thought you were meant to know all about this sort of thing. You've got a degree, haven't you?'

'Obviously, there are holes in my knowledge.'

'Don't be so pompous. I can't talk to you. Not about Sam at any rate.' Then I gave a despairing laugh and added, 'He isn't deaf.'

'You don't have to explain anything,' Sam said.

I bit my lip and looked up at him and felt a tingle of fear. 'Why did you come back?'

'Because you called me.'

Jonathan had gone very quiet. I think he was trying not to look horrified. He put his arm through mine and tried to steer me away, but I resisted. His voice was unsteady when he finally spoke. 'Maybe he'll vanish when you get better.'

'Maybe.'

'This can't go on for ever. Something will happen.'

When I replied I was looking at Jonathan but it was Sam I was really addressing. 'I just can't imagine life without him. Even if it does turn out to be something that can be fixed with drugs, I couldn't do it; I couldn't take anti-depressants. I'd feel like I was knifing him in the back.'

'That's exactly what you would be doing. Alice, please stay with me.'

I walked away from him with Jonathan, feeling desperately upset and a little shell-shocked. I wasn't hiding it well. I could feel Jonathan's concern in the way he slowed his pace to match mine. We found Emma and Brian in the café and Sam didn't reappear until we were ready to leave. When we'd paid up we decided to have a last stroll before getting back into the car.

Emma said something to Brian and turned to me. She tucked a loose strand of hair behind her ear and twisted the coloured glass beads of her earring. I had known her long enough to recognize a warning signal.

'Walk with me, Alice. Jonathan, why don't you go on ahead with your father?'

'There's a particularly interesting lintel I wanted to show you . . .' Brian had evidently been given his cue.

'I've been waiting for a chance to talk to you,' Emma said.

'I want to talk to you too.'

'Well, let me go first. It's a little bit delicate.' She hooked her arm through mine. 'You know that I care about you, don't you? You've been like a daughter to me. To Brian as well. We both want what's best for you.'

I could feel my smile slipping. Emma was worrying me now. 'You've always been wonderful. I'm so grateful to you.'

Was she going to tell me that she couldn't bear being with me because it was too painful, because of Rory? She looked at me and her eyes were gentle. She genuinely loved me, I knew that, but there was no escaping the fact that I had been driving that night. No matter how many times she and Brian told each other that it wasn't my fault, there would always be that thought, like a tiny bit of grit in a shoe, that had we left earlier and had I been more alert, I could have prevented it. And there was the part she didn't know. The part where Rory tried to insist we took the train and I dug my heels in and refused. I thought I would burst. The guilt inhibited every single conversation I had with her.

'There's no need. We don't ask for gratitude and nor do we deserve it. Oh, Alice, I'm sorry, but I am worried about you. I've seen the way you are with Jonathan.'

I hadn't expected that and my heart slumped into my stomach. I actually felt physically sick. I didn't realize she could read me so well. 'I don't understand. How am I with Jonathan?'

'Darling, it's the way you look at him. The way you brighten when he comes into the room. You have to be careful. You're a lovely young woman and you're struggling with life. He's a strong man who has always been fond of you and he's drawn to you because of what has happened and because of who you both are. It's created a bond between you. I can understand how you could confuse that feeling with love.' She paused and then said in a rush, 'That's why I wanted to have this talk.'

'Emma. Please don't. I adore him, but as a friend. Of course I like it when he's around. He's good company. But you mustn't read anything else into it. I know he loves Megan. And even if there wasn't Megan, we'd still just be friends.' My voice lacked conviction.

'It's very easy to fall in love when you're feeling vulnerable. I don't want to see either of you hurt. You've been through such a lot already.' She stopped and took my hand. 'You had an unhappy childhood and you've been damaged by that. You didn't have enough love and attention, and then later you and Rory were so close. When he died, I think you lost more than you realized and you're trying to get that back with Jonathan. But I honestly don't believe he can give you what you want. He certainly shouldn't fall into an affair with you because you're young and sweet and hurt. He mustn't feel he has to put you back together again. It's not fair on him and it isn't fair on Megan.'

I couldn't bear it. I broke in. 'I'll leave.' I was dying inside.

'No, please don't,' Emma said. 'If anyone goes, it should be Jonathan. I'm so sorry. I only wanted to warn you. The last thing I want is to hurt you or make you feel unwelcome.'

'But how can I stay now? It'll be so awkward.'

'You'll be fine and I'll help you.'

Did Emma know that Jonathan was having doubts about his wedding? Had he hinted at it? I felt sure that she wouldn't mention it even if she had picked up on the vibes. She wouldn't want to give me false hope. God, what a mess.

'Alice, you're like a daughter to me.'

I nodded sadly and she held my hand. There had been a time, not so long ago, when I really believed that.

Chapter Nineteen

THAT NIGHT I HEARD JONATHAN YELL OUT. I SAT UP, EVERY HAIR ON my body standing on end. Next to me, Sam's bed was empty. I didn't stop to think. I jumped up and ran downstairs, through the den and into Jonathan's room. Sam was at the end of Jonathan's bed, staring at him. Jonathan was sitting with his head in his hands and his feet on the floor, his shoulders hunched forward.

'What the hell are you doing in here?'

'Uh. It's my bedroom,' Jonathan said, rubbing his face and blinking at me.

I breathed out. He was fine. I felt awkward, hovering over him in my pyjama shorts and white vest, not knowing whether to come in or leave.

Sam muttered, 'I was only playing with him.'

'I heard you shout. Sorry, I'll . . . um . . . go back to bed.'

'Alice, I just had the weirdest experience. Like a nightmare that got real. I thought I was being suffocated.'

I'd reached my tipping point. I started to cry and, to my horror, I couldn't stop. It was like that time when I first met Rory – a dam burst. I felt as though there was nowhere to go. Jonathan jumped up and pulled me into his arms and I sobbed into his chest. Beside me Sam seemed to just slip away. When I looked round he was slumped against the door. He looked distraught and I wondered what he would do if Jonathan kissed me. But Jonathan behaved like a gentleman. He sat me down, disappeared into his bathroom and turned on the taps. A few moments later he came out rubbing a towel over his face.

I smiled wanly at him. 'I can't take this any more.'

Jonathan shushed me. 'We'll talk about it in the morning.'

'I don't want to go back to bed. I don't want to be on my own.'

He didn't say anything at first, although he looked like he wanted to, and then he scratched his head and smiled. 'You need to go back to your room, Alice.'

I didn't move.

'I'll come with you and stay until you fall sleep.'

We went upstairs and he sat beside me and stroked my hair; and all the while Sam was watching from the bedroom door. He reached behind him and opened it and Jonathan looked up and frowned, staring into the dark corridor, puzzled. I caught his hand and held it against my cheek.

'It's just a draught,' I said. I closed my eyes and after a minute or two I felt the bed creak as Jonathan stood up.

'Go on,' Sam said. 'Get out. Leave her alone.'

Jonathan reached for Sam's pillow and put it on the floor, made himself comfortable and leaned back against my mattress.

'Jonathan?' I murmured.

'I thought you were asleep.'

'I miss Rory so much.'

'Me too.' He drew a long, tired sigh. 'Christ, Alice, what are we going to do?'

I put my hand on his shoulder and he twined his fingers into mine.

'I don't know.'

He kissed my hand briefly and we whispered to each other in the darkness, about Rory and life. We never once mentioned Megan or love or even Sam. I didn't notice him go. I must have fallen asleep.

The next morning I ignored Sam and for the rest of the day took care that I was never on my own with Jonathan, frustrating his attempts to talk about last night. Megan had called first thing and by that evening she was with us and suddenly he had something else to think about. Emma's relief was palpable. Brian was just happy someone had broken the odd tension that had invaded the house.

I think Megan knew something was up. The look she gave Jonathan after their first greeting was both speculative and determined. But for the time being she overcompensated by talking like a magpie on speed. She had come for five days, leaving the wedding to her mother and the planners. She had finished filming and had left it all behind, forgotten the lot because she needed to. She was stressed. She needed some R and R. She had tales of page-boys who refused to wear knickerbockers, of Hannah who freaked when she saw the dress she was expected to wear. ('But it's green! I'll look like a sugar snap.') And wedding gifts that had been delivered to a surly South Londoner who denied all knowledge once the department store finally admitted their mistake and called him.

Megan held out her glass for more wine and said, 'Nightmare. I just hope the bastard appreciates Egyptian cotton.'

I did my best but, ever since that conversation with Emma, I could barely bring myself to look at Jonathan in front of her, so despite last night, or maybe because of it, everything I said to him sounded like lines spoken by a bad actor.

Still, as far as Emma and Brian were concerned, Megan's arrival redressed the balance. She looked gorgeous, she loved the house, adored the area and was evidently going to be easily pleased. She was exhausting.

'Didn't Matt say he had bought a place in Stapeley Gardens?' We were having breakfast and Jonathan was reading the newspaper Megan had brought out with her.

Megan said, 'I don't remember. Why?'

'Nothing. At least, I don't think it's anything. It just says that they've found the body of a man in a ground-floor flat.'

'He does live there,' I said. 'I hope he's all right. I sent him a text the other day, but he hasn't answered.'

Megan raised her eyebrows. 'Is there something you haven't told us, Alice?'

I went bright red. 'No. Nothing. He's just a friend. He came to Mum's wedding with me.'

'How's the book going, Jonathan?' Brian asked, sensing my embarrassment and intervening with characteristic generosity.

Jonathan tore off the end of a baguette and spread butter and apricot jam on it. 'I'm nearly there.'

'Brilliant,' Megan said. 'We can spend some time together. I promise I won't mention the wedding.'

Jonathan smiled at her and I could see her melt into his eyes. She really was in love with him. I don't know why that surprised me. They were engaged, after all. I suppose I had just hoped it didn't go so deep with her.

'I want to put in a couple more hours, but we could take the bikes out later. I'll show you around.'

'I'd love that. You don't mind me disappearing off with him, do you?' She looked at Emma, but I wondered whether she was really talking to me. 'We haven't been alone for ages and it was getting so awful in London. I don't blame you for escaping out here, Johnnie. It was just what you needed, wasn't it, honey? To get a sense of perspective again. You know, if I had realized what a juggernaut weddings have become, I think I'd have gone to Las Vegas and then come back and had a party. It's a nightmare.'

'It'll be worth it on the day,' Emma said. She pushed her chair back and wiped her mouth with her napkin. 'I'm going to pop into town this morning and do a bit of shopping. Anyone want to come?'

We all declined, except for Brian, who wanted to go to the bank. They left and Jonathan started piling up plates.

Megan watched, her gaze flicking between us. 'Why don't

you go and work, Johnnie. Alice and I can sort this lot out.'

'I really don't mind.'

He hovered close to me but I moved away from him, more alert to Megan's mood than he was. Intelligent men can be very stupid sometimes.

'No,' Megan insisted. 'Go on. It's not as if we have anything better to do.'

He loped away. Left on our own, Megan and I cleared the table and loaded the dishwasher. We didn't speak much at first, but I could feel the unasked questions.

'It sounds as if you've all been having a lovely time,' Megan said.

I shrugged. 'We've hardly done anything except that trip to Les Baux. We've been incredibly lazy. Just sitting around sunbathing and eating and talking. Well, me and Emma and Brian have. Jonathan's been working most of the time.'

'Has he talked to you much about the wedding? I think he was feeling incredibly hassled last week. We were almost at each other's throats.' She gave a little laugh.

I couldn't look at her. 'Not really.'

Megan took a cloth outside and wiped the table clean with, it seemed to me, unnecessary vigour. I made more coffee and we took our mugs and lay in the shade of the parasol and reached for our books.

'I'm thirty-five.'

Sam had been drowsing beside the pool but his head jerked up.

I turned to her. 'You don't look it.'

Megan ignored the compliment. 'When I first heard about you, when I saw that photograph of you and Rory and Emma on the boat – do you know the one I mean? It's in their sitting room on the oak dresser.'

'Yes.' The photograph had been taken when Rory and I were about nineteen. Both home from university for the summer holidays.

'Well, I asked Daniel about it. He said I'd better watch out because you had a crush on Johnnie.'

I dropped my book face down on my thighs and groaned. 'Daniel was stirring.'

'So you didn't have a crush on him?'

'Well, I sort of did. When I was a teenager, I thought he was cool. I hardly ever saw him though.'

Megan sat up and hugged her knees, her face turned towards mine, her green eyes watchful.

'But that's irrelevant, isn't it? I had a huge crush on a boy that I only ever met once. When I think about him, I still get this sense of having left something unfinished.'

'I also had a crush on my history teacher. And several of Rory's friends. And at least half a dozen pop stars.'

'But none of them meant as much to you as Johnnie.'

For some reason I looked at Sam when she said that. Really looked at him and I felt that jerk of love, the instant connection between us. He jumped up and came over to where I lay and put his hand on mine.

I pushed it away. 'Megan, what's this about?'

'Do you really need to ask?'

'You think I'm trying to take Jonathan away from you? I'm not.'

Megan shaded her eyes. 'You don't understand what damage you're causing. I love him, and if he leaves me, I don't know what I'll do.'

She bent her head so that her thick blonde hair fell forward. For a moment I thought she was crying and I quashed my irritation. 'I'm not in the slightest bit in love with him. He's like a brother to me, that's all.'

Megan lifted her head. Her eyes were clear and shining.

'Yes, you are, Alice. But he doesn't love you. He's just all mixed up because of Rory. He's vulnerable at the moment. So you have to back off.'

'Back off? Oh, for goodness' sake. This is a stupid argument. Either you believe me or you don't.'

Megan made a visible effort to control herself. 'OK. Sorry. I didn't mean it. It's just that I have my life all sorted out and Johnnie is an important part of it. I didn't want to say this, but really, you have to look at the way you behave round him and you have to stop coming on to him. He told me he's finding it terribly awkward.'

Speechless with anger and shame, I leapt up and walked away, to the boundary of the property and into the lane. Sam caught up with me and put his arm around my shoulders. I stiffened at first but he persevered.

'Hey.'

'Hey,' I said.

He stopped and made me face him. 'Are you talking to me yet?'

I shrugged and met his gaze reluctantly. 'I suppose so.'

We walked on and turned up a dirt path into the olive grove and I looked back at the house. There was no way I could relax there now.

'What're you thinking?' Sam asked.

'That I want to go home.'

He smiled. 'Same here. I've had enough of the Walkers to last me a lifetime.'

I didn't answer at first because I knew I'd made a fool of myself, and I knew Sam knew it too. Now Megan had arrived and made it perfectly clear that she didn't trust me to be on my own with her fiancé, I really did feel as though I'd outstayed my welcome. She didn't have to worry. I had got the message.

'I suppose we'd better go back,' I said. 'Or Megan will accuse me of throwing a tantrum.'

We wandered back into the kitchen. They were all there and there was an odd tension about the place. It felt as though they'd been talking about me. Brian was standing, his hand on the back of a chair, Emma unloading her shopping, Megan sitting with one leg elegantly crossed over the other, swathed in a beautiful ivory-and-green sarong that slid away to reveal a shapely knee. She gave me an odd look, part curious, part hostile.

Jonathan was standing beside her, but he looked up as I walked in and held my gaze for just long enough to tell me what I wanted to know. He felt bad that he had been disloyal to her. Seeing them together made me miserable, insecure and jealous. Being in the same room as them was pure torture.

My mobile, which was on the windowsill, plugged into a charger, started ringing. I picked it up. Private number.

'Alice Byrne?' It was a man's voice, clipped, with a hint of South London.

'Yes.'

'This is Detective Inspector Palmer from the Metropolitan Police. Do you have five minutes? I need to ask you a couple of questions regarding a friend of yours. A Mr Matthew Clarke . . .'

Chapter Twenty

I THOUGHT IT WAS A HOAX CALL BUT IT EVIDENTLY WASN'T. 'MATT? Why? What's happened?'

'I'm afraid Mr Clarke is dead, Miss Byrne.'

I felt the blood leave my face and automatically turned to Sam. He raised his eyebrows. 'But he can't be,' I said. 'I only saw him about a week ago.'

I looked round at the others. They were all politely pretending not to be curious. I pulled the cable out of my phone, walked out to the pool and sat down on one of the loungers. 'How did you get my number?' Was that the wrong thing to say?

'We spoke to the woman in the flat below yours.'

'Oh, yes, of course. Sorry.' I always left her with contact details if I went away, in case something happened, like a break-in or a plumbing disaster. She did the same. 'Can you please tell me what's going on?'

'Matthew Clarke was murdered on the night of the thirtieth of July.'

My jaw dropped. 'Murdered?'

The Inspector gave me a moment to allow the statement to sink in. My head was beginning to ache and I shifted my position so that I was in the shade of the parasol. Poor Matt. I couldn't take it in.

'As far as we can ascertain, you were one of the last people to see him alive. Would you mind just taking me through that day, Miss Byrne?'

245

I did as I was told but I could feel anxiety balling in the pit of my stomach. 'The taxi driver dropped me off at home. You'll be able to track him down easily. He was in the ranks outside Richmond station. He had short, thick grey hair and an earring in his left ear. Oh, and I spoke to my next-door neighbour. He was out walking his dog. I don't have his telephone number but his name's Charlie Clifford. He should remember. And then I let myself into the house,' I finished, adding, 'That's about it really. Not much to tell.'

I didn't mention the darkness of the flat or my jolt of fear as Sam's hand clamped down on my arm.

'What time did you arrive home?'

I wasn't altogether sure. I had been too busy making a fool of myself. 'Around eleven, I think. Not later than eleven thirty though, because I was in bed by midnight.'

'Did anything happen to upset Mr Clarke while you were in the cab?'

The line wasn't very good and I had to ask him to repeat the question. I was about to say absolutely nothing, but I realized in time that if they questioned the taxi driver, he had witnessed our kiss so there was no point in concealing it or lying. He had also witnessed my humiliation.

'I don't know if he was upset particularly.' I hesitated and looked round, but Sam wasn't with me. 'We kissed and he, well, he told me he wasn't ready.'

'He kissed you or you kissed him?'

'I kissed him. But it didn't mean anything.' I paused and then blurted out, 'How did he die?'

'We're not releasing that information yet. I'll need you to come into the station to make a detailed statement. When will you be returning to England?'

I told him the date and rubbed my temples.

After he'd hung up I sat staring at the pool for a few minutes, watching a dead beetle float slowly from one side to the other.

After a while the others came out and Emma sat down beside me.

'What on earth's happened?' she asked. 'You're as white as a sheet.'

'Matt Clarke is dead. That article in the newspaper – it was his body they found.'

'Oh my God,' Megan said, clutching Jonathan's arm. 'You're kidding?'

'I'm not.'

'Why did they want to speak to you?'

'Because they think I might have been the last person to see him alive.'

'They can't seriously believe you had anything to do with it,' Emma said.

I put my head in my hands. 'I have to go and make a statement once I'm back. I feel like a criminal.'

'Did they tell you how he died?' Jonathan asked.

I looked into his eyes and saw two things there: a genuine concern and a journalist's habitual curiosity. 'He was murdered.'

'Jesus,' Megan said.

'Poor chap,' was Brian's measured reaction. 'I wonder who he upset.'

'Well, he didn't upset me.' Hysteria bubbled inside me. 'Maybe a disgruntled client? God, why am I laughing? It's not in the slightest bit funny. The poor man is dead.'

'Alice, you have nothing to worry about,' Emma said. 'I'm sure the police will be able to corroborate everything you tell them and that will be the end of it. No one in their right mind could think you would have anything to do with something so appalling. You were just the easiest target. Of course they have to question you thoroughly. They wouldn't be doing their job otherwise.'

'That's right,' Brian said. 'Don't take it to heart. They're probably interviewing any number of people. Just forget about it for now and enjoy the rest of your holiday. There's nothing you can do.'

'I'm sorry. I'm going to try and get a flight home tomorrow. They want me to make a statement and I can't just leave it hanging.'

Jonathan moved away from Megan so that she had to drop her hand. 'Did they ask you to come home immediately?'

'No.'

'Then you don't have to,' Megan said. 'Stay a little longer. Have your holiday.'

She didn't sound all that sincere. I held her gaze. 'Yes, I do have to. It's for the best.'

Jonathan allowed me to use his laptop to change my flight and that evening I packed while Megan and Emma went to the super-market and the two men sat on the terrace drinking a convivial lager. Their voices were low-pitched and comforting. Sam was dozing and once I had finished I left the room, closing the door quietly behind me. I didn't want to disrupt Brian and Jonathan's conversation, so I walked past them, heading for the orchard.

Jonathan made to stand up but I shook my head.

'It's all right. I'm just going for a last look round.'

They raised their bottles to me and Brian shaded his eyes with his hand. 'Saying goodbye to the place?'

I smiled. 'Yes.'

I almost stumbled, I was so anxious to appear at ease in front of Jonathan. I didn't want him to know how incredibly screwed up I was feeling. If he felt the same, he was very good at hiding it.

In the orchard, I leaned on an ancient apple tree and took in the landscape. I wished I could turn back time. Not so long ago, my life had been straightforward and predictable. I had my flat, my work and a not bad social life, considering I wasn't great at people. Now look at me. I was a wreck.

I wondered if Jonathan and Megan had made love since she arrived. Of course they had. Thinking about it nearly ripped me apart. If I had been certain that he was in love with me, I would have fought for him. But I wasn't. I didn't doubt he cared, but I had a feeling Emma was right, he was confusing the instinct to help me with deeper feelings. Megan would have reminded him what he had with her.

God, I had far too much time on my hands.

I heard a step behind me and turned to find Jonathan approaching. He was tanned and his hair was beginning to bleach in the sun. The sleeves of his creased white shirt were rolled up and his large feet were bare and dirty. He put his hand on a branch and leaned forward.

'Are you worrying about this Matt business?'

I nodded.

'Well don't. Nothing bad is going to happen to you, and if there's any problem give me a call and I'll see if I can help. I'll be home by Thursday.'

'I expect you'll have a lot to do, what with the wedding and everything.'

Jonathan's smile faded. 'Alice, don't.'

When I was younger, I thought that Jonathan was infallible but I'd grown out of that misconception. He was as flawed as any other man and as prone to making mistakes. I had to face it. Something had happened between us, but I didn't know exactly what it was, and neither, I suspected, did he. Anyway, if it came to it, did I really want to be his final fling before he settled down with someone else? To my relief, this thought made me angry. I resented being used as a sounding board, or worse, a port to turn to if he and Megan split up. Second best.

'I'm not your bloody safety net.'

'What are you talking about?'

I shrugged. 'It's like you want to keep me around in case it doesn't work out with Megan. I've had enough.'

He reacted as if I had hit him. It gave me a certain perverse satisfaction to goad him into losing his cool.

'Jesus. You've had enough? Alice, sometimes you drive me up the wall.'

'You'll know what it feels like then. Be straight with me, Jonathan. Please. I want to know if you're just my friend or if there's something more. I want to be able to walk away from you and know it's over.' I clenched my fists. 'Not that there's anything to be over.' I was ashamed of my outburst. 'Oh, just go away, leave me alone.'

'I'm not going anywhere until we've talked this out.'

'There's nothing to talk about. I've said more than I meant to. You go and get married, that should send the right message.'

I sat down on the dry ground, defeated. Jonathan joined me. I could feel his eyes on my profile but I wouldn't look at him.

'No. I apologize, Alice. I've been selfish. You're ten years younger than me. You should be with someone your own age.'

I rubbed my forehead with the heel of my palm. I was on the verge of tears. That wasn't what I wanted him to say.

'What does anyone's age matter?'

'It doesn't any more.'

He leaned back on his elbows and turned his face to the sun. His eyes were closed and I couldn't stop myself. I ran the back of my hand against his jaw.

He groaned. 'Alice.'

And then Sam appeared, striding towards us from the house. He came right up to me and crouched down.

'Touch him again and I'll kill him.'

I hugged my knees. I was determined to ignore him.

'I'm sorry,' I said to Jonathan.

Sam raised his eyebrows but he didn't smile. He is not real, I told myself. Sam is not here. Maybe that was the answer, to behave as though he wasn't. To let him see that I could wrest control of my life out of his hands.

'Be careful,' Sam said.

I was so angry with him, I flipped. 'For God's sake. Leave me alone.'

'You want me to go?' Jonathan said, frowning. 'I'm not sure what's going on here—'

'Not you,' I interrupted. 'Sam. Shit.'

'Alice, whoever it is you think you can see, he's not here.'

He put his hand on my arm but I knocked it away. 'What about Les Baux? You told me you felt a presence. How do you explain that? Sunstroke?' I just stopped myself saying, *he tried to suffocate you in your bed.*

'It was a feeling. It was suggestion. Come on, Alice, give me a break. I don't have an explanation, but whatever did happen, Sam isn't real. He can't be. You have to hang on to that. We both do.'

He paused and I didn't speak. I was waiting for him to go on, hoping, I suppose, that he had the answer, but knowing that he didn't. Why should he understand? Why should anyone?

'Let me help you. I won't walk away, I promise.'

'I'm not going to drag you into my problems.'

'You know I don't care about that.'

'You only think you don't. Look at me, Jonathan. I'm a total mess. Sam's still here. He's with me most of the time. Are you willing to deal with that?'

'All I know is that I can't stop thinking about you and I can't get married. I made a mistake but it's not too late to put it right.'

'Don't,' I whispered, aware of Sam's narrowed eyes. 'It would never work.'

'What do you want? Do you want me to tell you I love you? Alice, honestly, I don't know. I'm not used to this. Normally, women just come along and I get attached without actually knowing what's happening.'

I laughed and I hoped it sounded sarcastic.

'Sorry, I know how arrogant that sounds. All I mean is, my relationships just seem to happen, without much effort on my part. I'm not used to longing for someone.'

251

My nose was about to drip. I sniffed and did my best with my sleeve. Jonathan waited.

'You don't understand,' I said.

'Then explain. Talk to me.'

'Don't bother,' Sam said coldly. 'He'll never understand. He'll just try and make you think he does. You can't possibly be so naïve that you can't see through him.'

I suppose I did, in a way. It didn't mean I could love him any less though. Couldn't Sam see that? Obviously not. 'Jonathan, you'd better go. I'll be all right. I just need a bit of time.' I added, looking him straight in the eye, 'With Sam.'

'This is lunacy. I can't leave you in this state.'

We stood up together and I made a bit of a deal about dusting off my trousers. Jonathan waited patiently, then took my chin in his hand and forced me to look at him. His steady gaze weakened me. I wanted to be swallowed up by him, to be pulled in and crushed until I lost myself entirely. His smile reached inside me and it was beautiful and unbearable. I closed my eyes. I thought if I couldn't see Sam, if Jonathan's touch obliterated him from my mind, then he couldn't hold his place in my brain, his tentacles would loosen and slip away. There had to be only room for one of them.

'Alice,' Sam shouted. My eyes flew open.

Behind Jonathan, Sam stooped to pick up a stone. He raised it above his head, his eyes blank, and I jerked back, away from Jonathan and threw myself at him and went down, hitting my knee hard on the impacted earth. Jonathan caught me before I fell forward on to my hands and pulled me back up, brushing the dust off my clothes. I was trembling all over, I could barely get the words out and my knee was agony.

'Are you all right?' Jonathan asked.

'Fine. I tripped.' I remembered Matt saying the same thing. Maybe Sam really had tripped him up. What else had he done? 'Please go back to the house. I'll be OK.'

'You're obviously far from OK. Tell me what to do.'

I limped away from him and pulled myself together. 'You can't do anything. I promise I'll come and find you. I need to do this on my own.'

He stared at me. 'Are you in danger?'

My heart was pounding. 'No. Absolutely not.'

He looked as though he had plenty more to say and I wondered if he was deliberately encouraging me to engage with Sam in front of him, and taking mental notes.

'You should go,' I said.

He evidently knew when he was beaten. He shoved his hands into his pockets and reluctantly walked away. Sam tried to follow him, but I grabbed his arm and he turned snarling to me.

'Let me go, Alice.'

I wanted to scream, but I made myself whisper. 'Are you completely insane? You could have hurt him.'

He pulled me round so that my face was close to his and I could see beads of sweat on his brow. 'What will you do if he leaves Megan?'

I stiffened. 'I have no idea.'

'I thought you had chosen me.'

'What choice do I have, precisely? You just won't go away.'

'I love you more than he does. You're my whole life.'

I looked back at the house, wondering if anyone was watching. I heard Brian calling me. Sam was still going on.

'If I knew I had you, I wouldn't behave like this. You do this to me, Alice. You frighten me. I can't lose you.'

'Oh God.' I pressed my fingers against my head, desperate. 'It's like talking to a brick wall. You think you can control me, but you really can't. I'm better now. Just go away. Please.'

'You told me you'd take care of me.'

'Sam, for God's sake. Be reasonable.'

I could feel panic rising. He was not going to understand or even accept my point of view, no matter how hard I tried. He was only thinking about himself.

'Were you lying, then?'

I rubbed the side of my neck. 'No, of course not. But I didn't know what you were capable of then. I do now.'

'Do you?'

I held his gaze. 'I think so. Frankly, I don't trust either of you.'

'What do you mean?'

'Nothing.' I wished I hadn't said anything.

'No. Tell me, Alice. There is something, isn't there?'

I shrugged. It was just a suspicion. Something I hadn't meant to voice. 'I'm probably wrong. But I think he may be writing all this up.'

Sam laughed. 'I wouldn't be surprised. It would be a waste if he didn't. As far as he's concerned, I mean. Why don't you ask him?'

'Because I don't want to. What difference would it make? He can't write and publish anything about me, not unless I agree.'

'I'm sure he knows the rules. Why don't you take a look?'

'Yeah. Right. I'll go and ask him now, shall I?'

'Of course not. Do it tonight, when he's asleep. I'm sick of being the bad guy. If he's pissing you around for the sake of his career, I want to know about it and you need to.'

'I don't want to snoop through his things.'

'Alice, Jonathan is a journalist. His morality is different from yours. Don't trust him. And don't think he's the answer to all your problems, because he isn't.'

I looked up. 'I don't think that.'

But had I? I wondered. In my heart had I hoped that Jonathan would step in and sort everything out for me? I was an idiot if I had. Why would someone like Jonathan want me, when he had Megan?

'I might not be what you want, but I'll never let you down.'

Sam's voice filled my mind, clouding it, so that I couldn't think straight.

I contemplated him in silence and then I shrugged, defeated. 'Fine.' At least I'd be doing something proactive.

I set the alarm on my phone for three a.m. The floors were tiled so there were no creaking boards, but I was still terrified that I would wake the others. In the den, Jonathan's computer whirred into life when I hit the space bar, and even that sound seemed alarmingly magnified. I don't know what I expected. Some polished piece, I suppose. What I found, when I checked his recent documents, was a series of disjointed notes. The digital equivalent of scribbles in a notepad.

Doesn't understand herself – not sure she ever has – can be contradictory.

Tendency to swing from open to guarded. Scared of showing she's vulnerable?

Childhood – possible root of Sam issue? Viz. lack of friendships amongst peers. Parents/benign neglect. Fear of rejection inbuilt or nurtured? Needs to be explored. Sam cannot reject her.

My brother. Where does she go from here? At the moment she feels besieged both by what is going on inside her head, and by her mother and father who, since the accident, seem to have finally realized she's as important as their other kids.

Myself. Am I too involved to see straight? Maybe persuade her to talk to someone who doesn't know her so well?

All too pat? Am I oversimplifying? Maybe there is something else.

I scrolled down.

She will be hurt, I think. But she has to stop trying to forestall the inevitable. Any relationships with men have the potential to devastate her – consequently unwilling to take risks.

And then:

> The strength of her conviction is affecting me. It's as if it's not something she's learned, or appropriated somehow, it's just part of what makes her. So much so that I could almost believe in Sam. But there are explanations: a nightmare; too much sun; a trick of the light. Or is it just me wanting her not to be crazy?

Crazy. My heart was pounding and I felt nauseous, as if I had been eavesdropping and heard people talking about me. Sam was still reading. I didn't want to believe that Jonathan, after everything he had said, could betray me so coolly. Was all that emotion just a way of manipulating me into opening my heart to him? How could I have been so stupid and gullible?

I said sharply, 'OK, that's enough.' And shut it down.

Chapter Twenty-One

JONATHAN OFFERED TO DRIVE ME TO THE AIRPORT BUT MEGAN protested and in the end a cab was called. It felt as if I was leaving in disgrace. The next morning I presented myself at the police station where I was greeted with a request from DI Palmer for my fingerprints. Palmer wasn't what I expected at all. I had imagined him as thin with beetling eyebrows. In fact, he was fleshy, with a double chin and hair thinning at the top. His eyebrows were rather ordinary.

'We need to rule you out,' he said. 'Forensics have a couple of prints that we don't have a match for.'

'But I was there. I went into his flat when I bumped into him a few weeks ago. He asked me in.'

'Did you touch anything?'

'Possibly. But I didn't stay for longer than ten minutes.'

A young officer brought in an inkpad and a form with two rows of five boxes printed on it. He wrote my name at the top and I placed each finger on the pad then pressed them firmly into the squares. My hands were shaking. Palmer waited in silence until the man had left.

'Do you have any proof you entered the flat on that day?'

I thought about it and nodded. 'His neighbour saw me leave. She was getting into her car and she caught my eye. I'm sure she'll remember. Her name is Carol Margulies.'

'Yes, we've spoken to Ms Margulies. She didn't mention that though.'

'It doesn't mean it isn't true. She may have forgotten. You can ask her, can't you?'

He picked away at that point, although it seemed barely relevant to me. I was beginning to think he actually wanted me to be guilty.

After a few minutes there was a knock on the door and Palmer stood up. He opened it, leaned out and appeared to be conferring with whoever was in the corridor. When he came back to the table he looked very serious.

'Miss Byrne, I'd like permission to search your flat.'

I was horrified. 'On what basis?'

'Your prints match those found on a photograph of the victim and his girlfriend. The photograph was in a drawer.'

'That's because Matt put it in there,' I protested. 'They only broke up recently and he didn't want to be reminded of her. Look, don't you need a warrant?'

'Only if you refuse permission. But I have to warn you that the application process takes time and I don't want to have to keep you hanging around here all day. I'm sure you're busy.'

He didn't look in the least bit sure of it. He looked as if he thought I had all the time in the world.

'I thought I was just here to make a statement. Am I a suspect?'

'You're helping us with our enquiries, and I hope cooperating. We won't take long. Would you mind handing over your keys?'

My hands were shaking as I pulled them out of my bag. 'But what do you expect to find? Matt never came back to my place.'

The detective gave me a reassuring smile. 'Just trying to rule you out, Miss Byrne. Don't worry. My officers won't cause any damage.'

'I'll go with them,' Sam said. 'I want to know what they're looking for.'

I nodded. Perhaps it would be better if he wasn't with me. He would only get angry. All the same, I wondered why he would desert me at a time like this.

DI Palmer asked if I wanted a lawyer but I refused. I had done nothing wrong. I just wanted to get it over with and go home. He went to the door and I thought I was going to be left with the WPC, maybe softened up, but she left as well and the door closed behind them with a decided metallic click. At one point, an officer came in with a cup of tea which I accepted gratefully. The hands on my watch moved very slowly. I wondered what Jonathan was doing and whether he was thinking about me and a lump formed in my throat. I had to stop this. Our paths didn't cross very often and it was possible that I wouldn't see much of him once he was married. I missed Rory suddenly and deeply. It came out of nowhere.

'Please,' I whispered. 'Rory, if you can hear me, please do something about this. Make it all go away.'

He would have calmed me down. That was what he was good at. He would have cracked a totally irrelevant joke and distracted me.

The door opened and the two officers walked in and pulled out their chairs. Palmer didn't apologize for keeping me waiting. He looked down at some papers he had brought in with him, then at me. His frown lines were pronounced.

'How would you describe your relationship with the deceased?'

'There wasn't one really, but I suppose you could say we were friendly acquaintances. I was a shoulder to cry on.' I added, 'Not literally.'

'Did he want more than that?'

'I don't know. Maybe.'

'And what about you, Miss Byrne? Did you want more?'

'No. I liked him but I hardly knew him.'

He referred to his notes again. I tried to read them upside down but I couldn't. 'You apparently knew him well enough to invite him to your mother's wedding.'

His tone, with its strong undercurrent of accusation, caught me off guard, as it had probably been meant to, and I felt myself redden.

'Mum wanted me to bring someone. I don't have a boyfriend and I'd recently bumped into Matt, so I just called him up on the off-chance. He came as a friend, nothing else.'

Palmer leaned forward. 'But you barely knew him. Surely, there was someone else you could have asked. Someone you knew better?'

'No. Not really.' I thought about Daniel, but it wasn't worth mentioning him.

'We managed to track down the driver of the cab, and he's made a statement. When he drove Matt home, they talked. Matt apparently said . . .' He paused and checked his notes. 'That you had "scared the shit out of him".'

'That's ridiculous.' Had the two of us been on completely different planets? I couldn't believe he would say something like that; something so vile. 'I kissed him because he was holding my hands and looking into my eyes and it was dark and we'd had a few drinks. I don't understand why he would feel that way. It makes me sound like some sort of sexual predator.'

The DI shrugged. 'Women are more aggressive than they used to be.'

'Well, I'm not.'

'Of course not. Now, we've looked into the logistics of you getting to Fulham and back. It wouldn't take you long at that time of night.'

I tried to convey, in the look I sent him, that I thought he was mad. 'As I expect you know, I was in an accident. My car was totalled and I haven't got round to replacing it. The insurance hasn't come through yet.'

'I apologize.' He added, unapologetically, 'It was still early enough for public transport.'

I stared at him in disbelief. 'I didn't kill him.'

'And then getting back. That would of course have been more problematical. However, not impossible. Buses run all night to Clapham Junction and you're only twenty-five minutes' walk from there. It's doable. Frankly, if you'd had to walk the entire distance it would have taken you less than an hour.'

I shook my head. I didn't know what to say.

'For the record,' the WPC said, 'Miss Byrne has shaken her head. Would you like a glass of water?'

'No, thank you.'

DI Palmer gave me a moment and then he started to pile the pressure on. 'Matthew Clarke was killed between one forty-five and two fifteen on the night of July thirtieth. Can you account for your movements during that time?'

'No. I can't.'

'I want you to talk us through the time between leaving Mr Clarke in the taxi, which we will verify, and the next morning.'

'I went to bed and I went to sleep.'

'Do you have a witness to the fact that you remained in your flat all night?'

'No, I don't. I live alone.'

'So it is conceivable that you could have left your home and gone to see Mr Clarke, had an argument with him and killed him and been back in bed by the small hours of the morning.'

I wondered if I looked like a killer to them. I said patiently, 'There is no way I would have dragged myself all the way from Battersea to Fulham, killed a man who weighs at least three stone more than me and then waited at a bus stop covered in blood.'

'We didn't say anything about blood.'

'No. Sorry. I just assumed there would be blood. I don't know. At any rate, I'm not a murderer and that particular night I was tired and I wanted to sleep so I took a sleeping pill and I slept. Alone. I was certainly not capable of working out night bus schedules. This is ridiculous. He was a friend. Why the hell would I want to harm him?'

'I don't know, Miss Byrne. That's what we are trying to find out. Granted, it wouldn't have been easy for you, but we are aware of your mental difficulties . . .'

'My what?' I was flabbergasted.

'You've had some emotional upheaval lately.' His voice was gentle again but his eyes were hard. 'It has been suggested that you may need help, with your condition.'

'My condition? I don't have a condition.'

'You were involved in a car accident and suffered severe head injuries. I'd call that a condition. And you've been to see a psychiatrist, so surely that proves that you think you have a problem.'

That completely threw me. 'How do you know that?'

'As I said, we spoke to Ms Margulies.' He smiled at me, as if he thought I was a bit dim.

'OK. Well, I went because my father asked me to. And anyway, whatever I said to her was confidential. If she told you anything, she was breaking the rules.'

'She certainly didn't tell us the details of your conversation. You can rest assured of that.' He paused. 'So it's your father who thinks there's a problem, not you?'

I had to remind myself not to take it personally. He was fishing, that was all. I had watched enough murder mysteries to know how it worked. Everything he said was probably carefully crafted to provoke me into making some startling admission.

'No. Well, yes, maybe he does. What has this got to do with Matt anyway?'

'Maybe nothing. We're trying to build a picture of the twenty-four hours before his death, and you feature prominently in that time frame.' His voice softened, became quite kind. 'Is there anything you want to tell me?'

I was exasperated. 'No. Explain to me how I did it? Did I call a cab?'

'Do you own a bicycle?'

'No.'

There was a tap on the door. DI Palmer stood up and went outside. When he came back in his expression was stony. He sat down again, his back very straight, his forearms resting on the table.

'There are bloodstains on one of your shirts, Miss Byrne. It was found bundled up in your washing basket. Forensics will be comparing those stains to Mr Clarke's blood, but you may be able to save us time. Where did the blood come from?'

'Which shirt? Sorry, I forget a lot of things since my accident. Did they say what colour it was?'

'White. There's a long smear of blood on one of the sleeves. Surely you'd remember if you hurt yourself?'

I closed my eyes and thought hard. Sometimes things came back immediately, sometimes half an hour later, sometimes days later. It was as though my damaged synapses were reaching blindly for each other. If I got lucky, they would connect quickly. This time, I got lucky.

'It was the shirt I wore to visit the psychiatrist. I chucked it in the wash but the stains didn't come out. I meant to bleach it but I forgot all about it.'

'So where did the blood come from?'

'It was Matt's.'

DI Palmer's expression didn't change. 'Matthew Clarke's blood?'

'Yes.'

I explained about Matt tripping up and the piece of glass, but he didn't look convinced. I couldn't believe this was happening to me, how Matt's death could have anything to do with our very tenuous relationship. It was just a terrible coincidence that he had died that night. Perhaps they should be interviewing Sam, not me. It was no more ridiculous. He had the motive and the opportunity and I was almost ready to believe that he had the capability. I wondered what Palmer would say if I suggested that Sam might be the killer. He'd send for a police psychologist, but I would have dug my grave. The words *of unsound mind* popped unbidden into my head. And would he be right? God. I really didn't know. I didn't feel mad, but neither did I feel altogether sane. I was somewhere in between and it wasn't an easy place to be.

'Miss Byrne, I strongly advise you to call a lawyer. If you don't know of any, I can organize one for you.'

How on earth had it come to this? I nodded mutely.

I was taken to a small office and given the use of the phone. I called Dad, who turned out to be on location in South Africa. He nearly choked when I told him what had happened.

'You are kidding me?'

'No, I'm not.'

'Jesus. Well, don't you worry, sweetheart. I'll call Shoba. Whatever she's doing, I'll make sure she's with you within the hour. How the hell did you get mixed up in this? Your mother must be doing her nut.'

I was trying very hard not to cry. 'Mum doesn't know yet.'

'Oh, Christ. You're going to have to warn her.'

'I can't speak to her.' I gave up holding back the tears. I sniffed. DI Palmer produced a tissue and I blew my nose. It pissed me off that I had cried in front of him. 'She's still on her honeymoon. I can't face it. And anyway, I'm not sure they'll let me make another call.'

'In that case I'll get hold of Olivia.'

'Please don't, Dad.'

'Don't be silly, sweetheart. You can't just pretend it isn't happening, and frankly, you need the support of your family. Do you want me to talk to the detective?'

'No. I don't think it would help. I'll call you as soon as I can.'

'I wish I was with you. Why am I never around when you need me?'

'You're here now. That's all that matters.' I said it to make him feel better. Why did he have to ask me questions to which there was no answer?

In the end, it was two hours before the lawyer turned up. Two long hours sitting on a narrow cell bed with no one to talk to. I contemplated my situation with a kind of stunned detachment. There was nothing more I could do or say that would convince the police. They smelled an easy victory.

I had spoken to Shoba at Rory's inquest, but I hadn't got much of an impression of her, beyond the air of professionalism and her diminutive size. Her mouth was uncompromising and her sloping, long-lashed green eyes were keenly intelligent. She was dressed in black, but her fingers and ears were laden with gold jewellery. The hand I shook was fine-boned and strong. We were given five minutes so that I could explain my side of what had happened. Kabir watched me throughout and only spoke once I had finished.

'Thank you, Alice. Shall we?'

She stood up and knocked on the door and we were taken back into the interview room. DI Palmer switched the tape recorder on.

'For the record, Miss Byrne's lawyer, Ms Shoba Kabir, has entered the room. Miss Byrne, we have a few more questions to ask you. I want to talk to you about the day you met Matthew Clarke outside his flat.'

I swallowed hard and nodded. We went through it, with Shoba repeatedly interjecting, much to the irritation of Palmer. He kept on referring to my 'vulnerable state'.

'And subsequent to that meeting, you invited him to your mother's wedding, despite disliking him. Why would you invite a man you didn't particularly like to an important family event?'

'I don't know. I just did.'

'Because in fact, Miss Byrne, you did like him, maybe more than he liked you.'

'You're making assumptions, Detective,' Kabir said. 'Alice, you don't need to comment.'

Palmer closed his eyes for a second. Then he opened them and nodded at Shoba. 'Thank you, Ms Kabir. Miss Byrne, you've told us that Mr Clarke invited you into his flat. For what purpose?'

I felt like asking why it was necessary to cover the same ground again, but there was nothing to be gained from irritating him so I answered his question civilly. I was very aware of the time and I was getting worried. I wondered how long they were allowed to keep me. Forty-eight hours? I wasn't sure and didn't want to ask.

'Let me check I've got this right,' Palmer said. 'You met for the first time at your father's wedding?'

'Yes.'

'And the second time . . .' He glanced down at his notes. 'Was at a supper party?'

'Yes.'

'You had recently been involved in a road traffic accident where you not only lost your best friend, Rory Walker, but you sustained head injuries severe enough to put you in a coma.'

'That's right.'

'And on the third occasion, you were coming away from a session with a psychiatrist. In the last two instances, you latched on to Mr Clarke as a means of emotional support and subsequently became obsessed with him—'

Shoba interrupted, 'Detective Inspector, might I remind you . . .'

He held his hand up apologetically, but he'd said it and it was too late to take it back.

'It isn't true,' I insisted. 'I didn't have any feelings for him. He's just a bloke.'

'Was just a bloke,' DI Palmer said. 'You said he rejected your advances in the taxi.'

I blushed. 'That's right.'

'So would it be fair to say you were angry?'

'No. I wasn't angry. I was embarrassed.' Under the desk I dug my fingernails hard into the palm of my hand, hoping that the pain would help me keep it together.

'Can we go back to the White Cross Pub in Richmond? You say that you mainly talked about the break-up of his three-year relationship with Celia Lyndes.'

Half an hour later we were still plodding through it. I was shattered but I sat up straight and kept my eyes on his face. I wanted him to think that I wasn't afraid but the truth was that I was desperately scared, even with Shoba Kabir beside me.

Palmer leaned forward as if to compensate for the space I had put between us.

'Give me some reason, any reason, to believe you.'

Shoba cut in: 'My client has no further comment. Either charge her or let her go.'

The detective slapped his hands on the table with a grunt of frustration. 'Ms Kabir, we have clear grounds for suspicion and I intend to hold Miss Byrne for a further twenty-four hours.'

My voice came out as a shriek. 'I can't do that.'

What if it got back to one of my clients? How on earth would I explain it? How could I tell anyone I was being held in a police station on a murder charge? The news would spread like wildfire. No one would ever use me again.

Palmer just looked at me.

I was struggling not to cry but with the panic the doubts were creeping in. If I could interact with Sam, it stood to reason that I could do other things too. What if he was just a dream or a series of blackouts, and those times when I thought I was with him, I was actually doing something else?

'DI Palmer,' Kabir said softly, 'that is completely inappropriate. She should at least be allowed to go home and get some rest. You've already searched her flat.'

Palmer looked grumpy. 'I would prefer it if she stayed here, but failing that, I would strongly recommend that she stay with a responsible relative. Not on her own.'

As I started to protest, the solicitor put a firm hand on my arm.

'That won't be a problem. At any rate, I suggest we get a

psychiatric assessment before we go any further. My client has suffered a head injury and is in no condition to be locked up in a cell. Miss Byrne's father has confirmed that she can stay with his family for as long as you deem it necessary.'

DI Palmer looked as if he was weighing up his options. I could hear a telephone ringing outside the interview room and for some reason it reminded me of something. Something important. I closed my eyes and listened, frustrated as the memory evaded me. It was like trying to catch feathers. The phone stopped ringing and I let out the breath I had been holding.

'Alice?' Shoba said. 'Is everything all right?'

And then it came back to me and I almost laughed with relief.

'I can account for where I was that night. I can prove I was at home in bed. I had a dropped call. I was fuggy because I'd taken something to help me sleep and I forgot all about it.'

DI Palmer frowned. 'Who was it?'

'I have no idea. That's the point of dropped calls. Whoever it was didn't speak to me and I was too groggy to check the call register. But it must have been at about the time Matt died.'

'Was the call to your mobile or your landline?' His expression was icy.

'My landline. But you'll be able to find out what time it was made, won't you? You have the technology for that?'

The DI's response was grudging. 'Yes, but it might have saved a lot of time and trouble if you had remembered this earlier.'

'Don't you think I would have told you if I had?'

Palmer sighed and turned to the WPC. 'You can turn the recorder off now, Elliott.'

Both the officers left the room and Shoba and I waited. I was embarrassed about wasting her time, but she seemed not to mind. We talked about inconsequential things like the weather and our jobs and, after a while, we fell silent. I was uncomfortable on the plastic chair and longing to get away, but it was a good three-quarters of an hour before Palmer came back.

'It was a wrong number,' he said. 'I spoke to the householder. Apparently he was drunk and trying to get hold of his girlfriend. Her number is one digit away from yours.'

'Oh.' It seemed an anti-climax.

'I assume Alice is free to go,' Shoba said.

She leaned over and picked up her briefcase and Palmer shuffled his papers together. He looked more puzzled than frustrated.

'Thank you for coming in, Miss Byrne. You are free to leave.'

When Shoba accompanied me out into the foyer, we found Olivia waiting on one of the blue seats. She glanced at me when the door swung open and leapt up.

'Alice, what on earth's been going on?'

I shook hands with Shoba before I answered. 'It's all right. It's over.'

Chapter Twenty-Two

I WALKED PAST OLIVIA, HITCHING THE LEATHER STRAP OF MY BAG ON to my shoulder. She grabbed my wrist.

'Hang on. I want to make sure you're all right.'

'Well, I am. They've let me go.'

'But why did they bring you in?'

All I wanted was to go straight home, not to have to explain things to anyone, just hide in my flat for a few hours, sleep and read until I'd got the bad taste out of my mouth. I had been accused of murder, and even though there was no way I could have done it, and the police knew that, I still felt, in some obscure part of me, that I was involved somehow, or that Sam was, which amounted to much the same thing.

'I can't talk about it. Not now. I'll call you.' I pushed open the glass doors and ran down the concrete steps.

'Alice, wait.'

I stopped and swivelled round. She was standing at the top, looking so gorgeous with her long black hair and high heels that a passing policeman lost his footing.

'Don't start on me, Liv. I'm at the end of my rag.'

'I know you are. You don't have to tell me anything if you don't want to, but I'm not going to let you go off on your own. Let me at least run you home.'

'It's late, Olivia.'

'Doesn't matter. James is at home. Come on, get in the car.'

I was too exhausted to argue so I climbed into Olivia's gleaming Chelsea tractor, did up my seat belt and settled into the comfort of the leather upholstery. Olivia twisted round and dropped her bag on to the back seat. She checked her mirror and pulled out.

'I'm sorry I snapped at you,' I said. 'It's not easy to talk about this.'

'You bottle far too much up, you know. You always have. Am I such a difficult person to talk to?'

'No, I don't suppose you are.' I closed my eyes for a moment. I was sleepy. I felt her slow down as we turned a corner. 'After the wedding, Matt and I went out for a drink.'

'Go on,' Olivia said.

I told her what had happened that night and she offered to speak to Mum for me.

'Could you?' I said. 'I'm so tired of trying to explain things.'

I thought about Sam, whose name I hadn't mentioned in all this. Where was he? He hadn't come back to the police station, so he must still be at home. I would have to face him, be calm with him, while my mind sorted through the things I'd learned and the things I felt. There was something about Sam that I didn't trust. A malevolent side to him that made me fear for the people who were close to me. He didn't take kindly to my focus being on anyone but him. I couldn't see any way out.

'It must have been awful,' Olivia said. 'I'm sorry you had to go through that on your own. Oh, by the way, are you around next weekend?'

'Yes. Why?' Perhaps she was going to invite me round for a family meal. James wasn't much of a house-husband, but he made up for it on Sundays.

'Mum and Larry get back on Friday and they need help packing up the house. We have to go through all our old stuff. I dread to think what's there.'

'Fine. I can do Saturday.'

'Great.' She switched on the radio and my mind drifted with the music.

When Olivia started to reverse her Range Rover between a scruffy Fiat and my neighbour's motorbike, I was tempted to tell her to go home, but some sense that I had to try harder with her prevented me. She had been kind and I appreciated it and was touched. Maybe, we could eventually be friends. Miracles happened every day. So I kept my mouth shut and let her follow me in.

Olivia chucked her bag on the sofa and went to switch the kettle on. No sign of Sam. Good. I looked around. The police had made a token effort to restore my flat to the way they found it, but there was evidence of their search everywhere. Books had been moved, cushions rearranged, drawers not pushed back in properly. And the place stank of cheap aftershave. It took me a while to even accept that I was at home, and I spent a few moments trying to persuade myself not to care about the invasion of privacy. But it was a miserable homecoming. The worst thing was the smell; it changed the flat's whole identity.

'Are you OK?' Olivia asked.

'Yes. Fine.'

I shook off a feeling of apathy and opened a window. It didn't help, because the night was muggy and the atmosphere close. The ghostly presence of the police would fade in time. I just had to hang on. That was the easy bit.

I wondered what the Walkers were doing. Emma and Brian had known I was making my statement today and I'd had a text from Emma that morning, which I'd replied to cheerfully. And one from Jonathan that I had read with a sick feeling in my stomach. All he had said was *Call me*. But I hadn't and I wasn't going to. I knew that saying goodbye to him was the right thing to do, but I couldn't say it to his face or any other way. So I stuck my head in the sand.

I found Sam in my bedroom, curled up on the bed looking ill. There were dark shadows beneath his eyes and his hair was lank. I tried to feel pity, but I couldn't. He had brought this on himself.

He turned his head and peered at me through pink-rimmed eyes. 'I tried to get to it before they did.'

'Get to what?'

'To your shirt. I remembered about the blood. But you're back,' he added. 'What happened?'

'They had to let me go.'

I studied his face. What was he thinking? Was he relieved? His pupils were dilated, darkening his eyes so that they appeared almost black. There was a faint blue line around his mouth.

'Olivia's here,' I said.

'I know. I heard you come in.' He closed his eyes again and sank into the pillows.

I didn't want to touch him but the urge to check that he was real, that I was right and everyone else was wrong, overwhelmed me and made me place a hand on his shoulder. He felt hot and clammy.

Olivia pushed open the door, holding a cup of tea. I still had my hand on Sam, so I suppose it must have looked as though it was hovering above the bed. I snatched it away and stood up.

'Who were you talking to?'

I took the tea from her and walked out of the room. She turned and followed me.

'Was it Sam?'

'It's none of your business, Liv.'

She stiffened. 'Hey. Don't get ratty with me.'

'I'm not ratty. I'm just tired and fed up. Nobody believes a word I say. As far as you and everyone else are concerned, I'm delusional. But I know what I can see and what I can't. He's in there, if you must know. If you can't handle that, then just go away and leave me alone.'

'Alice, for God's sake, can you stop it? You have this ridiculous idea that nothing you do affects the rest of us. You float around in your own little bubble and expect your family to accept it. Mum's had enough and so have I. I know you've been unhappy since the accident, and I know how much Rory meant to you. But honestly, you have to pull yourself together and get back into the real world. You're making yourself look ridiculous.'

I put the tea down. I didn't want it anyway. 'How exactly does it affect you, Olivia? Are you losing friends over it, or sleep? What?'

'You're worrying Mum and when she's worried she nags me.'

'And that's it? I might be in my own little bubble but at least I'm not desperately trying to be like everyone else.'

Olivia recoiled as if I had spat at her. Then she shoved past me into the bedroom and started dragging at the bedclothes. Sam leapt off the bed and backed away. She pulled off the duvet and flung it on the floor and then she beat her fist into the mattress.

'Where is he then? Is he here? Come on, Sam. Show me you exist.' She threw aside the pillows and pulled up the sheet. 'What's the matter? Don't you want to fight?'

I rushed forward and we began a tug of war which ended with Olivia bursting into tears and collapsing on to my bed. I was shocked.

'Liv! I'm sorry. I didn't mean it.'

'It's the last bloody straw,' she sobbed, pressing her fingers against her eyes. 'Why can't you be normal? It's all gone wrong.'

I had a feeling she wasn't talking about me. 'What's gone wrong? What's happened?'

She started twisting her rings. At first I didn't hear what she said and had to ask her to repeat it.

'James has been having an affair.'

'Oh, God. I'm so sorry, Liv. How long have you known?'

She choked back her tears. 'A couple of months.'

'You poor thing. But why didn't you tell anyone?'

'Because . . . because Mum has been so wrapped up in the

274

wedding and I didn't want to say anything that would upset her. And you've been busy with your invisible friend.'

I let that pass. 'You both seemed fine at the wedding.'

'It was Mum's big day.'

I fetched a box of tissues from the bathroom and handed it to her. She dragged some out and blew her nose. Poor Olivia. Her life had seemed so perfect. I had been the disaster, not her. She was the one with the besotted husband, beautiful daughters and plenty of money. That was how it should be.

'So what are you going to do?'

She shrugged. 'Nothing. He promised it didn't mean anything and begged me to forgive him, and I'm trying my best. I love him. So you see, I don't have it all.' She gave me a tearful smile and wiped her eyes. 'I'd better get back. Don't tell Mum, will you? I can't face the hysterics. Or Dad either, please.'

I saw her out of the flat and then went back to the bedroom. Sam was sitting on the floor, leaning against the wall. I didn't speak to him while I made the bed but he followed me with his eyes. I could feel his hunger, his need for understanding and kindness, but there wasn't going to be any ceasefire, not on my part. I had been telling the truth when I told Olivia I'd had enough. Sam lay down again. I left him and switched on the television and fell asleep with a rug pulled over me.

A clap of thunder woke me. I went to the window, stretching my arms behind my head to loosen my shoulders. It was dark and I could see my reflection in the wet glass. I had no idea what time it was, but I guessed it must be close to midnight.

'Alice?'

I didn't reply.

'Where's Olivia?' Sam came and stood next to me and peered out at the rain.

'She left hours ago.'

'What happened at the police station? Why did they let you go?'

'Because of the phone call.'

'What phone call?' He sounded genuinely curious, not guilty.

I turned and waited until he looked me straight in the eye. 'A wrong number. I answered it, so I had to be here. Where were you, Sam?'

A flash of lightning momentarily illuminated his face and threw his beauty into eerie relief. We waited in silence for the thunder to follow and I was aware that my heart was beating too fast. Was I scared of him? Was that it?

'I didn't go anywhere.'

'You're lying.'

I walked out and shut myself in my bedroom. I heard him moving around and then silence. I lay back with my arms behind my head and tried to work out what to do next, but Jonathan kept intruding and after a while I gave up and allowed myself to think about him. I thought about how it had felt to be held and the way he sometimes looked at me and the tears started rolling down my face. I curled up into a ball. What was happening to me? How could I have allowed it to get this bad? I wanted him so badly. I didn't care what he had done. I didn't care that I might upset Megan. All I cared about was that he was the person I was meant to be with and could never be with. I was stuck with Sam and Jonathan was sleepwalking into the wrong marriage. Because I knew he wouldn't break the engagement, not for me, his case study. He had as good as told me that he let women call the shots. Megan had worked hard for this and she wouldn't let him go.

In the morning I pushed myself wearily out of bed and wandered into the sitting room.

'You look tired,' Sam said.

'I am tired.' I sounded terse but he didn't flinch.

'It's my fault. I hate it that I've made things tough for you.'

Did he think he could wear me down? I went into the kitchen, switched on the kettle and popped a slice of bread into the toaster, all the while aware that Sam was waiting. He thought he only had to be patient, that sooner or later I would see that it was hopeless even trying. The weaker side of me felt lost, but a stronger part of me wanted to fight.

I took my plate and mug into the sitting room and sat down at the table.

'You can't pretend I'm not here,' Sam said.

'No, but I can wish it.'

He let me eat before he spoke again. 'Are you saying you want me to go?'

I looked up at him. He had gone very still and I decided to call his bluff. 'If I said yes, would you?'

He slowly shook his head.

Chapter Twenty-Three

VINCENT DROVE ME DOWN TO KITTY GOODWIN'S HOUSE IN KENT FOR the TeaCake shoot, accompanied by Sam, of course. Vincent's car was a battered and ancient hatchback with a passenger window that wouldn't open, a gear stick that needed a strong arm to jerk it into first and one windscreen wiper that didn't work. When we reached and crossed the M25 I knew that we were within a mile of the spot where I'd had the accident. I thought, I can't shut my eyes, because another time I might be driving. I had to anaesthetize myself by looking for the place and acknowledging it. It was almost impossible to tell, but there were signs if you knew what you were looking for. There was the bridge that I had been shunted into, with black scrape marks up its side, and there, immediately after that, was a section of barrier on the central reservation that looked newer than the rest. I could have easily missed it at the speed Vincent was going, but I didn't and the sight gave me a jolt that stopped my breath. As we drove on I tried to control myself but anxiety and misery washed over me. I had to look away and surreptitiously wipe my eyes. Then Vincent started to talk about a gig he had been to the night before, and gradually I relaxed.

The weather wasn't perfect for an outdoor shoot, but apart from a short spell in the early afternoon, when the clouds scudded over from the west, gathering above the house for a torrential but short-lived downpour, there was plenty of time for the shots I needed. While it rained, Kitty, Vincent and I sat around the kitchen table and went through the frames. The model, Emily, an English rose with chiselled features and a wispy, breathy voice, smoked a cigarette in the shelter of the veranda.

The pictures were evocative of England in late summer, with dappled sunlight and a soft breeze that rippled the fabric around Emily's legs. She posed in the herb garden, she posed framed by a bower of late-flowering pink roses and sitting on the swing under a gnarled and lichen-crusted apple tree. Kitty was very involved, and it irritated me a little whenever she made suggestions I didn't agree with, but I smiled and let her think she knew best.

Kitty sipped her coffee and then leaned forward and peered at the screen. 'Shame about this one. There's a funny mark on it. It's gorgeous otherwise.'

Overlapping Emily was a dark smudge, almost human in form. Sam grabbed my arm but I shook him off. He had been in front of the camera for two or three seconds; no more. I was so used to him that I hadn't reacted, just kept on snapping; kept up the chatter. Had I captured his energy or an echo of his presence? Maybe it was just a trick of the light. It was impossible to tell.

'That's me,' Sam said. 'I came through. That's amazing.'

'Maybe you have a ghost,' Vincent said to Kitty. His hand moved the mouse so that the cursor hovered over the delete icon. 'Shall I dump it?'

'No,' I said. 'I need to check there isn't something wrong with my camera.'

When Vincent dropped me back at the flat that evening, the first thing I did was switch on my laptop and retrieve the picture.

'You understand what this means?' Sam said.

He was leaning over my shoulder and the proximity of his body and the heat coming off him made me feel claustrophobic. 'I don't give a monkey's what it means. I want you to go.'

'It doesn't work like that. It's out of my hands.'

I picked up my bag and went out. I'd had enough, and not just of Sam. I'd had a message from Jonathan saying, 'Please call me, Alice. I need to know you're OK.' I didn't and I felt stronger for it. I had reserves that I'd never realized I possessed.

At the weekend, Sam and I went to Mum's to help pack up the family home. She and Larry had sold Birch Road and bought a flat in Richmond. As we approached the house, I remembered the things that used to make me smile. Simon slouching off down the road in his DMs, his skinny arms draped over the shoulders of his spotty mates. Olivia strutting along, her body moving as though she thought she was Sophia Loren, her hair as black and glossy as a raven's wing. And Sam as a little boy. The house was filled with memories of Sam. That's where it should have ended, when we were still children.

Bin-bags were piled in front of the house and beginning to spill out on to the street while an ancient zed-bed and a box of bits and pieces from the kitchen had been shoved up against the low wall. The windows looked grubby and sad without their curtains. I tried to imagine it smartened up by the new owners. They had young children, and this would be their first house. Mum had taken offence because they had referred to it as a *good starter home*, as if they planned to move on to something bigger and better the first chance they got.

She let me in, kissing my cheek, her phone pressed to her ear, and went back to her conversation. I wandered into the sitting room and stood looking around. The shelves had been cleared and the cupboards stood open. The edges of the dun-coloured carpet were grey. No doubt that would be the first thing to go.

'It doesn't smell the same,' Sam said.

I turned on my heel and he followed me upstairs. I glanced at the bathroom door where the dent from Jonathan's boot still had the power to take me back two decades. I was glad Mum had never bothered replacing it. I found Olivia in her bedroom, the one that used to be ours, kneeling on the floor, going through scrapbooks. The room seemed smaller and tattier than I remembered. Olivia paused to look up and smile.

'Isn't it sad?' she said.

She was wearing tracksuit bottoms and one of her husband's stripy shirts, the tails tied at her midriff, her hair messily clipped up. I liked her better when she wasn't perfectly turned out. She probably liked me better when I was. I felt a growing warmth between us though. She had confided in me, had allowed me to see that her world was fractured too, and that must have been difficult for her.

I nodded. 'Are the girls here?'

'In the garden.' She went back to what she was doing.

I hung around for a moment, watching her. 'Are you all right?'

She swept the loose strands of hair away from her face and tucked them behind her ears. 'I'm fine. We're working things out. Thanks for listening . . . and not telling Mum. And I'm sorry I lost it about Sam. It wasn't helpful.'

I cleaned out the bathroom, chucking out the packets of hotel soaps and sticky bottles of cough mixture, and then began on my bedroom. Mum had been using it for storage and there were boxes piled to one side, but it still felt like my territory. I started with my old books.

Sam was lying on the bed with his ankles crossed, watching me. 'What are you remembering?'

I rubbed some dust off my fingers. 'Things that made me happy.'

It was true. The stuff that had made me miserable, that had permeated my life, seemed to be finally slipping away. It was as if I was shrugging off that time, realizing it wasn't the end of the world. Some people have crap childhoods. It doesn't mean their adulthood has to be horrible as well. It was just a fact of life. You grow up. You move on.

I opened a black bin-liner and started dumping things in it: a comb, a lipstick, a tube ticket. Sam picked up a photograph of me, aged four, sitting on Simon's shoulders, beaming ecstatically.

He stared at me and said slowly, 'I'll love you until the day we die, you know.'

I felt a mixture of despair and resignation. 'Why do you have to say things like that?'

I was about to throw away an old train ticket, but my eyes lingered on it. Charing Cross to Wadhurst, dated eight years ago. Wadhurst was the nearest mainline station to the village where Gabby's parents lived. That was all it was, but it reminded me of Rory and the weekend we had all spent there. The ticket represented a lost piece of time. I breathed deeply and then folded it up as small as I could and put it in the bin-bag.

A sudden squall between Elizabeth and Lottie made me jump up and go to the window. Lottie was standing on the bottom rung of the ladder to the tree house, her big sister glaring down at her, a picture of indignation. Mum appeared with a cloth in her hand to tick them off and they shot inside, Elizabeth yelling for her mother.

'It was her fault,' Lottie shouted.

My two nieces got on about as well as Simon and Olivia had. Above us, in the loft, I heard Larry laughing. I rubbed at my temples.

'Are you OK?'

'My head aches. It's so stuffy in here. I'm going downstairs.'

We joined Mum in the kitchen and then Olivia came down and shooed her daughters into the front room. The television was switched on and peace restored.

'Can I do anything?' I asked.

Mum rinsed her rag out under the tap. 'You look pale. Get some fresh air.'

'I'm fine.'

I poured myself a glass of water and sat down at the kitchen table. Mum threw a jar of Marmite into a bulging bin-bag, tied a knot and took it out to the front. When she came back, she sat down with a sigh. I assumed that was meant to convey how hard she had been working compared to everyone else.

'I wasn't such a bad mother, was I?'

'Wow,' Sam said. 'What's this all about?

'You did your best.'

Mum frowned. You didn't give her the answer she wasn't expecting, not unless you wanted a scene. 'I was very young when I had children. Only twenty when I had Simon. I wasn't much more than a child myself. It took me a long time to accept adulthood.' She smiled wistfully. 'I don't feel particularly grown up now. I did love you all though, even if I wasn't very good at showing it. I still do.'

'I know you do, Mum.' I pressed my fingers against my temples and rotated them.

'You should have told me about Matt, instead of letting me hear it from your sister. I don't understand. I would have helped.'

'I didn't want to spoil your honeymoon.' I scraped my chair back. 'Sorry. I need some air.'

I wandered to the end of the garden and sat down near the tree house where Olivia's girls had spread the old tartan rug. Strewn across it was a half-empty box of chocolate cupcakes, a lot of crumbs and two empty cartons of apple juice, the straws chewed and twisted out of shape. Sam sat on the bench outside the kitchen, his arms resting loosely on his knees. This was where he often used to sit while he waited for me to call him. Back then, I had been able to summon or dismiss him at will and he would have done anything for me. Now, although he loved me just as much, the balance of our relationship had changed.

Olivia came outside holding two cups of tea. She wandered over and handed me one before settling down on the rug.

'You are so lucky you don't have kids,' she said, and followed the statement with a long pause. 'I never asked about your holiday.'

I picked at the grass. 'It was really sad but really lovely as well.'

'Apparently, Jonathan was there.'

Olivia could never just leave things alone.

'Yup. And Megan came out a couple of days after him.'

'Wasn't it awkward?'

'No. Why would it be?'

'Well, you know, Alice. You've always had a thing about that man. I used to feel really sorry for you because you made it so obvious. Do you remember that time we all went down to Kent and you went off in a terrible strop because Jonathan was paying me more attention than you?'

That wasn't quite how I remembered it. 'I'm a little older now,' I said. 'I can control my emotions.'

I felt lightheaded and Olivia's voice was beginning to sound bird-like. Cheep, cheep, cheep. Nag, nag, nag. She was still speaking.

'Alice! You are not listening to a word I say. I'm just trying to be nice, trying to talk to you.'

I squinted at her. 'Sorry. I've got a headache. I am listening.'

'I was talking about Sam. It's Simon's theory that—'

'I don't want to know Simon's theory.'

'OK. Calm down. He's your brother, so he's entitled to have an opinion.'

Sam laughed. 'How did she come up with that?'

He was right. Even I couldn't work out her logic.

'He was blaming us, that's all,' Olivia continued. 'And I was trying to apologize. We all did our best to pretend you weren't there. You know, to live our lives as if you had never happened. Mum as well, to a certain extent. And I'm sorry, I really am. I was a horrible sister. Simon's made me see that. He thinks it'll help me if I talk to you about it.'

I noticed that Olivia had tears in her eyes.

'Is this part of a twelve-step programme?'

I shouldn't have said it. It was beneath me. But it was always going to be like this with Olivia – her lurching from good sister to bad sister – and it was always going to wind me up. She meant well and it wasn't entirely her fault. Eight years had been too big a gap. I had a feeling that having daughters had made her question her relationship with me and I knew she wanted to put things right, but it was the wrong time.

Olivia's mouth hung open. 'You don't have to be like that.'

'Sorry. You know something? I don't dwell on that time. As far as I'm concerned, it really doesn't matter any more.'

'But it does matter. When I look back, I cannot believe the things Mum did. Leaving you on your own for two weeks. And that time she left you with Simon for the weekend. Jesus. The thought of doing that with my children, oh my God, it makes me shrink up inside. It was so wrong. If that happened now, Mum would be arrested and you'd be taken into care.'

I laughed and winced. 'I suppose Dad might have taken me in.'

'It's no wonder you were so attached to that family. They filled a vacuum.'

'Don't go on about it, Olivia. I wasn't a complete no-hoper.'

'So what about Sam? If that's not hopeless, I don't know what is. Things happen for a reason, Alice, and when they happen you have to realize that what you do affects everyone else to one degree or another. If you go on like this, you are going to become someone else's responsibility eventually. The mental stuff you're going through has a tendency to feed off itself, to grow beyond what is proportionate and rational. I've been seeing a counsellor for anxiety attacks so I know what I'm talking about.'

Sam groaned and I was saved from having to respond to this convoluted speech by my new stepfather, who appeared with a box in his arms, his wiry grey hair untidy, his white T-shirt covered in smuts.

'This is full of old dolls. Do you want to check the girls don't want them before they go to the charity shop?'

Olivia smiled at him. 'I'll have a look through them in a minute.'

I tried to stand but I was feeling distinctly unsteady. 'I need to find some Paracetamol.' Parrots eat 'em all. Rory. I tensed as I held out my hand to Larry.

He pulled me up and I stood staring at him for a moment, my hand still clasped in his.

Sam shouted, 'Alice!' But he sounded like he was far away.

Darkness and stars clustered about my eyes. I wasn't in Mum's garden any more. I felt buoyed up and cushioned, but insecure at the same time, as if whatever held me was too insubstantial to last. My eyes were open, but they might as well have been closed because everything was black. I could hear voices but not clearly enough to decipher words. And then nothing. Just dreams.

Chapter Twenty-Four

IN HOSPITAL I ENDURED BLOOD TESTS, MRI AND CT SCANS, TORCHES being shone in my eyes and the disconcerting sight of the female side of my family gathered round my bedside like they were waiting for my life to end. There was no sign of Sam, hadn't been since I woke, but I was too woozy to do more than wonder if he was coming back.

I dreamt Jonathan came. He was in the hospital bed with me, wrapped around me, and it felt so wonderful, so painfully sweet and perfect. I twisted my fingers through his and pressed his hand to my heart. He kissed my eyes and my mouth and it was such a relief. He said, 'It's going to be all right. Megan knows.' As I woke up I tried to cling to the dream and even after I surrendered the images the feelings remained hot and tight inside me.

I opened my eyes and saw someone sitting in the chair close to my bed. It was Gabby. No Sam then. I moved my head gingerly. The pain was still there but it had lost its intensity and had become a nagging pressure rather than agony.

'The doctor's going to check you over,' Gabby said. 'And then if all's well I can take you home. They didn't find anything wrong, thank God. They think it was probably just a severe migraine.'

'What day is it?'

'Monday afternoon. You've only lost a day and a half.'

I closed my eyes. Gabby was silent. If, by some miracle, Sam had gone for good, that meant I was free. I would be able to move on. I felt my mood lift and then drop like a stone to the pit of my stomach. What if he was waiting for me back at the flat?

Gabby was rummaging in her handbag. She pulled out a newspaper which had been folded back over an article. 'You won't have seen this.'

She handed it to me and I read it quickly and then read it again, more slowly, as I took in its implications. The police were following a new line of enquiry. According to the journalist, they believed Matt's murder could have been a case of mistaken identity. They had probed into the flat's history and discovered that the previous occupant had fallen out with a business associate over a deal that had gone wrong and after a series of threatening phone calls and letters he had moved away and the flat had been sold. The enquiry had shifted to Spain. I handed it back with a sigh of relief. Thank God.

'At least you never made the papers,' Gabby said, folding it away.

'Lucky escape.'

'A little more than that.'

I looked at her suspiciously. 'What do you mean?'

She smiled and went a bit pink. 'I mean, your journalist friend pulled a few strings. If it had gone any further, I doubt that it would have done any good.'

It was my turn to blush. 'Jonathan?'

She nodded. 'He is such a decent man.'

Was he? I restrained the feeling of euphoria that was threatening to engulf me. He probably didn't want anyone else to get their hands on my story before him. I had opened myself up to him and made myself vulnerable. Jonathan was a very clever man. I wasn't stupid, but still . . .

Anyway, even though I would have loved nothing better than to throw myself at his feet in weepy, abject gratitude and love, there was Sam to think of too. Had he gone or not? Funnily enough, it felt different to the other times when we hadn't been together.

Then, I was always aware of him on some level, but I wasn't now, at least, not in the same way. I really believed he had somehow faded away. All the same, I wasn't ready to go home yet.

'Gabby, can I stay the night with you?'

She brightened. 'Do you really want to? I'd love it, actually. Mike's not back till the end of the week and the kids are at my parents'. I'm rattling around on my own.'

Whatever her excuse, I had a feeling it had been her plan all along.

I stood at the window of Dad's spare bedroom, pressing my hands against the sill as I gazed out at the stucco-fronted houses on the opposite side of the street. I opened it and let in the air. I could hear birdsong. A couple strolled by the house hand in hand. At the end of the street, where it met the main road, a young mother picked up her little boy and hooked him on to her hip. I watched until they disappeared, then pulled the window back down.

I pressed my forehead against the cool glass. At any rate, I was free now, and that was something to be thankful for. I wasn't going to prison and I had been cured of Jonathan. France felt like more of dream than Sam did, more like an episode I could pretend hadn't happened. I only wished I hadn't been such a complete idiot. Seeing Sam was nothing to imagining that Jonathan was genuinely in love with me. He knew how I felt, since I had as good as told him, and even if he hadn't realized how deep it went, Megan or Emma might have hinted at it. Megan particularly. He had encouraged me just so that he could get inside my head and write some crap about my delusions. Megan was welcome to him.

'Is Sam with you?' Gabby asked.

We were in the garden sitting in a patch of sunlight on the deck. I brushed a biscuit crumb off my jeans. I didn't answer for a moment. I didn't trust myself enough to say it. There was something embarrassing about the admission.

'He's gone.'

'What? Just like that?'

I felt a rush of optimism. 'Yes. He was there before I collapsed and gone when I woke up.'

I was tempted to say that it felt as though the whole thing had been a dream, if only to excuse my behaviour. But I didn't have the energy to lie. I felt grief as well as relief. Not heart-broken misery, just a sense that something important had been lost. Sam had been extraordinary.

'Well, that's something to celebrate, isn't it?'

'Yes, I suppose it is.' I looked down at my hands for a moment and then turned my head and smiled. 'I feel like a completely new woman.'

'So,' Gabby said. 'Have you spoken to Jonathan?'

I shook my head. 'I'll text him.'

Gabby looked surprised. 'He put himself out for you, Alice. Surely he deserves more than a text.'

'He's getting married.'

She stared at me until I dropped my eyes. 'There's still time to tell him.'

How did she know? Was it really that obvious? I couldn't work out what to say, so I said nothing.

Gabby put her arm around me and gave me a hug. 'So, you're just going to let him walk up the aisle with the wrong woman. If you care about him, you've got to speak to him. And you do care, don't you?'

I nodded, ashamed. There was no point lying to Gabby.

'I thought so. So did Mike. You poor thing.'

'Am I that transparent?' When she didn't answer I added, 'He doesn't love me.'

I needed to talk so badly that I told her all about France, and it was so much less embarrassing than I had expected. She listened

290

without making me self-conscious and without interrupting. When I came to the end of my narrative, I stared down at my feet.

'All that stuff about caring about me – Jonathan was just getting me to open up. It was so underhand. And if he goes ahead and publishes, I'll look like a headcase.'

'But are you absolutely sure?'

'I found out by chance and he doesn't know that I know. The mortifying thing is that he knew how I felt. So did Emma and Megan. But I was wrong. And anyway, surely to fall in love with someone, you have to spend time together? I can probably count on two hands the times I've been alone with him.'

'My parents met when Dad tripped over Mum's bag on the train to Edinburgh. He always said it was a series of small events that led him to her. That's what life is, in a way, isn't it? Small things leading to big things.'

'Those small things can lead to bad things too.'

'Yes, I know. I really think you should talk to Jonathan, Alice. It's better to have it out.'

'I can't. I already feel like a stalker as it is. Why do I get myself into such toe-curlingly embarrassing situations? You'd have thought I'd have grown out of it. And now that Sam's gone, I feel so stupid. What world was I living in?'

'Alice, can I say something?'

'That's what Olivia says when she's about to say something bitchy.'

Gabby sighed. 'I'm not Olivia. Listen, sweetie. It's so easy to fall into a victim mentality.'

I felt as though she had never known me. 'I'm not like that at all.'

'You never rebelled against your mother; you just bottled it all up. You never put Olivia back in her box. And, quite frankly, she needs it.'

I turned and looked at her. 'That's not true any more. I can give as good as I get when I feel like it.'

'Good, I'm glad there's been progress there. It's no wonder you created Sam. He's just another side of you, your vengeful alter ego. If you had stood up for yourself back then, none of this would have happened. I'm sure of it.'

'Sam was just Sam. He wasn't a version of me, and I'm not a victim.'

'Maybe, but the fact is you were imprisoned by him. You must see that.'

I nodded.

'And whether it's Sam who's locking you away from your friends, or your head playing tricks, you have to fight it. He might be gone, but I don't think it's over.' Gabby glanced at her watch. 'Would you mind if I run out to the supermarket? I've just remembered there's nothing for our supper. I'll only be half an hour.'

I sat outside in the garden and cradled my mug and tried to feel optimistic. Sam wasn't with me any more. I could get on with my life and make something of it. The idea was going to need a bit of getting used to.

Gabby was taking ages and after a while I started to feel hungry and went inside. I opened the fridge and saw a couple of chops, a pack of chicken breasts and a drawer full of vegetables. Enough for three suppers. That was odd. I retreated to the sofa, covered my feet with a rug and picked up one of the Sunday papers. After a few minutes, I realized I hadn't taken in a single word. I folded it and leaned my head back on the cushions and chewed at my lip.

Gabby had a point. When I thought back over my relationships, they were all to do with keeping other people happy and avoiding confrontation. I just wanted people to get on with each other. And with boyfriends, I'd wanted to please, not challenge them. The only person I had been able to endure the odd spat with was Rory. Maybe Sam had been nothing but a primal scream – the real me battling for dominance. And maybe I had pushed Jonathan away because I thought he wanted the Alice Byrne I had chosen to show the world. The passive Alice.

Actually, maybe not. But that was before he wrote his sodding notes for an article. Why did he have to do that? Why did he have to make me lose faith in him?

The doorbell rang and I leapt up, jolted out of my thoughts. Gabby probably had her hands full. I ran to the front door and opened it and stood there with my mouth hanging open. Jonathan was framed in the doorway.

My first instinct was to smile, the second to slam the door in his face. I compromised by holding it open but not inviting him in. Behind him, his bicycle was propped up against the wall.

'What are you doing here?'

His big shoulders drooped, as if I had let out a little of his air. It pleased me inordinately that I could get to him.

'You've been ignoring my texts and not answering my calls.'

I set my chin. 'Maybe you shouldn't have bothered coming round then.'

'Gabby called me.'

'Why would she do that?' I was astonished.

'She said you wanted to see me.'

He stopped talking and waited. I tried to hold his gaze but it was too much for me and I looked away. 'I don't know where she got that idea. I suppose you expect me to say thank you for keeping me out of the papers.'

'You can thank me if you like, but it isn't necessary.'

'It depends why you did it.'

He frowned. He wasn't used to me being shirty with him. 'So, are you going to ask me in?'

'It's not a good time.'

'Alice . . .'

'I don't know why Gabby asked you to come round. It had nothing to do with me. I don't want to speak to you.'

'Not even as a friend?'

'We aren't friends.'

He looked puzzled. 'Alice, let me in. We need to talk and this may be the only chance I'm going to get. You're on your own for once. There are things that need to be said.'

'No, you're wrong. Nothing needs to be said.' I could see that I was hurting him but I pressed on. 'Jonathan, you shouldn't have written what you did. I told you I didn't want any of this to be made public.'

He frowned and scratched his head. He did it so well that I was tempted to think his bafflement was genuine. But he was a journalist, and journalists had to have a believable front or they'd never get their foot in the door.

'What do you mean?'

'You know exactly what I'm talking about.' I paused and then repeated the words that had stuck in my head since I'd read them on his computer: '*Or is it just me wanting her not to be crazy?* All the time we were in France, and maybe even before, you were only digging for dirt. I cannot believe I was so stupid. All that stuff about Megan. How could you do something so low?'

There was a long silence while Jonathan digested this. 'You went through my private things?'

I crossed my arms and stared him out.

'Why?' he asked.

For once I wasn't going to take the whole lot on my shoulders, even if it meant that I lost the person I most wanted. I was too angry and too hurt. 'Because I didn't trust you. And I was right not to. You knew that I didn't want you to write about me – we discussed it. But you just went ahead. Were you even going to tell me before you published it?'

'Jesus.' Jonathan pushed his fingers through his hair. 'I haven't written any article. I've written notes because I thought one day you might agree to talk about it and I didn't want to lose the immediacy. I didn't want retrospect. If you'd read them properly you'd have understood that.'

Before I could stop him, he lifted my arm and walked past me. I spun round.

'You should have told me.'

He was standing beside the banisters in his green T-shirt, baggy beige cardigan and ill-fitting trousers. There was something very engaging about his lack of dress sense. But I shouldn't be thinking like that right now. He was furious with me and stupidly, part of me was actually enjoying it. Fighting back was doing me good.

'Yes, I should have. But I didn't want to. It would have made it more difficult to get a realistic take on what was happening. We'd have sat there, analysing it and picking it to pieces. I just wanted a sense of how your life is, without you influencing me.'

'But can't you see how wrong that was? You manipulated me. You're manipulating me now. I'm sick of people thinking they can mess with my mind.'

Jonathan smiled, his anger dissipating as quickly as it had come, but I didn't respond.

'I am not messing with your mind. Do you want to read what I've written? I assume you only skimmed it, seeing as it was a covert operation.'

'I read enough, and anyway I don't want to see myself through your eyes. I'd feel . . .' I hesitated, trying to think what I meant. 'Distorted.'

He raised an eyebrow. 'You think I see you in a distorted way?'

'I don't know how you see me. I don't care. You're getting married soon, Jonathan. You can't come round here and . . .'

'And what?'

'And I don't know. I have no idea what you want.'

'I want you. I'm not getting married, Alice.'

There was a short silence. I swallowed. I couldn't look at him because I knew what would happen if I did.

'What sort of man treats his girlfriend like that?'

Jonathan didn't answer and I shrugged and opened the door. 'You'd better go.'

He shook his head slowly. 'Don't do this. You're talking about the rest of our lives. Even if you keep pushing me away, it won't change anything.'

'Are you still with Megan?'

A look of pain crossed his features. 'She's been on location, but she's back later this evening. I didn't want to do it over the phone, so I'll talk to her tonight.'

I stood in silence, thinking over what he had said, wanting to believe him, wanting to run to him. But I just couldn't. I would lose face. Instead, I said sullenly, 'You're confusing me.'

'OK. You've read some of what I've written and I can't take that back. So you know that I have my theories about Sam.'

I flinched and he pushed the door shut again.

'Alice, please don't think I don't take you seriously. Some of the stuff that's happened has been very hard to explain. I don't believe in a sixth sense or the paranormal, all I know is that whoever and whatever Sam is, he is completely real for you.'

'You just won't say it, will you? You won't admit that he attacked you in your bed that night. That you felt him even if you couldn't see him.'

He sighed. 'Alice, it was a nightmare. A very real one, I grant you, but a nightmare all the same. Look at me.'

He touched my cheek gently. 'There is no Sam. There is no possibility of Sam.'

I knew he was right but deep down my gut said something different. 'He's gone now. For good, I mean. At least, I think so. I fainted the other day and, when I came to, he had disappeared.'

He threw back his head and laughed. He was my Jonathan again; the scruffy, exasperating man with the beautiful smile.

'I think I love you,' he said.

I remembered what Emma had said and what Megan had echoed, that Jonathan simply wanted to rescue me. It was in his nature.

'Are you sure you aren't confusing love with pity? You're very like your mother.'

'For Christ's sake, Alice. Sometimes you say such stupid things. What I feel for you has nothing to do with pity.'

'But it has. Ever since I met your family, you've all tried to help me. What is it about me? Do I really look that incapable? I want to do it by myself now. My relationship with you is all wrong and, if we were together, it would go on being wrong. I'd never get away from who you think I am.' I took a deep breath. 'Just go, Jonathan. I've had enough. I want to start again.'

It's true, I thought. I am better. Sam had gone. Time to move on. My throat ached.

'I'm glad you wrote about me,' I added. 'I don't think you and me would work.' As soon as I said the words, I regretted them. I was lying and he knew it.

He released his breath. 'The fact is, I need you. I wouldn't be here otherwise.'

I reached out and touched his face and he held my fingers hard against his lips. I felt a tear slide down my cheek.

'It's not enough,' I said. 'I went through your files, remember? And you took notes on my life.' My chin wobbled. 'I just want to try and get back to who I was before all this started. Just go. Please. Before I make a fool of myself.'

I opened the door for him again and he waited a moment, as if he couldn't believe that I was actually chucking him out. I couldn't believe it either. I was so scared that he would try and kiss me that I pressed myself back against the wall.

Jonathan put his hand on my shoulder and wiped away my tears with his fingers. 'It's going to be all right, Alice. You'll see.'

Then he left the house. I didn't want to watch him cycle off, so I shut the door quickly and then leaned against it while I cried. I used to pride myself on my self-control. Where had that gone?

Seconds later, I heard Gabby's key in the lock and moved away so that she could let herself in. She took one look at me, dumped

297

the carrier bag she had been holding on the floor and gave me a hug.

'I've just seen Jonathan leave. Did I do the wrong thing?'

I couldn't speak so I just shook my head.

Gabby was genuinely dismayed. 'Alice, darling, I didn't mean to cause trouble. I wanted to help. I thought if you just spoke to him . . .' She held me away from her and her eyes searched my face. 'Oh God. Alice, I am so sorry. Sweetheart, I wouldn't hurt you for the world. You know that, don't you?'

I nodded. 'It's all right. Really. It had to happen sometime. At least the worst is out of the way.' My chin wobbled again and I tried to laugh it off. 'I need a drink.'

She smiled. 'Good girl. Just tell me I'm an interfering old witch.'

'Interfering maybe,' I conceded. 'But not the rest of it.'

Chapter Twenty-Five

I COULDN'T GET TO SLEEP THAT NIGHT. MY CONVERSATION WITH Jonathan was stuck on repeat. He'd said he thought he loved me and I spoilt the moment. But then he hadn't actually said, *I love you, Alice Byrne*, and he had been so aggravatingly unapologetic about what he had done, expecting me to forgive him and fall into his arms. As if that made everything all right. I wondered whether he would do what he had said he would do, and end his engagement, or whether he had gone home, disappointed in me, and found Megan, warm, beautiful and welcoming, waiting for him. I scrunched myself into the foetal position and cried until my throat hurt.

But at least one problem appeared to have resolved itself. I was alone again. And yet my dreams were hectic. I was being chased and trapped; I was screaming at Olivia and not being heard; I had blood on my hands. I was far too hot, but when I flung the covers back I felt vulnerable. When I woke up it was light outside and the bedroom had a late summer quality to it. That was my first sensation. Then I heard the sound of breathing. I closed my eyes again and exhaled.

'Shit.'

Sam was fast asleep beside me, a lock of hair draped across his forehead; a beautiful man, but his beauty left me cold. I wanted Jonathan's face with his broken nose and the smile that left me helpless.

Sam opened his eyes and stared straight into mine. I couldn't have felt more trapped if he had locked me in a cellar. The walls of the bedroom seemed to crowd in on me and his body was so close to mine I could feel the heat coming off him. He made my flesh crawl.

OK, I thought, try to be rational. There was no way on earth anyone was actually lying beside me. The irrational side of me, the side that could no longer untangle reality from dream, felt total and utter despair. Obviously, it was all in my head. Perhaps I should go to a neurosurgeon and have the part of my brain that conjured him up sliced out with a scalpel. A small curl of grey matter, carved away.

Sam yawned and stretched drowsily. 'God, I slept well.'

I stared at him. Didn't he know he'd been absent, or was he pretending nothing had happened? I didn't say anything because I didn't trust my voice. He would know everything; how relieved I had been; how I hadn't wanted him to come back. I was more frightened than ever now.

'Alice, relax.' He reached for me and I leapt out of bed, backing away from him.

His eyes searched my face. 'I've been gone, haven't I?'

'Yes.' Somehow he turned it into an accusation. He was entirely unpredictable; like a wild animal I'd failed to tame sufficiently. My instinct was to mollify him. 'Sam, I'm sorry. I have no idea why it happened. I fainted and when I woke up you weren't there any more.'

His eyes narrowed. 'I remember now. We were in Julia's garden. Everything went black.'

'We have to talk.' I was beginning to sound like Jonathan.

But he was already up and out of the room. I could hear him wandering round Dad's house, poking about. I wondered what he was searching for. Some sign that I had been unfaithful to him, a whiff of sex perhaps. Some hope.

I came downstairs in my pyjamas. Gabby was sitting on the

sofa reading a book, her feet up, a cup of tea on the floor beside her.

She looked up. 'Good morning.'

'Morning.' I went over to the cupboard, took out a mug and managed to drop it so that it bounced off the granite worktop and smashed on the floor.

'Oh, God, I'm sorry.' I got down on my knees and tried to scoop up the pieces.

'Don't worry,' Gabby said briskly. 'It's not Mike's. That's all that matters.'

I must have looked mortified because she laughed. 'I was joking.' She tilted her head and studied me. 'You look pale. Did you sleep OK?'

'Bad dreams.'

She fetched the dustpan and brush from under the sink.

'I'll do that,' I protested.

'Alice, are you sure you're all right?'

'I've always been clumsy. I'll buy you a new one today.'

'Don't be silly.' She swept up the broken china and tipped it into the bin, then gave me another mug and switched on the kettle, waiting for it to boil with her hands deep in the pockets of her long cashmere cardigan. 'What's the matter?'

I turned and stared at the door. Sam had come down and was watching me. When I frowned he walked across the room and went outside.

'He's back,' I said. My hands were shaking.

'Sam?'

I nodded. The kettle boiled and clicked and Gabby grabbed it before I could and made me a cup of tea. She glanced at her watch. 'I think you should see the psychiatrist again.'

'Oh, Gabby . . .'

She shushed me. 'You're going and that's final. You'll end up a nervous wreck if you're not careful, and then what use will you be to my kids?'

301

I smiled wanly. Sam was standing outside with his back to the house, his hands by his sides. He was very still. Unnaturally so. I felt the pull of him but I resisted it. I drank my tea and read the paper, took a shower and washed my hair. At nine o'clock I rang Carol Margulies and begged her to fit me in.

'Does Sam tell you he loves you?' Carol regarded me through her spectacles.

'All the time.'

'And your parents. Did they tell you they loved you?'

I was silent for a moment and then I sighed. 'I know what you're getting at.'

'You don't have to be Einstein,' Sam said.

'Would you rather not answer the question?'

'The answer is rarely, until recently. But Sam isn't a distress call.'

'Isn't he? If you didn't need him, Alice, he wouldn't be here. I am sure of that.'

'Then why did he vanish and reappear again? Why did it feel like he had gone absolutely, not that he was just out somewhere? Like I was free.'

I felt a bubble of panic rise and swallowed it down. Sam was leaning against the wall beside the window, his arms crossed.

'You know this is a waste of time, don't you?' he said.

I ignored him. 'I thought I'd beaten it.'

'It was a blip,' Sam said.

Carol leaned forward and I had the feeling that she didn't really know what to say. At this stage, I didn't care. I just wanted medication. A duller brain seemed like a small price to pay to get out of this situation. Nothing else was working; no effort of will on my part or persuasion on the part of my friends. It seemed the more I told myself he didn't exist, the more apparent his existence became. I couldn't win because whatever I did required thinking about him and me thinking about him was exactly what he wanted.

'How long was he gone?'

'Three days.'

'Seventy-one hours,' Sam said.

'Whatever.'

Carol frowned and made a note.

'How did you feel when you realized he wasn't with you?'

I turned to face him. He raised his eyebrows. My mouth felt dry.

'I was relieved. I felt excited about putting the last few months behind me and getting on with the rest of my life.'

The psychiatrist touched her glasses. I wondered what that meant in terms of body language. Did it mean that she was humouring me, that she thought I was lying, or that she was being dishonest herself?

'And when he returned?'

I closed my eyes. Awful. Awful. Awful. But I couldn't say it. 'Confused.'

'And Sam is with you now?'

I pulled myself together. 'Yes.'

'Where?' She didn't look round when she asked the question. She kept her eyes fixed firmly on me.

I jerked my head in his direction. 'Standing to the right of the window.'

'Sam,' Carol said. 'Tell me what it was like when you weren't with Alice.'

'Are you going to charge for both of us?'

I couldn't help smiling even though I didn't want to be on his side. I needed humour to get through this. I repeated what he said.

'No. I only charge clients I can see. Can you answer the question?'

I put my elbows on the desk and my head in my hands.

Sam said, 'I was lost.'

'I was lost.' At first I repeated his words without the emotion. But he soon got to me. There was a lump in my throat.

'I felt like a child who had let go of his mother's hand in a crowd, and I felt like I was submerged in nothingness. Then later, I was jostled and pushed by things I couldn't see, by my memories, my dreams. When I woke and found that I was lying next to Alice, it was as if all the burdens of my life, all the fears, had left me. So listening to her now, I understand. I know how frightening this is for her. But the fact is, I need her and it isn't possible for me to let her go. I don't have the strength and I'm not sure I even possess a conscience. What you have to understand is that I love Alice and I want her to be happy, but only if that means we are together. Anything less is impossible for me to contemplate.'

He stopped speaking and I looked round and shook my head slowly and Sam came and knelt beside me and put his arms around me. I pressed my forehead against his.

'I'm sorry. I'm so sorry.' I turned round. 'Please prescribe me something.'

'Anti-depressants? I'm not sure they would help.'

'Not anti-depressants. Anti-psychotics.'

Carol's pen stilled above her notebook. 'Do you consider yourself psychotic? You do understand that these are powerful, mind-altering drugs?'

'Yes. I need my mind altered.'

'But, Alice, they're mainly targeted at patients who can no longer distinguish reality from their delusions.'

'I can't though, can I? Sam is obviously a delusion, but as far as I'm concerned he is absolutely real.'

'On the other hand, you aren't in any danger and nor is the public. Taking anti-psychotic drugs is an enormous step. You need to consider all the implications extremely carefully before you go down that road. I really think some extra sessions with me would be more appropriate.'

I took a deep breath. 'No. This has gone too far. I'm admitting defeat. My delusion has overwhelmed me and I'm scared it will eventually destroy me. I am a danger to myself.'

There was a short silence. Carol seemed to be weighing things up. She was obviously unwilling, but I knew that part of her was fascinated by my case and she didn't want to lose me. Perhaps, like Jonathan, she wanted to write it all up and publish it.

'I see.'

I breathed a sigh of relief. 'Thank God.'

Sam stood up and leaned over the desk, breathing into Carol's face. She went very still.

'If you put her on drugs, I will kill you.'

I groaned, exasperated. 'Don't be so ridiculous, Sam. Dr Margulies, please. Just give me the prescription.'

'You'll need monitoring.' Her tone was reluctant but she was weakening.

'That's fine. You can monitor me. I'll come and see you every couple of weeks.'

'Days,' Carol said.

I wondered how I was going to manage that as well as taking on more work. I had a couple of shoots lined up and I couldn't afford to turn them down. But I couldn't worry about it now. I'd think about it later.

'All right.'

She frowned and started to type. Her printer disgorged the prescription, but when she took it out Sam reached to grab it from her. I leapt up and ripped it out of her hand and he recoiled in anger, swiping his arm across her desk. Her small stack of files went flying, as did her telephone, pens and notepad.

'Alice! What on earth are you doing?' Carol said, backing away from me.

'I was . . .' I stopped, the prescription crumpled in my fist. How was I supposed to explain that Sam had done that, not me? I knelt and started picking the stuff up.

'Leave it, Alice. Sit down.'

'My hour's up.'

'It doesn't matter.'

I shook my head, handed her back her stapler and went to the door. 'Thank you, but I can't stay.'

We left the house and I paused for a moment outside Matt's flat where a For Sale sign had already gone up. His windows stared at me, dead-eyed. I walked away, muttering under my breath to stop myself crying. When Sam caught up, he drew my arm through his.

'It's going to be all right,' he said. 'Don't fight me any more, Alice.'

'Oh, just get lost!'

A passer-by glanced anxiously at me and quickened his pace, dragging his snarling terrier behind him. I could have gone straight to a chemist, and I don't know why I didn't. Instead I went back to Gabby's. It was only later that I found the prescription ripped to shreds, the pieces muddled amongst the contents of my bag. I held them in my hand and stared at them. Had I done that? What did that mean? Somewhere in the depths of my consciousness, did I want him to stay? Was this my punishment? Was Sam to be a constant reminder that it was my bloody-mindedness that had killed my best friend?

Chapter Twenty-Six

I BEGAN TO WONDER WHAT WOULD HAPPEN IF I KILLED SAM. WOULD it constitute murder? Would I be left with an invisible decomposing body? I could smother him in his sleep but he'd most likely overpower me. Alternatively, I could stab him. But what if he bled all over the place? Perhaps I could drug him for long enough to go back to Carol and get her to reprint the prescription? But the already wary psychiatrist was hardly going to believe what had happened.

My mobile rang and I checked the caller display. It was Dad.

'Are you busy?'

'No. What do you need?' There was no other possible answer to that question, when put by my father, unless I was at work.

'Do you think you could go down to Sussex with Gabby? Your grandmother's in hospital. I'm back late tonight, but I'll try and get down tomorrow.'

'What's happened?' My heart plummeted and I braced myself for bad news.

'She's had a fall. Nothing broken, but they're keeping her in for a day or two. She's bored more than anything. I've tried Olivia, but her nanny says she's out for the day, doing a watercolour course. That girl needs to get a job.'

'Is it Paula?' Sam said.

I didn't reply. I hadn't spoken to him since we left the psychiatrist's house and I didn't intend to again.

There was a moment when Gran looked at Gabby, who had walked in ahead of me, and I thought she seemed puzzled. It was fleeting, but enough for my stepmother to feel she had to announce herself. Gran wasn't wearing make-up and without the powder and pink lipstick, she looked like she could be blown away. Her make-up had been a banner that read, *I'm perfectly fine, thank you very much.* It had made it easier for everyone, though maybe not for her.

'It's only me and Alice,' Gabby said. 'We've come to make you feel better.'

The room, a private one, was cheerful and bright, with nets on the windows and blue lino on the floor. A bunch of freesias in a glass vase sat on the windowsill. On the bedside cabinet there was a Penny Vincenzi novel with a torn edge of a magazine stuck in as a bookmark.

Gran's focus sharpened and she spoke too brightly, trying to cover up her momentary lapse. 'Gabby, my darling. How sweet of you. And Alice too. How lovely.'

She was treating the occasion as if we had just dropped in for tea and cake and her smile dispelled a little of my anxiety. I leaned over the bed and gave her a kiss, then sat down on the chair beside her while Gabby dug in her bag for the magazines and grapes she had brought. Sam took the small, wooden-armed seat by the window. He leaned forward and put his elbows on his thighs, resting his chin in his hands. I could feel the tension building in him. I had a nasty feeling this was going to be a repeat of last time, with him badgering her to admit that she knew he was there. Another battle of wills perhaps, or a Holy Grail that remained out of reach. I didn't know what I wanted more; for her to acknowledge his existence or for Sam to lose that last shred of hope.

Gabby stayed for ten minutes and then left us together while she drove to Gran's house to pick up the things she needed.

'I'll stop off and buy you some chocolate biscuits,' she said.

'A bottle of sherry would be nice,' Gran replied.

'How long are they going to keep you in?' I asked, after Gabby had closed the door behind her.

'I don't know.' She sounded worried. 'They don't tell me anything, but I want to get home as soon as possible. The longer you stay in these places, the more dependent they make you.' She changed the subject abruptly, catching me off guard. 'You don't look healthy. Have you lost weight?'

'A little. But I'm fine. What about you? Are they treating you well?'

'I feel like a prisoner.'

'You and me both.'

We sat for a moment in silence. My mind was my gaol – that much was indisputable – but wasn't it all my own fault? If I genuinely wanted Sam to go, surely he would vanish in a puff of smoke? I remembered what Carol Margulies had said at the end of our first meeting, that I was a happy person stuck in an unhappy person's shell. I didn't entirely agree because I didn't think I was that weak, but her words did have a kernel of truth. I didn't believe that finding some mythical happy place deep inside me was going to get Sam off my back, but I knew what she meant about wearing the wrong skin.

'I should have looked out for you more,' Gran said. 'But we certainly didn't see this coming. Your father is very worried about you. How's that head of yours?'

Discombobulated. 'Intact,' I said firmly.

'That's all?'

I smiled. 'You know that's not all.'

Gran didn't look in the least bit abashed. 'Last time I saw your father, he talked about Sam. Are you still seeing him? Or is that all over?'

Despite my best efforts to ignore him, Sam was as solid and real as ever. He opened his mouth to say something, then seemed to change his mind and shrugged.

'Seeing as in, going out with?' I said. 'No.'

'You know what I'm talking about. Seeing as in seeing things that aren't there. Are you?'

I swallowed. 'Actually, he's in the room.' I qualified the statement quickly. 'Well, obviously, I know he isn't, but then again, he is. Does that make sense? He's as real as you, Gran. I know it sounds mad, but that's the whole problem.' I grimaced.

'Go on.'

'If I could see through him, or if he vanished and reappeared, like the Cheshire Cat, it would be a hell of a lot easier. There's a big difference. How real was Fred to you?'

'Completely.'

I smiled, relieved. 'Then you know what I'm talking about. This wasn't meant to happen, but somehow it has, and I really need to fix things before I lose my grip on reality.'

Gran regarded me thoughtfully. 'You think I know he's here?'

'Maybe. Perhaps it's just a feeling, or perhaps you see him as well as I do but won't tell me. I don't know.'

She didn't reply immediately and the room went so quiet that I could hear my breath pulling in and out of my lungs. My body prickled with anticipation.

'What do you want, my darling? What can I do?'

My mouth dried. 'I want you to tell me what you see. I want you to understand what I'm going through. I don't want to do this on my own any more.'

'And if I told you that there was something, how would that help?'

'Because if he's real to you, then maybe, between the two of us, we can persuade him to go away and leave me alone.'

'I am here,' Sam reminded me.

'Something happened,' I said. 'Years ago, in my garden. You spoke to Sam. I know about false memory syndrome, but I'm not imagining it. I remember every tiny detail. I remember what I was

310

doing when you rang the doorbell. I remember what I had for lunch that day. So how can it not be true?'

'I wouldn't make a reliable witness even if I said what you wanted me to say. Anyone I spoke to would dismiss it as a sign of dementia.'

This was so frustrating. She was as slippery as an eel. 'But what do you actually believe?'

'I believe you don't tell lies. But truth is flexible, isn't it? It depends so much on point of view.'

I had to spend a moment figuring out on which side of the fence her answer put her, but Sam looked pleased.

'It is the truth. We were friends once, Paula. You remember that, don't you?'

I waited. She didn't answer.

'Do you?' I said.

'Do I what?'

'Do you remember being friends with Sam?'

She smiled. 'No. But I remember Fred.'

'One and the same,' Sam said. 'That was me. Why else would I know so much? I was there when you needed a friend and I never let you down. I won't let Alice down either. I promised you that. I keep my promises—'

Gran spoke over him: 'I had stopped seeing him by the time I was eight. My mother remarried and I had Adam for company, so I grew out of all that silliness.'

She must have seen the hurt on my face, because she touched my cheek. 'Alice, I do understand. I know what I felt when I had Fred with me and it was just the way you describe. But what's happening isn't right, and to tell you otherwise would only make things worse. You need to do this yourself, darling. I can't help you.'

'Yes, you can,' Sam said. 'You can admit that you believe her.'

He came and leaned across her, hovering over her like a dark shadow. I watched her expression. How aware was she? Was it just a sensation? Did she see, feel, hear and smell him? Did she feel the touch of his hand on hers?

'You don't need to be alone,' he said. 'How do you fill your time now that no one needs you? You used to be so busy, but what do you do these days? Wait for visits? Do you tell yourself your opinions still count for something? I can spend time with you as well as with Alice. Age is irrelevant to me.'

'This is what you do best,' I said contemptuously. 'You make us feel isolated and then step in and fill the gaps. You did that to me. You're not going to do it to my grandmother.'

'Don't worry about me,' Gran said. 'I grew up with rationing. I know how to deal with petty tyrants. You should know when to leave, Sam,' she added. 'We are finished with you.'

She was speaking to him, only she wasn't actually looking at him. It was like when you're watching an interview on television and the interviewee is addressing the wrong camera. She was humouring me. She was trying to help.

'Why should I go?' Sam said. 'I've as much right to an existence as you. Who decreed that I get squeezed like a sponge and then discarded when you have no further use for me?'

'Sam,' I said. 'Don't.'

He turned on me. 'I want to stay. Why shouldn't I stay? Because it means a sacrifice on your part?' He gripped my wrist, glaring at Gran. I could feel his fury. 'You know I'm here, Paula. You told me to stay and watch over Alice. You begged me.'

'When?' I demanded. 'When did she ever ask you that? You build things up completely out of proportion. She never asked you to stay.'

'You know she did. You were there.'

'I was a child. I lived in my head. It's different now. Whatever happens, you can't win, you're never going to get what you want, no matter how hard you try, because I'm not enough for you. You want the world to acknowledge you exist, and that's not going to happen. You're as trapped as I am, Sam. Maybe even more so.'

We were all silent for a moment and then Sam started speaking again. 'You're wrong. I'm getting stronger and you know it. I'm nearly there.'

I shook my head but he was talking to Paula now, his voice edged with menace. 'You forgot all about me when you went to live with Adam. That was a mistake.'

'Is this some sort of threat?' I asked. 'Because you're whistling in the wind if you think she can hear you. What are you going to do anyway? Attack us? I'd like to see you try.'

'For goodness' sake, Alice,' Gran said.

Sam whipped round. 'Do you have any idea what I'm capable of, Paula? Maybe I can light matches? What do you think?'

I could have sworn my grandmother reacted then. Her mouth opened and she looked straight at him, just like she had in our garden that time. I was sure because I felt the same prickle go through my body. But then she looked back at me and her eyes were clear.

'Gabby's taking her time,' she said tartly. 'What do you think she's doing?'

'She won't be long.'

Sam leaned in. 'I asked you what you thought, Paula. I know you heard me. Don't pretend.'

'Stop it, Sam,' I said. 'You're giving me the creeps. What good will this do?' I shoved back my chair and stood up, grabbing my bag.

Gran held out her hand and I took it. Her grip was surprisingly strong. 'Don't let him take over your life,' she said, narrowing her eyes. 'It's time to send him back where he came from, where he can't do any more harm. Try, Alice, please, for your family's sake as much as your own. You have to take control of your life and not let this insane situation pull you down.'

Her voice had dropped to an exhausted whisper. I felt terrible. I was supposed to be here to cheer her up.

Sam backed away from her. 'For Christ's sake, why the hell

don't you die and leave Alice alone? I can look after her now. She's mine. You and the rest of the Byrnes have had your chance. Why would she need me if her fucking family hadn't screwed her up so badly?'

'Sam, shut up!' I pushed him away, furious. 'Gran, I am so sorry.'

Her head was deep in the pillows. She had closed her eyes but she opened them and looked at me. 'This is my fault.'

'None of this is your fault. Please don't worry. I can sort it out.'

I rang the bell for the nurse and didn't leave until I saw my grandmother in safe hands. I was shaking as we walked out of the hospital to wait for Gabby. The main entrance stank of stale cigarette smoke. I moved out into the fresh air.

'She knew me,' Sam said. 'It was so obvious.'

'Don't be ridiculous. You know that's not true. You made a fool of yourself.' I felt a tremor of fear. He could hurt me if he wanted to. But he wouldn't want to, would he? Because if he hurt me, he risked his own existence.

His jaw tightened. 'You don't really believe that.'

I glared at him. But I wasn't sure what I believed any more. Gran had said she couldn't admit that he was there, that it wasn't possible, that it was to do with me. But she had never said, *I cannot see him or hear him.* I felt awful, putting her in a position where she felt she had to reassure me when she was the one who needed reassurance. She was elderly and this must be so confusing, especially dragging Fred into it when she had barely thought about him in eighty years. She had suffered loss as a child, with her father dying and then her stepbrother, and she didn't need to be reminded of that time. I shouldn't have let him come. I should have done something to stop him. I had been stupid and thoughtless. Dad would be furious if he ever found out how much I had upset her. I hung my head and Sam put his hands on my shoulders and a sensation of warmth spread like tentacles through my flesh.

'Please don't make me go,' he said. 'I'm sorry I made you angry, but I'm scared. It's empty out there without you.'

I shook my head and tried to blot out his voice, but there were few distractions: a couple of pigeons pecking around; patients and visitors walking to and from the car park; a bent old woman on a Zimmer frame edging her way towards a waiting minibus; a male nurse pushing a man attached to a drip in a wheelchair. It was no good.

He clasped my hands. 'You have the strength to do this, Alice. You don't need your old life. You don't need a family who've never cared about you, lovers who come and go. Or the Walkers, for that matter. You know that if you disappeared from their lives, you wouldn't leave much of a gap.'

I wrenched my hands out of his. 'Just get away from me! I hate you!'

He smiled softly, as if my sudden burst of temper proved something to him. 'No you don't. You're my best friend. Come on, calm down. We can have a good time together, we don't need to be at each other's throats. There's room for us both and I promise I'll try and compromise.'

'You want me to choose.'

He shook his head slowly. 'That was my anger talking. Of course I don't want you to cut your ties with everyone you love, I'm not a monster, whatever you might think. I want what's best for you. I want you to be happy.'

His voice was beginning to have a paralysing effect on me. It was as if he was erasing my thoughts and putting what he wanted in there. I was still pulsing with anger but it was ebbing away, leaving me feeling washed out and ready to cry. Then the sudden, plaintive wail of an ambulance siren brought me to my senses and I hurried away. Sam didn't follow me. Maybe he had run out of words. My breath shuddered from me. Even though I was angry, I understood. He was part of me, formed from me, an expression of myself, and I loved and hated him because of that. I thought about Jonathan, who I loved for no reason. The idea of life without him was intolerable.

'What happened?' Gabby asked as we left the hospital car park.

She had nipped into Gran's room with the things she'd picked up, while I waited in the car. I didn't open the door for Sam, but he pushed me out of the way and climbed over the seats and into the back. I rubbed my arm where he had shoved me.

'I don't know. I'm not sure about anything any more.'

Gabby hesitated. 'You wanted something out of this, didn't you?'

The car was stuffy so I wound down my window and looked out. 'I wanted Gran to back me up, but she couldn't. I think she understands what I'm going through, but she's scared of making it worse.'

'You've got to leave it now, Alice.'

I leaned my head back. 'Don't you think I would if I could? I'm stuck with this needy, manipulative spirit-man who won't be happy until I've lost all my friends.' I groaned and rubbed my eyes. 'It's a nightmare. He's a nightmare.'

'Don't talk about me like I'm not here,' Sam said.

I turned on him. 'As far as I'm concerned, you aren't.'

Gabby tapped her fingers on the steering wheel. She seemed anxious to change the subject. I was making her uncomfortable.

'I am sorry,' she said. 'You know . . . about the other day. I still feel rotten about calling Jonathan. It was none of my business.'

'It doesn't matter. When does Dad get back?' It was my turn to try and change the subject, but Gabby was blissfully unaware.

'Late tonight. His plane doesn't come in until ten. It was wrong of me, I know that now. I'm sure the two of you can manage perfectly well without my interference.'

It was too late to stop her and I felt the atmosphere freeze.

'You've seen Jonathan?' Sam said.

I flinched. 'Yes.'

'Well, that explains a lot. So what did you two talk about? And

316

where was Gabby while this cosy chat was going on?'

I rubbed my temples. 'Stop it. It's my life. I'll see who I want, when I want. You have to go, you really do.' I didn't have the energy to pretend. Let Gabby see me at my worst. I had lost my inhibitions. Sam was winning. I was losing it.

'To leave the field free for that cunt? I don't think so.'

'Don't you dare call him that!'

'What on earth is going on?' Gabby asked, flicking her gaze between me, the rear-view mirror and the road ahead. 'Are you having a row with Sam?'

'Keep out of it, Gabby,' Sam snapped.

'Gabby,' I said through gritted teeth, 'I'm sorry. Ignore me, please.'

'Easier said than done.'

'I thought there had to be a reason I felt so weak. Did you let him fuck you?'

It was as if he had shed a skin and was showing me who he really was. A man who would stoop to anything to control me. I wasn't playing his games any more. I didn't feel apologetic, and for once I didn't feel guilty.

'Don't be so vile.'

'Make love then. Did you make beautiful music together? Come on, Alice, something happened. You wouldn't walk away otherwise, I know you. You need some other poor sap to pick up the pieces. But I'm not going to let you do it to yourself, or to me.'

He waited for me to say something but I didn't respond. Poor Gabby, her knuckles were white from clutching the steering wheel. She kept looking at me, then checking the mirror. Every so often she muttered under her breath. I think it was, 'Oh my God.'

Sam was not going to let it go. 'It's not your life that's at stake. If you make me leave, I die. Do you understand that? Can you possibly stop thinking about yourself for one moment and look at this through my eyes? I lose everything when I lose you.'

'You don't know that,' I said, galvanized. 'You might go back to being a child; you might forget I ever existed. Surely, that's not so bad. Surely, that's what you're here for. Gran was right; you should have left me years ago.'

I fished around in my bag and found an old tissue and, beside it, a small rectangle of white card. Matt Clarke's. I blew my nose and wiped my eyes. Sam was silent. I hoped he was considering what I had said, because I was deadly serious. I turned the card over and then twisted round so that I could see his face.

'Where did you go the night Matt died?'

'I didn't go anywhere.'

I was desperately aware of Gabby beside me. What must she think? Well, it was obvious really, but I couldn't worry about that now.

'But you did,' I insisted. 'I know you did.'

'Alice . . .'

'Where were you?'

He sighed. 'OK, I went out. What did you expect? I'd been in all day, wondering where the hell you were and what you were doing. I felt cooped up and pissed off. After you went to bed I couldn't sleep and it was driving me mad that you could, after what had happened. I had to go out before I woke you up and said things I would regret. But I swear to you, I did not go anywhere near Matt.'

'So where did you go?'

'Don't look at me like that. I'm not a killer. I visited Rory's grave.'

I studied his expression. His eyes held mine, unblinking.

'In the middle of the night?'

'Yes. I wanted to be there. I don't know why. Maybe I wanted to feel what it was like, not to be here any more. Anyway, I just sat there for an hour or so and talked to him.'

'I don't believe you.'

There was a long silence and then Sam said, 'Then there's nothing else I can say.' He turned away from me, and looked out of the window.

'Sorry,' I said to Gabby. 'This must be so weird for you.'

'Alice . . . Look, we'll be home soon. I'll put the kettle on, we can sit down and have a cup of tea and talk about it.'

I spent the rest of the journey in silence and half an hour later she pulled over and parked. I got out of the car and, after hesitating, opened the back door for Sam. As I turned towards the house he took hold of my arm.

'Wait. Please.'

I glanced towards Gabby. She was waiting for me at the top of the steps.

'Are you coming in?'

'Two minutes.'

'Alice, please come inside. You can't do this out on the street.'

She was embarrassed for me as well as concerned then. 'Are you worried what your neighbours might think?'

'Don't be silly. Of course I'm not.' She looked stricken. 'Well, do what you like, but if you're not in the house in five minutes I'm coming out to get you.'

Sam waited until she pulled the door to before he spoke. 'I'm scared, Alice.'

'OK,' I said slowly, not knowing where this was going but feeling a tiny spark of hope.

'If I go, it'll be like dying, won't it? What if I can't get back, or if I can, I don't remember you or how we were together. All this will have been wasted.'

Did he mean what I thought he meant? I hardly dared believe it. His eyes seemed to melt around me and embrace me. I tried not to feel guilty and selfish, but the sense of my own part in this was lodged somewhere between my diaphragm and my heart. I took pity on him and didn't object when he took my hands in his.

'Surely it would be better if you didn't remember. You'd start again with another child. You'd make someone else feel less lonely.'

His grip tightened. 'But what if I don't, what if I finish up back in that terrible darkness. Like when I lost you last week. That's what hell is.'

'It won't be like that.' I twisted my hands and he let me go, and I practically had to shake the blood supply back into them. 'You're a good person, Sam. Everything that's happened has come about because you were never meant to grow up. You were only ever supposed to be a child.'

And that's what he was. That was why there was no sexual chemistry between us. I hadn't thought about it that way before and it struck me that this was right. He had the reactions of a young boy: the need for attention, the impulsiveness, the thought-lessness. A child in an adult's body.

'I'll go,' he said.

I released the breath I had been holding, and hugged him, feeling for the last time the vital signs of life; his warmth, his smell, his pulse, the almost desperate grip of his arms around me. Then I watched him walk away. He didn't vanish or fade like I had expected him to. He remained solid until he turned the corner. Then what? Out of sight, out of mind? When he wasn't with me, was he there at all? I had to believe that this was it. I rubbed the tears from my eyes and gathered myself together, then went inside and into Gabby's kitchen where everything was nice and normal.

'I think it's over.' Even as I said the words, I felt a tiny niggle of doubt. 'But I'm not sure. I don't want to jinx it.'

'Let's just take it slowly,' Gabby said, handing me a mug. 'See what happens.'

Chapter Twenty-Seven

IF I HAD ONLY LET RORY HAVE HIS WAY.

I wasn't thinking straight. Even with the best will in the world and a decent Sunday service on the trains, he and Daniel would never have made it to the christening on time, not in a million years. But the fact remained that I had persuaded him out of it. Even if he had wanted me to, even if the whole point had been to make himself feel better about taking advantage of my good nature, I had said, No, we're driving, that's final.

My fault. My Fault. My footsteps on the pavement beat time. My fault. I could never tell the Walkers. I kept moving, trying and failing to blank the memory. As I walked I looked around, still expecting to see Sam, expecting him to run up behind me and tuck his arm through mine. The outside world seemed to pulse, echoing my footsteps, and the morning light was so clear and bright that when it bounced off car windows it made me squint. There was nothing comfortable about the day.

I began to feel nervous as I headed towards the station and I soon found I was half running, half walking through the streets and past the black-painted iron railings of the communal gardens. By the time I reached the Underground I was sweaty and out of breath. I slowed down, bought a ticket and went through the barriers. I was being paranoid again. Sam had gone of his own accord. I really didn't need to worry any more.

But something definitely wasn't right. I had expected my world to feel the same as it had after I woke from my faint, with that sense of bright clarity, that knowledge that I was blessedly alone again. But it didn't. It felt oppressive. I was anxious, unable to convince myself that Sam wasn't still around, maybe even following me. And I was almost certain that people were keeping their distance. I shifted my overnight bag from one hand to the other. Stop it, I told myself. Keep calm.

Sam had given in too easily. How could he have switched so abruptly from threatening me to offering to leave me? It wasn't in him. I knew how badly he wanted to be part of my world. I was almost sure he was still around. I could feel it.

A District Line train pulled in and I got on, examining each face before choosing a seat. I studied my reflection in the window against the darkness of the tunnel. The double-glazing painted panda-like dark circles around my eyes and made me look scared. At one point, I thought I saw Sam in the reflection, watching me from the far side of the carriage. I turned my head, but it was only a young man reading a copy of the *Metro*. It was impossible to relax. I stood up and walked to the door between the carriages and peered through. He wasn't there. I tried to distract myself by checking my emails. There was a message from Olivia about me coming round for supper. I supposed I'd have to accept, or risk offending her. One from an editor about a three-day shoot in Cornwall. I replied to her and said, *Yes please*. The rest was junk.

Back home, I let myself in and almost missed the envelope lying on the floor amongst a scattering of estate agent magazines and junk mail. I picked it up, ran up the stairs to my flat, slammed the door behind me and double-locked it. When I looked out of the window, the street was empty.

This was stupid. He had gone. I looked around the sitting room, at the plumped-up cushions, the neatly stacked papers on the cabinet and the shelf of books that Sam had arranged in alphabetical order. I kicked off my shoes and chucked my coat over the back of a chair, my bag on the sofa. It was such a relief not to have to be tidy any more.

I studied the envelope – the handwriting was achingly familiar – started to open it and put it down, switched the kettle on and leaned back against the worktop, drumming my fingers against the drawers. But in the end I couldn't resist its lure. I tore it open. Inside I found a USB pen and a note.

Dearest Alice, this is everything I've written about you. I've deleted the lot from my PC. It's up to you now whether we do anything with it. And I mean, we. Destroy it if you like. I wouldn't blame you. I'm sorry I lost my temper. I was being self-righteous when my sin was greater than yours. I love you.

Jonathan

I grabbed my mobile and began to dial his number then stopped. What good would it do? It was only a gesture. It didn't cancel out what he had done. I peered out of the window again. The street was deserted and I felt very alone. I turned away, sat down on the sofa, hugged my knees and refused to think about him. Unfortunately, not thinking about Jonathan left room to question what had happened, why Sam had given in so quickly. It made me wonder again if he could have murdered poor Matt.

All that stuff about paying a visit to Rory's grave, that wasn't Sam. He was melodramatic but he wasn't sentimental. I tried to make sense of it all but my brain wasn't functioning properly; all I knew was that I was confused and frightened. In the quarter of an hour Sam and I had spent at Gran's bedside, there had been perhaps half a second when I could say that she saw him, and believe it. Just a tiny moment that I could easily have misread. Perhaps I had been over-sensitized. Perhaps I had been wrong. Perhaps it had been nothing but a product of desperation and hope, and I had merely seen what I wanted to see. And if that was the case, then Sam hadn't been there; and if he was a figment of my imagination, then he couldn't have taken someone's life.

But if it had been real, if my eyes and the prickle of my skin hadn't deceived me, then there was a chance that my friend, empowered by fury, fear and sheer determination, could have killed Matt. It opened up horrifying possibilities that I couldn't ignore. When he talked about Adam and being able to strike a match, that was the moment when Gran met his eyes. Even without being one hundred per cent sure, there was enough doubt in my mind to scare me. I picked up my mobile and phoned Dad.

'How did Gran's stepbrother die?' I asked.

'Adam? Why do you want to know?'

'I'm doing a bit of genealogy.'

'Oh, right.' Dad sounded dubious. 'A house fire. He was ill and the rest of the family had gone out for the afternoon, leaving him in bed. It was tragic.'

'Do you know what started it?'

'I haven't a clue. What's this about, Alice?'

'Nothing. Really.'

Sam hadn't left me. I had never really believed it, not in my gut. My fingers shook as I tried to call Jonathan. He was the only person Sam might be with if he wasn't with me. When Megan picked up, it caught me completely off balance.

'Alice.' Megan's tone was hostile.

'Is Jonathan there?'

'What the hell do you think?'

'I don't know. Why did you answer his mobile?'

'He forgot it when he left me.'

So he had kept his word and ended their relationship. I tried not to acknowledge how that made me feel.

'I'm so sorry.'

'Why would you be sorry when it's what you wanted all along? All that poor little Alice bullshit. He couldn't resist it.'

'How long ago did he leave?'

'Last night. I assumed he had gone to see you. Maybe he's at his parents'.' She paused and I didn't fill the gap. 'I used to think you were sweet. I didn't realize what a scheming cow you really are.'

That was too much. I refused to shoulder the entire blame, even to placate Megan. 'I didn't scheme.'

'Are you saying it's my fault?' There was incredulity in her voice but I didn't have time to argue.

'No, of course not. I am truly sorry, but I have to find him. It's desperately important.'

'Go to hell.' Megan hung up.

By the time the cab drew up outside the Walkers' house I was feeling deflated and my relentless pursuit of Jonathan across London seemed less heroic than ridiculous. Who did I think I was? If he was inside and unscathed, how was I supposed to tell him that I thought his life was in danger from a man no one believed existed? On the other hand, what if I did what I felt like doing and slunk away like a coward and something happened?

I paid off the cabbie and ran up to the house and pressed my finger against the doorbell, practically stamping with impatience. A light appeared as the kitchen door opened and I made out Emma's figure, distorted and misty through the stained glass, walking towards me.

'Alice. Darling, come in.' She held the door wide open.

'I'm so sorry to bother you.'

'Don't be silly. You never bother us.'

'Is Jonathan here?' I blurted it out and felt myself going bright red. Emma gave me a rueful smile. 'You've heard then?'

I nodded. 'Yes. I called the flat earlier. I spoke to Megan.'

Now Emma probably thought I was chasing him down because he was single again.

'It's not . . . I'm not here because of that. I just need to speak to him. It's urgent.' I kept looking past her in the hope that he would appear. Perhaps he knew I was there and didn't want to see me.

'Come in for a moment, Alice. I want to talk to you.'

My heart was pumping. The feeling of dread that had assailed me earlier was stronger now. 'He's not here?'

'No.'

Emma stepped back, expecting me to cross the threshold but I didn't move.

'Do you know where he is?'

'He's gone to the boat. He left about ten minutes ago.'

'The boat?'

I must have looked stupefied because Emma said kindly, 'He needs some time on his own.'

My hands curled into tight fists. I wanted to explain but I couldn't. I started to walk away.

'Alice, hang on!'

I stopped in my tracks and turned. Emma ran out, clutching a coat.

'At least take this. You're hardly wearing anything and it'll be cold on the river.'

I took it and gave her a quick hug, and then I ran.

Brian kept his boat at a mooring close to Orleans House in Twickenham. It was only a ten-minute walk, but I ran most of the way and by the time I reached the river I had a terrible stitch. I stopped and gripped my side until it had faded and then pressed on, hurrying down on to the pontoon.

He was still there, thank God. I was in time. But in time for what exactly?

There didn't appear to be anyone else about, but a Jack Russell belonging to the man who owned the boat next to the Walkers' was standing guard, his tail stiff, his muzzle pointing directly at Jonathan, who was busy rolling up the rain cover, so busy that he didn't notice me at first. Then the dog spotted me and started to yap.

Jonathan turned, took one look at me and broke into a huge smile. He let go of the cover and jumped down.

'I got your letter,' I said. 'Thank you.'

326

I was holding the bulky coat, its padded black fabric draped over my arms. Jonathan took it and tossed it aside, then pulled me against him, taking my head in his hands, his fingers threaded in my hair. When he kissed me it was spontaneous and clumsy but it was real and everything I'd hoped for; the feeling of his mouth claiming mine; the urgent pressure that told me how much he wanted me, how little control he had over himself; his hands exploring my body; the roughness of his jaw; the taste and smell of his skin. All I could think was *at last*. I never wanted to let him go again.

In the distance the terrier yapped but this time his owner shouted at him and I heard it walk away, its nails clicking along the wooden slats.

We pulled away from each other reluctantly.

'Hi,' Jonathan said.

He grinned at me and I couldn't help grinning back at him. Like an imbecile. But we were both imbeciles, so it didn't matter. How could I ever have thought I could put him behind me? He took my hand and scooped up the coat and we walked back to the boat.

'Do you want to come out for a ride?'

I nodded, glancing around. No sign of Sam. I was probably worrying for nothing.

'You can give me a hand with the ropes. Do you remember what to do?'

I said I did, although it had been a while. I managed not to mess up though and we were soon on our way. Jonathan held me firmly against him and it felt like this was where I should have been all the time. Every so often he took his eyes off the river and kissed me, and between those kisses I waited for the next one. The sun shone, sparkling on the fast-moving water, a heron perched on an overhanging branch, patiently waiting for an unwary fish. It was idyllic, quiet except for the hum of the engine. It was as if we had taken a moment out of time, just for us. I should have trusted Sam. He had been as good as his word.

'Do you love me?' Jonathan asked.

I nudged my head against his shoulder. 'I've loved you since I was six years old.'

He stroked my hair. 'I think I've loved you since that day you photographed Connie Wells. Do you remember? When you made a pass at me in the street.'

I blushed furiously. 'Thanks. I don't need to be reminded.'

'You're right. It was bloody disturbing.'

I giggled. 'So, your USB pen . . .'

'Yes?' he replied warily.

'I'm going to keep it. You never know, one day I might look back on all this and want you to put it down on paper. And I wanted to say I'm sorry. I shouldn't have touched your laptop without asking you. It was really bad.'

'You're forgiven. You were already forgiven.'

I thought I'd better tell him I'd spoken to Megan. 'I was trying to get hold of you,' I added, embarrassed.

Jonathan wrapped his arm around me, tweaked my shirt from under the waistband of my jeans and folded his hand around my waist. I managed it less deftly, but my hand found his bony hip and stayed there. The heat that my palm and fingers absorbed seemed to enter my bloodstream and flood my body. I had almost forgotten about Sam. My fears seemed ridiculous now. I had watched him walk away from me, willingly if not happily. The important thing was to believe it completely. If one thing was going to bring him back, surely obsessing about him would.

'Why didn't you just call my mobile?'

'I did. Megan picked up.'

'Oh, shit, yes. I left it there. I'm sorry.'

We talked until we reached the first lock and then had to stop while we manoeuvred the boat into position and Jonathan slung the ropes through the metal rings. Locks always made me nervous. It was their wet, dark walls, slimed with green. There was something Victorian about them; they made me think of dense fog and murder most foul.

Once we were safely through and out the other side I joined him at the helm again. I was keen to continue the conversation about how and when he fell in love with me, but my stomach was rumbling.

'Did you bring anything to eat?' I didn't have high hopes. Organization and advance planning had never been Jonathan's strong point.

He gave my hair an affectionate ruffle. 'There're some biscuits down below. Help yourself.'

I opened the door to the cabin and stepped down. My eyes took a while to adjust to the dimmer light but, when they did, my heart almost stopped beating. Someone was sitting on one of the banquettes.

'Hello, Alice.'

Chapter Twenty-Eight

SAM STUDIED ME WITH A MIXTURE OF COMPASSION AND IRRITATION. It wasn't something I was used to, coming from him, and it riled me.

'What're you doing here?' I said.

'I could ask the same of you.'

He looked easy and relaxed but I wasn't convinced. I could feel the tension in him, the pulse of suppressed anger. We both waited for the other to speak. I was the one to blink first.

'Well, you can't stay. You have to leave now.'

'Don't worry so much.'

He held out his hand to me and I flinched. 'I'm not worried. I'm angry.'

'Why?'

He leaned back again, stretching his arms along the back of the banquette. It was as if he was claiming ownership of the space. A very Sam-like thing to do. He had always been territorial.

'Why do you think? You told me you were going.'

He replied with a shrug. 'So I changed my mind. And maybe it's a good thing you're here. I've been thinking about us. I understand everything you said, but I'm not going to let you throw it all away.'

I clutched my head and closed my eyes, muttering, 'Oh God . . .'

'Come on, Alice. Think about it.'

'We said goodbye. Don't make it even more painful. You were a good friend to me when I needed you and I'm grateful and I'll always love you for it. But it's over.'

Sam wasn't taking it in. He was very good at not hearing things he didn't like. 'It's not up to you. My life, the blood in my veins, the air I breathe, I can't just put them aside.' He seemed to realize he was ranting, because his voice became quieter. 'It's just that I'm not yours any more. I have a will of my own.'

'I know you do,' I said. 'And I know this is hurting you, but I can't deal with you. I honestly can't.'

'If I go, it'll be because you've killed me. Do you really want that?'

'You know that's not what I want.'

'Then you're asking me to do your dirty work, to salve your conscience. I couldn't, even if I wanted to. You have to accept that we will never be free of each other.' He leaned forward, his gaze intense, and for some reason I didn't move. His eyes were beautiful. 'You know there's a reason I'm here, don't you? You know that without me you can't deal with what happened to Rory. You can't cope with the knowledge that you could have prevented all this.'

I hung my head and he reached out and stroked my hair. 'It's all right. I'll look after you.'

I pushed his hand away and looked at him through my tears. 'What do you know, Sam?'

'I know about the phone call. I know what you said.'

'I'll tell Jonathan now.'

I could do it. I visualized myself walking out on to the deck, standing beside him, not letting him hold my hand. I would stare at the river because I wouldn't be able to look at his face. I wiped my tears.

'He'll change towards you,' Sam said. 'Can you live with that? And what about Emma and Brian? Are you going to tell them as well? Or are you just going to hope they never find out?'

I let out a cry, and covered my mouth with my hand. Sam

looked at me with compassion. He was right and I was weak. I stumbled over my words. 'Stay then. But please leave Jonathan alone.'

I examined his face, searching it for signs that he was prepared to strike. There was sadness in his expression, but determination as well.

'Every time that man takes your mind off me, it saps my strength. He needs dealing with.'

Panic squeezed the breath out of me. 'Sam, you mustn't say things like that. You don't mean it.'

'Just say the word and I'll leave him alone. Tell him you've come to say that you want him out of your life. Don't talk about love or hate. Just tell him he got the wrong idea. You're not interested.'

'And if I won't?'

He grabbed my wrist and caught my chin in his hand and his eyes seemed to dig right into my mind. I kept very still, holding his gaze until he released me.

'I want you to go. I mean it, Sam.'

'It's too late.'

'I'll forget all about you.'

He laughed. 'There is no way you'll ever forget me. And while you remember, I'll be by your side.'

His words made my blood run cold. The idea that I would have to spend the rest of my life accommodating this man, compromising my happiness and becoming a virtual recluse, scared the hell out of me. And yet he had been right about my conscience. Whatever the logistical problems would have been, however easily justified my insistence on driving that night, I still had to live with the fact that it had been ultimately my decision. Sam knew what was inside me and that meant I wasn't entirely alone. Was this what it was all about? I was losing control and I didn't seem to be able to call up the will to fight. There was one thing I wanted to know, though.

'Did you kill Matt?'

His jaw tensed but when he looked at me his eyes were clear and bright. 'What do you think?'

'I have no idea.'

'What would you say if I admitted it?'

'I'd say you were a monster. I'd never forgive you.' I waited. 'So did you or didn't you?'

He smiled at me. 'Why should I tell you when not knowing the truth keeps you awake at night?'

I studied his expression, trying to understand him, but the effort to think cohesively drained me of energy. I waited until the silence threatened to drown out the engine before I spoke.

'I'm going to stop this. I'm going to speak to Jonathan.'

'Careful, Alice.'

'No, I will not be careful.'

I stood up but the space was so small that I knocked against the hob with my elbow, sending the kettle flying. Sam picked it up and put it back. I heard the hiss of gas. I tried to reach the knob to turn it off but he pushed me down on the banquette and slid in opposite me. He was holding a box of matches.

My heart dropped to my stomach but my voice was steady. 'Put that down.'

He smiled slowly at me and drew out a match. 'Aren't you curious to know if I can do it?'

'No, I bloody well am not. What do you want to do? Kill us all?' He can't, I thought. It's impossible. He's impossible.

He ran the match gently over the strike, grazing it, and then held it to his nose and breathed in. He raised his eyebrows, mocking me. 'I love the smell of gunpowder.'

'You're not frightening me, Sam.'

'Are you calling my bluff?' He stared at me and to my surprise, he started to cry. He held the match at striking distance from the side of the box.

'Sam. Don't.'

'I love you.'

I could barely breathe by now. I was choking on the foul-smelling air. 'Then turn off the gas. What the hell are you going to achieve by blowing the boat to bits? Sam, please. Think about it. If you want to stay, then stay. But you have got to find some way of compromising, of living amongst real people without me having to give up everything for you. Please be reasonable. I'll find room in my life for you, if you give me room to move.'

'You don't understand. I can't do that.'

I contemplated flinging myself at him, but the table was between us, so I'd have no impetus. I thought about kicking him in the shins but that was more likely to precipitate disaster than prevent it. And then Jonathan shouted, wanting to know what was going on, frustrated at being tied to the helm. Sam was momentarily distracted and that moment was long enough for me to lurch forward and grab the box of matches. I shoved it into my pocket, turned off the gas and squeezed past him to open the ceiling hatch. I sucked in fresh air and then jumped down, hooked open the door and leaned out.

'What were you doing down there?' Jonathan asked.

'I'll explain later.'

He frowned at me. 'Tell me now.'

'In a minute.'

'Alice . . .'

I grimaced an apology and disappeared again, sat down and leaned back, holding my sleeve over my mouth and nose. Sam looked wounded and childlike in the dim light. Like a figure in a pre-Raphaelite painting. It stabbed at me. Try as I might not to let him get to me, there were times when I had to acknowledge our bond. It wasn't his fault I'd brought him into my life and it wasn't his fault that I'd fallen in love with Jonathan. I couldn't blame him for his instincts. This was the hardest thing I'd ever had to do. The closest I would ever come to taking a life. It would be killing, as far as my conscience was concerned at least, because he was with me now, whatever the logic; three-dimensional; a man in all ways but one.

'Alice, listen to me. You do need me. I can feel it in you.'

I took his hands in mine and felt the heat of his. 'I'm sorry, Sam. I belong to Jonathan. It's over.' Then I let him go and hurried back up, stopping myself from breaking down by pressing my thumbnail hard into the back of my hand.

'You were ages,' Jonathan said.

'I used the loo.'

'That was brave.'

He tucked my hand into his pocket with his and his keys jabbed my knuckles but all I could think about was how to tell him the truth, how to find the words.

'Jonathan, would you mind if we went back?'

A few clouds had gathered. Two kayakers approached and he slowed the boat to let them pass and then turned it round in a wide circle. Even the river had begun to look brown and uninviting where up until a few minutes ago I had thought it beautiful. A runner on the towpath passed a cyclist coming in the other direction. I watched as the cyclist checked his speed and edged past and then braked and wheeled round, his bellowed obscenity exploding across the water.

'Charming,' Jonathan said.

The wind was against us now and we made slower progress. I felt chilly and put the coat on and zipped it up. Every so often we cut through the wake of another vessel and the boat rocked. I had to fight a desire to grab the controls and increase our speed. I would tell him now. The words were forming in my head and even though it felt like a huge hurdle to drag them into my mouth, to roll them on my tongue and actually speak them, I would do it.

'I need to talk . . .'

'Do you mind taking the wheel for a moment?' Jonathan said. 'The boat's a bit sluggish. I think there might be something caught in the propeller.'

'Oh. OK.'

It was a reprieve, but a temporary one at best. As I shifted in front of him to swap places he put his hands on my hips and kissed my neck and I nearly collapsed with need. I just wanted him to hold me and make all the bad stuff go away. I leaned back against him.

'Can we stay like this?'

Jonathan kissed me again and eased himself out from behind me, stepping down to the deck floor. I shook my hair away from my face and concentrated on what was happening ahead, trying not to think about what Sam might be up to down below. A school sculling team was rowing towards us, followed by their coach booming instructions through his megaphone. I gave the boys a wave as they passed.

And then I heard Jonathan let out an oath. When I turned he was on his knees, his hand rubbing his shoulder. 'What the hell was that?'

Sam was standing over him, his lip curled in derision.

'Are you all right?' I said.

He stood up and said brusquely, 'I tripped. Alice, careful, you're overcompensating.'

I had moved too far to the left. I adjusted our position. My heart was pounding and the movement of the boat combined with the gas I'd breathed was making me queasy.

Jonathan came back and took the wheel again. 'I couldn't see anything wrong. It's probably just the current slowing us down.'

'Are you hurt?'

'Not really.' He looked at me. 'You've gone as white as a sheet.'

'I feel a bit sick. I'm going to get a bottle of water.' I couldn't tell him Sam was here. I didn't want to remind him of that side of me.

I jumped down and stood, feet apart, steadying myself with a hand against the back of Jonathan's seat. Sam was holding the top of the hooked open door. We contemplated each other and I

336

suddenly knew what I had to do. He was out of control, and, to be honest, so was I. I saw so many things in that moment. I saw Sam as a little boy. I saw Rory coming out of the rain. I saw Jonathan smile and hold out his hand. My past wove through the present, muddling and muddying everything. The only thing that was clear was that Jonathan was in danger. If there was the remotest possibility that Sam was capable of taking a life, then it was up to me to stop him. There was only one option now. No other way forward and no way back.

I lunged at him, grabbing his arm and dragging him as far as possible from Jonathan. He fought me but I wouldn't let go and the two of us stood in a clinch, my leg pressed painfully against the side of the boat. His arms were like iron, his voice in my ear, cold.

'Let me finish it.'

'What's the matter?' Jonathan shouted. 'Christ. Stop that, Alice. You're scaring me.'

He slowed right down and cut the engine and the river went quiet. Locked against Sam I could hear the gentle lapping of the water against the rocking boat, the birds in the trees. Sam was breathing hard. In that moment I saw everything clearly. It was me. I was causing the problem. I was enabling Sam to hurt others. His existence was down to me alone; his power to menace was down to me as well, and this was not something I or anyone else could fix. It was futile. There was me and there was Sam and we would never be apart because I couldn't destroy something that was part of myself, however much I wanted to.

'I don't want to hurt you,' he said. 'It's only Jonathan who has to go. There's nothing you can do.'

But he was wrong. There were two people fighting for control of my mind and if I couldn't win, I'd make damn sure he couldn't either.

'There is,' I said, through clenched teeth. I hugged him hard, pressed my lips against his jaw. 'I'm so sorry.'

337

I pulled us both over the side of the boat and into the river. We hit the water together, came up for air together, but we weren't together for long. A ripping tide was taking me with it. I was confused. This wasn't what I'd meant to happen. We were meant to stay together; to leave together. My coat quickly became waterlogged and heavy and it took every ounce of power I possessed to keep my head above the surface of the water. I heard a splash and guessed that Jonathan had thrown the lifebuoy over. He couldn't know that that wasn't what I wanted. Something hideous had invaded me. I reached for Sam's shoulders, meaning to drag him down with me. I wanted to kill even if in doing so I killed myself. Sam moved away, flicking the wet hair out of his eyes.

Jonathan was shouting his head off. He had climbed over the back of the boat and was standing on the small platform beside the propeller, stretching out his hand. I screamed back that I was sorry, that I loved him. The undercurrent pulled at me but I was no longer rational enough to have the sense to take off my coat and boots. All I knew was that I had to fight it and get to Sam. I yelled for him to come to me, putting all the authority into my voice that I could muster. It wasn't much. A watery splutter at best.

This was the way it used to work when we were children. I told him what to do. He did what I told him. He might be his own person now, but the essentials remained the same, he was a product of me. There was still a chance he'd come if I asked him to, that I hadn't relinquished all control.

I could hear shouting as I met the surface gasping. The schoolboys had realized what was happening and had turned back with their coach. I could see them waving their arms, but my feet felt like lead in my boots, the quilted coat acting like a weight and my jeans sucking against my legs. I went down and kicked back up but it was getting harder each time I tried to break the surface. Why didn't he come?

'Sam!' I tried again but my voice was lost in engine noise as the rowing coach motored towards us.

Then suddenly Sam was there, smiling, triumphant. He thought he had won, that I'd given in and all he had to do was save my life. I had already made my decision. I wrapped my arms around him and let myself go slack and heavy against his resistant body, fighting the urge to panic as we sank. In the darkness I began to feel calmer and the water felt warmer, the current less vicious, a soothing backdrop to oblivion.

Sam's voice was in my head. It was everywhere. It swirled around me with the water, tugging at my mind. As my lungs filled I heard him say my name, I felt his hand stroke my cheek, his lips close to my ear.

'*Remember me, Alice. I'll remember you.*'

Always.

'*I remember your feet swinging from the tree house, attached to chubby legs and scabby knees; I remember them tanned and sandy as you ran across beaches; I remember them at the wedding, shoes kicked off to dance; and I remember your feet after the crash, caked with blood and dirt.*'

Yes. I smiled and released my breath. I wasn't frightened any more.

Epilogue

It is my love that keeps mine eye awake;
Mine own true love that doth my rest defeat,
To play the watchman ever for thy sake.

Shakespeare, Sonnet 61

LONELINESS IS A SICKNESS THAT GRABS AT THE RIBS AND HOLDS ON tight. Holly has the sickness. It doesn't show on her face, but everyone knows it's there, and nobody wants to catch it. I wish I could make her better.

I stand in the middle of the playground, my arms out, revolving. Children charge around and if I half-close my eyes, they become a kaleidoscope of pink, white and blue. They are never still. Each child moves with a force of its own but, even so, they are joined to each other by invisible threads. They know where they are going and they know who is with them and they understand the unwritten rules of the playground.

After a while, I begin to feel dizzy and sit on the ground and rest my chin on my hands. I wish Holly would call me. I watch her as she loiters in the shade of the walkway and I can feel what she's feeling: a despair that is as physical as a shove in the chest. In the playground, stillness is odd. Children stop moving, but only for a moment, and mostly if they've fallen over, to maximize the drama. But a child who stands still for minutes at a time upsets the picture.

Holly is only five, but she is so ashamed of being all by herself that she can barely stand it. In a minute, she'll go and hide in the loo. She is embarrassed but she is proud and her pride makes her stiff and the other children don't like it. She is beginning to realize that, no matter how hard she tries, she won't get it right.

The friendship bench sits at the side of the playground like a monster lurking in the shadows. To Holly, it is a symbol of failure and humiliation and she wouldn't dream of sitting on it. I've asked her why she doesn't go and talk to children sitting there, but she sets her chin. She would rather be alone than risk rejection.

Pride is her enemy. Pride means that, even at times like this, she won't ask me to join her. When she's not feeling so desperate, when she's home and with the people who love her, we play for hours in her bedroom or in the garden. She chatters like a magpie and we make up stories and plan great adventures. Her bed is great for bouncing on, her garden just brilliant for fairy circles. At home, she is a cheeky little monkey and the apple of her daddy's eye.

In the classroom, Holly sits at a table with three other children. They're the brightest of the bunch but Holly is the brightest by far. She doesn't know how to deal with it yet or that by thrusting up her hand, keen to tell every answer, she's making herself even more unpopular. Poor Holly.

And she's not even ugly. I think she's beautiful. She's tall for her age, and has nice round cheeks, a lovely smile and a neat ponytail. It's her eyes that do the damage. Dark and too intense, they seem to question everything anybody says, and that includes her teacher who hardly ever picks her when she puts up her hand.

I love her more than anything in the world. She is my world.

At picking-up time I wait in the playground beside Holly's mum. She's talking to another parent. She doesn't feel much a part of things either, I think. I like her though. There's something warm about her, something familiar, something like I would want my mother to be. She mixes with the other mothers for

Holly's sake, because Holly doesn't get asked for many play-dates.

'You're Rosie's mum, aren't you?' she asks, as the kids come tumbling out. 'Holly mentioned her the other day. Do you think she would like to come round for tea?'

Rosie is one of the most popular children. She is tiny and blonde with a big smile and boundless energy. The other kids follow her like the pied piper. The staff adore her. Holly occasionally tries to join in, but at that age, children don't care so much about hurt feelings and they tell her she isn't allowed to play with them.

Rosie's mother peers at Holly's mother through her sunglasses. She looks embarrassed.

'I'll have to check my diary when I get home, but I know Rosie isn't free for the next couple of weeks. She's only allowed one play-date a week, so it's usually one of her best friends.'

Holly's mum struggles to smile. 'Don't worry about it.' She waves at Holly and hurries over, wanting desperately to limit the time her child stands alone.

I wait for them by the gate. When Holly reaches me, I tuck my arm through hers. I am a bit smaller, but not too much. But even that's annoying when you're a boy. Maybe when I'm older, I'll grow taller than her.

'How was your day?' Holly's mum asks.

'Fine.'

'Who did you sit next to at lunchtime?'

Silence from the back seat. Then Holly says, 'I was a bit late so I sat with Form Two.'

'Oh dear. Why were you late, darling?'

'I was taking my book back to the library.'

It's true, although she did it deliberately to make herself late so that she could join a table that was already half full, rather than sit on her own and have the others squeeze on to another table together. She does that most days. She's good at finding ways around problems.

'Did you play with Rosie?'

'What?'

'Did you play with Rosie?'

'No.'

She turns bright red. She lied about Rosie to please her mother.

At home, Ezther, the Finnish au pair, hands over the baby. Holly's mum carries him to the sofa and sits down and dandles him on her knee. Holly joins her and they babble happily, making little Rory giggle like crazy, his feet and fists pumping the air as she lifts him. Rory isn't like Holly at all. He's the happy one, the little bundle of joy. He never cries, never whinges and everyone absolutely dotes on him, including Holly, who bursts into tears every morning when she has to leave him.

It's Friday and the family are going to stay at Holly's grandparents' house. They live in the countryside. Their bags are packed and Holly's dad is already in the car, eager to leave before the traffic gets too bad. He beeps the horn and they come out, Holly's mum carrying Rory, Holly holding on to her pink overnight bag. She waits patiently while Rory is strapped into his bucket seat. I am sitting on the doorstep, cross because I don't want to be left behind and Holly hasn't called me.

'Hop in.'

Her dad reaches over and holds out his hand to her with a huge grin. Sometimes I love Holly's dad but sometimes I'm scared of him. When she has his full attention I feel as weak as a kitten.

She almost takes his hand but then she turns and looks straight at me.

'Come on, Alexander.'

I leap up.

The air seems to go very still. Time stops. In the car, Jonathan is staring hard at Holly. Rory is waggling his little arms and blowing bubbles. Alice has turned away from the baby and her mouth is open. The sun reflects its heat off the car. Alice stares right at the door, just to the side of me, then at her daughter.

'Is Alexander here, Holly?' she asks, and her voice sounds all funny.

Holly shrugs and looks at her feet.

'Alexander's always here.'

Acknowledgements

My thanks to: Victoria Hobbs, Harriet Bourton, Pippa McCarthy, Jennifer Custer, Fanny Blake, Clare Bowron, Debi Alper, Liz McAulay, Anne Bayne, Jackie and Nicholas Taylor, Graham Minett, Steve and Lulu Smithwick, Katrin MacGibbon, Gordon and Jocelyn Simms of the Segora Short Story prize and Finton House School.

Brought up in London, Fleur studied French Literature and Language at Southampton University and has worked in various jobs, including twelve years as a school secretary, before becoming a full-time writer. As well as novels, she writes short stories and has won the Writers' Village and Segora competitions and has been shortlisted twice for prizes from Fish Publishing and *The New Writer*. She lives in London with her husband and two children. For more information on Fleur Smithwick, see her website at www.fleursmithwick.com.

Find her on Twitter: @FleurSmithwick.